THIRD WHEEL

MASTERS OF MARQUIS
BOOK 9

GOLDEN ANGEL

For every girl who ever experienced humiliation and heartbreak at the hands of an asshole and moved on to live her best fucking life without him.

CONTENTS

1

____

Amy

"What do you mean you don't know where Jeremy is?" Amy stared at Jeremy's best man, the man who was supposed to be standing beside him when she walked down the aisle, which she was supposed to be doing in less than ten minutes.

She was fully dressed.

Wedding gown. Makeup that had taken an hour to do. Hair that had taken nearly two. Veil. The only thing she didn't have on were her shoes, which were her something blue.

Wes cringed, avoiding her gaze and staring at a point on her bare shoulder. She didn't normally wear strapless dresses, but she'd made an exception for her wedding gown, stuffing herself into a strapless ballgown because Jeremy had once commented that those were the only dresses that truly looked 'bridal.' He'd had a lot of opinions about the wedding while they were planning it, which she'd thought was sweet. He'd shown more interest than many grooms she'd heard about.

Now...

Now, she was feeling trapped in a gown she couldn't move very quickly in, and it was far too tight around her. It didn't matter that she wore corsets on a weekly basis; the one she was now wearing under her dress felt as if it was tightening with every breath she took, cutting off her air. Her head buzzed as Wes cleared his throat.

"Well, uh... he didn't show up this morning..."

"Why not? He was with you last night, and you're here." Her voice was going shrill.

Reaching up to adjust the tie at his throat, Wes' gaze skittered behind her at her bridesmaids. Her mom. Amy could feel all of them staring from behind her. Silent. Waiting. Like she was waiting for Wes' answer.

"He, uh, wasn't actually with me last night." Wes was starting to sweat, his round, pale face slowly turning red as he continued to tug at his tie. His dark blond hair looked damp, though that might have been the gel he'd used to style it. "He promised he'd be here today, though, so I kept covering for him, but..."

But it was almost time for the ceremony to start.

Jeremy hadn't been with Wes last night. So, where had he been?

Amy felt lightheaded. She really couldn't breathe. Putting her hand on her stomach, she felt the lace and the boning beneath her palm and tried to focus on that sensation instead of the buzzing in her ears. Someone came up behind her, putting their hand tentatively on her shoulder.

"Maybe something happened to him," she said. "Maybe he was in a car accident. We should... we should call the hospitals. Or the police. Something."

"Baby, if he'd had an accident, we'd know. His parents are out there, remember? I told you, I saw them," her mom said gently, moving her hand to rub the center of Amy's back under the veil she'd borrowed from her. *Something old. Something borrowed.*

Jeremy wasn't coming. Deep down she knew that, could feel the truth of it in her core, yet she wasn't ready to admit it yet.

Behind her, she could hear her bridesmaids muttering to each other. Marissa, her maid of honor. Morgan. Carolyn. Sam. Her group of girls. Her besties. Well... almost all of them.

Her brain nudged at her.

Noelle was missing, too.

Not that it was that surprising. Amy hadn't heard from her all week. She'd been relieved. Relieved when Noelle hadn't answered her texts. Relieved when Noelle hadn't answered the one call she'd made.

Relieved when Noelle hadn't shown up today.

No. It's not possible. He wouldn't... she wouldn't...

Wes kept staring at her, sweating. Her mother was murmuring soothing platitudes—*it will be okay.* But it wouldn't. She already knew it wouldn't be. The wedding wasn't happening. It couldn't happen when the groom wasn't here.

And my bridesmaid is missing.

She was putting all the pieces together, but she didn't *want* to.

This couldn't be happening.

This wasn't real.

This was another bad dream. Another stress wedding nightmare, like the ones she'd been having over the past month. Not that she'd ever had one remotely like this. And none of them had lasted this long. Or been this detailed.

The annoying sound she'd assigned to Jeremy on her phone for this week rang out, filling the room. She'd wanted to make sure she didn't miss any important calls from him this week.

"My phone!" She spun in the direction of the table where she'd left it and lunged forward, one of her feet catching in the hem of her dress. Something ripped, but she didn't stop. She didn't care. She needed to know. Needed to find out what was going on.

Because this wasn't a dream.

Morgan was already at the table, picking up the phone. She hesitated a moment before holding it out in front of her toward Amy, her green eyes filled with worry.

Shame flushed through Amy.

Her bridesmaids knew. Everyone in that stupid little room where she'd been getting ready knew.

But she couldn't believe it.

Not really.

Not yet.

It was a video call.

She hit the accept button.

The screen blurred for a second, then cleared. Amy found herself staring at her missing groom and missing bridesmaid. Jeremy's handsome face smirked back at her while Noelle was beaming, neither of them appearing in any way upset, the way she was. Amy blinked, not quite believing her eyes.

Jeremy was wearing a bowtie, and his hair was styled the way he'd said he was going to do for their wedding day. Noelle was wearing full makeup, her hair pulled back from her face, and she had something white atop her head.

"Hey, Amy, how's it going?" Jeremy's smirk was mean. Amy wasn't sure she'd ever realized how mean his smirk was.

"Where are you?" Her voice didn't sound like her own; it came out in a high squeak.

"We're in Vegas." Noelle's eyes were bright as she held up her hand. There was a bright diamond ring on her ring finger.

A ring Amy recognized. Suddenly, her legs couldn't hold her up anymore, and she found herself crashing to the floor, surrounded by lace and tulle, as she stared at the phone in her hand.

"We just got married."

"I... I don't understand." Somewhere behind Amy, a door opened and closed. Someone had left the room, but she couldn't make herself turn to see who it was. It felt like she was about to break apart into a million pieces. A scream rose up in her chest, but it was trapped there, unable to get out.

"How dare you?!" That was Amy's mom, who knelt down on Amy's skirt, wrapping a supportive arm around her shoulder. "What the hell is wrong with you, Jeremy?"

"I'm sorry you had to find out this way, Mrs. Newhart, but your daughter has been cheating on me for our entire relationship." Jeremy might have started with an apology, but he didn't sound or look sorry. "She lied to me."

"I did not! You said you understood! You agreed!" Now, the tears were starting to come at the unjustness of his accusation. She would never—*never*—have done anything without Jeremy's consent.

"Your daughter is a filthy pervert," he continued, as if Amy hadn't spoken. "She told me she needed to be whipped and hurt, and I wasn't willing to hurt her that way. I tried to be understanding. I told her she could fulfill her needs at a club that she goes to, but she was cheating on me there."

"I was not!"

"I've seen the pictures," Jeremy sneered, his expression turning ugly for the first time. "Noelle was honest with me when you weren't. She showed me what you were really doing."

"I'm sorry, Amy. I just couldn't keep perpetuating your lies. Not when I saw how it was hurting Jeremy. Not when we were falling in love. Please don't hate us. You can't blame us for having feelings."

Everything was going grey at the edges of Amy's vision. She couldn't speak. Couldn't defend herself. Couldn't scream. Fight, flight, or freeze, and she froze. Hard. She wanted to throw her phone away from her, as far away from her as she could, yet she couldn't loosen her grip, clinging to it like she would tumble off a cliff if she did.

"None of this would have happened if you hadn't cheated on me. Noelle was there for me, Noelle—"

Someone plucked the phone out of her hand.

Marissa.

Amy felt her skirts move as her bridesmaids surrounded her like a phalanx, blocking her view from the phone. Blocking their view of her. It wasn't quite a group hug; it couldn't be because of this stupid, stupid ballgown skirt, but it was a protective barrier.

"You are both terrible people," Marissa said coldly. "Noelle, you can fuck all the way off and never come back. Jeremy, you never deserved Amy in the first place, you shriveled little dickhead. Do not contact her again."

"What's going on?"

Oh God, Amy recognized that voice. But what was he doing here? She hadn't even heard him come in.

This day just kept getting worse.

Something was wrong.

Kincaid looked over at his boyfriend, Zach, who was nervously adjusting his tie. Again. He tried to quiet the uncertainty that rose up inside him.

They were here for Amy Newhart's wedding, and Kincaid wasn't sure how his boyfriend felt about it. Zach and Amy scened together, platonically, at the BDSM clubs they all belonged to, but he wasn't sure how Zach felt about her getting married. He also wasn't sure he could ask.

Their relationship was still on shaky ground after a breakup. They'd just gotten back together recently. He still wasn't sure where he could push and where he needed to back off, but Amy was one of the subjects he didn't feel like he could push.

He couldn't watch Zach keep anxiously fidgeting without checking in with him, either. That wasn't who Kincaid was.

He reached over, putting a hand on Zach's thigh so he could lean a little closer, keeping his voice low since they were surrounded by wedding guests. Though they were hardly the only ones talking. Everyone had noticed that the wedding hadn't started on time.

"Are you okay?"

Rather than answering right away, Zach dropped his hand away from his tie and turned his head to give Kincaid a nervous smile. Kincaid smiled back as best he could, but he knew he wasn't entirely hiding his concern.

It wasn't just concern over Zach's anxiousness but some trepidation about what it meant for them. Amy was important to Zach, Kincaid knew that... but how important? Did he sometimes wish Amy was single? Or was Kincaid projecting just because he knew he was the first man Zach had been with?

"I'm fine. I think I might have tied my tie too tight." Zach slid his hand under Kincaid's to hold it. The touch helped soothe some of the emotions that were buzzing under Kincaid's skin.

Zach was here with him. In public. Showing affection. And he'd told his sister about their relationship, even if he hadn't worked up to telling his parents yet. *Baby steps.* As long as Kincaid could see some progress, he could live with that. He knew it was hard for Zach, but he was trying.

In front of them, Rick—another member of the BDSM clubs they went to—leaned over to his wife, not bothering to keep his voice down.

"What time is it? Isn't this supposed to have started already?"

Beside Kincaid, Zach glanced down at his watch, and Kincaid looked over as well, joining Zach in his frown. The wedding should have started five minutes ago. Zach twisted around and froze, and Kincaid looked up as well.

Sam, one of Amy's bridesmaids, was striding down the aisle with purpose—not walking slowly like she was starting the ceremony— and her gaze was locked on Zach. Shit. Something was wrong. He could see that the moment he saw Sam's expression.

She came to a halt in a sweep of chiffon, the stray curls from her coiffure swaying at the sudden stop.

"Amy needs you," she told Zach. "*Now*." She looked up to meet Kincaid's gaze. "You'd better come, too."

The audience all burst into murmured noise as both of them leapt to their feet. Zach didn't even look back as he darted down the aisle ahead of Kincaid, too intent on getting to Amy. Hurt darted through Kincaid, but he did his best to push it aside. Sam was not an alarmist. If she had come to get them, there was a damn good reason. Amy needed her Dom. This wasn't about him.

The moment they burst into the room Sam led them to—she could move damn fast, even in three-inch heels—any hesitation Kincaid felt washed away the moment he caught sight of Amy. They'd never been close; Zach had always kept them fairly separate, and Kincaid hadn't protested because, as far as he was concerned, Amy wasn't really part of their relationship.

Zach had certain needs as a sadist that Kincaid couldn't fulfill. He was fine with Zach playing with others platonically. Even when Zach had stopped scening with anyone else other than Amy, he hadn't made an effort to step in because their dynamics were all well established by then.

But it would take a harder, crueler person than him to be unaffected by the sight of her surrounded by her bridesmaids, her mom beside her with her arms around her, all of them huddled on the skirt of her dress where she knelt in the middle of the room, with the most anguished expression he'd ever seen on a woman's face.

Standing in front of Amy and the crowd was Marissa, a sub with a bad reputation at Stronghold, who was nonetheless one of Amy's bridesmaids. She wore the same sage green gown as the others, and for a moment, Kincaid thought she must be the one causing the problem before he realized she was speaking to someone on a video call on the phone she was holding in front of her.

"You are both terrible people. Noelle, you can fuck all the way off and never come back. Jeremy, you never deserved Amy in the first place, you shriveled little dickhead. Do not contact her again."

Jeremy. Amy's fiancé. Noelle... another problem sub at the clubs. Also, one of Amy's bridesmaids. What the hell is going on?

His brain was struggling to catch up, but apparently, so was Zach because he blurted the question out.

"What's going on?"

Everyone huddled on the floor looked up at him as Sam went on her knees to join them, her arms going around Amy and hugging her. Amy's pale face stared at him and Zach from over Sam's shoulder, the look in her eyes piercing Kincaid's heart.

He could see the shame, the humiliation, the pain, and it made his own chest ache in sympathy. He wanted to beat the hell out of whoever had put that look on her face.

"Noelle and Jeremy eloped, and they're blaming Amy for their shitty behavior," Marissa answered before turning back to the phone and glaring at it. "Do not ever contact Amy again. And Noelle, you can consider your membership to Stronghold and Marquis revoked."

She hit a button on the phone, cutting off their voices as the two on the other side of the call started yelling back at her.

As Zach went down on his knees to join the group huddled around Amy, his voice soothing as he murmured something Kincaid couldn't quite make out, Kincaid looked at Marissa and raised his eyebrow.

She shrugged.

"If anyone knows what it takes to get kicked out of Stronghold, it's me. Noelle crossed one of the lines Patrick won't compromise on—she took photos of Amy and shared them with a non-member. As soon as I tell him, she's out on her ass."

Kincaid would have replied, but a heartbreaking wail rose in the air as Amy flung herself into Zach's arms and finally started to cry, sobbing as she buried her face in the shoulder of her Dom.

Fuck.

2

———————

The look on Amy's face when he and Kincaid first entered the room terrified Zach. He had seen her in all sorts of emotional states, but he had never seen her look like *that*. She was stark white, hazel eyes so wide, he could see the whites of her eyes around them, making her look like a ghost among the sage green of her bridesmaids' dresses. Beside her was an older woman in darker green, who looked enough like Amy, she had to be her mother.

Now, Amy was wrapped up in his arms, sobbing her heart out against his shoulder, while her mother stared at them in consternation. She was the only one still on her knees, appearing unsure as to why Amy was crying on *him* and not on her.

"I'm going to go get us some vodka," Carolyn said, briskly brushing off her skirts as she straightened.

Her words made Amy's mother jerk out of her reverie, and the older woman slowly got to her feet. She looked like she was on the verge of falling apart, too, but she held it together.

"Can you stop in the ceremony room and tell the guests... tell the guests..." Mrs. Newhart's voice trailed off. She wrung her hands in front of her, looking lost. What were they supposed to tell the guests?

"I'll go find the event coordinator and tell her we need to move up the cocktail hour to *now*," Marissa said, interjecting when Carolyn made a face at the idea of having to be the one to tell the guests that the wedding was off. Though, most of them had probably guessed it by now, anyway.

Zach's arms tightened around Amy. He wasn't sure how much she was hearing of what was going on around her, she was so lost in her own headspace.

"Then I'm finding Patrick. Here." As she said 'here,' she tossed the phone at Sam, who caught it.

Morgan stood beside her, watching Amy with pure sympathy, wringing her hands in much the same way as Amy's mother. Marissa and Carolyn left the room together, talking in low voices before the door shut behind them.

Before anyone could do anything more, the phone buzzed in Sam's hands, and she looked down at it. Scowled, hot fury blooming on her cheeks.

"That fucking dickweed." She looked up, over Zach and Amy, to meet Kincaid's gaze. "He just texted to say that Amy needs to be out of 'his' house by the time he gets home from Vegas next weekend. He can't do that, right?"

Kincaid was a former police detective, not a lawyer, but he knew more about the laws than anyone else currently in the room.

"He can't. She has rights if she's been living there." Kincaid's hand came to rest on Zach's shoulder, offering support. "She'll need proof, but he can't just kick her out—"

"No." It was the first word Amy had said since they'd entered the room, and it came out in a gasp. He could feel her head moving against his shoulder as she shook it. "No... I don't... I don't want to be there when he... when they..."

Another sob cut off her words, and she shook in his arms. His chest ached with sympathy, tears welling in his own eyes at the sound of her pain. He was a sadist, but not like this. There was no enjoyment to be found here. However, he'd sure as hell enjoy causing fucking Jeremy some serious pain. His focus needed to be on Amy, though. She didn't want to be there when Jeremy and Noelle came home.

"I don't understand," Mrs. Newhart said, still wringing her hands as she looked between Amy and Zach. "What's going on? Are you the man she's been..."

"Yes and no," Kincaid answered before Zach could. "Zach is my boyfriend. He's also Amy's Dom, but their relationship has been completely platonic. Whatever Noelle showed Jeremy, it was a lie. Or pictures that could be easily misinterpreted. Holding Amy like this is the most Zach has ever done with her."

Zach nodded, jaw clenched as a little trickle of guilt flickered through him. There had been times when he'd fantasized about more... but he'd had Kincaid, and she'd had Jeremy, and fantasies weren't cheating. Kincaid was right. He and Amy had never done anything more than exactly what they were doing right now, albeit with fewer clothes, but she'd been wrapped in a blanket for aftercare.

All they had done at the club that was at all intimate was after-care. Then she would go home to Jeremy, where he'd reap the bene-fits of any arousal she might be feeling in the aftermath, though Amy usually came to the club to cry and relieve her stress, not to get horny.

"Do you know what a Dom is?" Sam asked, eyeing Mrs. Newhart warily.

"Yes, yes, I read Lexi Blake. I know what a Dom is." Mrs. Newhart sighed, putting her fingers to her temples. "I didn't realize my daugh-ter... anyway. Not important." She opened her eyes and huffed. "Jeremy is a shit."

Despite the situation, Zach choked back a laugh. He liked Mrs. Newhart.

Amy's tears were finally starting to slow. She hiccupped as she got herself under control, her breathing stuttering as it returned to normal. Rubbing her back, Zach rested his chin atop her head, glad Kincaid's steady hand was on his shoulder. It wasn't just the brides-maids there if something happened; he could trust Kincaid to take care of anything and everything else while he took care of Amy.

<u>*Amy*</u>

Everything was awful, and it was all real.

She wanted to hide in Zach's arms forever and never come out because coming out meant facing the real world. It meant facing her family. It meant facing her mom, who had never liked Jeremy and was probably dying to say, 'I told you so,' and Amy didn't think she could handle that right now. At least she didn't have to explain to her mom what kink was, though she was slightly disturbed that they read the same books.

Did that mean her mom and dad...

Nope, not going there.

Apparently, her brain was so desperate to think about anything other than her own terrible life that she'd rather think about her parents' sex life. That was how bad things were right now.

"Amy, baby, look at me." Her mom's gentle tone helped give Amy the courage to open her eyes and turn her head. Her mom crouched down beside her and Zach, a sympathetic expression on her face. "I'm going to go help handle the guests, unless you want me to stay."

Her mom was offering to shield her from everyone. Part of her wanted her mom to stay, but she didn't *need* her, too. She had her friends. She had Zach. And even Kincaid was standing like a stalwart buffer between her and the door. Wes had disappeared entirely; Amy wasn't sure when.

"It's okay," she said in a croak. "I'm okay. I... you should probably go tell everyone..." She choked a little, tears threatening to fall again. God, facing everyone and telling them that Jeremy had eloped with one of her own friends, one of her bridesmaids, on their wedding day... she couldn't do it. "I don't want to see them."

"You don't have to, baby," her mom said soothingly. "Don't worry, I'm going to take care of everything." A hard expression crossed her face. "I'm also going to have a word with Carrie." Carrie being Jeremy's mom.

Amy choked on the idea of having to see any of his family today.

She just wanted to go home. But home was the house she'd shared with Jeremy for the past year. He'd never put her on the lease, promising he'd do so after they got married. That probably should have been a red flag, but it had made sense when he'd explained it, and he'd sounded so reasonable...

"Do you want to come to my place?" Morgan asked, stepping forward. "Asad and I would be happy to have you."

"Or you can come stay with me, though Morgan and Asad might be better since they have an actual guest bedroom," Sam said.

Mom's expression changed, realizing that what seemed like a future problem was probably a more immediate issue. No, Jeremy wouldn't be back until the end of the week. He and Noelle were in Vegas on what was probably supposed to be his and Amy's honeymoon. He'd planned the honeymoon and hadn't told Amy where they were going, but it made sense that he'd be there all week with Noelle.

Like the wedding, it had probably already been paid for.

"You can come home with me and your dad," her mom said immediately. "You can stay with us as long as you need to."

"I don't think running away to a different state is going to help," she replied tearfully. "My job is here. My friends are here. And weren't you and Dad leaving for a cruise this week after you got back home?"

"Well... yes, but we can cancel. You're more important."

Immediately, Amy started shaking her head.

"Don't cancel. I've already upended everyone's plans enough, cost you enough money—"

"Don't think about that," her mother said sternly. "That is *not* your fault." She sighed. "But you have a point about your job and the fact that we wouldn't be home."

Amy didn't exactly want to go crawling back to her parents' house, anyway. It felt like a step backward at a time when her life was supposed to be moving forward.

"And apparently, I need to pack up my stuff this week and get it moved somewhere else." Her brain was finally working again.

Leaning against Zach's strength helped. She always felt safe with him. "Maybe a storage unit."

There was no way in hell she was going to be in Jeremy's house when he came back with Noelle, no matter what rights she had. Absolutely the fuck not. She was going to take her stuff and get out.

"You can come live with us," Zach offered. "We have a guest bedroom. And a pretty much empty basement."

She hesitated because living with Zach sounded the most appealing. In some ways, she was closer to him than she was to any of her other friends. If she hadn't been trying to respect Jeremy, she would have asked Zach to be her Man of Honor, but Jeremy had been completely weirded out by the idea, and she'd given in. Plus, she knew she was going to cry again. A lot. Zach was the only person she'd ever felt like she could really let go and cry for.

But she also knew things had been rocky between Zach and Kincaid for a while, and they were just getting good again. She didn't want to come in, dumping all her issues on them when Zach was finally happy.

Twisting her head, she looked up past Zach at Kincaid, who was standing just behind him. At this angle, it was really hard to read his expression. Heck, it was difficult at the best of times. Kincaid could be very closed off. When he looked down and met her gaze, his face was completely blank at first, then his eyes softened as he looked at her.

"We do. You'd be welcome to stay as long as you need," he said, reiterating Zach's offer.

"I don't think I can decide right now," she whispered, letting her head drop back down. Her throat, nose, and eyes hurt from her heavy sobs. Her chest ached with the shame of being an abandoned bride. All she wanted to do was melt into the floor and not have to deal with any of this.

"You don't have to, baby," her mom said, reaching out to pat Amy's hand. "You stay here for now. I'm going to go talk to the guests, then I'll come back and... oh, here are your friends with the vodka."

Vodka sounded good.

3

____

"I'm sorry," Zach murmured, leaning against Kincaid as they watched Amy do her second shot with her bridesmaids. He wondered how much Amy'd eaten today. Not much, he was guessing, because while the other women were getting tipsy, she was already well on her way to sloppy drunk just from the first shot. "I shouldn't have invited her to come live with us without asking you first."

"You shouldn't have." Kincaid's tone was deceptively mild. "And I'll take that out on your ass later. But I would have said yes, anyway, so it comes out in the wash."

Except it didn't, because he still should have asked, even though he'd known what Kincaid would say. But he'd been holding Amy, feeling her shaking, feeling her confusion, and he'd wanted—needed—to make it better. Deep down, he knew he was the best choice, too.

If she went to Morgan and Asad's, or anywhere else, she would feel like she had to pretend she was okay, the way she was doing now. She would act as normal as she could, all while she was slowly dying inside, unable to tap into her emotions, unable to focus on herself while others were around her. That was exactly why she'd come into the scene in the first place—to be forced to focus on herself.

It was what she needed, even if she wouldn't want to face it. And Zach could give it to her. Kincaid would help. He might not have ever been part of their dynamic before, but obviously, that would need to change a bit. Kincaid was a caretaker. A protector.

If Jeremy came after her for any reason, Zach would protect her, but Kincaid would crush the man for daring. Once she was under Kincaid's protective wing, he would consider her wellbeing one of his priorities. That was another reason Zach wanted her with them.

He was a sadist. A top. But Kincaid was a *Dom* in a way he'd never managed to be. He knew some people felt it was the same, but he never did. How could he call himself a Dom when Kincaid was dominant to him? When he submitted to Kincaid? Sure, he was a switch, but even when he was topping someone, he didn't feel like he could give them what Kincaid gave him.

Amy would need that, too. She wasn't just a masochist; she was a submissive. She would have needs Zach wasn't sure he could fulfill.

Between him and Kincaid, they'd be able to help her in a way no one else could. So, he couldn't regret offering the invitation or even the way he'd done it. He knew he'd been pushing Kincaid into a situation where he was going to say yes, regardless of how he felt, but at the same time, he was sorry because he knew he'd been wrong to do so. He'd also been right.

And he didn't mind at all if Kincaid was going to take it out on his ass.

Zach straightened up as the door opened, and Mrs. Newhart came back in, along with an older man holding her hand, whom he assumed was Amy's dad. He wondered how much Mrs. Newhart had told him. The relief that had poured through him when he realized she read kinky romance had been strong, but that didn't mean that both parents would be as understanding. He also wasn't sure her mom would understand how truly platonic he and Amy had been.

After Rae had started writing kinky romance, everyone in the club had gotten on board with reading her books, and he'd read a few more beyond that. None of them really featured platonic kink, even though it was highly prevalent in the club. He didn't want Amy's mom to think they'd been cheating. They hadn't been. Yes, he cared deeply about her, and yes, he found her very attractive, but he would never do that to Kincaid.

Yeah, I just hide our relationship outside of the club and hurt him that way instead.

Ruthlessly, he pushed that thought away. He was working on that.

He watched as Amy straightened up, putting a smile on her face for her parents as they talked to her. Maybe trying to convince her to come stay with them instead? Probably not; it really wouldn't make sense. He sidled closer to try to overhear what they were talking about, ignoring Kincaid's amused look. Yeah, so he was nosy. So what?

"Jeremy's family has left, but most of the guests are staying, and we're having a party. Do you want to come out? You don't have to. You can do whatever you want." Mrs. Newhart was firm in making that last part clear.

"I..." Amy's smile slipped a little, some of her pain coming back into her expression. "If I don't have to..."

"You don't have to," her dad said immediately, reaching out to take her hand in his and patting it. "We'll take care of everything. You should do what you feel like right now. Whatever you feel like."

Amy glanced over at her group of friends, who were now watching her with sympathetic expressions. He could see her hide her wince.

"Would it be terrible if I just stayed here and didn't come out at all?"

"Of course not. No one is going to blame you for that," her mother reassured her. She stepped forward, pulling Amy into a hug. "We'll take care of everything." With that sentiment repeated, she stepped back and gave her husband a nod right before he gave Amy his own hug. She buried her face in his shoulder, but when they parted, Zach wasn't surprised to see that her eyes were still dry.

She really did have issues about crying in front of people if it was about her own emotions. That was why she needed the club, why she needed Zach. The more he'd gotten to know her, the more he'd realized she didn't feel comfortable with people feeling like they had to take care of her—and if someone was crying, that was an indication they needed to be taken care of.

That was why it really was for the best if she came to stay with him and Kincaid. Otherwise, she was going to kill herself trying to keep it together for whoever she was with. Zach wouldn't let her get away with that.

KINCAID

"Get this off of me." Amy stared down at the dress she was wearing as if she'd never seen it before. Four shots in, and she was drunk as a skunk—and her bridesmaids weren't much better off. Zach had a few, too. Kincaid was the only totally sober person in the room at the moment.

"What?" Morgan looked at Amy in adorable confusion.

Reaching down, Amy started tugging at the bodice of her dress. "This. Get it off me."

"Okaaaaay." Morgan moved around behind Amy and frowned. "Um..."

"What's wrong?" Sam leaned over to see, a blonde lock of hair falling in her eyes.

"It's all buttons. Teeny tiny buttons."

"There's no zipper?" Marissa asked, taking a sip of her drink. "Sometimes, the buttons are fake, and there's a zipper underneath."

Morgan reached out to touch the back of Amy's dress.

"No zipper." She frowned in concentration, fumbling at Amy's back. "Why are they so small?"

"It's couture," Sam told her, then frowned. "They aren't even buttons. It's a bunch of tiny loops. What sadist designed this? Aren't wedding dresses supposed to be easy to get out of?" Her expression turned to one of horror as she realized what she'd said, what she'd implied, as if Amy needed the reminder that her wedding night was not going to happen the way it was supposed to.

"Get it off me!" Amy shrieked, pulling harder at the front, her expression turning to panicked desperation. "Rip it, whatever, just get it off!"

"Here..." Zach shouldered his way in, reaching for the back of her dress. He tried to rip it, and though there was a small sound of fabric tearing, the dress did not open up the way he'd obviously intended. Under other circumstances, his dumbfounded expression would have been funny, but Amy was clearly working her way up to hysterics.

"Stop." Kincaid's command dropped into the room, making everyone freeze. "Move, Zach, I've got it." He moved behind Amy. Yeah, a whole row of tiny buttons done with loops. Zach had managed to rip the very first loop out of the fabric, but that was it. Putting his hand on Amy's shoulder, Kincaid could feel how clammy her skin was, could feel her shoulder rise and fall as she panted for breath. "Deep breath, Amy. In... and out. One more time for me. Good girl."

He felt her sag against his hand at the 'good girl.' Poor little subby. She was having a hell of a day; she'd probably needed that.

"Everyone, just go back to what you were doing," he told them. What they'd been doing had been talking shit about Jeremy and Noelle, some of which had been highly entertaining. Marissa and Carolyn had both been incensed at Noelle's betrayal of the 'sisterhood,' something he found fascinating because Carolyn actually did cheat on her husband when she came to the club, and Marissa had never been known as particularly friendly among the other submissives.

Something about Amy brought out a protective streak in them, he supposed, though he'd also seen them treating her like a doormat. Maybe it was an 'only I'm allowed to walk all over her' mentality.

He could understand the protective streak.

As he made his way down the tiny row of buttons—seriously, who did this on a wedding dress? Unless the plan was to just flip her skirts up and— Nope, stop thinking about that. Thinking about what Amy was going to be doing on her wedding night while he undressed her made him feel incredibly awkward and incredibly guilty.

Undoing the buttons, he snuck a peek at Zach, who was watching them both.

He and Zach had shared women in the past, submissives, but never Amy.

And thinking about sharing Amy on what was supposed to be her fucking wedding day… what the fuck was wrong with his head? The intrusive thoughts were real. Though, maybe it wasn't entirely his fault since he was undressing her, and the more buttons he got undone, the more of her underwear he could see.

She was wearing a lacy white corset underneath the dress, exaggerating her hourglass figure. It was pure lace and boning and probably a bit uncomfortable. Amy was a masochist, but considering she'd been close to trying to tear the dress off her, he doubted she wanted the corset on, either.

"Do you want me to loosen this?" he asked, tapping the back of it once he had the last button undone.

"Yes, please. There should be a robe…" She looked around as her voice trailed off, and Sam immediately jumped up and hurried over to the other side of the room where Kincaid now noticed a white satin robe draped over the back of a chair.

"I've got it!" Sam called out as she picked it up.

Kincaid focused on loosening Amy's corset. She sagged even more than she had for being called a good girl, taking in a deep breath of relief. As Sam approached, holding up the robe, Kincaid stepped back and turned away slightly. Not like he hadn't occasionally seen Amy's breasts at Stronghold, but this was different.

When he turned back after a moment, she was now in the robe, which went down to her knees, and she was trying to tie the belt around her waist… and failing.

"Here, let me do that." He stepped forward, taking the ends of the belt from her and tying them in a bow, very aware of the way she was looking at him with big, watery doe eyes and a trembling lower lip.

"Thank you," she whispered.

"You're welcome." He didn't really know what else to say. There was something incredibly vulnerable about her at that moment.

"Okay, who wants another shot?" Carolyn asked.

"Me!" Vulnerability disappeared under a big smile as Amy turned away from him. "Me, me, me, me!"

This was probably going to end badly, but Kincaid couldn't find it in himself to tell her no.

4

AMY

Everything was awful.

Everything hurt.

Especially her head.

And her mouth felt like something had died in it.

She recognized the symptoms as she clawed her way out of sleep, trying to wake up. Her brain was buzzing. Something important had happened, and she felt like shit. Why was she thinking so slowly?

Oh.

_Oh._

Today was supposed to be the first day of her married life with Jeremy.

It was still the first day of his married life... with Noelle.

The shame, the embarrassment from yesterday, welled up inside her. She wasn't a wife today. She hadn't been a bride yesterday. Everyone knew. Everyone had seen what she'd suspected. She'd told herself she was imagining how close Noelle and Jeremy had gotten. Had believed Jeremy when he'd told her that he and Noelle were planning something special for her. Had believed Noelle when she'd said she and Jeremy were just good friends.

And now everyone, *everyone*, knew what a fool she was. Knew what a failure she was.

If I got dumped yesterday, why am I in bed with someone?

Amy's eyes popped open as she felt the heat of the body beside her naked body. That got her awake and searching her memories from the day before, her mouth somehow going even dryer when she saw the dark head of hair and handsome face and recognized Zach. And did not recognize the bedroom.

Oh my God, I slept with Zach.

How the hell did I end up in bed with Zach?

Did he and Kincaid have a fight? Did I sleep with both of them?

If I slept with both of them, where is Kincaid?

Her thoughts had gone from moving like molasses to running through her aching head like a freight train. She lifted her hands to press her fingers against her temples, practically whimpering as she tried to make it stop.

Tried to remember.

Jeremy and Noelle's call.

Her mom finding out she was kinky.

Her parents taking care of everything—and God, she hoped her dad didn't know she was kinky—while she hid away with her friends and didn't have to face anyone. How she was ever going to face anyone ever again, she didn't know.

At least she didn't have to face work yet since she was supposed to be on her honeymoon this week.

Focus. How did I end up in bed with Zach?

Vodka.

Carolyn had brought in vodka. And she'd drank and drank... and Kincaid had helped her out of her dress, and she'd felt like a really fucking terrible person because, for just a moment, she'd pictured him helping her out of her dress for an entirely different reason while Zach watched them.

Oh God... had she done this? Had she thrown herself at them, and they'd given her a pity fuck because she was that pathetic?

Her gorge rose. She was going to throw up.

No... wait.

Reaching down, she breathed out a sigh of relief as she realized she wasn't totally naked. She had on underwear. Her vagina was not sore in any way. It did not feel like she'd been fucked. And with two men, she would feel it, right?

Logic reasserted itself.

Neither Kincaid nor Zach would ever touch her while she was wasted drunk. Neither of them was that kind of guy.

She was just really freaking slow this morning.

But she *was* in their bed, she assumed, in their room. Blinking, she looked around. It looked like a main bedroom and not a guest bedroom. Huge bed and she was in the center of it. There was an empty space beside her and a pillow with an indent, which was probably where Kincaid had slept. Big, dark, masculine-looking wooden furniture. Two dressers. Several doors, which probably led to closets or maybe a bathroom, or both, and one must lead out to the hallway.

Amy didn't remember which one. She couldn't remember anything after Kincaid helped get her out of her dress. Which was extremely disconcerting. She'd never gotten blackout drunk before.

I've also never had my groom elope with one of my friends on my wedding day before, either.

The door directly across from the bed started to open, and Amy squeaked, pulling the sheets up to cover her breasts. Which was dumb because Kincaid had definitely seen her boobs in the club and had probably seen them last night, even though she couldn't remember it.

He appeared in the doorway, grey sweatpants hanging from his hips, a tray in his hands, looking like he'd stepped right out of a viral internet video. Amy did her best to focus her eyes on his face, not on his bare, muscular chest and abs, and definitely not on the sweatpants that were clinging to him. A slow smile moved over his lips.

"You're awake. How are you feeling?"

"Okay... um." She reached up, pressing her fingertips to her lips because the smell of the food hitting her made her stomach churn in a painful manner. Her vagina might not be sore, but her stomach muscles were.

"Do you need to throw up again?" Kincaid asked, coming over to put the tray down on the nightstand beside his side of the bed. There was bacon, eggs, biscuits, orange juice, and coffee. Also, a pill bottle.

She didn't know what she wanted first—the coffee or the headache medicine.

But there was something she needed to ask first.

"Again?" Please no...

His sympathetic gaze made her want to shrivel into a tiny ball.

"You don't remember?" His tone was gentle and nonjudgmental, but she still felt the shame wash over her. Because she didn't remember. Because he'd definitely seen her throw up. Which meant Zach had, too.

She wanted to sink through the bed, into the mattress, and just never come out again. If only that was possible.

"No. I'm so sorry."

"Hey, don't worry about it." One side of his lips hitched up. "But that's how you ended up in here, in case you were wondering. The guest bedroom should be ready for you again by tonight."

"Oh, no." Amy buried her face in her hands. She'd thought she couldn't get any more mortified, but apparently, there was still room on the scale. If only she could make herself disappear. She'd not only gotten so drunk they'd had to take care of her, she'd thrown up all over their guest bed, so they'd been forced to let her sleep in theirs. "Oh my God, I am so sorry."

"Hey, don't worry about it." Zach was awake, though his voice was still thick with sleep. Amy cringed because now she had to face *two* of them. He pushed himself up beside her in the bed, stretching and yawning. "We knew it might happen. You said you were nauseous the whole way over here. We had a bucket and everything... you just... missed a little."

Tears sparked in her eyes, and she gritted her teeth against the little sob that wanted to escape. She didn't want them to feel like they had to comfort her on top of everything else.

"I should go."

"You should take this." Something cold nudged her shoulder, making her jerk, and she looked up to see that Kincaid was holding out the orange juice and two little white pills. The stern look on his face made her tongue tied, even though she wanted to argue with him. "You're not going anywhere until you've had something to drink and eat. You need to rehydrate. Then you're going to take a shower and brush your teeth. Sam is bringing over some clothes for you, then we're meeting everyone at your... at... the house to grab your things."

"I... oh." Amy was about to at least try to argue when some of her memories from yesterday started to trickle back in at his words. She'd insisted that she wanted to be out of Jeremy's house *today*. She didn't want to wait. At least she hadn't then. Now, faced with the fact that she was probably going to be living with the two men whose bedroom she was currently in, she wasn't so sure.

To give herself some time to think and try to remember more, she took the orange juice and the pills from Kincaid, who smiled approvingly at her. That smile sent warmth flooding through her body in a way that made her blush, and she quickly popped the pills into her mouth and raised the glass of OJ to her lips to try to hide it. Behind her, Zach yawned again before reaching out to rub her shoulder. She felt the bed shift as he got up.

"Morgan and Asad volunteered to get boxes on their way over because there's a place by them that always has a bunch that people can pick up. Carolyn has to work, but Marissa said she would come help. Your mom and dad are going to meet us there with food for everyone who is coming to help." Kincaid rattled off the list of things that were happening like he was ticking little boxes in his head of how they were going to take care of everything. "On our way over, we'll stop by the U-Haul to get the truck I rented. We've also invited everyone who is helping over for dinner tonight."

Tears welled up again, for an entirely different reason this time.

When was the last time anyone had taken care of her like this? Made it so that she didn't have to think about a single thing? Jeremy always expected her to plan everything. To arrange everything. Every single guy she'd ever dated had expected that of her. Even the ones who asked her out first never just planned the first date. She always told herself they were being respectful, making sure she had input when they didn't really know her that well, but getting to know her better had never resulted in them doing more planning. The most Jeremy had ever planned was the proposal, and he'd gone for a classic—the ring in a glass of champagne during dinner at a fancy restaurant. Not exactly tailored to her.

Kincaid had taken care of organizing everything, renting the truck, *and* had a thank you planned for the helpers. And there were so many helpers coming to assist. It made her feel warm and fuzzy all over, despite everything. Amy knew she sucked at asking for help— she'd rather just do things on her own—so to know that everyone was just jumping in... it made her feel guilty and relieved and so loved, all at the same time.

Yesterday, while she'd been getting drunk, she'd been dreading having to figure out how she was going to get all her stuff out of Jeremy's house and to Zach and Kincaid's. Part of her had also been wondering if it would be smarter to go live with one of her girlfriends... but honestly, she wanted Zach. Not like, *want* wanted, but she felt safest thinking of being near him.

Plus, Zach would be preoccupied with Kincaid. They'd just gotten back together. Hopefully, she'd be able to just exist in the background while they focused on each other. If she went to Morgan or Sam's, both of whom were in settled relationships, they'd end up focusing on her. And if she went to her parents while they went on their trip, not only would she not be able to go to work, but she would be entirely alone with nothing but her own thoughts.

Which sounded horrible.

If her parents canceled their trip so she wasn't alone, she'd feel even worse than she already did.

Zach and Kincaid's place was the best solution now that she was able to think through it again soberly.

"I'm going to take a shower, then I'll be ready to go," Zach said. Amy glanced at him. Unlike Kincaid, he was wearing nothing but boxers. He sniffed the air and shot an accusing look at Kincaid, who was rounding the side of the bed now that he was satisfied Amy was eating. "Where's my coffee in bed?"

Kincaid just chuckled as he walked over to smack Zach's ass.

"If I brought you coffee in bed, you'd never get out of it," he said, turning from spanking Zach toward the door in one smooth motion. "Yours is waiting for you in the kitchen when you're out of the shower."

Zach grinned at him and headed to the door that Amy now knew led to the bathroom. She'd have to find another one to use soon because she needed to pee, but... coffee first. And time to gather herself.

She felt guilty for sitting in their bed, which she'd invaded, eating breakfast while they weren't even there. On the other hand, it would probably be more awkward if they were unless they were eating, too, and it sounded like Kincaid didn't make that an option for Zach.

Food helped settle her stomach, strangely enough, and the coffee was doing its job waking her up. Her head was starting to hurt less. So, physically, she was on her way up, and emotionally... emotionally she was in a million different places.

Hurt. Disappointed. Shamed.

Humiliated.

She hated knowing that everyone she cared about knew what a failure she was. Not just at failing to get married, but failing at picking out a good man to marry.

Yeah, Jeremy was the jerk who'd decided to elope with her bridesmaid on what was supposed to be their wedding day, but she was the dumbass who'd thought marrying him was a good idea in the first place. She was the one who'd missed all the signs leading up to the wedding that things weren't as they were supposed to be. She was the one who'd ignored all the red flags he'd waved in her direction.

She knew there would be some people who were wondering what was so wrong with her, what she had done that Jeremy felt like it was okay to leave her that way.

She was pretty sure he'd be telling everyone that she'd cheated soon enough. But she hadn't. She never would have.

So, why did she still feel so guilty?

Quietly eating, listening to Zach in the shower, she knew her conscience wasn't entirely clear.

5

KINCAID

Amy appeared shell-shocked at the number of people who had shown up to help her move out of Jeremy's house. And embarrassed. And so damn grateful she was running around nearly in tears, trying to help everyone who was trying to help her.

Eventually, Kincaid made her sit down on a chair in the bedroom, so everyone in there could show her things, and she could say keep, donate, or "not mine," and ordered her not to move from that spot. Because while some things were obviously hers, not everything was, and there were some things she decided not to take with her.

She didn't want to touch the bed, which was why he'd put her in the chair.

After they were done, he moved her to the kitchen while Morgan, Asad, Q, and Sam packed up everything they'd sorted in the bedroom. Her parents, Zach, and Marissa, all pitched in for the kitchen, holding up the things they'd pulled out that they thought might be hers.

While they packed up, Morgan and Amy went into the bathroom while he and the other three moved around the living room and television room, pulling things out that were likely Amy's.

"Pretty sure these DVDs are all hers," Q said, running his hand over his dark, bald head. "Unless Jeremy is a big chick flick fan." He held his hands up when his girlfriend gave him a suspicious look and grinned. "I'm not saying there's anything wrong with chick flicks. I'm just saying Jeremy seems like the toxic masculinity type who would think there is."

Sam huffed in agreement, sighing as she came over to look.

"You're not wrong, but I think all the DVDs are hers. I don't think Jeremy owned any."

"Because who still has DVDs, much less a working DVD player?" Kincaid quipped.

"Well, if you're going to make fun of me about it, you don't have to watch them," Amy said from behind him, a large thread of anger in her tone. As they'd gone through room by room, he'd noticed that she'd started moving from gratitude at the support from everyone to sadness. That she was heading toward anger didn't surprise him, but he also didn't deserve her ire.

He turned and gave her a hard look.

"I wasn't making fun of you; I was making fun of me. I have a DVD player and a collection. Which Zach often makes fun of me for, so if you're going to take it up with someone, take it up with him."

Amy immediately blushed, the rosy hue filling her cheeks as her shoulders slumped. Ah, dammit. He'd preferred seeing her a little riled up with more fight in her over back to being sad.

"Sorry," she said, reaching up to nervously tug on the end of the ponytail. "Being here is starting to get to me." Her gaze skittered away from his to scan the room, a mournful expression replacing the remorse. "It wasn't all bad, you know."

"It never is," Zach said, coming up behind Amy and putting a comforting hand on her shoulder. She turned her head to look at him, giving him a little smile.

Something about that little glance between them made Kincaid's chest squeeze tightly. He pushed the sensation away.

"If it was all bad, you would have broken up with him a long time ago. No one is terrible all the time."

"Most people aren't terrible until you're in too deep to realize that they're terrible. Like Noelle," Sam said, scowling. "Though I don't think any of us could have actually seen that coming. There aren't words for her."

"Yeah, but she was a good friend... until she wasn't." Amy frowned. "Though the more I think about it, I'm pretty sure all the times she was there for me, encouraging me to vent about Jeremy, all the times she let me cry on her shoulder... she was probably already fucking him, wasn't she?"

It felt odd to hear Amy curse. Kincaid didn't know her that well, but he couldn't remember ever hearing her curse before. He was pretty sure he remembered Zach saying something about that, too. It was a mark of how upset she was that she said it that way.

Zach moved his hand from one shoulder to the other, putting his arm around her and hugging her into his side. On one hand, Kincaid approved. On the other, Zach was not an affectionate touchy person, so he normally wasn't touchy with anyone but Kincaid and only in private. Stifling the rising jealousy that Zach clearly had no problem touching Amy in front of others was difficult.

Considering what she went through just yesterday, what kind of heartless asshole wouldn't give her comfort right now?

Especially because she clearly needed it. Amy leaned into him for a long moment, taking a deep, shuddering breath.

"It's okay, no one answer. We can't know for sure, but..." She tilted her head back to stare up at the ceiling, and now Kincaid's chest hurt for an entirely different reason as his heart ached for her. "I'm pretty sure. Anyway, I'm going to go to the kitchen and help finish up in there."

"I was actually just coming to tell you that we're done," Zach replied apologetically. "This is the last room, then we can take everything to our house until you can get a storage unit."

Amy blinked.

"Oh. Wow... that was fast."

It was fast. Everyone had come together to make it go a lot faster than it would have if she'd been on her own. Which had been

Kincaid's plan. He didn't want her to have to be in this house one second longer than absolutely necessary. Even though she could stay here, even though she had rights, he was glad she wasn't going to be here when Jeremy and Noelle got back.

She deserved a hell of a lot better than what they'd likely put her through if she was.

ZACH

Getting Amy out of that house was a relief. Zach was grateful for how her friends had come together to help so that it didn't take long. It had been a hard day for Amy, though she was doing her best to pretend like everything was fine. He'd seen how tense she'd been when they'd been in the house, surrounded by her and Jeremy's combined lives, then the way all that tension had drained from her when they'd left.

Now, she was just exhausted and limp, picking at the pizza Kincaid had ordered, long after everyone else had finished. The pizza and beer after a day of moving made him feel like he was in college again.

Couple by couple, her friends said goodbye and headed out until it was just them and her parents left. They were worried about her, he could see it, but they were also looking at Kincaid like he was their hero. Which Zach could understand. He knew he was looking at Kincaid in the same way.

The Dom had done a good job of organizing everyone and assigning jobs to get everything in place for today and then a masterful job of ensuring Amy didn't fall apart during the process. It had been close a few times before Kincaid had finally made her sit down and give directions rather than trying to do everything for the people who were trying to help her.

She wasn't used to sitting back and letting others help her, which had been more obvious today than ever before.

Now, her parents were sitting beside her on the couch, talking softly to her while he and Kincaid cleaned up in the kitchen. Zach had already taken care of the sheets on the guest bed so Amy could retreat to her room whenever she wanted. Part of him didn't like that she'd be so separate from them...

What if she needed them?

It was going to be her first night alone.

They hadn't told her because she'd already been embarrassed enough, but she'd begged not to be left alone last night. Even before she'd thrown up on the guest bed, they'd already been moving toward letting her sleep in theirs. That had just clinched it.

"She's going to be okay." Kincaid put his hand on Zach's shoulder, murmuring in his ear.

The view from the kitchen into the living room where Amy and her parents were wasn't completely open, but it was obvious what Zach was looking at.

He sighed and leaned against his boyfriend, feeling Kincaid's strength at his back. Kincaid's arms went around his shoulders, and Zach reached up to rest his hands on Kincaid's wrists, hugging him back in the only way he could in their current position.

"I'm just worried. It was a rough day for her."

"It was. She seems like she's doing okay, though."

"I think she's faking it for everyone." Yes, she'd gotten better and better throughout the day, but Zach was pretty sure she'd just worked harder at covering her true emotions.

"What do you want to do?"

That was the question, wasn't it?

Amy needed to cry. She hadn't cried since yesterday in the dressing room when he was holding her. She hadn't cried once today while they packed up her life and moved it from the house she thought she was going to live in with her husband. She'd gone from what she'd thought was a permanent living situation to a friend's guestroom and hadn't shed a single tear.

He wasn't sure she even realized how upset she was, but he could see it. In the past, the worse off she was when she came into the club, the more okay she'd seemed until he'd gotten her into the scene.

Sometimes, he thought she felt like it was okay to be a little upset, but not a lot, and so the more upset she was, the more compelled she felt to hide it.

The fact that he could now hear her laughing at whatever her dad had just said had him far more worried than if she was crying on his shoulder.

Zach knew what he needed to do to make her cry; he just wasn't sure she could handle it.

He wasn't sure Kincaid could handle it.

Yes, he and Amy had platonically scened in the past, but that was when they'd both been in committed relationships, when she hadn't been so vulnerable. When she hadn't been dependent on him, which she was now that she was taking over their guest bedroom. Whether Kincaid would be okay with continuing to scene together with her new lack of relationship... well, that was part of why Zach had wanted her to move in here with them, but he'd realized today that he hadn't talked to Kincaid at all about it.

He sighed.

Now was apparently the time for that.

"I think she needs a scene, if she'll accept one," he admitted. "She's bottled everything up so hard, I'm afraid she's going to explode."

Behind him, Kincaid didn't tense, his muscles remaining in place, which was a good sign. He wasn't upset at what Zach was saying, which relieved Zach's biggest worry. As concerned as he was about Amy, he had to put Kincaid first. Their relationship wasn't exactly on shaky grounds anymore, but they hadn't been back together very long, so it wasn't as strong as it had been when they'd negotiated him scening with others in the first place.

"Did you want to do it tonight?" Kincaid asked quietly. "Or wait 'til she'll go to the club?"

"Tonight, if she's agreeable. I'm worried about what will happen if I let her keep everything bottled up." Although he and Amy had never agreed that he was her Dom, he'd topped her enough to feel responsible. And he knew he wasn't the only one. Now that she was under their roof, Kincaid was going to feel responsible for her wellbeing, too. Hell, he already did, or he wouldn't have agreed to let her take over their guestroom for an indeterminate amount of time.

He felt Kincaid's deep breath.

"Okay."

"I want you there, too," Zach said, squeezing Kincaid's wrist. "If Amy agrees. You might see something I don't. I think we need both of us keeping an eye on her."

That and he wanted to make sure Kincaid didn't feel jealous or like he was being kept out of anything. Plus, he knew Amy was going to feel sensitive to the cheating accusations Jeremy and Noelle had flung at her. She would probably be more comfortable with Kincaid watching, so she was assured he didn't feel the same way.

Plus, doing anything in the house was going to be different from doing it at the club where they'd always been in public. Zach wasn't sure how he'd feel about scening with Amy in private, in his home. That felt so much more intimate than at the club.

He hadn't cheated on Kincaid, he fully believed that, but somehow, doing it at home felt different.

But he might be getting ahead of himself because everything he was thinking required Amy's consent, and he wasn't sure where her head was going to be.

6

Amy

Saying goodbye to her parents, Amy sagged as she shut the door behind them. She was so freaking tired. She knew they'd been staying because they wanted to make sure she was okay, but trying to pretend she was okay so they'd feel confident about leaving had been exhausting. And it wasn't that she wasn't okay exactly.

She was... numb. Mostly.

All she wanted to do was go curl up in bed and watch something. Or doom scroll. Start figuring out where she was going to live after this. She shouldn't take up their guest bedroom for more than a month. Two at most. Though she wasn't sure she could take looking for another place at this exact moment when she'd just finished moving everything.

She could plan something really nice to do for Kincaid and Zach as a thank you for all they'd done for her today and for letting her move in with them. Actually, that sounded like the best idea.

Doing something nice for someone else was sure to make her feel better. And it might relieve some of the guilt she felt about how little she'd done today while everyone was doing everything for her. She should probably make cookies or something for her friends. Write thank-you notes.

Her brain was still churning when she turned around to see both Kincaid and Zach standing there, looking at her.

For one beautiful, brilliant moment, her brain froze in appreciation of their pure male beauty. They looked so good, and they were both looking at *her.*

Then, her brain kicked in.

They're looking at me. Both of them.

They were waiting for me.

Why?

"Um, so thank you for everything today," she blurted out. Maybe they were waiting for her to express gratitude? She hadn't gotten a chance to yet today. Or maybe they wanted to reassure themselves she was okay before they went to bed, too. Just thinking about that made her feel even more tired, but they, more than anyone, deserved that reassurance. She just had to get the energy for it, then she could collapse in bed.

Alone.

Don't think about that. You'll be fine.

She hated sleeping alone but there was no way she was going to ask to join them again. They'd already let her do that one night. She was not invading their room again.

"Of course." Zach didn't smile as he answered, though. "Can we talk to you for a minute?" He gestured with his hand toward the living room where she'd been with her parents.

Oh, they probably wanted to talk about house rules or something. That made sense. Amy felt the sag of relief again. Rules she could do. All she had to do was nod and agree with everything they said, which she knew she would, even if they were unreasonable. But she trusted Zach not to be unreasonable, and if he was with Kincaid, then she trusted Kincaid. Plus, she knew enough about Kincaid from things Zach had said and from club gossip to know he was a really good guy.

So, whatever they wanted, she'd agree to, and not just because she didn't have a whole lot of other choices. They'd take care of her. She trusted that. Hell, she'd been experiencing it.

"Sure." She summoned her brightest smile and headed back into the living room, returning to the couch where she'd been sitting with her parents. To her surprise, rather than going to the couch across from her, on the other side of the coffee table, Zach and Kincaid came and sat down on either side of her, putting her in the middle. "Oh... um..."

She wasn't sure which one she was supposed to be looking at. Or why she was in the middle of them. Her brain was doing that fritzing thing again, as it had when she'd turned around and seen them standing there, waiting for her. She was trying desperately to reboot it, but she was so tired...

Zach took her hand, so she turned to look at him. He looked concerned. God, she was so tired of everyone looking at her with concern, even though she understood why, but that expression was just another reminder of how horrifically she'd failed at life. People weren't concerned about someone who was succeeding; they were only worried when you were falling apart.

"I..." he started to say, then stopped. Hesitated. Looked over her head at Kincaid. Her head turned with the change in his focus.

Kincaid met her gaze with compassionate eyes, which was almost worse than Zach's concern. With Zach, she could tell herself that he knew her well enough to be concerned. They had a long-time connection. He was a caring guy, of course—like all her friends and family. He was going to worry about her.

Her only connection to Kincaid was through Zach, and they'd been kept pretty separate in his life. So, while he wasn't a total stranger, it wasn't like they had a relationship that made him invested in her wellbeing. Her stomach turned over in embarrassment that he had to spend his time worrying about her because of the terrible choices she'd made.

"Zach and I want to know how you're holding up," Kincaid said gently.

He wasn't the first to ask, obviously, but it was the first time Amy hesitated before answering. It was the first time she tripped over the 'I'm not great, but I'll get there' lie that had been her standard for the whole day.

She was so far beyond 'not great,' and something about Kincaid's penetrating gaze made her feel like he would immediately know that she was lying and that he would be disappointed in her.

She shrugged instead of actually answering, dropping her gaze to her lap where Zach was holding her hand.

The silence between the two men was deafening, and she got the feeling there was a nonverbal conversation happening over her head. Would they be insulted if she just said she was tired and retreated to her room?

She was about to make the attempt, in the nicest way possible, when Zach spoke again, about a second before she would have opened her mouth.

"Do you want a scene tonight?"

Amy froze. That was the very last thing she'd expected him to say.

Okay, well, no, not quite. The last thing would have been an invitation to get naked and get in bed with him, but asking if she wanted a scene was ranked nearly as high on the list.

A scene.

He was asking if she wanted a scene.

The kind of scene they'd always done at the club.

But they weren't at the club.

Her mouth opened, but she didn't actually know what she wanted to say, so nothing came out.

"I..." That was all she had.

Flight, fight, or freeze, and she froze. Again. Like she always did. Her brain felt like it was buzzing with energy, but no comprehensible thoughts were actually emerging.

"Amy." Kincaid's deep voice cut through the buzzing, calling her back to the moment.

She turned her head again, looking into his dark eyes. They were so serious, so caring, as though he really saw her, which was utterly terrifying in its own way.

"May I touch you? Not sexually, but I would like to touch you."

Numbly, Amy nodded. She wasn't sure what he meant, but she didn't mind being touched. Touch was comfort.

And God, did she need to be comforted today.

Kincaid's arm lifted, then she felt his hand curve around the back of her neck, almost as if he was going to draw her toward him to kiss, but instead, his fingers slid up and pressed into the soft points just under her skull. It felt really, really good. Not in a sexual way. In a massage way.

She sighed out a long breath of air, letting her head drop, her eyes closing as he pressed his fingers in, kneading softly and releasing the tension from the little muscles there. Her shoulders slumped. Zach squeezed her fingers.

"Zach thinks you need a scene," Kincaid said gently but firmly as he continued to rub her neck. "I don't know you as well as he does, but I agree with him. We want to make you feel better."

God, she wanted to feel better. The awful block of emotion sitting in the pit of her chest, which she'd been successfully ignoring all day, pulsed, as if it realized it was being threatened. It would feel good to let it all go, wouldn't it?

This was what Jeremy hadn't understood. That it wasn't about sex. It was about release. It was about getting all the things she held inside of her *out* of her. And right now, she had more emotions clawing at her insides than normal, trying to trip their way through her skin, through her tears, and out into the world, yet she felt like she couldn't let them.

It wasn't like crying was productive. It never helped a situation. But she knew she held the tears in for too long, and it got to a point where the lack of crying did start to harm her. All those ugly emotions would come out in bursts of anger or meanness if she held them back for too long, and that wasn't the kind of person she wanted to be.

Which was why she needed to get them out.

She nodded her head.

"I want to feel better." She also wanted to sound less pathetic, but that apparently wasn't an option right now.

"Good girl."

All the air rushed out of her lungs as tears filled her eyes unbidden. She was so on edge, she was about to start weeping at being called a good girl. Something settled inside her stomach at the acknowledgment that even though Jeremy had dumped her in a spectacularly humiliating manner, even though a bunch of people probably thought she was a cheater and a scum human being now, even though she'd had to upend her entire life and move it out of the house she thought she'd be living her married life in… she was still a good girl.

"Come here, Amy." Zach tugged on her hand gently, letting her be the one to control her movements but indicating he wanted her to move. "I want you over my lap."

This was easier than having to say, 'Yes, I want a scene.' Because agreeing to a scene, knowing how Jeremy felt about them now, made her feel guilty all over again. But this wasn't agreeing, it was just doing. It was following direction.

It was being a good girl.

Reluctantly pulling away from Kincaid's hand on her neck, she felt his fingers trail down to the center of her shoulder blades and give her gentle guidance forward and over Zach's lap. Resting her face against the leather couch, she took in a deep breath, inhaling the rich scent, which reminded her of the club and helped her relax even more.

Zach's hand came down on her lower back, rubbing in a similar manner to the way Kincaid had rubbed her neck.

"What's your safe word, Amy?"

He knew her safe word, but he asked her every time, anyway, as a good Dom would.

She felt his hesitation, the brief pause in his hand when he realized.

Her safe word was 'Jeremy.'

Obviously not a great safe word anymore.

"Red." She'd go with the stoplight system until she could think of something unique. If she wanted to pick something unique again.

"Good. I'm going to lower your pants, though we'll keep your underwear on." He wasn't asking; he was telling. She had her safe word if she wanted to stop him.

Amy relaxed against his lap, closing her eyes as he briskly pulled down the yoga pants she was wearing. She knew Kincaid was probably staring right at her butt in her ugly granny panties, but she didn't care. She wasn't trying to be attractive for him or for Zach. This wasn't about that.

She wondered if Jeremy had ever truly understood that. Or if he would look at her like this and see her pants being pulled down and assume it could only be sexual rather than the simple fact that a spanking over pants just wasn't as effective. Without knowing what pictures Noelle had taken of her and shared with Jeremy, Amy couldn't be sure, but she was willing to bet that was how he'd taken it.

Even though she often didn't come home horny from a session with Zach, and the few times she had, he'd been the one to benefit. Or maybe the lack of coming home horny had been what made him think she was cheating.

She didn't get the chance to think much deeper about what was going on because Zach's hand came down on her ass.

Hard.

Hard enough to take her breath away and make her cry out.

Normally, he gave her a bit of a warmup before getting into everything heavy.

But normally, they didn't do an over-a-lap spanking with just his hand. Normally, he had some kind of implement and something planned out he wanted to do. Normally, she would be bound to some piece of equipment, not pressed up against his body.

Right now, nothing was normal, so it made sense this wasn't either. And she was grateful this part wasn't normal.

Being held on his lap, his body against hers was comforting. He was holding her, even as he was spanking her, his hand coming down again and again, her breath coming in short, sharp gasps every time his palm connected. Yet the tears weren't spilling over yet.

It didn't hurt enough yet.

More.

She wanted—needed—more until the external pain matched the agony that was clutched tight in the little ball of emotion in the center of her chest.

Her hips moved, lifting her ass up as she clutched the couch cushion she had her face pressed against.

Someone wrapped their hand around her hair.

No, not someone. Kincaid. It was him because Zach was the one holding down the middle of her back while his other hand went to town on her ass. The burn was growing, even though it didn't match the rock of emotion in her chest. She needed it harder. Though the tingling sensation as Kincaid tugged on her hair helped.

She sensed more than saw him kneel down beside her.

"You're a good girl, Amy." His voice was low. Firm. Not gentle, but soft and utterly controlled, and his words completely undid her in a way that she would have never expected. "You didn't do anything wrong. You deserved so much more than what Jeremy did to you."

They were all the right words, and they made her choke as the sobs she'd thought were still tightly locked away were suddenly in her throat. Zach's hand came down again, right on her sit spot, and a small cry leaked out.

It was too soon. Normally, she needed a lot more pain before she could cry, but the combination of Zach's palm and Kincaid's voice was ripping her defenses apart like a seam ripper through thread.

"Jeremy should have never treated you like that."

Zach's hand came down on her other sit spot.

"You deserve someone who loves you."

Another burning slap against her heated skin.

"You deserve someone who treats you like a queen."

And another.

"You're a good girl."

Amy's raw cry as the sobs erupted from her was akin to a wounded animal.

7

Waking up to a woman between him and Zach for the second morning in a row was an odd experience. Especially because it didn't feel as odd as it probably should.

He turned his head to look at the woman in question. She appeared much more peaceful this morning, though the skin around her eyes was mottled. She'd cried so hard, she'd burst some of the capillaries in the delicate skin around her eyes. But her breathing was deep and even, the lines on her forehead that she'd fallen asleep with had smoothed out overnight, and all the distress had been wiped away.

Which was a relief.

He didn't think that was quite how her and Zach's scenes normally went, though he knew she went to Zach to help her with emotional release. That had definitely been a huge pressure valve bursting last night.

Afterward, he and Zach hadn't needed to talk to know that she was sleeping in their bed again. There was no way either of them was going to leave her. She'd dropped and dropped *hard* at the end of the scene. Kincaid wouldn't leave his worst enemy going through that all alone, much less someone he actually liked.

Quietly, he slipped out of bed, leaving her a robe to put on since they didn't have any of her clothes in here, and went to get breakfast ready again. Just like yesterday. He was just glad there was something he *could* do. Last night, he'd felt helpless while she was crying her heart out because it was what she'd needed, and there had been nothing he or Zach could do to fix it.

They'd already done all they could.

She'd fallen asleep clinging to both of them, still shaking from her excess of emotion.

This morning, she would need coffee and something to help restore the energy she'd expended last night.

As he was getting breakfast ready, his phone beeped at him. He glanced over at the display—Mitch was calling. His best friend, outside of Zach. They hadn't been at the wedding. Amy was friendly with Mitch and his girlfriend Domi, but Domi and her group of friends didn't get along that well with several of Amy's other friends, especially not with Noelle.

Quickly rinsing off his hands from the eggs he'd been cracking, Kincaid swiped the answer button and put it on speaker.

"Hey, what's up?"

"Pretty sure I should be asking you that." As usual, Mitch's voice was filled with amusement. He walked through the world, finding the fun in it and constantly clowning around, right up until it was time to torment his submissive, at which point he turned into a sternly sadistic Dom. "I hear you have a new housemate."

Kincaid wasn't surprised. The gossip train at Stronghold and Marquis would be running strong. It wasn't just Amy's bridesmaids who were members of the kink clubs; there had been plenty of them among the guests, too. He bet the word had started spreading that something was happening—even though no one had known what— the moment Sam had come to get him and Zach.

"We do." He hesitated. "What are people saying?"

"Oh, all sorts of crazy things, you know how it is. Everything from

Amy and her groom had a big fight right before the wedding because she caught him cheating or he caught her cheating, to he was kidnapped, to he eloped to Vegas with one of her bridesmaids." Mitch cracked up at that last one because it was so freaking unbelievable.

Even having witnessed it, Kincaid was still having trouble believing it. Because who the fuck even did that? Who thought that was an acceptable thing to do?

"It's more of a combination of the first and last one. Noelle convinced Jeremy that Amy was cheating on him, and apparently, the correct reaction to that was to fly to Vegas and elope with Noelle on what was supposed to be his and Amy's wedding day." Kincaid stabbed the cantaloupe, which allowed him to vent his feelings a little.

"No fucking way."

"Way. Marissa, of all people, said she's going to talk to Patrick. Apparently, Noelle took pictures of Amy inside the club and shared them with Jeremy as proof."

"Hell, I scened with Amy... in the past, before Domi and I got together. I fucking believe her when she said she told him what she was doing and that he'd consented to her being there. She was very clear about the boundaries. It was all platonic kink, nothing sexual at all." The indignation in Mitch's voice matched how Kincaid felt about the whole situation.

"He's an asshole," Kincaid said flatly. Even though he'd never actually met the guy, that was clear. His emotions were coming out in the way he was cutting up the cantaloupe, which did not need the aggressive movements he was using because it was actually very ripe and easy to cut. But it helped him feel a little better. "Even if he didn't truly understand what he was agreeing to, he deliberately chose to hurt and humiliate her in the worst way possible. He could have called off the wedding beforehand. He didn't. And he didn't have to elope with Noelle on the wedding day. He did it because he wanted to be cruel."

"Noelle, too. I know we're not supposed to speak badly about the submissives, but..." Mitch's voice trailed off. "Between what she did to Iris and what she's done now to Amy..." Suddenly, he laughed, startling Kincaid. "Domi just called her a cuntcake."

Obviously, Mitch wasn't on speaker because Kincaid hadn't been able to hear Domi at all. He couldn't help but laugh, too, despite the situation.

Maybe the Dominants weren't supposed to speak badly of the submissives, but that wasn't going to stop the submissives from doing so. He doubted Noelle was going to find any welcome at Stronghold, even if Patrick didn't revoke her membership. Everyone loved Amy. On top of that, no one was going to take it well that Noelle had secretly been taking pictures inside the club. She'd broken trust on just about every possible level.

"I mean..."

"She's a total cuntcake," Amy said from behind him, making him jump about a foot in the air and spin around, knife held up high, heart racing from the surprise.

He hadn't heard her moving around. She smiled at him. Her eyes were still puffy and red, but the smile looked more real than any of the ones she'd worn on her lips yesterday. His navy-blue robe was far too large on her and yet she looked like she was happy to be snuggled into it.

"Is that Amy?" Mitch asked from the phone. "Hey, sweetie, how are you feeling?"

"Better than yesterday," she said, which was a good non-answer. Considering she'd been as low as a person could be yesterday, it wasn't like that was a high bar to clear. "I'll be even better if that's fresh coffee I smell." Her hazel eyes met his with pleading hope.

"It is. Mugs are in there." He nodded his head toward the correct cabinet, then turned around to finish cutting up the cantaloupe.

"Thanks. Sorry for interrupting, but I woke up, and my stomach was growling," she said apologetically. He heard the cabinet opening behind him.

"Well, we are talking about you," Mitch said, back to his normal cheerful tone. "Might as well have you join in, right? For some reason

Domi is telling me she's got a shovel as if that has some sort of special significance. However, I have to tell you that I do not approve of any plans that involve actual body burial, no matter how a person might, theoretically, deserve it."

As always, Mitch got the laugh he was looking for. It was one of his superpowers and one that Kincaid was rather envious of, especially right now. He was happy to see Amy genuinely laughing.

"So, make any murder and body burial plans when you're not around, got it," she said teasingly as she poured herself a cup of coffee.

"Hey, now, I can't be hearing this either. Former police officer, remember?" Kincaid protested. He knew they were joking.

Probably.

"Since it's 'former,' it's not really an issue though, right?" Mitch asked. "You've moved into personal security, and as long as it's not a client..."

"Oh, yes, that automatically is going to stop me from doing the right thing." Kincaid shook his head. "If she gets caught, she'll be in jail. The best revenge is living happily."

"Oh, so it's for practical reasons and not just because you're Dudley Do-Right," Mitch teased, making Amy laugh and Kincaid grimace.

He did try to do the right thing, always, and it had bitten him in the ass more than once. It was a large part of the reason he'd made the job move into personal security, but that was his burden and not something Amy needed to hear about when she was actually laughing and smiling.

"But if they get caught, you'll be the first in line with bail money, right?"

"Of course." He winked at Amy, pushing aside his own issues. "It would be the right thing to do."

She laughed again, bringing the coffee cup up to her lips to hide her smile.

Kincaid grinned at her. For this moment, at least, he was pretty sure she actually was okay.

Zach

No one was in bed with him and the sound of laughter was trickling down the hall and into the bedroom as he hit his alarm. Zach frowned grumpily. Apparently, everyone was having a great time without him.

What was with both Amy and Kincaid being early morning risers?

He wanted as much sleep as he could get.

He was tempted to call out of work again today because he was a little worried about how Amy would be doing after last night, but since he could actually hear her laughing, maybe it wasn't going to be a problem.

That or she was faking it again.

Which he thought was the far more likely scenario.

Amy was really damn good at compartmentalizing, so that even when she was enjoying herself, even when she was laughing and having fun, there could very easily be a part of her that was dying inside. Though she'd gotten some of that out yesterday, he knew it was too soon for her to be fully okay. She'd be even better at faking it, though, now that she wasn't holding herself together by inches.

The urge to check on her was what propelled him out of bed and into some pajama pants. Normally, he'd spend his time getting ready for the day before heading into the kitchen, but today, he wanted to see what was going on with Amy before anything else. As he walked toward the kitchen, he recognized Mitch's voice, and it only took him a moment to realize the man was on the phone and not in the kitchen with the other two. Kincaid gave him a knowing look when he walked into the room, as if he'd anticipated Zach's change of routine.

The all-too-perceptive Dom probably _had_ guessed how he'd react.

"Good morning," Kincaid said, handing him a mug of coffee.

"Morning." Zach did his best not to clutch at the mug in an obvious manner, but even the smell was helping him wake up.

"Morning Amy. Hey, Mitch, what's up?" As the words came out of his mouth, he realized he knew exactly what was up.

The gossip train was running full steam ahead, as usual.

"Morning, sunshine." Mitch chuckled. "I was just calling to check in and see how everyone was doing."

Uh-huh.

Well, hell, if he was the reason Amy was laughing this morning, Zach would take that. She probably needed a break from all the heavy emotions of the past two days, even if they were still lingering under her smile, and Mitch was definitely the guy to provide.

"We're good," Zach said easily, trying not to be too obvious about how he was looking Amy over. It had only taken him a moment to recognize the robe she was wearing—he wouldn't be surprised if Kincaid had left it out for her, so she didn't have to walk around in the tank top and underwear she'd fallen asleep in last night. She appeared tired, eyes still puffy and red, but the smile on her lips was sincere. At least for now. He didn't know how long it would last, but he liked seeing her smile. "Just getting up and getting ready for work."

Amy's smile faltered.

Ah, shit. He inwardly cursed his unthinking response.

She wouldn't be at work this week unless she was going to call in and tell them that she'd been left at the altar. The company she worked for was pretty large, and she worked in HR, which was why she hadn't invited any of her co-workers to the wedding, though she'd told him they'd thrown her a bridal shower. That was the kind of thing her department did.

They'd all be very sympathetic, but he doubted she wanted to face having to actually tell people about the wedding right now.

"Well, let us know if you need anything," Mitch replied. Since he couldn't see Amy's expression, he likely didn't realize how Zach had just fumbled. Kincaid did, though, and was shooting Zach an entirely different kind of look now.

Zach lifted the coffee to his lips, partly to keep himself from saying anything else stupid. Partly because he hoped the caffeine would wake him up enough that he wouldn't have to worry about what was coming out of his mouth because his brain would be working.

"Thank you," Amy replied to Mitch, pushing the smile back onto her lips.

Zach could tell it wasn't real this time, though. He'd managed to break the spell by reminding her of everything she was going to have to face.

Co-workers. Family. Returning gifts—she'd made them take all the gifts she and Jeremy had received yesterday because she didn't trust him to do it in a timely manner. The list went on and on.

"We'll talk to you later. Seriously, call me if any of you need anything."

"Thanks, Mitch." Kincaid leaned over the counter to where the phone was sitting in front of Amy and pressed the end call icon. It put him and Amy standing very close together, and an odd twinge went through Zach's chest as he stood across from them.

Not a jealous twinge, just a...

He didn't know.

All he knew was that he'd never expected to be standing in his home in the morning, drinking coffee, with the two most important people in his life standing there together. They'd always been kept so separate. It felt both strange and familiar at the same time, like déjà vu, even though he knew it had never happened before.

There wasn't a good way to explain it.

Amy took a deep breath, avoiding both his and Kincaid's gazes as she moved around Kincaid to take her empty coffee mug to the sink, rinsing it out and putting it in the dishwasher as she spoke.

"Right. So, thank you for breakfast. I need to go take a shower and... figure out what I'm going to do with my day." She skittered out of the kitchen before either of them could respond, not that Zach was sure what he was going to say.

Lifting his gaze to Kincaid's, he looked at his partner helplessly. Kincaid's mouth twisted in unhappiness, but he shrugged one shoulder.

"We might need to give her some space," he said softly, obviously wanting to make sure that Amy wouldn't be able to overhear him. "She was pushed pretty far yesterday. It might be good for her to have some time alone to think."

Right. Zach nodded.

Watching him, Kincaid tilted his head to the side, then stepped forward, opening his arms to wrap them around Zach. He hugged the other man back, resting his chin on Kincaid's shoulder and letting out some of the tension he'd been holding. Since they'd gotten back together fairly recently, he appreciated moments like this far more than he had before their breakup.

He closed his eyes, leaning on his boyfriend and wishing he knew what to do for Amy.

He also believed they'd figure it out.

Together.

8

―――――――

The week of her honeymoon felt entirely surreal and not just because she wasn't on her honeymoon. Her life had fallen apart, yet she didn't feel as bad as she probably should. That was largely due to Zach and Kincaid.

They had to go to work every day—though Kincaid's hours were more flexible than Zach's, and he was also working at home part-time—which meant she had the house to herself most of the time during the day. Even when Kincaid was working from home, he spent most of his time in his office on the phone or the computer, leaving her to her own devices.

She didn't love that part.

But she also didn't feel totally alone.

Zach texted her multiple times throughout the day. Whenever Kincaid was home, he was constantly checking to see if she needed anything—hiding away in her room didn't keep him from doing so. If anything, it seemed to make him more concerned and more interested in what she was doing, so she still couldn't wallow alone in there.

Every evening, one of her friends surprised her by stopping by for dinner, except for Marissa who had had to leave town for work again. But she called on the evening no one was coming over. Amy was surprised, though Kincaid and Zach weren't.

It was Sam who quietly confirmed that Kincaid was behind the scheduling.

To keep from going crazy while she was alone, Amy spent her days being as busy as possible. There was a lot to do, and as long as she didn't think about why she was doing it—like mailing back unopened gifts and answering emails from concerned friends and family members—she was just fine. If she thought about it as though she was her own secretary doing admin work, it became downright easy.

I'm not Amy, devastated by having to explain to yet another concerned cousin that I'm doing just fine... I'm writing this email on behalf of Amy.

I'm not Amy, so I don't need to cry over going to the post office with an armful of boxes for four days in a row... I'm mailing these gifts back on behalf of Amy.

Though, she did deliberately go to a different post office each day. The drive as she went farther afield helped clear her head, and that way, she didn't feel like the workers were wondering what the hell she was doing there for four days in a row, mailing multiple boxes. She didn't need the judgment of strangers; she was already judging herself hard enough.

Her parents checked in every other day, too, despite being on their trip. At least those calls were brief.

The catharsis she'd felt after the scene Zach and Kincaid had given her was slowly wearing off over the week, but at the same time, she didn't feel like she could ask them for more. They'd already done too much. *Were* doing too much. Giving her a room to stay in, helping her move her stuff, having her friends come over...

They didn't need a needy, clingy houseguest hanging on them all the time just because she was dumb enough to get engaged to a total asshole.

I think I might be working my way toward the anger portion of grieving.

Except she was as mad at herself for grieving as she was at Jeremy for being such a jerk. She was even more mad at herself for trusting Noelle so much. For trusting both of them.

The madder she got, the harder she scrubbed at the spot on the stove that she was trying to get out. It was Friday afternoon, both the guys were at work, and she was determined to make their house spotless before they got home. She'd spent the morning listening to the *Martinis and Murder* podcast while she cleaned, but for the afternoon, she'd switched over to the *Tortured Poets Department*.

Everything but the last two songs fit her mood perfectly.

She'd turned the volume all the way up, so when it suddenly cut off completely, she jumped and screamed in surprise, whirling around. Kincaid stood there, one eyebrow raised, hand hovering over the speaker she'd connected her phone to.

"Sorry, I didn't mean to scare you," he said a little sheepishly. Even hunching his shoulders a little, he couldn't exactly make himself look small.

Today, he'd gone to work in a suit, and he must have taken the jacket off when he'd come home because now he only had on the light blue button-down shirt he'd been wearing beneath it. The sleeves were rolled up, showing off his forearms, which she tried very hard not to look at because it reminded her of Sunday night, even though Zach had been the one to actually spank her. Her scalp tingled, as though she could still feel his fingers in her hair.

Get over yourself, Amy. Stop lusting after men you can't have.

Probably shouldn't be lusting at all.

But with heartbreak came the urge for a rebound, and there was definitely a part of her that wanted to lose herself and her mind in a night of really hot, amazing sex. Just, obviously, she couldn't do that with Kincaid. Or Zach. Or both of them. *Oh my God, stop thinking about it.*

"It's okay." She made herself smile at him, even though her heart was still racing, and her head was full of impure thoughts about two men who were just being nice to her and trying to help her out. God, she was pathetic. "I just didn't realize you were going to be home so soon."

"Finished up my meeting early." He leaned against the counter, his gaze scanning over the kitchen. "Wow. It looks amazing in here. Thank you for cleaning."

She snorted, waving her hand in deprecation.

"I figure it's the least I can do, considering how you and Zach have opened your home to me and taken care of me all week."

Kincaid tilted his head to the side, his gaze sharpening as he focused in on her. "You think we've been taking care of you all week?"

She stared at him for a moment, wet sponge squishy against her palm, before she answered.

"Um... yes." Duh.

"You do realize you've made dinner every night this week, right?" The eyebrow he raised now was twice as effective as the one he'd greeted her with. "You also made lunches for us every morning."

"Oh, well... I mean, you're both working. I've just been here."

"You also tried to take out the trash on Wednesday. And you did gather up everything in the house before Zach or I realized what you were doing and actually took it out."

"Well... I'm just trying to be a good housemate."

"How many of the rooms did you clean today?"

Okay, now she was starting to feel a little pissy about how he was questioning her. Couldn't he just accept the gesture? Why did he need to poke and prod at what she was doing?

"Are you saying it's a bad thing to help out around the house? That it's bad that I want to do something for you and Zach since you're letting me stay here?"

"No." He said it so definitively, she couldn't even argue.

Amy shifted her gaze away from his, feeling uncomfortable with exactly how deep it pierced.

"I'm saying you shouldn't feel like you have to earn staying here. You're paying rent, we already talked about that, remember? Which means we should be sharing in the chores around the house. I just don't want you to think that you have to do this next week, too, after you go back to work. If you're working off excess energy around the house this week, I get it, but you are part of this household even if you hadn't lifted a single finger."

Now, she was definitely uncomfortable. And pissed, though she wasn't sure why she was mad. Her skin was hot, and her stomach was churning the way it did before a fight. The excess energy he'd mentioned was buzzing underneath her skin and making her want to lash out, but that wasn't any way to thank someone who had opened their house to her. Yes, she was paying rent, but she was also well aware that she was an intruder into his and Zach's life.

"You could just say thank you," she muttered, then dared to peek at him to see how he reacted.

The dark, piercing gaze that met hers was full of contemplation, and he was silent for a long enough moment that she wanted to squirm, then melt into a puddle of shame. If she was a puddle, she'd be able to slide away, unnoticed, instead of having to stand here with someone who saw her far too clearly.

"Thank you for cleaning up the house, Amy," he said very formally after a long moment.

Somehow, it made her feel even worse. She kind of wished he'd yelled at her instead for being bratty. Or chastised her. Something.

Him being nice to her after she'd just gotten mouthy with him felt wrong.

She felt on edge, waiting for the back end, waiting for the rest of whatever he was going to say.

Instead, there was just silence, like he was waiting for her.

"No problem," she said after an excruciatingly long moment. "I'm, um, gonna go take a shower."

"Okay. I'll make dinner." A ghost of a smile flitted around his mouth, but Amy barely took notice of it as she fled the room.

What was wrong with her? What had she been waiting for? Her skin still felt too tight, like her body was buzzing and humming beneath it, vibrating with extra energy as she waited for... something.

Something hurtful.

Something that she was bracing herself against.

Jeremy would have said something mean in the same situation. Well, if he'd even noticed that she'd cleaned the house. Or made him dinner. Or any of the other things Kincaid had both noted and listed.

God, was she really that used to being invisible? Taken for granted?

Knowing Kincaid was making dinner rather than letting her do it made her want to run back to the kitchen to help, but she'd already said she was going to take a shower. Plus, as he'd pointed out, she'd already made dinner every night that week.

He and Zach had been incredibly grateful every night and insisted on doing the dishes. The first night, they'd had to practically kick her out of the kitchen.

Okay, so maybe he had a point that it's been a little excessive.

Sighing, Amy closed her bathroom door behind her and pulled her phone out of her pocket rather than getting straight to undressing. She had the group text, but she didn't want to talk to *everyone*. So, she called Sam, who answered after only one ring.

"Hey, girlfriend."

"Hey, got a minute?" She'd picked up quickly, which meant probably yes, but Amy always wanted to check.

"Sure." Sam's tone was overly cheerful and encouraging, and Amy had the feeling that even if Sam didn't actually have the time, she'd make the time. Which meant Amy would have to be quick because she didn't want to hold Sam back in case she was doing something important.

"If I was living with you and I made dinner every night, would you think that's going overboard?" Ugh. Saying the words out loud made her cringe because she could hear how that might be a little overboard now that she'd said it.

Sam's brief silence in answer spoke volumes.

"Um... did we discuss you making dinner every night?"

"Well... no."

"Am I ever helping? Or doing the dishes?"

"You do the dishes every night." Amy decided not to mention that she'd tried to fight Kincaid and Zach on that. Sam had only asked about what was being done, not whether or not she'd tried to do that, too.

"Well... I guess that seems fair. I probably would have wanted to talk about it first or make a schedule. Is everything okay?"

"Yeah, I just... Kincaid seems to think I've been doing too much around the house." Which made her grumpy, but Sam laughed.

"I kind of wondered if this was going to happen," she said.

"If what was going to happen?" Some of Amy's frustration was starting to leak into her voice, but she really didn't know what Sam was talking about.

"You and Kincaid are both caretakers. Put two caretakers in a house and you're both going to try to take care of each other. I kind of wish I was Zach, just so I could watch you two dance around, trying to be the one to do the caretaking."

Amy opened her mouth, then closed it.

Huh.

Sam might have a point. It had felt a bit like a dance with Kincaid, and although Zach had been firm in insisting he do the dishes, she was butting heads with Kincaid more than Zach over the day-to-day stuff.

"Just make sure to let him do some things for you," Sam continued. "He needs it."

Crap.

Now, she felt guilty.

At least she was letting him make dinner tonight. She'd have to do more of that, even though it felt wrong to sit back and let someone else handle everything. Well, obviously, she didn't feel that way in the bedroom, but in everything else, it felt like she was supposed to be doing something.

Crap.

Was this how she'd been making Kincaid feel by doing everything? Like he was itchy and useless because she'd taken over doing everything around the house?

Turning to face the wall, phone still to her ear, Amy gently banged her head against the flat surface. She couldn't do it too loudly because she didn't want Kincaid or Sam to hear her.

She couldn't believe she hadn't noticed that about Kincaid and hadn't been thinking about how she might make him feel. No wonder he'd been slow to thank her. No wonder he'd been pointing out everything that she'd been doing. She just hoped he didn't think she was deliberately trying to take his place or something.

Maybe they could figure out a chore chart.

"Right. I will definitely make sure I let him do some things for me."

"You've been doing everything, haven't you?" Sam's amusement was unabated.

"Not the dishes."

"Uh-huh." Then Sam's voice shifted, and Amy kind of wished she'd stayed amused. "Is everything else okay? How are you doing?"

"I'm fine." Standard answer. And true. She was as fine as she could be.

"Are you sure? Even with Jeremy and Noelle coming home tomorrow?" Sam's voice had softened; she was apologetic, but she was still asking. Still prodding at the wound.

"I don't see how that's going to affect me." At least she was going to do her best to make sure it *didn't* affect her. That nothing either of those people ever did ever affected her again.

"Well, good. But if you need me, all you have to do is call. That goes for all your friends. Or... do you want to hang out tomorrow?"

"Aren't you going to the club tomorrow?"

"I don't have to."

As if she was going to keep her friend from doing something she enjoyed just to babysit her. She wasn't that pathetic.

"No, go. If I need you, I'll come there." Even as she said the words, her nose wrinkled in reaction. She wasn't quite ready to return to Stronghold or Marquis yet, and she knew it.

But there was no way she was going to burden Sam with her issues. Jeremy and Noelle coming home was a non-issue, anyway. It wasn't like she was going to see them. They were no longer part of her life.

Period.

9

———

"So.... when are you going to tell Mom and Dad about you and Kincaid?" Krista asked, the question echoing around his car as he pulled to a stop at the red light.

"Don't make me regret calling you for my drive home," he joked, even as his chest tightened. His sister meant well, but she was the only one in his family who knew he and Kincaid were a couple for a reason. Eventually, he was going to have to tell his parents or lose Kincaid; he knew that, yet he kept pushing that day off.

"I don't think they're going to react as badly as you think they will." She'd been supportive when he told her he had a boyfriend and delighted to meet Kincaid, but she was also far more progressive than either of his parents.

"Uh-huh. You mean like how when Uncle Mark told us that Jaime had come out as gay, Dad said he was happy to Uncle Mark, then as soon as he hung up the phone, he started shaking his head and talking about how hard that was going to be on everyone?"

Krista was silent for a long moment, which was not her normal modus operandi.

"I forgot about that," she finally admitted.

Zach hadn't. It had happened a week after he and Kincaid had started dating, and it was burned into his brain.

At the time, he'd told himself there was no point in telling his parents anyway because it wasn't like he was sure it was going to stick.

That wasn't the case anymore, but it didn't make telling his parents any easier. They'd hung up a pride flag that June, but his dad still talked about his brother with pity for having a lesbian daughter.

"Remember how Mom asked Jaime and her girlfriend how they're going to choose which of them is biologically related to the baby, and she didn't stop to question whether or not Jaime and Leslie even want a baby? And when Jaime reminded her that they'd only been dating for a month, she said that she'd read online that that's like a year in lesbian relationships?" It had all happened so fast, it had taken Zach and Krista that long to recover from their shock to intervene, much to his cousin and her girlfriend's relief.

His mom had come back and apologized after a long talk with Krista, which Jaime and Leslie had been gracious enough to accept, but still. He could only imagine what kind of questions his mom would have for Kincaid if she found out he was more than Zach's roommate.

"Okay, but Mom is going to do that regardless of who your partner is. Remember how when you were with Jill and I was single, she asked me when I was giving her a grandchild, and I told her to bother you since you actually were with someone, and I didn't have a boyfriend? And she told me that I don't need a boyfriend to give her a grandchild?"

Zach laughed as the light turned green.

"I'd forgotten about that," he admitted. Sometimes, the things that came out of his mom's mouth... No wonder he and Krista remembered different, slightly horrifying things. There was so much to choose from.

"Yeah, being straight isn't going to stop the invasive questions," she said dryly. "Trust me."

"You have a point. But I feel like they're a lot more invasive to anyone she doesn't understand."

"Well, you're not wrong there." Krista sighed. The car was silent as Zach made the final turn onto his street. "You do need to tell them, though. Mom's been talking about trying her hand at matchmaking. Apparently, one of her friends has a very nice, newly single daughter who's only a few years older than you."

Groaning, Zach pulled into the left side of the driveway, making sure to leave room between his car and the garage door in case Amy decided she wanted to go out. He and Kincaid had insisted she put her car in the garage, in large part because neither of them wanted Noelle or Jeremy to drive by and see it there. Just in case they decided to come harass her some more.

If she took the garage spot, they'd never know whether she was home if they were watching. He wouldn't put it past them. Assholes.

"I'll tell them. Soon. I'm just waiting for the right moment." It was the same thing he'd said to Kincaid multiple times now. Though Kincaid hadn't asked again in the past couple of weeks.

Either he was leaving it entirely up to Zach, or he'd given up. Zach really, really hoped it was the former. Though, this week, it was understandable why Kincaid hadn't asked. Maybe having Amy move in with them was enough of a distraction that he'd set the matter aside for now, which would give Zach a little more breathing room.

"Sometimes, you have to make the right moment."

"Yeah, yeah, I know. I'm home now, so I'm hanging up. Talk later, bossy pants."

"Good luck, kid."

Zach chuckled as he ended the call. When they were kids, Krista had wanted to call him 'squirt,' just like the big sister in one of her favorite books. He'd balked, and they'd negotiated and then settled on 'kid.' It didn't matter that he was now half a foot taller than her and an adult; the nickname had stuck. On days like today, it was both reassuring and made him long for a simpler time.

Walking into the house, he breathed in deep as he recognized the scent of Kincaid's tomato sauce. *Hell, yes.* Whatever Kincaid was making, Zach was excited. Amy had been cooking for them all week, and she was a very good cook, but Kincaid's tomato sauce was his favorite. He also wanted Amy to take a break. She'd been keeping herself busy all week, which he understood, but she also needed some downtime.

He was starting to worry that she was avoiding her feelings by burying herself in housework.

"Something smells good," he said, dropping his briefcase next to the door and heading into the kitchen. Kincaid looked up from where he was standing, butterflying some chicken breasts, and grinned.

"Someone looks good." Kincaid winked at him. Laughing, Zach rounded the peninsula counter and went in for a kiss. Because his hands were full of raw chicken and a knife, Kincaid couldn't put his arms around him, which meant Zach's hands were free to roam while they kissed.

"Is Amy here?" Zach murmured, keeping his voice low just in case she was.

"Taking a shower." Kincaid leaned over to nip at Zach's earlobe as he pulled away, though Zach left his hands on Kincaid's hips, standing behind him.

They hadn't had sex all week. They'd been too distracted by Amy's presence. Zach had been too worried she might need him—them—in the middle of the night.

But the week had gone by, and she'd slept through every night without a problem since those first two. He didn't need to feel guilty about wanting intimate time with his boyfriend.

"She'll probably be out soon." Kincaid refocused on the chicken, picking it up to start it through the dishes he'd prepared with egg and breadcrumbs. Yum. Chicken parmesan. "How was your day?"

"Pretty good. I talked to Krista, and she says hi." At the very least, he could remind Kincaid about the family member who did know about their relationship. Kincaid's quick flash of a smile made him feel even better than he had. "Want a beer?"

"No, I'm good, thanks."

Nodding, Zach headed over to the fridge to get his own. He didn't think Kincaid would take him up on it—he could have gotten his own if he'd wanted—but he liked to offer.

"How was your day?" he asked as he popped the top off the bottle.

"Good, though it affects this weekend." This time, the smile that Kincaid shot him was apologetic. "I've gotta go out of town tomorrow. I'm going to escort Cassidy up to her new place."

They'd been planning to spend tomorrow night with their friends, but obviously, this changed things. Cassidy was a submissive who'd left her abusive relationship, and recently, her ex had started stalking and harassing her. Proving it was him had been difficult.

"Cassidy is moving?" Amy, freshly washed and scrubbed pink from the shower, came into the room from the hall, her long hair damp and darker than usual. Her doe eyes were wide. "I hadn't heard. Hey, Zach."

She'd been kind of busy and preoccupied with her wedding plans, but there was no way in hell Zach was going to point that out.

"Hey, how are you doing?" he asked, walking over to envelop her in a hug. She hugged him back, then stepped away, moving around the outside of the counter to take a seat on the other side, opposite him and Kincaid.

"I'm good." She sat down and smiled, though her smile was a little odd. Forced, but not in the way it had been, as if she was trying to hide some negative emotions. No, this was forced in a different way, though he couldn't quite put his finger on how. She directed it at Kincaid. "That looks good."

"Thanks." Now, Kincaid was also awkwardly smiling.

Ah. Zach wondered if maybe who was cooking dinner had been a bit of a power struggle between the two. When a service top and a service bottom face off... who ends up serving who?

KINCAID

Sitting down to dinner with Amy and Zach while he served them felt like relief. He liked feeding people. It had been nice to be the one being fed for a few days, but he'd also been concerned about how Amy had buried herself in housework. She wasn't pausing to take any time to feel her feelings or do something nice for herself because she was so focused on 'paying' him and Zach back for letting her move in.

She was already literally paying for her spot in the house, so he didn't want her going overboard trying to fulfill a debt that wasn't owed.

"So, you have to go to Pennsylvania tomorrow?" Zach asked. He'd been kept apprised of the Cassidy situation the whole time. She'd actually decided she should probably move several months ago but then had procrastinated on taking the final step. Kincaid couldn't blame her. She was leaving literally everyone and everything she knew, and it wasn't really by her own choice. She was being forced to do so because of her ex's stalking behavior.

"Yeah, Cassidy is ready to take the final step. She's all packed up and everything." Kincaid grimaced. "I think the final straw was earlier this week when she was grocery shopping and saw her ex there. He just stood there, staring at her, then followed her out to the parking lot and stared at her until she was in the car and driving away. She said she nearly had an accident because she was shaking so hard."

"Why can't the police do anything?" Amy asked indignantly. "It's not right that he gets to harass her like this."

"Well, for one, there's no proof that he's done a lot of the things that we know he did. The law is reactive, not proactive, and there's only so much the cops can do." He grimaced.

What he didn't say was that some of them might even be on her ex's side or find his actions 'harmless' because he wasn't doing anything physical to Cassidy. The emotional damage or her fear wouldn't move them. Too many of them were willing to overlook certain behaviors from men because they identified too closely with those behaviors—something that he'd learned about his ex-partner a little too late.

Besides, he'd made sure that the cops taking Cassidy's reports were among those who were the most sympathetic, the most proactive, but there was only so much they could do. Her ex wasn't doing anything to break the law.

"There's no law against being in the same store as someone unless she has a restraining order, and he hasn't done enough for her to be able to get one of those." Zach scowled, though the fierceness of his expression melted a little when he took a bite of his chicken parmesan, which lightened Kincaid's heart.

Sometimes, good comfort food really did help, and after hearing that Cassidy was taking the final step and that he was going to have to cancel his plans, he'd wanted comfort food. There was no way he was going to let someone else handle taking her up, though.

"Why are you the one taking her up?" Amy asked curiously, twirling spaghetti around the fork.

"She's being protected by Black Fox Security once she gets up there. Patrick's cousin works for them, and he helped arrange it," he explained. "And I'm helping with the D.C. office, which isn't open yet, but I'm here, and she needs an escort. Someone could come down, but they're in the middle of something else right now, so I volunteered to take her up."

Zach's eyelashes flickered, but he didn't protest. He knew that Kincaid would always volunteer to do the right thing, and he'd been just as worried about Cassidy as Kincaid was. Kincaid would make up for the canceled plans with him.

"Is there anything I can help with?" Amy asked, obviously concerned. "Does she need anything?"

He smiled warmly at her.

"She's covered, but if something comes up, I'll let you know." Truthfully, Cassidy was completely covered, and there had already been offers of help that had been rejected. Everyone in the clubs felt protective of the sweet submissive and wanted to help her.

If only they'd been able to find a way to keep her here... but hopefully, Pittsburgh wouldn't be a permanent move for her. Once she was away, her ex would hopefully lose interest entirely and move on with his life, then maybe she could come back home. That or maybe he'd do something stupid enough that they could actually get him locked away, but Kincaid only hoped for that under circumstances in which no one else got hurt.

Too many times, someone had to get hurt before there was anything that could really be done.

"You can keep me company since my boyfriend is abandoning me," Zach joked, winking at Kincaid to let him know he wasn't actually upset. Even knowing that, an odd feeling stirred in Kincaid's chest. It felt like... jealousy.

Not that he thought Zach would ever cheat on him, but it did kind of suck knowing that he was being replaced for a night, even platonically. However, he was the one canceling plans, so it wasn't like he had room to protest.

And Zach and Amy were close. Maybe Zach would be able to get further down to the root of what was going on with her without Kincaid there. Did it chafe a little, knowing his absence might help more than his presence did? Sure, but since he was going to be gone, anyway...

Thankfully, it was only for one night.

What could happen in one night?

10

———

After doing the dishes—which he wouldn't let Amy help him with, causing her to pout before sighing and heading off to her room to read before bed—Zach went in search of his boyfriend. No one was in the main living room, so he didn't have to look far. Amy wasn't the only one who had decided to read in bed, though obviously, Kincaid was in his and Zach's bed, not Amy's.

"Hey, there," Kincaid said as Zach entered the room, immediately stopping what he was doing and picking up the bookmark he'd laid on his chest. He was stretched out on the bed, feet bare, wearing his favorite sweatpants and nothing else. Dark hair sprinkled his chest and down his abs, making a happy little trail down to the waistband of his pants.

"Hey." Zach sauntered over to the bed and crawled onto it, crossing from his side to invade Kincaid's while his boyfriend watched him coming with a slightly amused gaze. He placed the book on the nightstand beside him. "Whatcha doing?"

"Right now?" Kincaid asked, reaching up to slide his hand around the back of Zach's neck and pulling him down. "Kissing my boyfriend."

Heat bloomed in Zach's body as his lips met Kincaid's, the strong fingers around the back of his neck holding him in place where Kincaid wanted him. While Zach might be a sadist and a top, something about Kincaid had always drawn him in from the very beginning. He'd fought it for a while, both the attraction and the submissiveness that Kincaid instilled in him...

But it had felt so damn good when he finally gave up the fight.

Kincaid moved, rolling both of them so Zach was on his back, with Kincaid kneeling between his legs. Zach's cock swelled, pressing against the tight front of his pants as Kincaid planted his hands on either side of Zach's head and lowered his mouth to kiss him again.

Their bodies pressed together, Kincaid's cock rubbing alongside Zach's. He moaned against his boyfriend's lips as the pleasure, the need, surged. Zach reached up to run his hands across Kincaid's hard body, his muscular chest and shoulders, moving them to his boyfriend's back as more of Kincaid's weight came down on him. Kincaid rocked against him, making both of them groan as Kincaid broke off the kiss and moved his lips along Zach's stubbled jaw.

"How do you want it tonight?" Kincaid murmured, making his way toward Zach's ear. His breath was hot along Zach's skin, and when he caught Zach's earlobe in his teeth, Zach moaned at the pleasurable sting.

He shuddered. It had been too long since they'd had sex, and they were missing out on tomorrow night. He wanted to feel it. He wanted it rough and hot and filthy.

"Hard. Fast. I want to feel used."

He could practically feel Kincaid's grin, even though he couldn't see the other man's expression. Kincaid raked his teeth over Zach's earlobe again, making him cry out. His hips thrust upward, and he shuddered again, clinging to Kincaid's shoulders.

He knew Kincaid understood what he was asking for.

The buttons on his shirt flew across the room as Kincaid ripped the sides of his shirt open, and Zach scowled.

"Dammit, do you know how much that shirt cost?"

"I'll buy you a new one." Kincaid was slightly more careful with his pants, probably because they were harder to rip than his shirt had been. His hand wrapped around Zach's cock, stifling any further protest he might have made as hot pleasure lanced through him. Kincaid moved his hand up and down, a rough, callused handjob that was pleasurably painful. "A better one. Now be a good little fuckboy while I suck this gorgeous cock."

Oh, good, Kincaid was going for total domination with a dash of humiliation.

Just the way Zach wanted it right now.

So, like a good little fuckboy, he kept his mouth shut other than a low groan as Kincaid's hot mouth enveloped his cock, Kincaid's free hand tugging at his balls.

<u>AMY</u>

Oh, fuck... that wasn't what she thought it was, was it?

Amy's head lifted up from the latest *Trinity Masters* book, her ears straining for more. Maybe it was just because she was reading about a hot trio—two men and one woman—where the woman was watching the two men get it on, but she could swear that sounded like a sex moan.

A really hot sex moan.

She'd figured she'd dive into the *Trinity Masters* because she loved the series, and the trio relationships wouldn't make her think of Jeremy.

Or maybe, subconsciously, because she was kind of living her own little trio situation right now, just without the hot sex.

I was supposed to be getting married a week ago. I shouldn't be thinking about having hot sex.

That sounded like another moan.

So much for not thinking about having hot sex.

She was glad her presence wasn't keeping Zach and Kincaid from enjoying each other. She really was.

But...

God, her brain was doing horrible things.

Right now, instead of thinking about her heartbreak, instead of minding her own business, her brain was pushing the image of the three of them as a trinity. The two of them together, in robes, coming to meet their third... her. And when her identity was revealed, they were excited. Relieved.

Desirous.

Amy bit her lip against her own low moan as she pressed her thighs together.

Of all the times for my libido to suddenly return. Fuck.

She tried to refocus on her book and block out the noises, but reading about people having sex wasn't exactly helpful. Maybe if she could just speed through the sex scene...

Another moan—she was sure that it was Zach who was moaning —nearly had her throwing the book across the room as her body pulsed in response. Shit. She couldn't remember where she'd put her vibrator.

Was it gross to masturbate when listening to her housemates having sex? It felt like it was maybe a little gross. Sure, she'd seen them at the clubs together before, but this was different; this was in their home. They weren't putting on a show for everyone to watch.

Remembering they were both exhibitionists who occasionally fucked for an audience at Stronghold did help some of her guilt. Just a little. And she'd been reading a sexy book, so it wasn't like her arousal was all for them.

Maybe she didn't need to feel so guilty about wanting to get herself off, too.

Maybe just this one time, then I'll buy a TV to put in here, so next time they're having sex, I can turn that on and tune them out.

That seemed reasonable.

KINCAID

Sliding his mouth up and down Zach's cock, Kincaid ran his tongue along the mushroom head, just like he knew Zach liked.

"Fuck!" Zach's hips thrust upward, trying to bury himself in Kincaid's throat again.

Gripping his boyfriend's hips, Kincaid pushed him back down, holding him in place so he couldn't move so easily. Zach's fingers gripped his hair tighter, making his scalp tingle, trying to push Kincaid's head back down, but he wasn't letting that happen yet.

Pulling his lips off of Zach's cock with a small popping sound, Kincaid laved his tongue over the sensitive head.

"Shhh, you don't want Amy to hear us, do you?" He felt Zach's shudder as the other man panted for breath. "Or maybe you do. Maybe you'd like it if we invited her in here to watch me fuck you, so she could see her top bent over, bottoming for someone else."

His cock ached harder as he described the scenario, one that had happened in the past when they'd included a woman in their play. Hell, Amy had seen them at the club before, too. Maybe he shouldn't be using her as an example now that she was living with them and in the room right next door. She hadn't consented to being part of their fantasy... though he supposed no one ever did consent to being part of someone's fantasy. That was the whole point of fantasies.

Zach's reaction was electric, his cock jerking so hard, it bounced off his stomach, his eyes glowing even hotter with desire before he closed them.

"Fuck... Kincaid..." His voice was lower, hoarser, than before, but Kincaid knew the image had gotten to him.

"Do you think she'd like watching you get off in my mouth? Then watching me turn you over so I can fuck your ass until you're crying for mercy?" Almost before he'd finished speaking, Kincaid lowered his mouth again, sucking Zach's cock between his lips and taking him in deep. The thick head nudged against the back of his throat, and he swallowed, working the muscles so he could take Zach down to the root.

His boyfriend cried out, fingers flexing against the base of his skull. Kincaid felt the first pulse against his tongue before the stream of liquid jetted down his throat. He swallowed again, sucking and pulling the pleasure from Zach's cock, drinking it all down as the liquid heated the inside of his stomach.

"Fuck... fuck... fuck..." Zach panted, his hips trying to push upward, despite Kincaid's weight pressing down on them, until he went limp beneath him, and the stiff ridge of his dick began to slowly soften between Kincaid's lips.

Kincaid let the suction lessen. His own cock was hard as a rock, and he wanted to be buried inside Zach... now.

Zach had said he wanted it hard and fast.

Pulling his mouth away from Zach's cock, he used his leverage—and Zach's passivity following his climax—to turn him over onto his knees, shoving a pillow beneath his hips for good measure.

"I hope you're ready to be my little fuckboy," he said, leaning over to rest the length of his cock between Zach's upturned buttocks so he could open the drawer to the nightstand and get the lube.

"Yes, Sir," Zach said, still panting. He whimpered slightly as Kincaid pulled away. They'd had sex often enough that he didn't always stretch Zach, especially when he wanted the other man to really feel it. He knew he wasn't going to injure Zach; he just had to go slow on entry.

Zach

His own softened dick nestled against the pillow, Zach felt the tip of Kincaid's hard cock press against his hole. Slick, hard, and hot, he groaned as Kincaid pushed forward, burying his face in the sheets to try to stifle the noise. This was exactly what he'd wanted tonight.

The dirty talk.

The roughness.

The stretch of Kincaid's cock opening him up without the benefit of fingers or a toy beforehand.

It hurt, in a good way, burning as his sphincter was forced open by the thick cock. A sting that ached but wasn't more than he could handle as Kincaid began the long slide into his ass.

"Good job, little fuckboy," Kincaid said, sliding his hand over the back of Zach's head, gripping him by the hair, and pulling him back so Zach was impaling himself on Kincaid's cock. "You feel so good, so tight, around my cock."

Zach whimpered.

This was the part of him he'd been scared of. The part of him that loved being called a little fuckboy. The part of him that loved taking Kincaid up his ass and being praised for it. The part of him he'd tried to deny for so long, he still felt slightly ashamed of even as he reveled in it.

"You're going to take my whole cock, then I'm going to use this sweet ass for my own pleasure. And you're going to love it, aren't you?"

"Yes, Sir." Zach gasped as Kincaid retreated slightly, then thrust in deeper, harder.

His opening ached around the thick girth of Kincaid's cock. Unlike a toy, it was thick the whole way down, and Kincaid actually got wider at the root, which meant the deeper he went, the more Zach's muscles had to stretch to accommodate him.

"Oh, fuck..." Zach tried to muffle his groans as Kincaid bottomed out, the tip of his cock pressing against Zach's prostate as he passed by. Whimpering, Zach pushed back against the man, his muscles clenching Kincaid's cock, massaging it.

"Good little fuckboy." Kincaid growled the praise right before he began to fuck Zach into the mattress.

<u>AMY</u>

Oh God, oh God, oh God...

She needed noise-canceling headphones.

Or a TV she could turn up really loud.

Something.

There was no way she was going to be able to live here with them while they were making those kinds of noises on a regular basis. She would spontaneously combust. She felt utterly filthy as she rubbed her clit, listening to them, but she couldn't stop herself. She needed to cum so badly.

It was like all the tension that had built up inside her all week long had wound her tight, and she was so close to release...

"*Fuck!*"

Zach's voice, muffled though it was, followed by Kincaid's low, guttural groan, was all she needed to tip herself over the edge.

She rubbed her slippery clit harder, her arm muscles aching, but it didn't matter because the spirals of pleasure that soared through her were far more powerful.

"Oh, fuck..." She whispered the words, all too cognizant of how thin the walls were, but she couldn't help but make *some* noise. "Oh, fuck... oh, fuck..."

The wet slickness of her pussy was hot against her fingers as she finally went limp, panting for breath and staring up at the ceiling. Her body felt hot, not just from the orgasm but from embarrassment.

She really hoped they hadn't heard her—the way she'd heard them—because it was *really* quiet over in their room right now. They were probably cuddling or something. Hopefully, they weren't quiet just because they'd heard *her*. She was pretty sure she'd been quiet enough that they wouldn't have.

Please let me have been quiet enough.

Still lying on her back, staring up at the textured paint on the ceiling, she let out a long sigh.

It was very clear to her that she was going to need to try to find a place of her own sooner rather than later. Not because Zach and Kincaid weren't accommodating—they were, and they'd said she could stay as long as she liked—but now that she was here, she knew it couldn't last long.

Her feelings for Zach had always been something she'd denied. They only saw each other at the club, after all, and they both had partners... but now she was single and apparently incredibly pathetic, not to mention rebounding hard. She needed to find a proper rebound, not someone whose friendship she didn't want to lose.

And she needed to get out of this house before she did something really stupid—like throw herself at two men who didn't want her.

11

Escorting Cassidy into the main office of Black Fox Security, Kincaid smiled down at her reassuringly. The pretty sub's long dark hair was pulled back in a ponytail, so he could clearly see the anxious expression on her face. She was paler than he liked to see, though the relief in her hazel eyes was evident as her shoulders slowly relaxed.

He wasn't sure whether it was being inside or the large sign above the receptionist's head that said "Black Fox Security" that she found reassuring, but he'd take it. The whole ride up, she'd been quiet and anxious, and there hadn't been anything he could do about it.

"Hello," the receptionist chirped. She hadn't been here the last time he'd been up—a woman named Mrs. Dartmouth had been, and she'd been cheerfully on her way to retirement. Apparently, that day had passed. The new receptionist was young, maybe even just out of college, but professionally dressed in a navy-blue suitdress that set off her mahogany skin and dark eyes. The shape of her eyes and cheeks hinted at Asian heritage mixed with Black, and her shoulder-length hair was perfectly straight and shiny. "How can I help you?"

"Kincaid Cavill. I'm bringing in Cassidy Simone to meet Lincoln."

He smiled at the receptionist as she brightened with recognition when he introduced himself.

She hopped to her feet, leaning forward to reach across the desk to shake his hand, which he quickly offered.

"Oh, hi! I'm Jennifer Johnson. I just started last week. It's nice to meet you."

"Nice to meet you, too. Does this mean Mrs. Dartmouth is officially retired?" He was aware of Cassidy watching the interaction curiously, but she hung back rather than jumping in. She tended to be pretty shy, he'd noticed, except around people she was comfortable with when she became much more animated.

"Not yet, just on vacation this week to see if I can handle things on my own." Jennifer grinned, her eyes gleaming. "She'll be back next week for her final week. There's going to be a retirement party if you want to come."

"Maybe. I just met her pretty recently myself, and it's a bit of a drive." He smiled to take any sting out of the rejection.

"Makes sense." She turned her gaze to Cassidy. "Sorry, not trying to ignore you. I'll let Mr. Black know you're here. He's expecting you." She gave Cassidy an apologetic but friendly smile.

Cassidy smiled back, though she was still clutching the purse she had slung over her shoulder right around the bag.

"Thank you," she said softly.

"Come on, let's sit down," Kincaid said, gesturing. The spacious lobby had four chairs and one large couch, all set to the right of the doors they'd entered through. Jennifer's desk was set up to the left, facing the television that was situated on the wall beside the chairs and couch, which faced each other rather than the television.

The news was playing, though it didn't appear that anything of note was currently going on since they were covering a story about a waterskiing squirrel. Then again, he was glad there wasn't anything depressing on to make Cassidy's mood even worse. She actually smiled at the footage of the squirrel.

They'd barely had time to sit down before Lincoln Black appeared, coming down the hall behind Jennifer's desk with the captain of his team beside him. The office was split in two directions. To the left behind Jennifer's desk was Lincoln Black's side, and just past the seating area on the right was a hall that led to the other side of the office, which was where HR and Lincoln's brother's team made their home.

Immediately, Kincaid jumped to his feet.

"Kincaid, good to see you," Lincoln said, smiling widely as he turned his attention to Cassidy, his expression immediately softening. Lincoln was not only part-owner of the security firm, he was also a Dom and a member of the local club, the Outlands, so he was fully apprised of Cassidy's past. "And this must be Cassidy."

David, his team captain, stood slightly behind him with a bored expression on his face that had Kincaid bristling. The two of them had met a couple of times before, and he would have said that he liked the guy, but something about his demeanor made Kincaid feel like he wasn't taking Cassidy's situation as seriously as he should. A little shorter than Kincaid, he was all bulky muscle underneath the suit he was wearing, and he'd grown a beard since Kincaid had last seen him. The red hair on his beard was the exact same shade as the hair on his head, though the texture was more coarse and not nearly as shiny.

"Hi," Cassidy said quietly, stepping forward and bringing her hand up to meet Lincoln's and shaking it. "I'm sorry about this."

Behind Lincoln, David raised his eyebrow, and Kincaid scowled at him. Not that David noticed. He was too busy giving Cassidy a once over, as though he was trying to figure her out. As if Kincaid hadn't sent an entire file over about her.

"It's not your fault," Lincoln reassured her, patting her hand. "And we're going to keep you safe. This is David. He's my team captain." Lincoln turned slightly, gesturing to David and dropping Cassidy's hand as he did so. David did not step forward to shake her hand, his hands were firmly in his pant pockets as he gave her a nod. A civil nod, not a friendly one. Kincaid would have to have a talk with him. "He's going to help you get settled."

"We've found a place for you to stay with some housemates, so your name won't be on the lease," David said briskly. If he was aware of Kincaid's glare, he didn't show it, his entire focus on Cassidy. Well, at least that was how it was supposed to be. "You'll have to find a job yourself, but Jennifer... you met Jennifer? Okay, Jennifer has bookmarked a bunch of listings you might be interested in. The first three months of your rent have been paid for, so you have a bit of time before you have to look."

Cassidy nodded, keeping her gaze averted from David's, as though she sensed the same thing Kincaid did—the man wasn't particularly friendly to her. Though he didn't need to be friendly in order to protect her, Kincaid would prefer that she was surrounded by friendly faces.

"Who is she going to be living with?" he asked.

"One of our team, the youngest, but he's solid, so don't worry about that," David replied. "He has a housemate, and they had an empty room. The house has a solid security system, and Jensen knows that as long as she's there, he'll be spending every night there. If something comes up where he's unable to, another team member will take his place."

The drawling way he ran down the list made it clear that he thought this was excessive. Kincaid scowled at him.

"Good. If Don figures out where she is and follows her up here, you'll need to warn Jensen that he may become a target, too. Several members of our club had strange things happening to them, along with the escalation directed at Cassidy." Kincaid put his hand on the small of her back to reassure her. He knew she felt guilty about how Don had started harassing not just her but the people she knew, the people who were protecting her.

Right now, he wouldn't object to David receiving a little harassment if it meant he stopped acting like this was no big deal. Cassidy was extremely sensitive to emotions, and from the way she was shrinking in on herself, he could tell that David's demeanor was affecting her.

Maybe Lincoln could, too, because he stepped in.

"Okay, Cassidy, why don't I take you around to meet the rest of the team?" Lincoln turned slightly, away from David, offering his arm. "We'll let Kincaid and David talk through any further details, then Jensen will take you to the house to get settled in."

From David's scowl, Kincaid assumed that had not been the original plan. He would be willing to bet good money that Lincoln had asked his team leader to take care of that. So, at least Lincoln wasn't blind to David's attitude, and he was taking steps to prevent it from affecting Cassidy.

As soon as the two were down the hall and out of earshot, Kincaid lit into David.

"What the hell is your problem?"

"Excuse me?" David had been watching Lincoln and Cassidy walk away, and now he turned back to Kincaid with a glare. Behind him, Jennifer was looking down at whatever was on her desk—either not listening or doing a very good job of pretending she wasn't.

"What. Is. Your. Problem." Kincaid repeated, enunciating each word and biting it off at the end. "Don't act like there isn't one. Even Lincoln noticed your shitty attitude because I bet you were supposed to give Cassidy the tour and take her to the house. Otherwise, there was no point in you being here to meet her."

David scowled even harder, obviously not liking having it pointed out that his boss had subtly reprimanded him by taking him off the duty he'd originally been assigned. Well, too bad. Kincaid wasn't going to let him get away with making Cassidy feel worse than she already did, and he was glad to see that Lincoln was on the same page.

"There was no point in me being here, anyway. First of all, what's the likelihood of her ex following her up here? And secondly, if it was that high, why the hell didn't she report him to the police?"

"You know why. I put all of that in the report unless, of course, you didn't read the report."

"Of course, I read the report," David snapped. "I read all about how your little club tried to handle everything themselves instead of filing a report, just so she could save some face and not have to admit that she was at a BDSM club when the incident happened. Did any of you think about what happens after that? What if he had left her alone and gone to do exactly the same thing to someone else, all because she didn't file an actual report, and he faced no real consequences?"

The heated anger that filled Kincaid's chest had very little to do with David's question and far more to do with the reality of the situation—a reality David clearly didn't understand. While Kincaid might find that frustrating, even angering in this day and age, it was nothing compared to the rage he felt about how the system worked.

"And you think he would have faced real consequences if she'd filed a report?" he snapped back. "There's a fifty percent chance— hell, probably even more—that if she tried to file a report, the officer would hear BDSM club and immediately write her off. Or tell her that there's no point because, obviously, she invited that kind of treatment. If she gets lucky and gets someone who takes her seriously and takes the report, all those things will come up in court and worse. Any attorney would go through her entire sexual history to make her out to be some sort of slut, on record, then he'd walk away scot-free."

"But at least there would be a record for future women," David insisted, though his vehemence had dropped a few notches. "That way, if they look him up, they'll know."

"He's blackballed from every BDSM club in a four-state radius. Any submissive who tries to go to a club with him will immediately find out, and most of the people who choose to throw house parties rather than go to the clubs have some kind of connection to those in the know, so they've been warned, too. Not to mention, several of our submissives had taken it upon themselves to watch the dating apps and FetLife in case he pops up there."

With every sentence, David wilted a little more, but it wasn't enough for Kincaid. He wanted this point hammered home if he was going to leave Cassidy under Black Fox's care.

"We can't protect everyone, but we did our best, and as a former police officer, I can tell you that we did far more than they would have. And we protected Cassidy, which is now your job, and if you'd rather throw her to the wolves, if you don't care what reporting and a trial would have put her through as a person, and you only care about some hypothetical future women—which, by the way, would have still had to look him up and then believe what they found—then I'll ask Lincoln to assign her to someone else.

"She already feels guilty as hell for what he's been putting her friends through, on top of her fear for herself. She doesn't need your self-righteous bullshit over a situation that you would never, ever find yourself in and therefore could never fully empathize with or know what you would do if it did happen to you."

Applause sounded from behind David, making both of them jump. David spun around to stare at Jennifer, who was now standing behind her desk, hands high in the air as she clapped. Her fierce gaze was focused on the redheaded team leader, whose shoulders sagged even further.

"You tell him, Kincaid."

"Oh, come on, Jennifer, what if you or one of your friends dated him or someone like him after?" David's tone had turned almost whining as he pleaded with the younger woman to see his side. "I know you all research your dates like you're the FBI. You'd turn up the fact that he'd been taken to court, and you'd be forewarned."

"We'd find it, but a lot of these guys are good at explaining things away. Oh, it was a vindictive ex. Oh, she was lying because she didn't truly understand kink. Oh, it was a false accusation. And people believe that shit." Jennifer put her hands on her hips, narrowing her eyes at him. "Not only that, but because I'm a woman, I have friends who have tried to get restraining orders. I've had friends who have been dismissed by the police for 'lack of evidence' or because it was his word against theirs.

"Have you ever had to stand by a woman's side while the cops rip apart her 'story' while she's still shaking from the trauma? No? Okay, then. You're so obsessed with what the 'right' thing to do is, sometimes you forget that what's right for one person might not be what *you* deem is right for society. And that's why you're wrong."

"I'm not a bad person." David's immediate response was one that Kincaid sympathized with because, damn, hadn't he been there before? When he'd been the cop who hadn't been able to help. When he'd found out that his own partner was an abuser, and he hadn't seen it.

"I didn't say you're a bad person, but you are an uncompromising and often judgmental one who needs to work on their empathy. Especially when it comes to situations that you, as a white, straight man, will never understand because you will never have that lived experience." She raised her eyebrow at him.

David threw his hands in the air in defeat.

"You're right. No, I know. I see it sometimes, but I am always on the outside." He sighed. "I'll try to be nicer to Cassidy."

"Glad to hear it," Kincaid said. "She deserves a break."

Now, he was very glad that he'd decided to spend the night in Pittsburgh tonight to make sure she was fully settled in. Yeah, he'd given up an evening with Zach, but this way, he'd also be here to make sure David understood what his assignment was and the fact that Kincaid was going to kick his ass if he did anything to hurt Cassidy.

12

———————

AMY

Being alone in the house with Zach was odd. She'd always known that Kincaid had a big presence, but at Stronghold and Marquis, there were always other people around. Lots of other people. Who also had big presences. Lots of Doms who exuded confidence and strength.

Not that Zach didn't, but he didn't to the same extent Kincaid did. There were some Doms who just had a little extra 'oomph,' and Kincaid was one of them.

The house felt kind of empty without him.

"So, what do you want to do tonight?" Zach asked as she wandered into the living room. He was seated on the couch, scrolling on his phone, though he did glance up to smile at her before looking back down at the screen.

"Oh, you don't have to hang out with me if you still want to go to the club..." Her voice trailed off.

"I thought you were supposed to be keeping me from feeling abandoned." He looked up again to wink at her, and her stomach did a funny little flip. "We could go to the club if you wanted to, though."

"I'm not sure I'm ready yet." Especially not if it was just the two of them. If they walked in, both of them, without Kincaid, would everyone assume they *were* cheating? Not something she felt up to dealing with right now. Plus, she was going to have to face all the inevitable questions from everyone, and to be perfectly honest, she would feel better if Kincaid was there for that, too.

He and Zach weren't perfect shields, but as long as Kincaid was there, it would be clear to everyone that she and Zach weren't cheating and that anything they did together—or had done together —was sanctioned by him. Plus, he and Kincaid were two of the Doms all the subbies thirsted over, so they were distractions in their own right. No one was going to pay attention to her if she was hanging out with both of them. They would be too busy lusting over the two hot Doms.

Yeah, if and when she went back to the club, it would be when they could both go. Preferably on a slow night. Like a Thursday. Not the busiest night of the week.

"How about a movie night?" Zach suggested.

"Sure, as long as it's not a romance or something that will make me cry." Amy plopped down on the couch next to him. "Maybe something superhero."

"Um, superhero movies have both romances and scenes that will make you cry." Zach put his phone down on his lap, turning off the screen and focusing on her entirely.

"It's not the same as watching a romance where that's the whole point of the plot. Or something like *The Notebook*, where, again, the whole point of the plot is to make you cry." The last thing she wanted to do right now was watch someone else get their happily ever after. Even if it was a bittersweet one like *The Notebook*. Eventually, she'd get to that part of the breakup process, but not today.

"I feel like the point of the *Infinity War* movies was to make people cry," Zach muttered.

"I've never seen them." She knew what he was talking about, obviously, but she hadn't taken the time to watch them. When he stared at her in complete speechless shock, she shrugged her shoulders. "I was always more of a Batman girl. I've seen all of those movies."

"Wait, you haven't seen *any* of the Marvel movies?" He reached up to his collar, like the button-down he was wearing was too tight around his throat, even though the top buttoned wasn't buttoned. He was even starting to turn a little red.

Amy shrugged, enjoying his reaction to her casual indifference.

"I saw part of *Ironman* once, but I was sick, so I fell asleep halfway through."

The sound he made was indescribable, somewhere between a bird squawk and a moose bellow, and he was tugging at the neckline of his shirt again. Amy pressed her lips together to keep from laughing because she could tell he wasn't pretending to freak out. He was actually freaking out a little.

Such a boy.

"Okay. Okay." He took a couple of deep breaths while she watched in amusement. "It's okay. We can fix this. We're starting tonight with Ironman."

"Wait, are you going to make me watch the whole series?" Because it really was a series of movies, and if he said 'starting with,' that implied there was going to be more.

"Yes, except I'm not going to have to make you; you're going to be begging to once we get started." He shook his head. "We can maybe get through two, maybe three, movies tonight. We'll do more tomorrow. Kincaid will back me on this when he gets home."

"I said I didn't want to cry, though."

The look he gave her was pitying. "There's no way we're getting to the *Infinity Wars* for days. It's fine. I'll order some pizza and get out the snacks. We need to get comfortable. Go to your room and get into some pajamas."

Amy bounced to her feet without thinking, automatically following his direction. She was halfway to her room before she scowled, realizing that she'd jumped straight to his marching orders. Should she have put up more of a fight? Protested that he was making the decisions for her?

That had been something that bothered her about Jeremy. He had a tendency to push his own agenda without thinking about what she might want to do. They never watched what she wanted to watch; they only ever watched what he wanted to. He'd never watched any of her favorite movies with her because they weren't 'his thing.'

No, this was different. She'd specifically said superhero movies, and that's what Zach was going with. Granted, he seemed pretty excited about sharing the movies he loved with her, but she was pretty sure that if she told him she didn't want to watch *Ironman*, he'd let her choose something else.

Still.

After getting changed into some pajamas and running a brush through her hair, she came back out to find that he'd somehow already changed into sweatpants and a t-shirt and had a popcorn bag slowly rotating in the microwave. He was also on his phone again.

"How does pepperoni pizza, mozzarella sticks, wings, and cheesy bread sound?" he asked, not looking up from his phone as she walked into the kitchen and leaned against the counter.

"It sounds like a lot of food for two people."

"Yeah, but then we'll have leftovers. I'll add a salad too, so we can pretend we're being semi-healthy, and some chocolate cake. Sound good?"

"Sure." She couldn't help but be amused at how intently he was studying the menu. "Hey, what if I don't want to watch *Ironman*, though?"

Immediately he looked up, more with concern than anything else. He didn't seem at all bothered that she was changing her mind about him.

"Then we don't have to watch *Ironman*. Did you want to watch a Batman movie instead?" Again, concerned and not at all mad or upset that she wanted to watch something she'd seen before, even though a few minutes ago he'd been barking orders at her over watching the movies he wanted to share with her.

Amy shook her head.

"No, we can watch *Ironman*. I was just wondering."

The way Zach looked at her made her squirm a little where she was standing. He might not quite have Kincaid's aura or penetrating gaze, but he did just fine on his own, and his scrutiny made her feel like he was seeing right into her. Probably seeing way more than he wanted to.

He nodded slowly.

"Okay, then."

Okay, then.

<u>Z</u>ACH

Tonight felt like a test, though Zach wasn't sure what he was being graded on. Amy had been on edge a little earlier, though as they'd watched the first movie, she'd slowly relaxed. Though, she did give him a hard time when she ended up sobbing on his shoulder over the death of Dr. Yinsen.

In his defense, he'd kind of forgotten about that.

He usually got a little teary-eyed over it. Amy's reaction had a few of those tears slipping down his cheek as her emotions affected him.

But after that, she'd really enjoyed the movie.

"Time to take a break?" he asked her once the after-credits scene was over—they'd fast-forwarded through the actual credits so they could get to it a little faster.

Amy sat up from where she'd been snuggled up against him. Once she'd taken the position to cry on him, she'd just stayed there. It had been nice.

"Yeah, I need to go to the bathroom." She glanced down at the coffee table, which was covered in food boxes. "We should also probably put some of this away if we're done eating it."

"I've got it." He leaned forward to start closing the containers, but she was already bending down to do some as well.

"No, no, I'll help at least."

"You said you needed to go to the bathroom."

She rolled her eyes at him.

"I can hold it for two minutes to help clean up."

The sassy way she said it made his palm itch. Especially with her bent over the way she was. It was like she was asking for her ass to be spanked.

But...

No.

It was too weird when they were here alone.

Especially when he hadn't asked for consent. But the urge to playfully swat at her was strong.

He filled his hands with takeout containers to keep them busy and away from her ass, getting to his feet and turning away from the temptation. Amy went around the other side of the couch, carrying the pizza box, and they went to the kitchen.

Which, of course, caused a traffic jam at the fridge.

She giggled as she managed to get her pizza box in before him, but his longer arms crowded around her, trapping her in between him and the open fridge while he put his containers in.

"Okay, now you're just doing this on purpose," she said, laughing as she twisted around, looking for a way out that didn't exist.

"Doing what?" He opened his eyes wide with innocence, straightening up.

Which put them standing far too close to each other. He looked down at her. She looked up at him.

If they were in a movie, this was where he'd move in for the kiss.

His gaze dropped to her lips.

And his phone rang, making both of them jump.

Zach jumped back, putting about a foot of space between them as his hand went to his back pocket, pulling his phone out to see Kincaid's name flashing on the screen.

Guilt welled up inside him.

But nothing had really happened.

"I'm gonna go pee!" Amy scampered from the room, slamming the fridge door shut behind her as she fled, hair trailing behind her.

Taking a deep breath, Zach swiped his phone to answer it.

"Hello?"

"Hey, there, am I interrupting anything?" Kincaid's casual tone turned the question into a joke, but Zach's stomach turned over, anyway.

Guilty, guilty, guilty.

But he hadn't done anything. And he wouldn't. He wouldn't have kissed Amy, even though he'd wanted to. Because he loved Kincaid. Love was about choosing the person you wanted to be with, and he chose Kincaid.

"You called at the perfect time. We just finished watching *Ironman* and were taking a bathroom break before starting the second movie." Zach shook his head, his body calming as he relaxed into the conversation. "She's never seen them before."

"Wait, she's never seen them before, and now, you're watching them without me?" The mock aggravation in Kincaid's voice made Zach chuckle.

"Shouldn't have decided to stay the night in Pittsburgh," Zach teased. "Though, if you hadn't, we probably wouldn't be watching a movie, and I wouldn't have known that Amy had never seen them. So, you'll just have to join in a little late. We've got the whole series to get through."

"Wait, she's never seen *any* of them?"

"She says she watched some of *Ironman,* but she was sick and fell asleep."

Kincaid made a strangled noise, echoing Zach's sentiment.

"So Ironman 2 and Thor tonight?" he asked.

"Yeah, if we have time. I thought about throwing The Incredible Hulk in there, but..."

"But we always skip that one."

"Pretty much. We can go back and watch it later if she's really interested. She really liked the first movie, though, so that's a good sign. She says she's more of a Batman girl."

"Well, who doesn't love Batman?" Kincaid laughed, making Zach laugh because they both knew he was a pretty big Batman fan. They had their own little DC vs Marvel rivalry going on between them, though they both agreed that overall the Marvel movie as a series was better. But Batman had a longevity and popularity that even Ironman couldn't match.

Yet.

"How was your day? Is Cassidy settled in?" Zach asked.

"She's good. She's going to be living with one of the Black Fox guys and his roommate, so she's secure. They've got a really good security system, and she won't be left alone at night, ever." There was something in Kincaid's voice though, like he wasn't saying something. Zach knew his boyfriend too well to miss it.

"But..." He let the word trail off, encouraging Kincaid to keep going.

"But the team leader, David, is being kind of a hardass about her. He doesn't understand why she didn't file a report with the police. He's got a very black-and-white way of looking at the world."

"Hmm, I wonder what that's like." Zach rolled his eyes. If anyone knew what having a black-and-white way of looking at the world was like it was Kincaid. Granted, he had learned how to be a little more flexible since Zach had first met him, but he still had a very strict sense of what was right and wrong and a lot of impatience with grey areas.

"Don't you roll your eyes at me."

"How do you know I was rolling my eyes at you?"

"Because I know you."

"Yeah, well, I know you, too," Zach teased. "I think your problem here is that you and David disagree on what the right thing to do was. If he agreed with you, you'd be all over his support."

"He's wrong on this one, and I tore him a new one about it. Then the new receptionist applauded."

"Applauded?" Zach laughed, leaning back against the counter, crossing one arm over his chest while the other still held the phone to his ear. Out of the corner of his eye, he saw some movement and looked over to see Amy walking past the doorway as she headed back to the couch.

"Standing ovation. And then she ripped him up, too." Kincaid chuckled. "It was pretty great. I liked her."

"Of course you did. She agreed with you."

"That's not why." Kincaid paused for a moment. "It might be part of it." Zach laughed again. "Okay, well, I'm going to let you go so you can continue Amy's movie education. I'll see you both tomorrow."

"Good night."

"Night."

They hung up, and Zach took another deep breath before walking out of the kitchen.

"I'm just going to run to the bathroom, and I'll be right back if you want to get the movie cued up," he said as casually as he could. Right now, the best tactic was to pretend like nothing had happened.

Because nothing *had* happened, and nothing was *going* to happen.

Which was why, when he got back from the bathroom, and saw Amy sitting on one end of the couch—rather in the center where they'd been before—he sat on the other.

And they watched the movie.

13

———

AMY

The first day back at work was going to be the worst. That's what she told herself. Though, she'd at least made the smart decision of telling Sherry, their receptionist and the biggest office gossip, why she was returning to the office without a ring on her finger as soon as she walked in. Sherry would make sure everyone knew, which meant Amy wouldn't actually have to explain what happened more than once.

She just had to put up with everyone stopping by to express their sympathy and support. Which wasn't the worst thing. It was just humiliating that everyone had to know her business, had to know what had happened to her.

Granted, she hadn't told Sherry *everything*.

Just that she'd found out on the day of her wedding that Jeremy had been cheating on her with one of her bridesmaids, and so the wedding had been called off. If Sherry assumed that Amy had been the one to call things off, giving her a tiny scrap of dignity in the story, that wasn't Amy's fault. Besides, not everyone needed to know every humiliating detail.

Bad enough that all her friends at the club knew.

Though Sherry had asked Amy if she'd gotten tested, and Amy had frozen.

She hadn't even thought about that.

Making an appointment was the first thing she'd done that morning after talking with Sherry, and thankfully, her doctor had had an appointment open that afternoon. Going to the appointment also got her away from the office and the overwhelming sympathy for a bit, which she welcomed.

While she was waiting for her name to be called in the waiting room, she checked her phone.

The group text chat was blowing up.

Sam: Have a good first day back at work. Remember, you don't have to tell them anything you don't want to.

Morgan: You've got this, Amy!

Carolyn: Has anyone heard from Jeremy or Noelle?

Marissa: Noelle tried texting me, but I haven't responded. Don't worry about it, Amy. Like Morgan said, you've got this.

Sam: What the fuck does that cuntcake want?

Marissa: I don't know. Like I said, I didn't respond. She just said, 'Hey, can we talk?' and I left it on read.

Morgan: She hasn't tried to reach out to me.

Carolyn: Jeremy tried to call Harvey, but I told Harvey that if he even thinks about talking to that asshole, I will leave his ass and take all his money.

Which would be quite the feat considering that Carolyn had been cheating on Harvey for years. If he ever got proof... but as far as Amy could tell, he either didn't have a clue or didn't care. She was also kind of surprised that Carolyn was taking such a hard stance, considering her flexible morality when it came to cheating, but apparently, it was different when she did it versus when it was done to one of her friends.

> Sam: I hope she reaches out to me.

> Carolyn: Do we know if she got kicked out of the club?

> Morgan: Yeah, she did. I don't think she'll care that much. She never seemed that interested in being there.

> Sam: I think she was only interested in being there because Iris was there.

Which would make sense. Noelle and Iris had been best friends and roommates, then after Iris had gotten involved in the club, Noelle had ended up joining, too. But not until after their friendship had ended in an explosive fashion.

Noelle had always said that Iris had left her, they'd had an argument, and that she wanted to be friends again but that Iris was bullying her... Amy had tried to take a lot of it at face value, but it had gotten harder and harder over the months. Now, she wouldn't be surprised to find out that every single thing Noelle had said had been a lie.

If only she had paid more attention in the first place. If only she hadn't believed every single thing Noelle had said without asking Iris for her side of the story. Granted, she'd figured that Iris had some side, but she'd become friends with Noelle, so she'd chosen Noelle's side without even bothering to find out what Iris' perspective was.

And now she was paying for that.

Carolyn: Well, she sucks. When is Amy going
to text back?

Sam: She's probably actually working, unlike
the rest of us.

That got a few laughing emojis in reaction from the others, and that was it, as if they were waiting for her to come back and catch up.

Amy: Today is going okay. I just told our
office gossip that Jeremy cheated on me,
and the wedding was called off. Right now,
I'm at the doctor's office to get tested for
STDs.

Immediately, her phone started buzzing as the replies came in a wave.

Sam: Oh my God, I didn't even think about
that!

Carolyn: Aren't we supposed to get tested to
be a member at the club?

Marissa: Oh, shit

Morgan: We are supposed to get tested, but
who knows what Jeremy has done if he was
willing to cheat on Amy with Noelle.

Amy made a face. She really hoped Noelle was it, or she was an even bigger fool than she'd thought.

Sam: Fingers crossed that nothing comes
back.

Morgan: Let us know if you need anything,
Amy.

Carolyn: If he's given you anything, I'm going
to kill him.

Marissa: Don't say that in a text!

Carolyn: No body, no crime.

A snort escaped from Amy, and she immediately put her hand up to cover her mouth. Laughing in the doctor's waiting room just seemed disruptive, and sure enough, when she looked up the older woman sitting across from her was giving her a disapproving look.

Amy ducked her head back down, refocusing on her phone.

Amy: I'll hope for no issues, thanks.

Morgan: We should get together sometime
this week. Friday? Saturday?

Marissa: I'm out of town.

Carolyn: She's talking about the rest of
us, duh.

Marissa: Just wanted to make sure my
absence is appropriately mourned.

Sam: I could do either night.

Carolyn: I can't do either. Harvey has work
functions both nights this weekend that I
have to go to. But you should still get
together, so Amy isn't just stuck hanging
around with two men.

Amy: They've been really great, actually.

Sam: Carolyn's right, though. It's not the
same as girl time.

It wasn't. Watching superhero movies with them was fun as long as she didn't think too hard about the very awkward moment between her and Zach on Saturday night. For one wild second, she'd actually thought he was going to kiss her.

Thank goodness she'd been wrong. She wouldn't want to hurt Kincaid that way.

But... well, if anything was going to fuel her Trinity Masters-inspired fantasies, that had added another log to the fire. Those books and fantasies were probably why she was thinking such ridiculous things. Zach had probably been trying to figure out how to ask her to get out of his personal space without being mean about it.

Which was why she'd sat at the end of the couch after that.

He had sat on the opposite side, so they'd been on the same page.

And last night, when Kincaid had been back, and they'd had another movie night, Kincaid had sat in the middle. Which hadn't done much for her fantasies, either. She'd wanted to crawl onto his lap, then have Zach join them. Not for sex but for comfort.

Which told her just how badly she needed to go to the club. Maybe even have a scene. She had a lot of pent-up emotions that needed to get out before they made her do anything crazier than Zach almost kissing her.

Amy: Girls' night sounds good. Stronghold on Saturday?

Morgan: Are you ready for that?

Sam: Only if you're ready for it.

Morgan: Jinx

Sam: Jinx.

Sam: Dammit, two seconds too late.

Now, Amy was working not to giggle again. The old lady sitting across from her was still watching her, like she expected another unladylike snort from Amy at any moment. Amy coughed, clearing her throat at the same time to swallow the giggles. Of course, coughing just made the other woman look even more askance.

Oops.

Oh, well. She'd tried.

> Amy: I'll feel better if I go with you guys. And the sooner I go, the better. If I keep putting it off, I might never go back.

> Marissa: I think it's a good idea. Plus, the Doms are going to come flocking. And now you can fuck them if you want.

> Carolyn: She's living with two of the hottest Doms at the club.

> Morgan: Yeah, but she's not going to fuck them.

Sadly true.

> Carolyn: They've had threesomes before.

> Marissa: The last one they did was months ago.

> Carolyn: So they're in a dry spell. Break the dry spell, Amy!

> Sam: I mean… if they're down for it. But they did just get back together not that long ago. It might be too soon.

> Amy: It could also make living together really, really awkward.

> Carolyn: But what a rebound. #worthit

Thankfully, the doctor called Amy's name, saving her from the need to answer immediately.

> Amy: Getting called into the doctor's office.
> I'll talk to you guys later.

She felt her phone buzz as she got up, but she didn't look at it again. The last thing she needed to be thinking about while she was getting tested for possible STDs from Jeremy or Noelle or whoever else he might have been sleeping with—and why did it make her feel better to think that maybe he was sleeping with some unknown so that he was cheating on Noelle, too?—was a rebound.

Especially a rebound with her housemates.

Talk about a terrible idea.

Although if I'm determined to move out within a month anyway...

No.

No. Don't even go there.

Zach

When his mom called for the third time that afternoon, Zach sighed and picked up the phone.

"Hey, Mom, I'm at work."

"I know, sweetie. I just have a quick question." His mom's cheerful voice made him both smile and sigh. Just a quick question, which could definitely be a text message, but his mom hated texting. She hadn't left a voicemail either on the previous calls because she knew he didn't check them at work. She'd usually leave one on the weekend if he didn't pick up, but it was always just asking him to call her back when he got the chance.

Somehow, he'd never managed to get her to understand that he saw when she called, and he would call her back as soon as he could, regardless of whether or not she left a voicemail.

"Okay, what's up?" He turned slightly away from his open door.

Personal phone calls weren't prohibited, but they were frowned on. He hoped it really was a quick question.

"Well, I'm out shopping, and I found a pair of swim trunks I think you'd like... you did say you needed some new ones for the summer, right?"

Bending forward, Zach closed his eyes and gently banged his head on his desk. Of course, his mom would think this warranted a phone call.

"Sure, Mom, thanks." Quickest way to get off the phone before anyone at work realized that he was taking a personal call rather than talking to a client was just to agree.

"Okay, I'll get them." She sounded so happy when she got to do things like this. He took a deep breath. "What time will you be home tonight? I can swing over and bring them by."

"How about I pick them up on my way home from work? That way, I can say hi to Dad, too." Plus, then he wouldn't have to explain to his mom why he and Kincaid were sharing a room and there was a girl in the guest bedroom.

Not that she'd be going into their bedrooms, but she'd be curious about Amy's presence, and he couldn't exactly warn Kincaid and Amy to lie to his mom for him without making Kincaid feel like shit. Zach would tell his parents—he would—but this definitely wasn't the time.

Thankfully, his mom always called or texted before 'dropping by.' When he and Kincaid had first moved in together, his parents had seen the whole house. They just hadn't realized he and Kincaid would be sharing a bedroom, and Kincaid had been very understanding about letting them have that belief... then.

He didn't think Kincaid would out him if his parents showed up and wanted to know where Amy was staying if she was staying with them, but he also didn't want to put Kincaid in a position where he had to lie. And he knew that it would hurt Kincaid to have his parents show up and obviously still not know what was going on between them.

Kincaid hadn't given him a deadline for telling them, but he knew he was going to need to soon.

"That's fine, honey. I might get you some shoes, too. I saw some on sale."

"Thank you, Mom. I really appreciate it, but I'm at work, and I have to go."

"Oh, okay, sweetie. I'll see you when you stop by then!"

"I'll see you then." Zach hung up the phone, then looked out of his office door. The hallway was empty. He sighed and leaned back in his chair, rubbing his head.

He would tell his parents.

Soon.

Just... not today.

14

———

Sharing dinner duty with Amy made things a little easier for both of them. This way, neither of them felt like they were uselessly sitting back and not contributing. Plus, she was fun to cook with. He really needed Zach to see her cooking techniques because he would flip out.

"What are you doing?" He asked, watching her stack zucchini slices on top of each other on the cutting board.

"Dicing the zucchini." She took one of the little stacks and made all the slices line up and then started slicing it one way... and then the other while Kincaid watched in utter bafflement. Yup, he really needed Zach to see this.

While Kincaid was cooking, he usually kicked Zach out of the kitchen because Zach had very strict ideas about how things were 'supposed to be done' in the kitchen. Amy's way of dicing would not pass muster.

"So, why are you dicing the zucchini?" he asked, leaning his hip against the counter as he watched her. Since he was done breading the chicken and had just popped it in the oven, there wasn't much else for him to do but wait.

"Well, I don't really love vegetables that much, so I try to sneak extra ones into everything I eat. I don't notice diced zucchini and shredded carrots when I simmer them in chili or spaghetti sauce for long enough that they go soft." She smiled sheepishly, glancing at him before she started on another stack of zucchini slices. "I know it's weird."

"Hey, whatever works. It's good that you've figured out ways to get more of what you need. So, broccoli, cauliflower, and green beans are all okay on their own?" Those were all vegetables she'd made for dinners last week, and now he made a little mental note in his head.

"Yeah. I actually like carrots and zucchini on their own, too, but I'm not a huge fan of salad. I eat it, but..."

"But just the lettuce and carrots. No peppers, celery, tomatoes, or radish." That was something else he'd noted last week. She'd made them a salad, but hers had been in a separate bowl that she'd put to the side ahead of time.

"Yeah." She shrugged, still sheepish. "So this is how I sneak extra veggies into my diet because sometimes I don't eat what I should at breakfast or lunch."

"Smart." He didn't get a chance to say anything else—or ask anything else—because the front door opened, and Zach was finally there. "Hey honey, you're home... a little later than expected." He said it teasingly because it wasn't a big deal; sometimes, Zach's work ran long.

Today, though, Zach didn't smile the way he normally did. Instead, he ducked his head.

"Yeah, I had to run by my parents after work to pick up something my mom got me." He lifted a plastic store bag in his hand. "She wanted to chat for a bit. Sorry."

"No problem." Kincaid studied him. Yeah, Zach hadn't told his parents, and he was feeling the guilt of having seen them again but not telling them. Kincaid wasn't sure what to do. On one hand, he really didn't want to live his entire life in the closet. On the other, he didn't feel right pushing Zach before he was ready.

What he did know was that he didn't want to fight about it again right now. Zach had told his sister. Yeah, it had been several months since then, but that had been a big step. He just had to hope that Zach would take the next big step sometime this year.

How long would he be willing to wait? He didn't know. But now that Zach had told at least one family member and had promised to talk to his parents—eventually—that was enough for now.

"Whatever you're making smells good." Zach smiled as he put down his bag and came over to look at what Amy was doing at the counter. Kincaid stifled his laughter as Zach realized what was happening, his expression going from interested to horrified.

"Um... Amy? Are you... dicing those zucchini? Like that?" Zach asked, his voice strained like he was in pain. It was starting to physically pain Kincaid to keep his laughter inside. Zach was trying so hard not to sound judgmental, but it was clearly difficult for him.

"Yes." She didn't bother to look up, just moved the little pieces she'd finished to the side, then grabbed the next pile of slices.

"You know there's an easier way, right?" The strain in Zach's voice was much more intense now, and Kincaid practically choked on holding back his laughter.

Leaning back against the counter, he moved his hand up to cover his mouth. Not that Zach was paying attention to him. The other man was too distressed by the atrocity of Amy's dicing technique—or lack thereof.

"If you cut it in long slices and then—"

"This is easier for me." Amy cut him off.

Zach's nostrils flared as he clamped his mouth shut, taking in a deep breath. Then he forced a smile onto his face, which also looked painful.

"Okay, great. Well... I'm gonna go change into something more comfortable."

"You do that." As Zach moved away from the counter, Amy peeked over at Kincaid, and when she saw him looking at her, she winked.

He doubled over laughing, no longer able to hold it back, even if Zach could hear him.

Amy

Sitting down to dinner with Zach and Kincaid was really nice. They were both appreciative of what she made. Then again, Jeremy had been, too, in the beginning. But Zach was also appreciative to Kincaid, and they'd been living together for a while, so apparently, that appreciation didn't disappear for everyone. Jeremy had stopped appreciating and started expecting her to make meals for him as soon as they'd moved in together.

Which had made sense at the time, since he hadn't been much of a cook. He'd also always had trouble remembering what she would and wouldn't eat. So it had been easier to just make dinner for both of them. That way, he was happy, if not appreciative, and she got to eat things she liked.

Which was why it had been a little surprising to realize that after one week, Kincaid had already noticed and remembered what vegetables she'd made. She hadn't expected him to. Why would she, when she and Jeremy had been together for years and yet the one time she'd asked him to make dinner in the past year—because she'd been sick—he'd made peppers and onions as the side? She didn't eat either and never had. Sure, she'd made them for him sometimes because she knew he liked them, but somehow, it had escaped him that she'd never eaten them.

The more she remembered about their relationship, the more she contrasted it to just living with Kincaid and Zach, who weren't even romantically interested in her, and the angrier she got at Jeremy... and at herself for putting up with him.

"How was being back at work?" Zach asked as he finished telling them about the swim trunks his mother had bought for him. And how adorable was that, that his mother still did that? Especially for someone like Zach, who, unlike Jeremy, was incredibly independent.

"It was okay." She smiled, though it felt more like a grimace. "I think today was probably the hardest. By tomorrow, hopefully, my canceled wedding will be old news. Everyone was very sympathetic. I did run out during the afternoon to go to the doctor, though... for a test." She made a face. "Our receptionist asked if I had gotten tested, and I realized it hadn't even occurred to me."

"That's a nosy question." Kincaid frowned, putting his fork down on the side of his plate and straightening up with a protective air that would have made her heart flutter if he'd been single.

"Yes, but I'm glad she asked. It hadn't occurred to me that I should go get tested. If Jeremy was cheating on me with one person, he could have been cheating with more than one. And even if he wasn't..."

"Yeah, no, it's best to go get tested." Zach shook his head. "That sucks. How long until you hear back?"

"By the end of the week, she said, which is good because I'm meeting Sam and Morgan at Stronghold on Saturday. Not that I'm planning to hook up with anyone, but at least it would be an option if I wanted to." Amy stabbed at a piece of chicken on her plate, perhaps a little harder than necessary, and ignored the look that she saw Kincaid and Zach exchange out of the corner of her eye.

"You never really seemed like a hook-up kind of person to me," Zach said gently.

That was true, but at the same time, it made her hackles rise.

"Well, being the relationship kind of person put me in a position where I stuck it out with a guy who did the bare minimum, if that, while I ignored red flag after red flag and then was about to marry him despite all that because I thought that's what I was supposed to do." The bitterness that coated her voice was so thick she could taste it, and she hated that Kincaid and Zach were hearing it, too, but once the words started, she couldn't stop them.

"I'm not even sure I loved him by the wedding day or if I was just there because I couldn't bear to admit that I'd wasted years with him. And then he left me anyway, in the most humiliating way possible, so you'll have to excuse me if I think maybe being a hook-up person sounds a little better right now."

Panting by the time all of it had spilled out of her, Amy stared down at her plate; she couldn't bear to look at either of them. They hadn't done anything wrong. If anything, they'd done everything right. She was starting to open her mouth to apologize when Zach reached over and put his hand atop hers, which she hadn't even realized was clenched in a fist.

"You deserved a lot better than him," Zach said gently. "It's not your fault that he turned out to be shitty."

"It's my fault for putting up with it for so long. I just..." Her voice trailed off... because what was she supposed to say?

That part of her had liked that he'd needed her to do things for him, even as she'd resented him for making her do everything?

That she hadn't thought she could do any better?

That she'd rather have been miserable with him than face the uncertainty of being single?

Pathetic. There wasn't a thing she could say about why she'd stayed with Jeremy for so long that didn't make her sound utterly pathetic.

"And now you won't again. Sometimes, you get into a rut, and it's hard to get yourself out of it, and the longer it goes on, the deeper it gets." Kincaid's voice was firm, gentle, yet somehow distant, as though he wasn't really talking about her but about himself, as if he really did understand, which made her feel a little better. "And when you're in the rut, it's hard to see what's outside of it. But it doesn't really matter how you got out; the important thing is that you did, and now you know what to avoid."

Amy took a deep breath.

"That sounds a lot better than 'man, I'm stupid,'" she confessed, causing both men to focus their attention on her in a way that made her squirm in her seat. Holy crap. One Dom giving her 'the look' was bad enough... having it doubled?

Scary.

Also hot.

It made her think of what her friends had said about them having threesomes.

Which was such a bad idea.

Stay out of the gutter, brain.

Easier said than done.

Because now her thoughts were in a rut.

"So, how was your day, Kincaid?" she asked, doing her best to change the topic of conversation and the direction her thoughts were going in.

It worked for the conversation, at least.

15

Z_{ACH}

Saturday night at Stronghold was crowded and full of predators. Zach scowled at yet another Dom, who looked as if he was headed toward Amy's group of friends, who were hanging out in the Lounge area of the club. Not that the Dom was doing anything wrong. The Lounge area was where available submissives gathered.

But everyone knew who Amy was and what she'd recently gone through, and she didn't need anyone taking advantage of her vulnerable position.

Even if she was considering rebound sex.

Maybe, especially because she was considering rebound sex.

She was in a bad place, and he didn't want her making a decision she would regret later. Most of the Doms here were good people who wouldn't deliberately hurt her. But Amy needed her confidence built back up *and* to be taken care of *and* for someone to take her through a scene where she could let her emotions go. So far, Zach hadn't seen a single Dom looking at her that he would trust with such an important mission.

The Dom looked over at where he and Kincaid were in the bar area, where the Doms and couples tended to gather, then hastily changed course to another group of submissives. Amy and her friends kept chatting, blissfully unaware.

"Are you planning on scaring off every Dom who's thinking about approaching Amy?" Asad asked, sounding amused. The other man was standing across from him at the bar table they were gathered around, so he could see everything Zach was doing.

"No," Zach said at the exact same time as Kincaid. He looked at his boyfriend, who looked back at him with some consternation. Zach had assumed Asad was talking to him, but apparently, Kincaid had thought the same thing.

Had Kincaid been glaring at the other Doms as well?

"Yes, you're both doing it," Q said, chuckling from beside Asad.

As the two Doms in currently in committed relationships with Sam and Morgan, Q and Asad had joined Kincaid and Zach at their bar table. They all knew each other, of course, but they hadn't really spent much time together before. Zach had known them more by reputation than anything else.

Q had joined Stronghold as a Dom before realizing he was a switch, and he'd eventually hooked up with Sam, who was also a switch. Club gossip also said they'd had a past, though Zach wasn't sure of the details. The subs described Q as tall, dark, and nerdy. He was the only person Zach knew who occasionally wore a t-shirt with a funny saying on it to the club.

Everyone at Stronghold knew Asad as the Persian Excursion—a nickname he'd given himself—who had been the club player for a while before taking Morgan to his brother's wedding as a fake date and somehow ending up with a real relationship out of it. Both of them normally hung out with Master Law and Connor, who had recently revealed himself to be a submissive, because they'd all come into the club around the same time. Kincaid and Zach tended to hang out with Mitch and Brian since they'd all been in the same introduction class when they'd first joined.

It didn't help that Mitch's wife, Domi, and Brian's girlfriend, Rae, had been in the same submissives class as Morgan and Sam, and not everyone had gotten along at first. Then Rae and Domi had become friends with Law's girlfriend, Iris, and Noelle had shown up and joined Amy's group of friends and the rift had widened. Sam was the only go-between who regularly hung out with both groups. Amy got along with everyone, but she'd been as loyal to Noelle as she was to Jeremy, so while she was as friendly with Iris as she was with everyone else in the club, she'd also felt compelled to mostly stay away from her.

Zach didn't intend to let her loyalty be given to someone who didn't deserve it again. Not under his watch.

The other Doms knew she was under his and Kincaid's protection, which was why they kept checking in before heading her way.

"She's not ready to scene with anyone yet," Zach said sternly, hoping he didn't sound too defensive. "It's only been a couple of weeks since the wedding didn't happen."

"True, but I'm pretty sure that's her decision, not yours," Asad pointed out. "Did she say she's not ready to scene yet?"

"She said she wants to have a girls' night with her friends tonight," Kincaid came in smoothly to the rescue when Zach hesitated since Amy had sort of said she might want a rebound.

"Uh-huh." Q and Asad exchanged a look.

"What?" Zach asked, trying not to be irritated.

"You know people are laying bets that y'all are going to end up hooking up with her, right?" Q asked. "Not by me, but there are some people."

"Yeah, Q has learned his lesson about placing bets," Asad smirked.

"I didn't mind dressing up as Princess Leia for Halloween. I just mind that I missed out on Sam dressed up as Princess Leia for Halloween." Q scowled at the other man. "And I mind that I still don't know whether I actually lost the bet."

Asad shrugged, lifting his beer to his lips to take a sip, smirk still in place.

Zach shook his head. He tried to stay out of the betting pool stuff, but even he'd heard about how Law and Q had made a bet over whether or not Asad would join the "pegging pack," as some of the male submissives called themselves.

Somehow, Asad had found out about the bet and convinced both of them that they'd lost. Q had shown up to Halloween as Princess Leia to his girlfriend's Han Solo, whereas Law... well, he must have done whatever he'd agreed to because he was even more irritated at Asad than Q was. It must have been something private because Zach hadn't seen anything out of the ordinary. Or possibly he'd missed it.

"If anyone mentions a bet to you about us, you can tell them to fuck off and mind their own business," Kincaid said irritably, causing Zach to look at him with curiosity. Protectiveness he would have expected, but irritated? That was out of left field.

"Ah, yes, because that will definitely work," Asad commented dryly.

"It'll work about as well as telling someone to calm down in the middle of an argument," Q agreed, chuckling.

Privately, Zach thought they were right. He glanced at Kincaid again, watching his boyfriend watch Amy.

Maybe there was something to the betting pool. If Amy wanted a rebound, and he and Kincaid wanted to make sure that whoever she chose didn't hurt her...

If you want a job done right, do it yourself.

<u>Amy</u>

"So, no STDs, thankfully. Also, not pregnant, though that would have needed a minor miracle." Amy made a face. She'd chalked her lack of libido up to wedding planning stress, but looking back, not wanting to have sex with her fiancé in the weeks before their wedding looked like just another red flag. How many of them had she blatantly ignored because she'd felt like she was already in too deep?

Once the deposits were down, everything had felt... inevitable. Which was not actually a good reason to get married. She couldn't help but wonder how long she and Jeremy would have lasted, even if he hadn't been cheating on her with Noelle.

Would she have finally seen the light—realized he didn't love her the way he should if he was going to be a life partner—and ended things?

Or would she have stuck around, tolerating his indifference the way he tolerated her love until he left her? Cheated on her with someone else?

Maybe she should thank Noelle for saving her because she had the awful suspicion that the latter was the more likely scenario. God, she was so pathetic. Needy. Clingy. All the things Jeremy had accused her of being over the years. Because what kind of sad sack of a person clung to a relationship like that if they weren't clingy? What kind of person put up with so little if they weren't so needy?

Sam poked her in the boob, making Amy jump and cover the top of the soft mound. She'd dressed for Stronghold in a corset and short skirt, even though she didn't feel sexy. It was what was expected. Plus, it helped her fit in better.

"Stop thinking about him. Or her. Or them." Sam wagged her finger at Amy. "They don't deserve another second of your time or energy."

"I was just thinking maybe I should be grateful to Noelle for saving me from marrying him," Amy replied, rubbing the spot where Sam had poked her before dropping her hand. "Like, I could be married to him *right now.*"

Sam and Morgan's expressions turned to pure disgust. Yeah. Amy felt that disgust, too; she was just also disgusted with herself because she would have married him.

Pathetic.

"Hey, can we join you?" The question came from behind Amy, and she jumped in surprise, twisting around to see who had spoken. Domi, Rae, Avery, and Iris stood behind her. It was Domi who had asked the question. Rae and Avery stood beside her while Iris hung back a little.

Poor Iris, who had been Noelle's friend before she'd joined

Stronghold and she and Noelle had their falling out. Iris, who was the reason Noelle had come to Stronghold in the first place. Iris, who looked at Amy with pure guilt on her face.

Amy glanced over her shoulder to make sure Sam and Morgan were okay with it—really, Morgan, since Rae and Domi hadn't always been nice to her. They'd been more indifferent to Sam than anything else, but they'd had an actual problem with Morgan for a while. It seemed to have resolved, but... as much as she wanted to reassure Iris, she wasn't going to make Morgan uncomfortable to do so.

The redhead nodded serenely. Morgan wasn't the type to hold a grudge. Sam was. She nodded, too, though.

"Sure, come sit," Amy said. As the other women moved to take seats around them, Amy glanced over to where Kincaid and Zach had been hanging out with Sam and Morgan's Doms. They were now joined by Mitch, Brian, and Law, who were Domi's, Rae's, and Iris' partners. Avery's Dom was also her boss, and they both worked in the kitchen at Marquis, Stronghold's sister club, so on weekend nights, they almost never were both able to get a night off.

Actually, she was surprised Avery was able to get a Saturday night off period.

Sam obviously had the same thought.

"I didn't realize you'd have off tonight," she said to Avery as the pretty brunette sat down next to her.

"Nick is training a new sous chef, so I get a night off," Avery replied cheerfully, settling into her seat. The blue dress she was wearing would have fit in at a dance club, though it still worked for Stronghold.

The other group was far more diverse than Amy's group of friends. Avery was white with light brown hair and hazel eyes, a smattering of freckles across her face. Domi was Puerto Rican, while Iris identified herself as Latina, and Rae was Black. Amy had always been jealous of Domi's tightly wound curls—and her confidence.

Domi was petite in every way, but she was fierce. Rae was taller than her and just as confident, but her personality always seemed somehow softer than Domi's. Maybe it was just because Domi was a masochist with an edge while Rae was more of a babygirl—though she never called Brian "Daddy," even though he was a Daddy Dom. Amy had internally cheered when they'd managed to work things out despite that; anyone could see they'd belonged together from the way they'd circled around each other for months.

True to their dynamics, Rae dressed more like a babygirl. Tonight, she was wearing a pink tutu skirt with a white corset that had little pink bows at the top. Matching pink braids were threaded through the dark brown ones and tied into pigtails with more pink bows. Beside her, Domi was wearing a black leather skirt, a dark purple corset, and her collar had spikes on it. The fact that she'd hooked up with sunny, laughing Master Mitch had always amused Amy. They were the definition of opposites attract.

"We just wanted to come say we're sorry about your wedding and see if there's anything we can do for you," Domi said forthrightly, which was her way. She was definitely not the type to beat around the bush.

"Like bury a body or two," Rae muttered, which made Amy smile. Rae might look like a fluffy princess babygirl, but she could be just as ruthless as Domi. Maybe more so.

"Thank you, I appreciate that. I mostly just want to never see them again, and if I can make it so I never think about them again, that'll be even better," Amy joked. Except she wasn't really joking, but no one needed to know that.

"I know how that feels." Iris was seated in one of the chairs across from Amy. The PVC dress she was wearing clung to her body, and her legs were pressed tightly together to keep the material of the short skirt from riding up. Her hands were clasped on her lap, guilt practically shimmering from every line in her body. "I'm so sorry. I... should have said something to you when she started making friends with all of you, but I didn't know if you'd believe it, and I kept thinking maybe she'd changed... maybe she deserved another chance..."

"Hey, her shitty behavior is *not* your fault," Sam said, using her

Domme voice and reaching over from her own seat to put her hand on Iris'. "You are not responsible for someone else's actions."

"I know but... I've always been the kind of person who says something. Does something." Iris took a deep breath with a little huff. "I don't know why, but she's always the exception. She just gets me so twisted up..."

"We probably wouldn't have listened anyway," Amy admitted. "Even if I'd believed you, I would have also agreed that she deserved another chance. And Carolyn and Marissa would have probably made friends with her just to be contrary." Because they could be like that. They weren't always easy people to love, but she'd always been willing to forgive them their faults.

In some ways, they were very similar to Noelle, which was probably why they'd been drawn to her in the first place, but they would *never* have crossed the lines she did.

"Yeah, but you would have at least had some warning." Iris reached up, running her fingers through her hair, shaking the silky black strands away from her face.

"Trust me, she was very convincing about how you'd wronged her." Amy smiled apologetically. "I didn't believe everything she said, but even taking it with a grain of salt, I was gonna be sympathetic. If anything, I'm sorry I didn't come to ask you your side of the story. I was trying to be a loyal friend, but..." She sighed. Well, now she knew better.

"Trust me, I don't blame you for that," Iris reassured her. "I know how it is."

Out of the corner of her eye, Amy saw Domi and Rae quietly talking with Morgan, who was smiling happily, so whatever they were saying couldn't be bad.

Look at that. Somehow, now that Noelle was gone, she was bringing people together.

Go figure.

16

AMY

Their larger group had gotten smaller again. Though Rae was sticking by Avery since she didn't have her Dom here tonight, Domi and Iris had been collected by Mitch and Law for scenes, one after the other. Then Q had come and stolen Sam away. Interestingly, Morgan and Rae were deep in conversation about being in business for themselves and making social media content—Morgan had an ASMR channel, and Rae had become an author—and seemed to be getting along incredibly well.

Avery appeared to find the discussion fascinating. And it was, but Amy was also distracted.

The main floor of Stronghold wasn't for scening. They were sitting in the Lounge area, which was where the submissives gathered—there was no rule; it had just happened that way. The main floor also had the bar on one side and a stage for demonstrations on the other, with a dance floor in front of the stage. The stage was empty tonight. The dance floor was not, but it also wasn't where anyone scened.

That was reserved for upstairs in the private rooms or downstairs in the Dungeon. There were three private rooms down in the

Dungeon, too, though the majority of the space was taken up by spanking benches, St. Andrews Crosses, and various other equipment for public scenes. There was also the aftercare corner.

So, she wasn't being distracted by any scenes happening around her, but she was very distracted by the happy, beaming submissives who were being picked for a scene and the sultry, satisfied submissives who returned to the Lounge, mussed up and satiated. It had been a long, long time since she'd felt the way they looked.

In the past, it had been easier to ignore the envy tingling in her stomach because it wasn't like she could do anything about it. She had her scenes at Stronghold and her sex at home. The two were separate.

But they didn't have to be.

Don't I deserve a wild night?

It doesn't even have to be a rebound.

I'm not looking for a date.

I just want to look like... them.

When Sam returned, her blonde hair rumpled, her corset looser than it had been before, and her face glowing from post-orgasmic bliss, the envy that was swirling around Amy's belly felt like it was going to come up and swallow her whole.

"What?" Sam asked when she realized Amy was looking at her.

"I want to look like you."

"What?" Now Sam was looking at her weird.

"I mean, I want to look like you do right now... happy, satisfied, glowing from having a great scene and great sex." The yearning was so powerful, it actually hurt the inside of her chest. "I need to find a Dom to scene with me. If I can."

"Well, if you're going to get a Dom to scene with you, you're going to have to call off your attack dogs," Sam said, making Amy wrinkle her forehead in confusion.

"What attack dogs?"

Reaching up to run her fingers through her mussed hair, Sam paused and tilted her head at Amy. One blonde eyebrow went up.

"You didn't notice that every Dom who started to come near us suddenly veered away when he glanced at Kincaid and Zach to see if they were okay with them approaching? No... no, you didn't notice that." Sam laughed. "I don't think you need to worry about finding a Dom who wants to scene with you, honey. You just need to make sure the two Doms who have taken you under their protection don't scare them off."

Amy's mouth opened and closed as she tried to find a response and came up short multiple times.

Finally, she managed to get some words out.

"They've been scaring off potential Doms?"

Sure, she understood what it meant to be under someone's protection in the club, and she could even understand why everyone would assume Kincaid and Zach had taken that position for her. But she hadn't wanted them to. And she sure as hell hadn't asked them to.

There had been Doms who wanted to scene with her?

And they'd been scaring the Doms away?

Indignation rose up inside her.

"Multiple times after we first got here," Sam confirmed with a nod. "The Doms stopped trying after a bit."

Amy scowled. Well. Now that she knew, she was going to handle that right now. They might be her housemates, but that didn't give them the right to deny her orgasms! Maybe in the house, they'd have some say. At least she wouldn't have sex at their house in their guest bedroom out of respect, but this was here at the club! Totally different.

"Well. I am going to go have a talk with them. Excuse me." She got to her feet, her righteous indignation fueling her march over to the table, even as her heart stuttered a little when the table full of Doms turned their joint attention to her. It was a lot of hot to face all at once, though thankfully, it wasn't the full contingent.

"Amy. Everything okay?" Zach asked, coming around the side of the table.

"Can I talk to you and Kincaid for a moment?" She lifted her chin, trying to hide the way her heart was frantically beating. She hated confrontation, but now that she'd marched all the way over for it, there was no way she was going back.

Zach frowned but nodded his head and glanced over his shoulder at Kincaid, who also nodded. They both came forward and stepped to the side. Amy turned to face them, putting her back to the others. It helped with the whole audience factor; it did not help with the fact that Kincaid and Zach were incredibly intimidating all on their own.

Especially when they were both looming over her, totally focused on her.

Yikes.

But she'd already come this far.

"Are you scaring off Doms who want to scene with me?" she asked... no, demanded to know. And got her answer immediately, before they'd even spoken when they glanced at each other before either of them said a word. Frustration bubbled up inside her. "What the hell? Did you want me to hate myself?"

"What?" Zach's slightly guilty expression turned to bafflement, and he stared at her in confusion. "Why would you hate yourself?"

"Because I'm here, I'm single for the first time—ever—and I know the whole club knows it, yet not a single Dom came over to even see if I wanted to scene." Frustrated tears started to threaten, making her eyes burn, but she blinked them away. "I thought I was going to have to go beg someone to scene with me."

Kincaid frowned at her.

"I think you need to work on your self-confidence," he said. "Any Dom would be lucky to scene with you, and you shouldn't assume otherwise."

Despite the compliment, Amy could only focus on the first part of what he said. She talked fast and low, her voice brimming with emotion, but keeping the volume down so she didn't alert the whole club to her issues.

"What self-confidence? The guy I was going to marry left me at the altar. He didn't even have the courtesy to break up with me beforehand. He thought I sucked so much that I deserved to be humiliated like that. And that's the guy I chose to marry. No matter which way you look at it, I'm a fucking hot mess. Who the hell is going to look at me and say, 'Oh, yeah, I want to tap that,' when the guy I was supposed to marry didn't even want me?" She sucked in a deep breath. "Now, I'm going to go find someone to scene with, and you two are going to stay the hell out of it."

She started to storm past Kincaid, but she didn't make it more than two steps before his hand came up in front of her. With as fast as she was moving, she saw it coming but couldn't swerve to avoid him, and he caught her around the throat, turning with her movement so he didn't jerk her to a halt.

His fingers pressed on the side of her throat as he maneuvered her around him rather than past him, and she ended up standing between them, with Zach at her back. Wide eyed, she blinked up at Kincaid, her pulse fluttering against his thumb, mouth suddenly very dry as he bent over her, his dark gaze meeting hers as one eyebrow lifted at her temerity.

Shit. Shit. Shit.

She'd poked the Dom, and the Dom was poking back.

"Where do you think you're going?" he asked, his voice a low growl.

Amy whimpered as her legs pressed together, and she felt Zach move up behind her, the heat of his body against hers making her feel completely surrounded by them. Her brain scrambled, trying to catch up with what was happening.

What *was* happening?

<hr>

KINCAID

Dammit.

Between the way Amy had been putting herself down, her obvious hurt, and Zach's pained expression when she said she was going to scene with someone else, Kincaid had reacted without thinking when she tried to breeze past him. All he'd known was that he needed to stop her.

Now, she was standing between him and Zach, his hand around her throat like a collar, and Zach's eyes were hot with desire and hope. Kincaid much preferred methodical planning to spur-of-the-moment decisions and actions, but sometimes, they were unavoidable. This was one of those moments.

"I... um... to find someone to scene with?" It came out as more of a question than an answer, her voice light and breathless, pupils dilating as she looked back at him.

She was aroused.

By them.

Or by the situation.

Both.

"Is there a reason you don't want to scene with your usual top?" He nodded his head slightly, indicating Zach behind her, just as Zach put his hands on her bare shoulders. The corset she was wearing had her breasts pushed up high, and they lifted even higher as she took a deep breath.

"Well... our situations have changed, haven't they?" she asked, turning her head slightly, but Zach's hands on her shoulders kept her looking at Kincaid.

Sliding his hand along her throat, he cupped her chin, tilting her head back, so she had to look at him and couldn't try to hide her face. As he did so, her shoulders squared, the way they did when she was bracing herself to be brave, chin lifting in defiance. Courageous little subbie, no matter what she thought of herself.

"Zach and I scened together because we were both in relationships, but I'm not anymore."

"So?" Kincaid shrugged one shoulder. "I wouldn't have minded him topping you even if you had been single. You're not the only sub he's topped." Because Zach had needs that Kincaid couldn't fulfill for him. Topping Kincaid—who was not a submissive and not a masochist, though he'd be willing to try for Zach—was not satisfying for either of them.

Some emotion flashed across Amy's face, too quickly for him to decipher, before she went back to her stubborn expression.

"Besides, Zach topped you recently. After... well, after." He didn't say the words out loud because he didn't want to rub salt in the wound. "We both did."

"Right, well." She huffed. Damn, she was cute. "We also always scened platonically. I don't want to scene platonically tonight. I want to come upstairs from the Dungeon looking like the other subs. I want orgasms, dammit." Her cheeks flushed bright pink, but that didn't stop her from saying it.

Kincaid wondered if the bravery was coming from courage or defiance, maybe a little bit of both, but she was being very clear about what she wanted.

He looked up over her head at Zach. Zach's gaze met his. They didn't need to talk for Kincaid to know that Zach wanted to scene with Amy.

Non-platonically.

If this had happened before Kincaid had spent the past couple of weeks with her... but it hadn't. And Zach had never given him any cause for jealousy with Amy before, during all the time they'd been scening together. He'd known that Zach cared for her. It was obvious she was an attractive woman. They were both attracted to her.

They were going to need to talk about this later, especially since she was living with them, if any kind of arrangement was going to continue... but for right now, he didn't see the harm in going with the flow. Everything had been fine after the scene they'd done before; this was just another step up. Amy was looking for a night of pleasure and release, which was something he and Zach could definitely satisfy.

This way, neither of them would have to worry about her because they would be the ones taking care of her.

Everyone's problems were solved.

He ignored that Q and Asad were smirking at him from their places, where they were watching intently. While he doubted they were catching every word, they definitely had a good idea of what was going on right now.

Might as well give them something to talk about.

"What if Zach and I offered to scene with you?" he asked. "Non-platonically."

Amy's mouth dropped open in shock.

"*You* want to have sex with me?" She said it like the idea had never occurred to her, that she didn't realize how damn attractive she was.

Hell, of course, the idea had occurred to him, including when she and Zach were scening platonically, but she'd had a fiancé. Otherwise, they'd probably have already done a joint scene with her.

"Is there a reason why you think I wouldn't?" He raised an eyebrow at her. "And be very careful if your answer isn't complimentary toward yourself because you've already earned a spanking for some of the things you've said tonight."

"I... I..." She started to turn her head, and Kincaid let her chin go so that she could. She twisted around so she could look at Zach. "You?"

"I would never have had sex with you before because we're both in committed relationships, but if you hadn't been with Jeremy, I would have talked to Kincaid about scening all together a long time ago." Zach smiled and looked up at Kincaid. "I think he probably would have said yes."

"Yes, I would have. And I'm saying yes now. But if you don't want us, then we'll help you find someone to scene with."

Zach's lips tightened at the offer, but he didn't protest. Both of them knew that if she chose not to scene with them, they would feel better having some control over the situation. Most of the Doms at Stronghold were good Doms, but for her first scene post-wedding breakup, Amy deserved better than 'good.'

Kincaid was going to make sure she got it, one way or another.

"If I don't want you?" she sputtered, turning back and forth to look at them with an expression of incredulity on her face. The same incredulousness that was in her voice. As though it was unfathomable that she wouldn't want them.

A slow smile spread across Kincaid's lips.

"So, that's a yes, then?"

17

———

Amy

Did she want to do a scene with the two hottest Doms in the club? Yes. Yes, she did.

But she was also having a moment of panic because...

Two of them? How was she supposed to satisfy two men when she hadn't been able to hold on to *one?*

Kincaid's fingers cupped her chin again, turning her head toward him so she couldn't look away, and her insides quivered. She liked that. She liked that a little too much.

"We need an answer, Amy," he said gently but firmly.

"I'm worried about making things weird," she confessed. "We live in the same house now."

"Was it weird after we scened together in the house?" he asked.

She hesitated. It had been a little weird, but not as weird as it probably should have been. She'd felt far more awkward about listening to them have sex and fantasizing about being between them.

Girl. Stop hesitating and let them make all your dreams come true.

"If it helps, we'll keep all the scening stuff to here at the club," Zach offered, his fingers starting to rub her shoulders gently, smoothing some of the tension out of them and making it harder for her to think. Making it harder to just not blurt out the word 'yes.' "Just like we did before."

But they hadn't been living together before.

But they had done a scene with her already, at home, and it had been fine.

But they hadn't had sex.

Sex changed things.

Or did it? She'd been in a relationship so long, she didn't know.

"We want to take care of you, Amy." Kincaid's coaxing was like slow, smooth honey, sweetly slipping past her defenses and sticking up her thoughts. "Whether that means we do it ourselves or we help you find someone else... but I think Zach and I would both prefer the former."

"Hell, yes," Zach murmured, digging his thumbs into her shoulders, pushing even more of the tension, more of her hesitation, out of her body.

Amy nodded.

"Okay," she whispered.

Z*ACH*

Something inside Zach relaxed when Amy nodded. He hadn't realized what Kincaid was doing until it was already happening, but he didn't disagree with a single thing his boyfriend had said. He cared too much about Amy to let her go scene with any other Dom. He would much rather she chose him and Kincaid.

He knew what she needed when it came to pain, and Kincaid was the kind of Dom that he'd privately thought she'd always wanted. Jeremy hadn't done anything for her.

They could show her the kind of treatment she deserved, then eventually, she'd find a partner she deserved. In the meantime, he could fulfill some of the fantasies he'd had about sharing her with Kincaid, fantasies he no longer had to feel guilty about or try to suppress because she was single, and Kincaid was obviously on board.

The Stronghold-Marquis gossip train would be working overtime, but he didn't care.

"Let's go downstairs then," Kincaid said, glancing up at Zach. He nodded. Downstairs made the most sense. On a Saturday night, all the private rooms would be full. They might get lucky and get a semi-private alcove. Kincaid gave the others a little wave over Amy's shoulder.

Zach didn't bother. He didn't really feel like seeing the smirking that he was sure was going on behind them. His focus was on Amy, who managed to look both flushed and pale at the same time.

"Anytime you want to stop, all you have to do is say so," he reminded her, bending forward to murmur the words in her ear. Though he really hoped she didn't want to stop. She shook her head, and his heart skipped a beat before she spoke, and he realized that she wasn't trying to stop them before they even got started.

"I want this," she said, turning her head to look up at him. "I'm not sure it's the best idea in the world, but I still want it."

Kincaid chuckled as he moved, putting her between him and Zach, his hand going to the small of her back while Zach's hand slid up to the back of her neck. They started moving her forward toward the stairs to the Dungeon. Zach was aware of multiple heads turning as they passed and the disappointed expression on some of the other Dom's faces.

Too bad, assholes, she's ours.

For tonight, at least.

"Let us worry about whether or not it's a good idea," Kincaid reassured her while Zach looked around. Catching the eye of one of the club submissives, he made a motion with his hand, and Tracey immediately nodded, recognizing that he and Kincaid wanted their club toy bags delivered to them. "You don't have to think anymore tonight. You can just relax. Feel. The only thing you need to worry about is if there's something you want us to make sure we do."

"I just want kink and an orgasm combined." Amy sounded so wistful, it made Zach's heart twist in his chest.

He'd always wondered if Jeremy did *anything* for her when she went home, if he made any kind of effort to meet any of her needs. From the way she'd just said that, Zach was guessing no.

"Heck, I'll just take some orgasms that aren't self-inflicted at this point, but I'd really like to be spanked first."

Zach shook his head at the idea of "self-inflicted" orgasms. It was very telling that she called them that instead of personal pleasure or masturbating. Like she hadn't even enjoyed them. Since she'd gotten tested, he knew that she and Jeremy had had some semblance of a sex life.

He wondered when the last time she'd had an orgasm with her ex, though. If he were to be betting on anything, it would be on the fact it had been a while since her ex had done anything worthwhile for her in that regard.

"So, sex is on the table?" Kincaid asked as they began their descent down the stairs.

"Sex is definitely on the table." Amy sighed. "If we're going to do this tonight, I want to go all in. I've never had a threesome before, but I'd be lying if I said I'd never fantasized about the possibility. Jeremy would have never gone for it, unless it was with another woman."

That didn't surprise Zach in the slightest.

Amy looked up at both of them as they reached the bottom of the stairs, turning her head back and forth between them.

"As long as this doesn't change anything between us. I don't want to lose either of you as friends, and I don't want anything to get messed up between you."

"We've done this before," Kincaid reminded her, as delicately as possible, and without actually mentioning they'd done it with other women. Though, it had been a long time since that had happened. "That was never what messed us up."

That was true enough.

"It helped us," Zach told her. "Kincaid doesn't make the best pain slut, and he's not a very good bottom, either. So I always had to get some of those needs met in other places." Kincaid chuckled at the massive understatements. "Really, you're helping us because otherwise, we'd have to find a Dom for you *and* someone to help us out."

Though, granted, that didn't necessarily mean a threesome, but overall, it was still true.

"Well, when you put it that way," Amy said with a laugh.

Either she wasn't noticing the stares they were garnering as they moved into the Dungeon, or she didn't care. Zach was willing to believe the latter. It was hard to miss the many wide-eyed gazes directed at them. Damn. He didn't mind a bit of exhibitionism, but he was starting to wonder if they had bitten off more than he would usually chew.

They were going to have quite an audience, even if they did manage to secure one of the alcoves instead of having to use the spanking benches in the middle of the room.

"Let's walk around this way; I think I see an alcove at the back," Kincaid said, veering to the left. The privacy rooms lined the walls along the left while there were multiple scenes happening to the right of them. The alcoves were all along the other back walls, and Zach could see straight ahead to what looked like an empty space with a St. Andrew's cross set-up.

Not a bad spot, and maybe being at the very back of the room, they wouldn't feel quite so exposed.

They passed by the Interrogation Room and were almost at the door to the Jail when the door into that room suddenly opened in front of them. Master Will and his very pregnant wife Gina came out, his arm around her, supporting her while she had her hand on her swollen stomach, which protruded from between the leather bikini pieces she was wearing. Her blonde hair was down and around her shoulders, swinging with her movements.

Immediately, Kincaid rushed forward, hands slightly out in front of him, and the only thing that kept Amy from joining him was Zach's tightened grip on the back of her neck. Kincaid had it handled. This was one of the good things about there being two of them—they could tag team.

"Everything okay?" Kincaid asked as he moved forward.

"I'm fine... just super nauseous." Gina moaned, rubbing her stomach. "Everyone said morning sickness goes away eventually, but they all lied. And I don't know why it's called morning sickness when it's *all the damn time.*"

Master Will smiled down at her with sympathy.

"I think we're done for the night, sweetheart. Let's go to the aftercare corner, and I'll rub your feet." He smiled wider when she grumbled something unintelligible under her breath, then he looked up at Kincaid, Zach, and Amy. His eyes widened, sharpened. He glanced at the rest of the Dungeon, then back to them. Despite his distraction, it was clear he very quickly took in the situation, assessed it, and came to the correct conclusion. "Would you all like to use the room, since we won't be needing it?"

"That... would be very appreciated, actually. Thank you," Kincaid replied. "Do you need any help with Gina?"

"No, I've got her. Nothing to do but wait for the baby to get here. Just a couple more weeks." Will's eyes brightened with excitement while Gina rubbed her stomach harder.

"Or now. Now would be fine, too." She sighed heavily as Will laughed and gave her a little pat on the butt to get her moving. "Have a nice night, y'all."

"Feel better," Amy replied sympathetically, watching as Gina walked past them, Will at her side, supporting her all the way.

Kincaid held the door to the Jail room open, and Zach moved Amy forward once Will and Gina were past them. He felt bad for them but, at the same time, happy to have access to a private room. It was like the universe had seen all the attention they were getting and decided to give them a break.

The Jail was set up like an old-west sheriff's office, with a small part of the room in the back left corner sectioned off with real bars. It wasn't a huge part of the room, but it didn't need to be since it wasn't meant to hold anyone for more than a few hours at the very most.

The rest of the room had several large cupboards along the walls, all of which would be filled with implements and toys for sale, as well as a desk with multiple drawers. Even though most people brought their own, and some members kept their bags in their lockers—like him and Kincaid—Stronghold always had items that would be for sale.

They would just have to make sure that the change from Will to them was listed, so Will didn't get charged for anything they used, and it went onto their tab instead.

Speaking of...

Releasing Amy, Zach went back over to the door, opening it enough... perfect timing. Tracey was just coming down the stairs with his and Kincaid's club bags. They had larger bags they carried with them when they knew they were doing a scene, but both of them also kept a small bag at the club with the bare necessities. The perky blonde lit up when she saw him, hurrying forward to hand off the bags to him.

"Thank you," he said, taking them from her. Tracey ignored him, trying to peer past him even as she gave him the bags.

"Have fun, Amy! You lucky bitch!"

Rolling his eyes, Zach shooed her out the door so he could close it behind her, then turned back to the room.

Amy was standing in the center of the room, appearing awkward as she wrung her hands in front of her, watching Kincaid. His boyfriend didn't seem to notice, though his hand was still on the small of Amy's back. He was in the headspace he got into when he was planning something, thinking through what he wanted to do.

Then Kincaid turned his head and said something softly to Amy, and Zach could see she immediately relaxed.

Good.

"So, Kincaid," he said, striding forward with the two bags and swinging them up onto the table. They landed with a thud that made Amy jump, her face lighting up with eager trepidation. "What should we do with our naughty girl?"

18

Amy

Naughty girl.

Her thighs pressed together as the need between them pulsed. She was so in over her head, and right now, she liked it there.

"I think she needs a spanking," Zach said with a wicked grin that made her tingle all over. She knew that grin very well.

He wanted to make her scream.

Amy wanted him to make her scream.

Normally, she would say a spanking wouldn't do it, but he and Kincaid had already proven they could break her with nothing more. This was no longer the expected, like what she'd had before with Zach. They were moving into the unknown. Into places she couldn't anticipate.

"I think she has too many clothes on," Kincaid said, circling her.

Amy almost whimpered as she felt her corset move against her skin, his fingers tugging on the laces.

This was really happening.

They were going to get her naked and spank her, then fuck her.

Please, oh please, let them fuck me.

A kind of anticipation she hadn't experienced in years welled up inside her. It wasn't that platonic scening was bad. It wasn't that she hadn't been getting what she needed. If she was in a room with anyone other than Zach and Kincaid, she didn't think she'd be this excited, this aroused.

She would have gone through with it because she wanted a scene and sex.

But it was Zach and Kincaid, and she didn't just want a scene and sex—she wanted *them*.

Part of her knew that was dangerous, but it also made sense. She trusted Zach, and by trusting Zach, she trusted Kincaid. And who wouldn't want them? There was a reason Tracey had been happy for her, knowing who she was scening with. Yes, they'd done two-on-one scenes with submissives in the past, but it didn't happen often, and Amy couldn't remember the last time they'd chosen to do so.

She'd won the subbie lottery.

On top of that, after living with them for the past two weeks, she *liked* them.

Not that she would ever try to get between them for more than a scene, but she couldn't help but be thrilled that they liked her enough to want to scene with her, too.

The way Zach was looking at her, as Kincaid loosened her corset, with hunger in his eyes... he'd never looked at her like that before, even though this would hardly be the first time he'd seen her breasts. Of course, he'd never had an invitation to touch before. As the corset sagged loose, Zach began to stalk toward her with an intensity that made her automatically step back—right into Kincaid.

She let out a little 'eep' that was met with a dark chuckle from behind her.

"Going somewhere, little subbie?" Kincaid's breath was hot against her ear, the heat chasing the shiver down her spine as Zach came closer, a predator on the prowl while she was trapped against his partner. Kincaid's hands slid around to her front, where the corset clasps were, and she felt his thumbs push against her breasts as he gripped the two sides and popped them open.

The sudden coolness against her skin made her nipples pucker, and she sucked in a breath as she was exposed to them both.

It felt different.

It *was* different.

She'd never scened with Zach anywhere but the public spaces.

They'd never included sex into their scenes.

And they'd never had Kincaid with them.

Her shoulders started to hunch forward, arms instinctively coming in front of her, but the corset dropped to the floor, and Kincaid's hands were on her body, on her sides, rubbing away the imprints the boning had left in her skin. Zach came closer, close enough she had to tip her head back to look at him, his gaze locked onto hers as he cupped her chin to hold her in place.

"What's on the table, Amy? We said sex, but is there anything you don't want to do?"

She gave her head a little shake, not that his strong fingers allowed her to move much. Kincaid's hands were still rubbing up and down her sides, and she felt herself leaning back against his hard body, letting him hold her up as her knees went weak under their combined assault on her senses.

"No limits. I want... I want *everything*." A shiver went up her spine as Kincaid's hands curled around from her sides to her stomach, stroking the soft flesh there, the sides of his hands and arms brushing against the sensitive undersides of her breasts.

Instead of answering her, Zach studied her for one long moment. Then his gaze lifted to Kincaid, making her want to turn to look and see what Kincaid's expression was, but she couldn't with Zach cupping her chin. Then it didn't matter anymore because suddenly Zach was lowering his lips to hers.

He kissed her.

He kissed her, and Kincaid's body moved in behind her, pushing her against Zach as her hands went up to press against his chest, and Kincaid's hands moved up to cup her breasts. The soft mounds were crushed against his hands as he and Zach trapped her between them, aching from the squeeze, her nipples peeking through Kincaid's fingers to brush against Zach's chest.

Amy whimpered, her mouth opening under Zach's as his tongue slid between her lips to dance with hers. It felt like her whole body was suddenly aflame with sensation, heat, and need. Her head tipped back against Kincaid's chest as Zach devoured her while Kincaid's hands kneaded her breasts, holding her in place as though he was offering her up to Zach.

Zach's head lifted, leaving her lips feeling swollen... leaving her yearning for more.

"My turn," Kincaid whispered in her ear.

They spun her around, switching places with an ease that left her dizzy. Zach's hands found her breasts, Kincaid's lips found hers, and she whimpered against his kiss as his hand delved between her legs.

Where Zach's kiss had been ruthless, Kincaid's was firm. Zach had demanded she open her lips for him, Kincaid coaxed.

Not that the differences mattered. Both kisses left her head spinning, her toes curling, and that was even before she got into the differences in how they touched her.

Kincaid had massaged her breasts, squeezing and kneading, like he just loved touching them. Zach's hands were much rougher, his fingers going for her nipples and pinching them tightly, so she cried out, the sound muffled by Kincaid's mouth. While Zach tormented her breasts, making her nipples throb from his pinches, Kincaid's fingers stroked along the outside of her soaked thong before slipping beneath the fabric.

Trying to keep her balance as his fingers moved against her pussy, Amy's hands went to his shoulders, clinging to him as the two of them touched her. Stroked her. Kincaid firm and pleasurable, Zach's touch deliciously painful. The dichotomy was even more arousing than if they'd just gone straight for her masochistic tendencies.

Two fingers pushed inside of her, and Amy moaned again as Kincaid lifted his head to look down at her.

"She's soaking wet," he said, pushing his fingers deeper, making her rock against the heel of his palm, her little clit throbbing as he rubbed against it.

Amy whimpered, going up on her tiptoes, clinging to his shoulders, as his fingers moved inside her while Zach pinched her nipples even harder, twisting the little buds. Pleasure and pain flashed through her in a chaotic clash of sensations.

"Of course she is, she's our little slut." Zach's voice was harsher than Kincaid's, crueler. They'd played with verbal humiliation in their scenes before, but not this far... he'd never called her a slut before, so she'd never known how much she would like it. Especially when he called her *their* slut. Her muscles quivered around Kincaid's fingers as he moved them inside her, finger fucking her while she rode his hand, and Zach tormented her breasts.

"Oh, she liked that... and I like feeling how wet you are for us, princess," Kincaid said right atop him, his voice soothing where Zach's was edged, warm where Zach's was cold. The combination was far more potent than either would be on their own.

"She's wet because our filthy little slut who wants both our cocks, aren't you, princess?" Where Kincaid's 'princess' was an endearment, Zach's was almost mocking.

Amy gasped, shuddering between them, her pussy clenching around Kincaid's fingers again. She couldn't find the breath to answer, but then, she didn't think they cared. Zach released her nipples, only to pinch down and twist, sending pulses through her that brought tears to her eyes even as she moved against Kincaid's hand, rubbing herself on him because she needed to come so badly.

"You're a dirty whore who wants both of us."

"Oh God..." Amy was spiraling as the combination of their different touches, their different demeanors, were sending her out of control.

"We're going to fill you with cock, and you're going to love it because you're our nasty little slut, aren't you?"

"Come for me, princess, that's a good girl."

They were practically speaking together.

Amy cried out as they held her up, her knees buckling as her orgasm rolled up from her clit, pulsing through the muscles around Kincaid's fingers, heat fluttering through her body as she leaned back against Zach and gave herself over to the sensations. She went completely weak between them, and they held her in place, Kincaid's fingers still moving, Zach still tugging on her nipples, sending multiple waves of ecstasy through her.

She felt tears slide from her cheeks from the sheer relief.

Even if they stopped now, it would be the best orgasm that had ever happened to her.

But she really hoped they didn't stop now. Because she *was* a dirty whore who wanted them both. She *was* a good girl who wanted to please them. She *was* a little slut who wanted to be filled with their cocks.

Please don't stop.

<u>*KINCAID*</u>

Fuck, Amy was perfect.

Her pussy was hot and wet around his fingers, her eyes glazed from the pleasure, lips slightly parted like she was asking for another kiss. Her reddened nipples stood out from her pale breasts as Zach continued to massage her breasts, though he'd backed off on the pain —for now. Kincaid was sure his boyfriend had further plans for those gorgeous breasts, and he was looking forward to watching.

Something he'd discovered was that while he was not a sadist for himself, he loved watching Zach work. He loved watching the masochist's reactions, even though he wouldn't have wanted to do it himself.

Watching Amy get off on his hand while Zach ruthlessly tormented her nipples, while Zach degraded her, and Kincaid praised her...

Fuck.

So fucking perfect.

His cock was aching with envy of his fingers as he slid them from the warmth of her pussy. They were coated in her juices. Kincaid met her gaze as she opened her eyes, lifting his fingers to his mouth and taking them down to the knuckles so he could suck her honey from them. Her eyes widened in shock, pupils dilating as she watched him.

Damn, she tasted sweet. Sweet and salty and utterly delicious. He wanted to bury his face between her thighs and taste her directly from the source.

"Up on your feet, Amy," Zach said from behind her. "We're not done with you yet."

Hell, no, they weren't.

She swayed slightly as she was put upright. Kincaid pulled his fingers from his mouth with a small popping sound.

"I think we need to get the rest of her clothes off her."

"I agree," Zach grinned. "And then I want to decorate her."

Kincaid chuckled. Of course, Zach did. And Kincaid was going to enjoy watching.

This was the difference between them. After Zach was done with her nipples, Kincaid would have left them alone. They were already tightly budded, bright red from the abuse he'd put them through... Kincaid might have put loops on them to keep them nice and hard, but that would be about it. He was pretty sure Zach was going to go for clamps.

Tight ones.

He couldn't wait to see her reaction and hear the noises she made when Zach put them on.

It only took them moments to strip her skirt and thong off, leaving her completely naked between them. She was still glassy-eyed and panting for breath. The indents in her skin from the corset had mostly smoothed out of her soft stomach, leaving only the barest of lines visible, beneath which her pussy was shaved bare, allowing him to see the puffy lips and the gloss of her arousal.

"Such a pretty pussy," Kincaid said admiringly, the taste of it still lingering on his tongue. "I'm going to take another taste while you decorate her."

"Works for me."

Amy whimpered, and Kincaid grinned as he moved around her, putting his hand on her back so he could guide her where he wanted her—right over to the desk.

"Sit up here, princess, and lean back so I can taste that sweet pussy again." He patted the desk where he wanted her to sit, then helped her into position—butt right on the edge of the wood and legs spread wide enough for him to get his head between. He draped her lower legs over his shoulders, kneeling between her thighs so her pussy was right at his mouth level.

Looking up at her, he could see her watching him, that glazed look still in her eyes.

It was almost like she'd never had a sexy kink scene before.

Hell, maybe she hadn't. He needed to ask her. Or Zach might know. Regardless, it had probably been a really fucking long time since she had... and he doubted it had been with two men. They were going to overwhelm her senses in the best way possible.

She wanted to be satisfied? Satiated?

He was going to make sure they had to carry her to the car after this.

Goal in mind, he slid his arms under her thighs, forcing her to lean back and thrusting her breasts in the air as she placed her hands against the desk behind her. The position helped tip her hips back. He curved his hands around her buttocks, pulling her right to the edge so he could bury his mouth in her sweet pussy.

The fucking sweetest he'd ever tasted.

Even sweeter than her cry of pleasure as his tongue delved between her swollen lips, and he began to feast.

19

———————

Zach

Watching Kincaid bury his face in Amy's pussy brought the most intense feelings of arousal and jealousy stabbing through Zach's chest.

Part of it was jealousy that Kincaid's focus was on someone else—something that always fueled him during their scenes—but part of it was envy that he was the first between Amy's thighs. The first to taste her. Then again, Zach had gotten the first kiss.

And now she was pushing her breasts in the air, her reddened nipples begging to be decorated.

He moved beside them, smiling cruelly as she opened her eyes to look at him, the sensual haze still clouding her vision. With her hands firmly planted on the desk to keep her in position, he didn't need to bind her to keep her still.

"Do you like what he's doing, little slut?" he asked, moving around to the other side of the desk so he could cup her breasts from behind her, looking over her shoulder to watch Kincaid feasting on her pussy. His boyfriend's dark head moved up and down as he licked and suckled her sweetness.

Zach put his hands on Amy's stomach, just above Kincaid's head, and slowly slid them up to her breasts, caressing the soft flesh of her body with appreciation. She moaned, her head falling back as he reached her breasts. From the soft touch he'd been doing, he now changed, gripping her breasts hard enough to make her cry out as he pinched her nipples tighter than ever, flattening the little buds between his fingers.

From his vantage point, he could see the way her thighs moved, squeezing Kincaid's head between them in reaction to Zach's tormenting fingers. His cock ached from her sharp cry, and he turned his head into her shoulder, biting down on the sensitive flesh.

Something he'd never been able to do before.

He couldn't get his mouth on her pussy right now, but he could do this, and it assuaged some of the hunger he was feeling. He felt her pulse fluttering against his tongue and heard her tiny whimper as he sucked hard, leaving a small mark behind by the time he lifted his head again.

Only then did he give her nipples a final twist before releasing them, making her cry out again.

Time to decorate the pretty little buds.

He'd already picked out the adjustable rubber-tipped clamps, even though she could definitely handle more, just because he wanted most of her focus to be on him and Kincaid, not on the clamps. Reaching into his pocket, he pulled them out.

He could tell she was getting closer and closer to orgasm as Kincaid pleasured her with his tongue, the soft moaning noises she was making, the way her body shuddered. The pain would either pull her back or tip her over, and he was betting on the latter, though either way, he looked forward to finding out.

The more he discovered about her body, the better he'd be able to satisfy her.

The sound she made when he closed the first clamp around her nipple made him grin, his cock throbbing in response. Kincaid paused what he was doing, looking up with some concern, then heat flared in his eyes when he realized. His gaze caught with Zach's and made his dick pulse in an entirely different way, his insides tightening before Kincaid returned to his efforts.

Amy panted for breath, whimpering, and Zach hefted her other breast in his hand, closing the clamp over that nipple as well. This cry was smaller, possibly because she was expecting it and possibly because Kincaid's tongue was working magic on her pussy... or a combination thereof.

"Oh, fuck..." The little sobbing breath she took was music to his ears.

"What do you think, Kincaid?" Zach asked, sliding his hands up to toy with the clamps, tugging and twisting on them, watching her shudder as she tried to hold herself in position. "Should we let our little slut come? Or should we make her wait?"

Her breath hitched, and she whimpered again, turning to look at him with pleading eyes. Kincaid chuckled, lifting his head just barely away from her pussy so he could answer Zach.

"I think our sweet girl needs as many orgasms as we can give her," he said. "Until she's begging us to stop."

Zach wholeheartedly agreed, but he did like to see her worry, her anxiety, and then her relief.

"As you wish."

He squeezed to open the clamps—not all the way, just a touch, just enough to ease some of the pressure on her nipples for a brief moment—then let them go so that they closed down around the little buds again. Her scream of pained pleasure was glorious.

Amy

It hurt, it hurt, it hurt so good.

It hurt in ways she'd forgotten. In ways she hadn't known it could. Because it didn't just hurt; it ached. She ached. Throbbed. All over.

The pulsing agony from her nipples melded with the pleasure from Kincaid's tongue as he licked and sucked along her pussy all the way up to her clit. Her brain had turned off almost entirely, lighting up only for the little comments Zach was making.

When he asked if they should make her wait to come, she'd almost cried.

When she'd realized she wasn't going to have to wait, she would have cheered if she hadn't been screaming from what Zach had just done to her poor, abused nipples. Yet, part of her loved that viciousness, the way he played with her senses, the way he and Kincaid were double-teaming her in every possible way.

Not just touching her, not just Kincaid's praise against Zach's degradation; it was also Zach's pain against Kincaid's pleasure. The combination was exhilarating. It felt as though she was truly, wholly alive again, as if she'd just woken up from a dream, and now, she was aware and feeling *everything*.

And she wanted more.

"Come for us, our sweet slut," Zach whispered in her ear, his voice low, his warm breath wafting over her skin. His hands cupped her breasts, squeezing and kneading, making her nipples pulse with agony as blood tried to move through them, cut off by the clamps.

As if he knew she was close, Kincaid's mouth moved higher, up to her clit, and he sucked the swollen nub into his mouth as her thighs tightened around his head.

"Come for us so I can hurt you some more."

Her elbows buckled as her orgasm slammed into her. Zach caught her, holding her up, the back of her head against his shoulder as she writhed between them, the waves of ecstasy flowing over her. Everything still hurt, but it didn't matter because the pain felt so good.

Sensations crowded her body until they were so packed in, they didn't have anywhere else to go, then exploded outward, again and again.

It wasn't until she was finally limp against Zach that Kincaid lifted his head again, this time letting her legs slide from his shoulders. Her pussy felt so soft and used and wet, her body still humming from the orgasm. Kincaid stared up at her, licking his lips, which were glossy and wet from her juices.

His gaze darkened as it shifted to Zach.

"Do you want a taste?" he asked.

Amy didn't know what he meant until Zach nodded, and Kincaid reached for him. He wrapped his hand around the back of Zach's neck, pulling him forward and trapping her even more between them as his lips crashed against Zach's.

He was letting Zach taste her pussy from his mouth.

It didn't matter that she'd just cum—again—her insides quivered, and she wanted to whimper. Her nipples felt like they were throbbing even more insistently against the clamps, though the initial pain was all but gone. She watched in fascination, feeling their bodies against her, the sound of their mouths and tongues so close to her ears, and ached with envy.

Then, suddenly, as if they could hear her thoughts, feel her envy, they broke off the kiss and turned to her as one.

If she'd ever thought about three people kissing at once, she would have thought it sounded awkward. Two mouths coming together made sense... but three? How would their mouths close around each other?

They didn't. Not exactly.

She felt Kincaid's and Zach's lips against hers, at the same time, and knew they were feeling both hers and each other's as well. The heat of their mouths, the wetness of their tongues, they all wound together, and it didn't feel awkward at all. She could taste herself on Kincaid's lips, feel Zach's tongue seeking that flavor as well, feel them pressing against her. When Zach tugged off one of the clamps from her nipple, and she cried out, they both muffled the sound.

Not for long, though. One moment, she was crying out in the middle of their kiss, and the next, she was lying on her back with both of them bending over her. Kincaid's hot mouth closed around the nipple Zach had unclamped while Zach pulled the clamp free of her other nipple before joining his boyfriend in sucking her nipple into his mouth.

Her cries echoed around the room as the pain of her blood rushing back into the tiny buds crashed against the pleasure of their mouths suckling her sensitive nubbins. So much more sensitive than they had been before the clamps. She writhed on top of the table, and someone's hand pressed down on her mound, fingers slipping between her pussy lips to caress her clit.

She grabbed both of them by the hair, not because she wanted them to stop sucking her nipples, but because she needed something to hold on to before she levitated straight off the earth.

KINCAID

Damn, Amy was hot as hell. Needy. Sweet. And he and Zach were both enjoying her far too much. His gaze met Zach's as they suckled her nipples, connecting across her body, and his cock throbbed. With his free hand, he reached down to adjust himself and also put some pressure against the growing ache.

Zach's hand was between Amy's legs, busily stroking her... but despite what Kincaid had said, he didn't want her cumming again yet. Not so soon. They would wind her up, though.

When he lifted his head and looked down at her breast, he couldn't help but grin with satisfaction. Her nipple was plumped and harder again, but so much darker than it had been before the clamps. Zach lifted his head as well, revealing the same. Amy released their hair as they both straightened up, reaching above her to grab onto the edge of the table.

From how unfocused her eyes were, Kincaid wasn't sure how aware she was of everything going on around her.

"Let's get her turned over," Zach said, still moving his hand between her legs while Amy panted for breath. "I want to plug her ass."

"Works for me." Kincaid ran his thumb over her pouting lower lip. "I want her pretty mouth." He pushed his thumb between her lips and felt her teeth graze the digit, her tongue flicking against the tip as she automatically closed her mouth and started sucking.

Fuck, yeah, he wanted her mouth.

He was assuming she'd never been double penetrated before, so it made sense not to jump straight into things, but they could still tag team her. With a plug in her cute little ass, she would feel even more stuffed. For her first time in a threesome, that was about as far as he wanted to take it.

Would there be other times?

He didn't know yet, but he already hoped so. He was pretty sure Zach was on the same page. So, it would just depend on Amy.

And the better a time they gave her, he assumed, the more open she would be to more times.

So far, it seemed like she was really fucking enjoying herself.

Pulling his thumb from the suction of her mouth, he helped Zach flip her over. She whimpered a little as her breasts and tormented nipples were squashed flat against the hard table. Kincaid grinned, running his hands over her upper back and shoulders, digging his fingers into her muscles while Zach did the same with her very cute little ass. The heart-shaped cheeks tensed and relaxed as he filled his hands with them. She let out a little moan, the top of her head rubbing against the bulge in Kincaid's pants.

She was at exactly the right height for what Kincaid wanted to do.

Sliding his fingers through her hair, he took a firm grip on the silky strands and lifted her head, turning her to face him rather than looking to the side. Her lips were slightly parted as he freed his cock with the other hand, allowing the thick length to spring out and land right on her lower lip.

"Open up, princess," he said. "You're going to suck my cock like a good girl while Zach plugs that pretty little ass of yours."

20

The world was floating around her, none of it feeling quite real, as Kincaid's voice filtered through her brain, calling her princess and telling her to open up. There was a cock in front of her mouth.

Amy opened her lips, letting his hand on her hair hold her in place as the cock slid into her mouth, hot, hard, and meaty on her tongue. She licked the underside, savoring the distinctly male flavor as he pushed in deeper.

"If you need to safe word, just slap the desk twice, okay princess?"

The words flowed around her.

The grip on her hair tightened, and the cock slid away.

"Amy, do you understand your safeword?"

Kincaid crouched down in front of her, looking her directly in the eyes. She blinked, trying to gather her wayward thoughts to remember what he'd said.

"Yes?" It came out as more of a question than a true answer.

"What do you do if you need to safeword?"

'I won't need to' was not the correct answer, and she knew it.

It took her a moment to remember what he'd said.

"I slap the desk twice."

"Good girl."

Warmth buzzed through her at the accolade, making her pussy clench right as she felt something cool, hard, and slick press against her anus. She cried out. Her sex life with Jeremy had dwindled under wedding stress—or so she'd told herself—and it had been a really, really long time since she'd had anal sex. They'd barely made time for regular vanilla missionary much less anything more adventurous.

The stretch hurt. It hurt really, really good. Zach was relentless with the plug he was using, pushing it in slowly but firmly, forcing her hole to widen to accommodate it.

Before she could beg him for a moment, Kincaid was already standing up and pushing his cock back into her mouth. Her hands curled over the edge of the desk to keep from slapping it. She didn't want them to stop. Not when they'd just gotten started again... not when she finally had one of their cocks in her and knew the other one was coming soon.

Zach had paused, letting Kincaid start to fuck her mouth. Her tight hole ached around the thick silicone. How big was the plug he was using? It made her whole backside ache, which she both loved and hated. The fact that it was moving inside her while Kincaid's cock was as well made her feel like she was having an out-of-body experience.

She'd dreamed of being between two men like this.

Between *them* like this.

Kincaid's thrusts into her mouth were gentle, slow, taking his time as he used her mouth for his pleasure. Amy moaned around the thick length as Zach paused again, this time pulling back just enough to give her a tiny bit of relief as her ass was allowed to contract again before he began to push in again. This time felt a little easier because she was already partially stretched, but she could feel the plug widening. Her opening burned as it was stretched, making her pant around Kincaid's cock as it became nearly unbearable.

Her toes curled as the immense pressure made her cry out, and she gagged on Kincaid's cock as he thrust in deeper, moaning as her mouth slid down nearly the full length of his cock. Amy gripped the desk so hard, she heard the wood creak, and she was about to lift her hand to slap the desk...

Then the plug popped all the way in.

She cried out again, the sound muffled by the cock down her throat, as her body sagged with relief, her muscles untensing. All the muscles except the ones around the plug now deeply embedded in her bowels. Those ached, straining from their new dimensions, her poor little hole throbbing around the stem between the base and bulb of the plug. Thankfully, that stem was far thinner than the thickest part of the bulb, which gave the tight ring some relief.

The feeling of uncomfortable fullness made her pussy clench, and she sucked hard as Kincaid's cock retreated and then thrust in again. Sucking gave her pent-up energy some relief, her body quivering as she adjusted. Now that she was no longer so focused on the toy pushing its way inside her, she was more aware of her nipples still pulsing and the way Kincaid's cock felt as it bumped against the back of her throat.

"How's her mouth?"

Zach's crude, almost casual, question made her pussy clench, and she shuddered again.

"Fucking perfect," Kincaid replied. He looked down at her.

Looking up to meet his gaze made her crane her neck painfully, but she did it for a moment, anyway, wanting to see him watching her swallow his cock. His handsome face had a hungry expression, which made her quiver internally. The grip on her hair tightened, tugging at her scalp like a slightly painful massage.

"She's a good little cocksucker."

"I bet she is." Zach's hands ran over her ass, caressing, then one of them lifted, and he gave her buttocks a sharp slap that had her wriggling. It didn't hurt nearly as much as it could have, and it sent a flash of pleasure through her overwhelmed senses. Her muscles clenched around the huge plug, which made them ache all over again. "She likes sucking cock, don't you, my little slut?"

She couldn't answer, but that wasn't the point.

Zach just wanted to spank her.

And he did. Over and over again, his hand peppered her backside while Kincaid casually thrust in and out of her mouth, holding her in place by her hair, enjoying the way her cries sent vibrations over his dick. The pace and intensity of the spanking became faster, harder, and every time Zach's hand came down, she clenched around the plug. The discomfort from those little spasms lessened as the pain in her cheeks grew hotter, as if she could only contain so much.

Then, suddenly, his hand was no longer coming down on her heated backside. No, his hands were curling around her hips. The tip of his cock slid up and down the length of her pussy, coating the mushroom head with her arousal. Amy moaned around Kincaid's dick, pushing back.

As full as she was with the plug in her ass, she wanted more.

Needed more.

Her pussy was so empty.

"I think our little slut wants to be filled at both ends," Zach said, his voice floating over her head as if from very far away.

"Then let's make that happen," Kincaid replied.

They both thrust in, and Amy screamed from the sudden jolt of painful pleasure.

Neither man was small, and Zach's cock sliding alongside the huge plug in her ass made her feel fuller than she ever had in her life. She hadn't known she could feel like this, as if every centimeter of space inside her was taken up. She couldn't breathe, and not just because Kincaid's cock was blocking her airway.

The slap of Zach's body against her heated cheeks as he thrust home gave her another jolt of pained pleasure, and she sobbed against Kincaid's cock as he buried it in her throat.

Oh, fuck... oh, fuck...

Thoughts flew into the air, her head no longer able to contain them. There was nothing but sensation as they used her, rocking her back and forth between them in an erotic rhythm. They were two sides of the coin, and she was the center, a vessel for their pleasure, her own body buzzing with the ecstasy rolling through it.

She didn't know when she started to orgasm.

She wasn't even sure she could call it that.

It was just waves of sensual bliss, washing over her, again and again, washing away all thought, all sense, all care, and leaving her floating on air.

Pain? Pleasure?

One and the same.

And she was drowning in it.

———

Z*ach*

Their pretty little subbie was floating in subspace; Zach was fairly certain of it. His eyes caught Kincaid's gaze over her bare back, both of their cocks buried inside her. He could see the pleasure on his boyfriend's face, see the satisfaction from a job well done... watch as Kincaid's features tightened, his eyes closing.

Amy hummed as Kincaid groaned, her pussy tightening around Zach's cock as his boyfriend came down her throat.

Fuck, that was so fucking hot.

As hot as her pussy. As hot as the surface of her ass as he pressed against it from behind, the base of the plug bumping against his body.

He could only imagine what it would be like to have her between them, one of them in her pussy, the other in her ass. Feeling her writhing against them, clenching around them simultaneously.

Even though Kincaid had had his cock in her a lot earlier than Zach, he was pretty sure he wasn't going to last much longer than his boyfriend.

She was too hot. Her pussy felt too good. And finally sharing her with Kincaid... finally being buried inside her... thinking about all the filthy things he wanted to do with them...

"*Fuck.*"

As Kincaid disengaged, stepping back and stroking Amy's hair, Zach no longer had to worry about her choking on his boyfriend's dick. Gripping her hips, he started fucking her harder, faster, letting out all the pent-up need he'd collected over the months of scening with her but never sexually. He was aware of Kincaid watching, of his boyfriend's appreciation of Amy's whimpers and moans of pleasure, of the sight she and Zach made while he took her from behind.

Letting go of Amy so she could rest her head on the desk, Kincaid came around the desk. Zach felt his muscles tense as his boyfriend moved behind him. Kincaid's hand cupped his ass, his finger sliding between Zach's cheeks, and he automatically bent forward, groaning as Kincaid's finger teased his entrance.

"Make her cum again for me."

Kincaid's order sent a shiver through him.

Sliding his hand between Amy and the desk, he pressed his fingers against her sloppy clit. She made a sobbing noise, her body stiffening beneath his, pussy clenching around him.

He circled his fingers, drawing back to thrust in, while Kincaid's finger still rubbed against the entrance to his own ass, his palm cupping Zach's ass. The image of himself in this position with Amy, but with Kincaid behind him, fucking Zach's ass while he fucked Amy, popped into his head.

Sheer lust rocked him, and he slammed into Amy hard, his fingers rubbing circles around her clit. She sobbed out in ecstasy, her pussy spasming around his cock as he held himself still, emptying himself inside her.

"Oh, fuck..." he groaned. "Oh, fuck."

Kincaid pressed a kiss to the back of his neck as his cock throbbed inside of Amy.

It felt like everything he'd ever wanted.

Kincaid

Carrying Amy to their door—they'd done aftercare at the

club, but she'd fallen asleep while they were cuddling her and stayed asleep for the ride home—Kincaid paused to wait while Zach got the door unlocked and open. Definitely one of the benefits of there being two of them. He didn't have to try to figure out how to handle their passed-out subbie on his own with the door.

Zach gave her a fond look as Kincaid passed him, holding the door open.

"She's really out of it, isn't she?"

"I think she needed it." Kincaid got her through the door without banging her head or her feet.

"She definitely needed it," Zach murmured.

Kincaid headed toward the hallway with their bedrooms. Behind him, he could hear Zach closing and locking the door before following them all the way down the hall and into her room. Which was good because that's where Kincaid had to pause.

They'd had threesomes before, but they'd never taken the third home with them. Aftercare ended at the club, not in their guest bedroom.

Still holding her curled up against his chest, her head on his shoulder, legs draped over his arm, Amy was fully clothed. The corset was loose on her, but it was *on* her. Putting her into bed like this felt wrong. So did undressing her without her consent.

Yes, they'd just seen her naked and had their hands all over her and their dicks inside her, but that had been at the club where they'd talked about what they could do. Where there were clear boundaries. Now they were home, and the lines were fuzzy, and she was in no place to be able to communicate what she wanted.

"Do we put her in pajamas?" he asked Zach.

His boyfriend hesitated, dark eyes widening. Kincaid could practically hear him going through the entire thought process that Kincaid had just gone through.

"Um..." Zach cleared his throat and looked at her. He gave Kincaid another glance, as if asking him to take the lead, but on this topic, Kincaid thought it was better if Zach made the decision. His relationship with Amy was more long-standing, and he knew her better. "Yeah, pajamas."

Amy sighed in Kincaid's arms, stirring against his chest.

"Pmas."

They both stopped and looked at her.

"What did she say?" Zach asked, bewildered.

"I think she was trying to say pajamas." Considering how out of it she was, that wasn't exactly fully informed consent, but from what he knew of her and what Zach knew of her, they both thought pajamas, too. It was about as good as they were probably going to get.

It was another tag team effort to get her out of her clothes and into a nightgown, mostly because she didn't want to let go of Kincaid. They did manage to get her to let go long enough to get her night-gown on by transferring her to Zach's arms as they did it.

Then they ran into another problem when Zach tried to put her in her bed and move away. Her arms clung around him, gripping onto his shirt. He turned his head to look at Kincaid, obviously trying to figure out what to do now.

"No, no, no... no lone." Her eyes were still closed, her voice thick with sleep, but her intention was clear.

She didn't want to be left alone.

Strangely, the emotion Kincaid felt the strongest was relief.

He didn't particularly want to leave her alone. Considering what an intense scene she'd had, he was worried about sub drop. If she was alone in her bedroom, they wouldn't know if she woke up in the middle of the night needing something, and because it was Amy, he was pretty sure if she did, she wouldn't come get them. Even if she was in the middle of sub drop.

Maybe especially if she was in the middle of sub drop.

Staying with her felt like the better solution.

"I'll go get into my sweats, then come trade places with you," he told Zach. "We can all sleep in here tonight. Just to make sure she doesn't wake up with sub drop."

Some of the strain dropped from Zach's expression, turning to the same relief Kincaid felt.

"Okay," he said. "That sounds good. Maybe we should plan for us to all sleep together on scene nights in the future. I can't blame her for not wanting to be alone afterward."

Kincaid nodded.

"Agreed. We'll talk to her about it in the morning."

It made the most sense, after all.

21

———————

AMY

Waking up between Zach and Kincaid was not as surprising anymore, but the fact they were in her room and not theirs did make her blink. She couldn't remember anything that happened last night after Zach slid into her pussy in the Jail while Kincaid was still fucking her mouth. Remembering that made her stomach do cartwheels and her sore pussy clench.

Ow.

Not just a sore pussy, either. Sore everything.

Shifting, she could feel that both of her holes hurt. She was kinda sad she didn't get to see the size of the plug Zach had used on her ass. It had felt huge. She couldn't help but wonder how much of that had been in her head or if she was going to feel proud of what she'd taken.

Her nightgown, which was incredibly soft, brushed against her nipples as she sat up between the two men, and she winced. Ow. Those hurt, too.

Everything hurt in the best way.

And they'd stayed with her. She could only assume they'd also been the ones to put her in her nightgown. The combination made her feel all sorts of mush that she was going to have to fight off.

It doesn't mean anything.

Other than they were concerned about her. Just like they had been when they'd done the scene here in the house. It wasn't like she was waking up in their bed again. She was in hers, and they had joined her. Because they were good Doms.

And that's it, so don't read anything into it.

The fact that she'd woken up before Kincaid meant he was tapped out, too. A little thrill of glee went through her. She could make breakfast for them!

She was feeling energized. Good. Sore but satisfied. So far beyond what she'd hoped when she'd been watching all those other subbies come up from the Dungeon last night. She'd gotten everything she'd wanted and more.

Making breakfast seemed like a good way to repay them.

Carefully, she slid toward the headboard to get out from under the covers, sliding her legs from under Kincaid's arms. Zach's brow furrowed as she moved, and she froze, waiting until it smoothed out before she started moving again.

Once she was out from between them and off the bed, Kincaid made a disgruntled noise, reaching out and finding Zach. Amy watched, amused, as the two of them shifted closer together, filling in the space she'd left behind. Damn, they were cute.

She kind of wanted to take a picture, but that felt too much like an invasion of privacy.

That reminded her to grab her phone. It took her a few minutes to realize that it wasn't in the bedroom. Pulling on her robe she went exploring and found it a few minutes later, plugged in to charge alongside the guys' phones on the kitchen counter. She had always slept with hers by the bedside, but she didn't hate that it was in the other room, especially when she checked and saw the number of text messages racked up in the group chat.

With a small groan, she put the phone back down. She wasn't

ready for a full-on discussion with the chat yet. Maybe after she'd had something to eat.

It didn't take her long to get things assembled for scrambled eggs, hash browns, and sausage. She also pulled out some apples to slice, but not until right before she was ready to serve because she didn't want them going brown while she was cooking everything else.

Humming under her breath, she cracked the eggs while the oven was heating for the hash browns. Every move she made hurt a little, and she liked it. Especially the ache between her legs. How long had it been since she'd ached like this?

Have I ever ached like this? Or felt this satisfied?

Why she felt guilty for thinking about how Jeremy hadn't been able to satisfy her when he'd also been cheating on her, she'd probably never be able to figure out. Part of her head wanted to make excuses—it wasn't really his fault. She'd figured out early on in the relationship that he wasn't kinky; the spark had started to die, anyway... But deep down, she also knew he'd never made the kind of effort Kincaid and Zach had last night.

He'd never said he wanted to give her as many orgasms as she could take. Heck, during the last year, he'd barely seemed to care if she orgasmed at all. She'd chalked it up to wedding planning exhaustion. Or maybe it had really been her reaction that had been wedding planning exhaustion. She'd been too tired to fight for herself, to fight for what she wanted. Too emotionally exhausted by doing... well, pretty much everything. And for very little, if any, gratitude in return.

Did it make her feel pathetic? Yes. But also angry. And not just at herself now. It wasn't as though she had asked for very much. It would not have been that hard for him to make her feel special. Wanted. Loved.

Her phone buzzed, making her jump, and she looked over at the screen.

"Think of the devil, and he appears," she muttered, staring at Jeremy's name. Should she pick up?

If she didn't, and he didn't leave a voicemail—which he almost never did because he hated leaving voicemails—she was just going to spend all day wondering what he wanted. It would drive her crazy.

Worse... what if she'd left something at their... no, *his* house? What if she didn't answer, and he threw it away instead of trying to get back in contact with her? She absolutely believed he was capable of that.

Gritting her teeth, she set down the whisk she'd been planning to use for the eggs and picked up the phone, swiping to answer.

"Hello?" She made her voice as coldly neutral as she could. She didn't want him to know that he affected her at all.

He doesn't affect me. I just had the night of my life with the two hottest Doms in the club and orgasmed until I basically passed out.

Jeremy didn't bother with a hello.

"I'm going to need two hundred dollars for your portion of the electric bill by the end of this week."

Her head blanked. Hearing his voice again made her skin crawl, his dismissive tone making her want to shrink inside herself. When his words actually registered, they halted her thoughts in their tracks. And not in a good way, like Zach and Kincaid had.

"You expect me to pay the electric bill?"

She could practically hear his eyes roll.

"You lived here during the past month, right? You used electricity. You owe part of the bill."

When looked at that way, it almost made sense, but...

"But you kicked me out."

"Yeah, and I'm not asking you to pay for the part of the bill after—"

His words were cut off as the phone was plucked out of her hand, making her jump and scream in surprise. Whirling around, she stared at Kincaid, who frowned back at her as he put the phone to his ear.

"Amy isn't paying for shit, and you are not calling her again," he said calmly. She couldn't hear exactly what Jeremy was saying at that point, but she could hear the sound on the other side of the phone cutting off at the sound of Kincaid's voice. "If you have any questions, you can direct them to me, Detective Kincaid Cavill, or to her lawyer, Alfred Johan of Addison, O'Shane, and Smith. Though, I would look him up before you made that move."

Something muffled on the other side of the phone while Amy kept staring at Kincaid, frozen in place. She didn't know what was worse—what Jeremy was demanding, the fact she knew she'd already been on her way to caving and paying the bill just to get him to leave her alone, or being humiliated at Kincaid knowing what an absolute dick nozzle she'd almost married.

But having him stand up for her was making her heart do all sorts of swoony, swoopy things that had nothing to do with his bare muscular chest and the grey sweatpants hanging off his hips.

"Yes, I *can* do that. You didn't have Amy on any kind of lease, and technically, you did not give her the proper amount of time to move out. She could have made your life far more difficult than she has, and she chose not to. Out of deference to her, the rest of her friends have also chosen not to, but we can change our minds at any time. I'm going to text you my number and Alfred's number. Do not call her again."

And with that, Kincaid hung up the phone and set it down on the counter, looking at her like he hadn't just done the hottest thing ever. She kinda wanted to jump him right now, no matter how sore she was.

But that was for the club.

She was going to give him the best damn blow job the next time they got to the club.

"Want some help with breakfast?" he asked right as the oven beeped. It was done pre-heating.

"Sure, can you put the hashbrowns in the oven?" She'd already dumped the shredded potatoes into the dish, so there wasn't much else to do.

"Yeah... mind if I add some peppers to it?" Amy hesitated. Kincaid raised his eyebrow at her. "I know you don't like peppers in salad, but we haven't done cooked peppers yet, and some of the things you don't eat raw, you do eat cooked."

She shrugged one shoulder a little weakly.

"Peppers are flavor rapists."

"What?" Kincaid stared at her, a shocked laugh bubbling up out of him, which made her smile a little more authentic.

"If you put peppers in something, everything else just tastes like peppers. They completely take over. They're flavor rapists."

Putting his hand on the counter, Kincaid doubled over laughing, which made Amy huff. It wasn't *that* funny. She knew it was a little weird, but... it was true. Seafood did the same thing. She'd gotten really good at picking things out of dishes she didn't like, but some things, it didn't matter if you picked them out because they left their flavor behind.

Flavor rapists.

Since he was still laughing, she decided to take charge of the situation.

"Here, I'll divide it into two dishes so that you and Zach can have yours with pepper." And it wouldn't touch hers and spread the flavor. Her declaration just made Kincaid laugh even harder, which made it really hard for her not to giggle, but she didn't want to encourage him.

ZACH

Once again, Amy and Kincaid were in the kitchen together, laughing. Zach tried not to feel left out as he came down the hallway. Yeah, he was the one who loved to cook, but he just got up later than they both did. It wasn't a big deal.

It hadn't bothered him before today. Not really.

Probably because they hadn't had a night together like last night. Last night, they'd all three been equally involved. Waking up alone while the two of them were in the kitchen...

He knew it didn't mean anything, but he still couldn't help but feel left out.

Maybe he needed to start getting up earlier.

Doubtful.

Strolling into the kitchen, he felt a little better when both Amy and Kincaid looked up to greet him and smiled. Kincaid was wearing his sweatpants and nothing else, like he usually did on weekend mornings, while Amy was in her navy-blue robe. He assumed she was still in the nightgown they'd put her to bed in. Her hair was tousled, and she was smiling, but there was something off about her, too.

"Good morning," Kincaid said, moving over to slip his arm around Zach's waist and give him a brief kiss. "Breakfast should be ready in about five minutes."

"Morning." He smiled at his boyfriend. Why did this feel so awkward? It wasn't like they were really leaving Amy out. This was how they were every morning. Yet, it felt different now while she busied herself at the stove. "Is the coffee ready?"

"It is." Kincaid let him go, turning away to grab a prepared mug before turning back to hand it to him.

"So, what was so funny?" Zach asked. "I could hear you laughing all the way down the hallway."

Amy and Kincaid exchanged a look, identical smiles lighting up both of their faces.

"Flavor rapists," they said in unison, to his utter confusion, then both cracked up.

Zach lifted the coffee mug to his lips to help cover his uneasy smile. They weren't deliberately trying to leave him out. He knew that. They'd just been up and talking already, and he'd missed some things. No big deal. Not at all.

If only that logical reassurance did anything for the uncomfortable way his stomach turned over.

"Sorry, sorry," Amy said, still snickering and sharing another glance with Kincaid, who started laughing again. Zach was torn between enjoying watching Kincaid laugh so hard, which didn't happen often enough, and feeling out of the loop.

Of course, by the time she was done explaining how peppers— and seafood, apparently—were flavor rapists, Zach was chuckling, too. They hadn't been leaving him out; he'd just gotten left out because he'd woken up later than them. That was something he could fix.

Probably.

He was sure as hell going to try. That would be better than feeling like the third wheel with two people who weren't in a relationship— one of who *was* in a relationship with him.

22

———————

AMY

Updating the group chat meant going over a hell of a lot more than the night before. It also meant updating them on everything that had happened during the morning. Jeremy's call. Kincaid's defense. The fact that, apparently, Freddy was her lawyer.

She sat on the couch in her robe, the texts flying fast and furious, while Zach and Kincaid cleaned up in the kitchen behind her.

> Morgan: Freddy will kick his ass.

> Sam: Forget Freddy, I'm going to kick his ass
> if he calls you again.

> Amy: I'm pretty sure Kincaid and Zach are
> going to kick his ass if he calls me again.

> Carolyn: That's so hot.

Carolyn was not wrong.

Once Zach had heard about Jeremy's call, he'd gone on a pretty impressive rant, and she wasn't entirely sure he wouldn't have gone storming out to confront her ex if Kincaid hadn't caught him.

It had been just as hot as Kincaid taking Jeremy on over the phone.

They were both really freaking hot. She still couldn't believe she'd had sex with both of them last night.

If she wasn't so sore, she would have had trouble convincing herself that she hadn't just dreamed the whole thing.

> Marissa: You should burn your wedding dress or something.
>
> Sam: Oh my God, yes!
>
> Sam: If YOU want to, that is
>
> Sam: But I vote yes
>
> Carolyn: I vote hell yes
>
> Sam: Can we make s'mores?

She started to type out 'we are not burning my dress' when she paused. Why not? Kincaid had already ripped the back of it open. It wasn't like she wanted to wear it ever again.

When—if—she ever got married, she would be getting a completely different dress. One that had a zipper instead of a million tiny buttons. And that was a big 'if' as far as she was concerned. Right now, she couldn't imagine ever wanting to plan another wedding.

Ever.

> Amy: Yeah, let's burn it.
>
> Marissa: Yay!
>
> Carolyn: Yay!

Morgan: Yay!

Sam: Yay! But seriously… s'mores?

Snorting laughter, Amy leaned back against the couch.

"What's so funny now?" Zach asked. Sauntering around the side of the couch, he leaned against the armrest rather than sitting on the couch with her. She didn't mind that he didn't sit down with her; he had the look of someone who was just stopping for a moment before heading back to take a shower. And put on some clothes. Amy took a brief moment to admire his upper torso before answering him.

"The girls and I are going to burn my wedding dress, and Sam wants to make s'mores." She grinned as he laughed in response, shaking his head.

"Is it made out of natural materials?" he asked. "If there's too much polyester and plastic, I wouldn't want to eat something cooked over it."

That was a good point.

"I have no idea," she admitted.

"You should probably check on that," Kincaid called from the kitchen. Amy twisted her head around to see him appear in the doorway behind her, wiping his hands dry on a dish towel. "You might not want to stand too close breathing in the fumes while it's burning either."

"Good point." She texted that point to the chat.

When she looked up again, Kincaid was moving to sit in one of the armchairs to the right of her, having left the towel in the kitchen. He leaned forward, resting his elbows on his legs as he looked at her, hands hanging between his knees.

"I think we should talk a little this morning," he said. "We did things in a bit of a rush last night… not that I have any regrets." A little glint of pleasure lit up his dark eyes as relief shot through Amy. "But there are some things we didn't get a chance to talk about. Like, last night, when we got home, Zach and I got you undressed, then put you in a nightgown and joined you in your bed, which is what it seemed like you wanted at the time... but we never explicitly talked about it."

Amy relaxed even more. For one awful moment, she'd thought he was going to say that they could never repeat last night again, and while she would have understood it, she would have been very sad.

But Kincaid just wanted to talk about the aftermath, which there would be no point in doing unless they were going to do it again... so this was a good sign.

<hr>

KINCAID

As nervous as he'd been to bring up the night before, Kincaid had always believed in taking the bull by the horns, which was why he wanted to get right into it this morning. From the way both Amy and Zach relaxed as he brought up the subject, he knew it had been the right decision. Talking things out now would keep them from getting awkward in the future.

"I'm really grateful you put me in my nightgown instead of leaving me in my corset," she said, smiling. "And also that you stayed with me. I woke up feeling pretty good this morning, but I think if I'd been alone, I might not have felt as good."

"I was worried about sub drop. We both were." Kincaid glanced at Zach, who was still perched on the couch arm, hands on the leg that he had crossed over his knee.

"I appreciate that. And it's definitely a valid concern." She sighed, wrinkling her nose. "You don't have to do it every time, though. I don't want you to feel like you can't sleep in your own bed."

He and Zach exchanged another look. They probably should have anticipated that response.

"We slept where we wanted to," he replied evenly. "Zach and I talked about it, and, with your agreement, we'd like to establish a rule that on nights we scene together, we all sleep in the same bed, so we don't have to worry about you sub dropping when we're not there."

Amy started to open her mouth, as if to protest, then stopped.

This time, the look that he and Zach exchanged was amused. Kincaid had deliberately chosen to lay it out like she'd be doing *them* the favor. Instead of needing to be watched over, she was preventing them from worrying.

Since it was true, it was an easy perspective switch.

"Oh. Yeah, that makes sense." She nodded. "I would like that, too."

"Good. Then we're agreed." Zach tilted his head at her, smiling. "I guess the next question is whether you'd like to scene again any time soon."

"Oh... um..."

Yes. The answer was all over her expression, yet she hesitated. They were going to have to work on her ability to advocate for herself and to ask for what she wanted. Kincaid made a little mental note in his head.

"We have a table for Friday at Marquis, and we'd like you to join us." There. Not asking what she wanted—telling her what they wanted. And from the way she lit up, it was what she wanted, too. He was going to have to watch her carefully to ensure she didn't say 'yes' when what she really meant was 'no.' But how she felt about this invitation was easy to see.

"Yes, please. I'm doing the whole dress-burning party on Saturday."

"Perfect. Zach and I will go over your limits this week unless there's something you want to change, and we can talk through any fantasies you might have."

"Oh... whatever you guys want to do is fine. I mean, great. Not fine. Whatever you want is more than fine. It's great." A blush was rising in her cheeks. Yeah, they were definitely going to be working on having Amy ask for what she wanted. They could start on Friday.

At some point, he was sure she and Zach had talked about her needs while they were negotiating. He'd talk to Zach first, and they'd start there.

"Great."

"So, for today…" Zach said. "Are we all still down for watching some more movies and continuing Amy's Marvel journey?"

"Yes!" Amy lit up again, this time with something like hope. Surprise. Even though they'd talked about it before, it was as though she'd thought they would change their minds. Which was crazy, especially considering what they'd done together the night before.

He wondered how often her ex had said he'd spend time with her or do something with her, then not followed through. She shouldn't be this surprised and excited that they were going to do what they'd said they were going to do.

Having heard the jerk demanding she help pay the electric bill, after he'd kicked her out of the house, he was betting the asshole let her down a lot. Well, the least he and Zach could do was help raise the bar for her next boyfriend… and not just inside the bedroom. She might only be having rebound sex with them right now, but they could show her how she should be treated when she decided to move on from them.

It was silly to already feel a pang at the thought of her moving on from them, but… well, he cared about her, and he'd taken her under his protection. It was only natural to feel protective.

"Great." Kincaid slapped his hands against his knees and got to his feet. "I'm going to go get dressed, and we can get started once we're all ready."

Did he miss the way Amy's gaze slid over his body, exactly the same way Zach's did, once he was standing?

No, he did not.

Had he worn his grey sweatpants on purpose?

Maybe.

But he wasn't alone. Zach was wearing them, too. And as far as he was concerned, Amy's blue robe was the female equivalent. It was short enough to show off most of her legs and looked soft and fluffy enough to touch. Maybe she didn't mean to have him fantasizing about pulling the tie free and using it to bind her hands together while he and Zach laid her back on the fluffy bulk of the robe and touched her all over… or maybe she did.

He'd never had these kinds of thoughts about other women they'd scened with, but it might just be because he wasn't used to having their third come home with them.

Normally, they came home, and he didn't think about the sub again until they were back at the club, if they scened with her again. Obviously, everything was already different with Amy.

Part of him was already wondering if she'd be amenable to scening at home too, but... one step at a time. He didn't want to spring too much on her while she was in a vulnerable state. They'd see how things went keeping it to the club, then maybe if she was in a good headspace but not ready to move on yet, they'd talk about doing some scenes at the house, too.

He had a tendency to get ahead of himself, so he needed to pull back hard on his plans until he had a better idea of where everyone was emotionally. So, he just smiled at them and headed to the bedroom. It didn't surprise him when he heard both of them following, and Zach joined him a moment later.

Seeing Zach smiling so broadly made Kincaid feel happy. He'd realized that Zach had felt a little left out with him and Amy hanging out together this morning before he was awake. There hadn't been anything Kincaid could really do about that, but it seemed to have resolved itself.

"That went well," he said.

"It did." Zach's smile slipped. "I can't believe fucking Jeremy wants her to pay the electric bill."

Kincaid didn't have words, but a growling noise escaped from his throat, rumbling through his chest as he picked out a pair of jeans and closed the dresser drawer. Sadly, he could believe it, but he'd also seen a lot more fucked up shit than Zach had. Some of which he'd told his boyfriend about, some of which he hadn't because he hadn't wanted to burden him with it.

Still, when it came to mind games and mental and emotional abuse, Jeremy was definitely up there. Cheating on her, humiliating her at her wedding, kicking her out of his house, and now calling to tell her she owed on the electric bill?

Kincaid couldn't do anything about the first three things, but there was no way in hell he was going to let Jeremy continue his bullshit. Not under his watch.

"We could always go pay him a visit..." he murmured. When he was met with silence, he glanced over at Zach, who was now standing, holding a shirt in his hands, head tilted to the side, as if he was thinking about it.

After a long moment, he seemed to realize Kincaid was looking at him and met his gaze.

"I don't think she'd like that." Zach sighed. "As tempting as it is."

Zach was probably right. She might even be upset with them. Amy was a peacemaker, from what he could tell, and she wasn't going to want to be responsible for creating more conflict. It would likely do more harm than help.

He was still going to keep it in mind for the future. If Jeremy was smart, he wouldn't try to reach out again.

23

Zach

The week somehow both crawled and zipped by until Friday. Work felt slower than ever. His mom called to chat on Wednesday night, and he hid in his and Kincaid's bedroom so that she didn't hear Amy's voice while he was talking to her. And his sister texted to see if he and Kincaid wanted to get together on Saturday night to meet *her* new boyfriend.

To which he and Kincaid had said yes. Amy was having her dress-burning party tomorrow, so getting together with his sister then worked out. Otherwise, he would have felt bad about leaving her at home alone.

Which might sound weird since it wasn't like she was part of his and Kincaid's relationship, but...

Their evenings during the week had been what zipped by. Watching her watch some of his favorite movies was incredibly fun. Though, she did yell at him every time she cried, which was more than he'd thought she would. He was expecting a *lot* of yelling when they got to *Infinity War* and *Endgame*. Totally worth it.

Amy might not be part of his and Kincaid's relationship, but she wasn't exactly *not* a part of it anymore. They'd spent every evening this week together, and neither he nor Kincaid felt like she was an intruder on their time. In fact, it had almost been odd to go back to their room just the two of them, and when they'd had sex, he'd almost felt bad about her being alone in her room. He'd even considered asking Kincaid how he would feel about them inviting her to join them.

He was starting to feel like he didn't want her to ever leave.

But he couldn't think like that.

Eventually, she was going to go.

This was temporary.

Unless everyone agreed it didn't have to be.

Stop thinking like that.

It was way, way too soon to be thinking like that. He didn't know if Kincaid felt the same way. Though... he thought the other man might. Kincaid was almost treating her like he did Zach when it came to being around the house, and Zach really didn't mind.

Other than that one morning of feeling left out last weekend, this whole week, he'd adjusted to it being the three of them. Sometimes, he and Kincaid were having their own conversation; sometimes, he and Amy were; and sometimes, Kincaid and Amy were. And they shared whatever the third party missed once they were all together.

Living with a third person was way easier than expected, though he was pretty sure that was due to the third person being Amy. He doubted it would be like this with anyone else.

"Ready for tonight?" Kincaid asked, coming out of their closet. He and Zach had opted to wear suits for tonight. Well, Kincaid was wearing a suit jacket and pants. Zach couldn't consider him fully dressed in a suit without the tie, which Kincaid wasn't wearing.

Zach was wearing a full suit. Both suits were grey, though Zach's was a steel grey and Kincaid's more of a morning dove grey. He'd picked out a grey and navy-blue patterned tie to wear, which matched the navy-blue and silver cufflinks on his shirt sleeves and the tie clip that he was sliding on.

"Hell, yeah," he said, admiring how Kincaid's shoulders filled out the suit. Even if he did refuse to wear a tie, he looked hot as hell. Zach loved it when the other man dressed up. "You look good."

Kincaid's gaze sharpened, a slow smile spreading across his lips, and he changed course from wherever he was headed to come closer to Zach, sauntering with the cocky confidence Zach enjoyed so much.

"So do you," he said, coming into Zach's space. Zach tipped his head back slightly, smiling, as Kincaid's body pressed against his. Kincaid's arm wrapped around Zach's back, pulling him fully against him as they kissed. He groaned against Kincaid's mouth as he felt the other man's cock hardening against him. His own dick thickened, lengthened, rubbing against Kincaid's through their pants.

Devouring his mouth, Kincaid held him there for several long seconds before releasing him.

"If we don't go now, we'll never get out the door," he said, his voice low and husky.

"Right, right." Zach huffed, sighing when Kincaid let him go. They had plans for tonight. Big ones. And not just because they'd be watching Justin, Chris, and Jessica perform. "Let's go."

It was worth it. Amy was waiting for them in the front room, and her eyes lit up as they came in, her gaze bouncing back and forth between them like a pinball. She hopped up from where she was sitting in the chair, facing the hallway as she waited for them, and brushed her hands down over her skirt. They'd told her how they planned to dress so she could match them, and she did.

Some people used the back entrance of Marquis to head straight up to the club, rather than going through the front door where the restaurant was, and they tended to dress in fetgear.

Although that was always an option, it wasn't one they would need to use tonight. Amy's dress was sexy as hell, but definitely not fetwear. It was a little black dress—emphasis on little when it came to the skirt. Made of what looked like a very soft, clinging material, it was stretched over her curves and ended just below her ass. She'd been sitting with her knees tightly pressed together and tugged the hem of the skirt down as she stood because it threatened to ride up higher.

The neckline dipped low, showing off her cleavage, which was pushed up high with some kind of lacy bra that peeked out from beneath the dress, hinting at the sexiness beneath. Zach couldn't wait to get the dress off her and find out exactly what it looked like.

"You look amazing," he said, walking forward and holding out his hand to take hers. She blushed when she slipped her fingers into his, and he bent over to kiss her knuckles.

"You really do." Kincaid came up on her other side, taking her other hand, though rather than kissing her knuckles, he lifted her hand up and turned it so he could kiss the inside of her palm.

Amy's quick intake of breath made Zach grin.

"Um. Thank you. You guys both look great." She managed to rally after stumbling over her words, obviously taken aback by their intense interest. "I always love a man in a suit."

Zach chuckled.

"Well, tonight, you have two of them to enjoy." He winked at her. "And we're going to enjoy you. Let's get going."

He couldn't wait to start.

Amy

It didn't matter how long ago high school had been, she felt like the prom queen walking into Marquis with two men.

They'd chosen to go in the front entrance since they were all dressed for it. More than one group of women in the dining room broke off their conversations to stare at Kincaid and Zach. They looked damn good in their suits. Zach was all buttoned up and GQ with his neatly trimmed facial hair, while Kincaid looked a little more devil-may-care with the full-on beard and lack of tie. The top button of his shirt was unbuttoned as well, adding to the appeal.

And she got to walk between them.

She was very aware of her short skirt and the way it was threatening to ride up her ass, but she couldn't pull it down when she was walking between Kincaid and Zach with her hand on each of their arms. At least, not until they finally passed through the dining room, past Victor—who was guarding the stairs to the second floor—and were about to go up the stairs. That's when she finally let go of Kincaid's arm and tugged the back of her skirt down. Not that it went very far. It hadn't started riding up over the curve of her ass the way she'd been worrying, but she still felt better.

Both men paused, looking at her with amusement. The towering heels she was wearing didn't quite put her on eye level with them, but she wasn't too far off.

"I'm ready." She took Kincaid's arm again, and he chuckled, bending his arm at the elbow so she could hold on to him.

Walking up the stairs between them was another one of those 'princess' moments, and she felt like it as they emerged into the lobby of Marquis' second floor. This was where the kink happened.

The lobby was innocuous enough with lush carpet and everything decorated in red, with black-and-white art on the walls in gold frames. The art was erotic but tasteful, titillating without exposing everything. Behind the black desk next to the door to the theater, Freddy and Morgan were standing and grinning at her.

She pressed her lips together.

She happened to know that neither of them was originally supposed to be working the desk tonight. The schedule must have changed.

Or they'd changed it.

Since Freddy was in charge of the front desk, that was very likely.

"Hello." Freddy was bright enough already, wearing a neon pink netted shirt and pink leather pants, but his megawatt smile somehow kicked it up another notch. His blonde hair was sticking straight up and had what looked like glitter running through it. "How are you three doing this fine evening?"

Kincaid gave him a long look.

"We're good, Freddy, thank you," he said dryly. "I didn't know you were working tonight."

"Oh. Well." Freddy beamed again, picking up the menus for tonight's dinner. The upstairs served the same menu as downstairs, with the caveat that if you were going to eat upstairs, you had to arrive by a certain time. They didn't want to interrupt the show for food being brought in.

Amy had to stifle a laugh at Kincaid's head shake. Freddy's non-answer was so very lawyer-like, she loved it.

Sometimes, looking at him in the club, it was hard to believe he was one of the toughest divorce lawyers in the area, but she felt like that's why he dressed the way he did at the club. This way he got to really let loose.

"Have a good night," Morgan called after them. When Amy glanced over her shoulder right before they left the lobby, she could see Morgan already on her phone. Amy rolled her eyes. She had no doubt that Morgan was updating the chat, though what she could possibly tell them was a mystery.

Arriving was not that exciting.

Freddy showed them to their booths, giving Amy a little wink before he whisked away. She shook her head, still amused at her friends. They were acting like this was some big romantic gesture or something, but she and the guys were just here for a scene.

For sex.

Which she was very excited about.

And why she didn't mind at all when Kincaid got straight to business after they'd ordered their food.

The circular booths lined the walls of the room, while a circular stage took up pretty much the entire center space. Each booth had both sheer curtains and privacy curtains, or they could be left entirely open, which was what their booth had right now. The lights were pretty dim, but she was able to see into the currently empty booths across from them.

Once the lights went down and the show started, she wouldn't be able to see much of anything that wasn't happening on stage, even without the sheers.

Kincaid and Zach were seated on either side of her, and as soon as they handed their menus to their server—who immediately whisked away to put in their orders—they moved in on Amy. She didn't know if they'd had some kind of little signal or something. One second, they'd been mostly in their own space, though sitting close enough to her that their legs were basically touching, then the next, they were both pressed up against her with her trapped between them.

Which she really, really liked.

Zach's arm went up and across the back of the booth—she could feel the heat of it against her shoulders and the back of her neck—while Kincaid's hand landed on her bare thigh. His fingers slid between her legs, pushing their way in, his pinky only a few inches away from her pussy and the thong barely covering it.

Immediately, heat and need bloomed inside her. She hadn't been sure what to expect during the dinner portion of this evening, but she wasn't disappointed. This whole week, waiting for tonight, had been pure torture. Especially the times she'd overheard them having sex again. Now that she knew *exactly* what it felt like to be between them, she hadn't needed anything to help put her libido into overdrive.

"So, Amy..." Kincaid gave her inner thigh a gentle squeeze that made her whole leg tingle. "Zach and I have discussed some of what we want to do with you tonight... but we also want to know what *you* want to do."

"I want what you want." Wasn't that the whole point of being the submissive? She just wanted them to do what they wanted, and she could go along for the ride and enjoy herself.

No thinking, no wondering, just pleasing them and being praised for it.

Zach's fingers stroked the top of her shoulder, making little circles on her skin. She could feel them all the way down her body, her nipples hardening as her body flushed with arousal.

"You're saying you've never had a fantasy before that you wanted to fulfill?" he asked. "When we first scened together, you had a little list that you were hoping to check off."

Oh... well. That was true. But that had been different.

Though she couldn't exactly put her finger on why.

Kincaid squeezed her thigh again, making her squirm as her

pussy clenched. His fingers were so close to her pussy, yet so far... too far.

"Let's start with something easy. I'd like to have you between us, one of us in your sweet little pussy, the other in your tight little ass. Would you say that's a fantasy of yours?"

One beneath her, the other one on top of her, moving as one... just remembering how it felt to have Zach fucking her while she was plugged was enough to make her cream her panties again.

That was an easy one.

"Yes," she whispered.

"Good girl." Kincaid's hand moved a little higher on her thigh, pushing against the hem of her skirt.

Oh, fuck.

"Zach wants me to fuck him while he fucks you." His tone was so casual, if she hadn't looked down to see the huge bulge at the front of his pants, she would have thought the conversation affected him about as much as the weather. Zach's bulge was just as big. His hand dropped from her shoulder to slide over her dress, his fingers dangling next to her nipple. "Is that something you'd like to try?"

Of course.

But they wanted to hear her say it.

"Yes, Sir," she whispered again, squirming as Zach's hand closed around her breast and Kincaid's fingers slid under her skirt, stroking against the outside fabric of her thong.

"Now, those are two of our fantasies. Can you tell us one of yours?" His fingers rubbed against her clit through the wet fabric of her thong while Zach's fingers circled her nipple.

The rising arousal, the way they were teasing her, was wildly distracting. She couldn't focus.

Kincaid had told her theirs. It was only fair that she shared hers, right?

"Cream pie," she whispered, bringing her hands up to cover her face, which inadvertently trapped Zach's arm against her breast. She couldn't look at either of them. Jeremy would *never*. "That's... that's when..."

"Oh, we know what that is," Zach said, his voice silky smooth as he gave her nipple a hard pinch as a reward. "And we are definitely going to make that fantasy come true."

To punctuate his words, Kincaid gave her clit a hard rub, making her moan and shudder.

"Very good girl."

Amy melted.

24

———

Amy was pouting. They didn't let her orgasm before their dinner came, and it was cute. She was very aroused, which apparently made her stab her food aggressively with a knife as she sent little glares at both him and Zach. But squirming and needy was how he wanted her right now.

Last weekend had been all about giving her as many orgasms as she could handle. Tonight was about making her wait a little bit. Especially because once they got started, he wasn't going to want to stop. So, they needed to eat first.

As they did, he and Zach had a whole conversation while Amy pouted and squirmed between them, helped along by the little caresses that they were both giving her at random intervals. It was no wonder she was pouty and jumpy. Kincaid smirked every time she glared at him. This was fun.

While Zach submitted to him and was submissive to him, he didn't have the fun little reactions Amy did. He could tell that Zach was enjoying tormenting her as well. They were part of a team.

As soon as they were done eating, Kincaid pushed their plates to the edge of the table, so their server could easily pick them up. Amy perked up, looking incredibly hopeful. But the show on stage hadn't started yet, and he was pretty sure Zach was enjoying edging her as much as he was.

"Did you bring anything to decorate our pretty little sub with?" Kincaid asked, knowing perfectly well that Zach had done exactly that.

"Of course." Zach grinned, reaching into his pocket as Kincaid shrugged off his jacket.

Amy watched him roll up his shirt sleeves, her focus entirely on his forearms and hands, and he couldn't help but grin. As she watched him, she wasn't paying attention to Zach bringing out the clover clamps that he'd packed away. They weren't Kincaid's preference, but he knew Zach liked them, and apparently, Amy did as well.

"Let's see these pretty breasts," Kincaid murmured, reaching for the front of her dress. Amy sat still like a good girl while he and Zach pulled the V-neck of her dress open, revealing the lacy bra beneath. Her pink nipples were already hard, pressing against the black lace. Kincaid paused to pinch and roll the one closest to him, making her give a little moan as the lace rasped over the sensitive bud.

"Very pretty," Zach said from the other side, pinching her nipple hard and tugging. Amy squirmed between them, and Kincaid grinned as she ended up with one hand on his thigh and the other on Zach's.

"Now there's an idea..." He looked up at Zach. Yeah, they were on the same page. It only took them a moment, then Amy was between them, a hand on each cock, squeezing and holding on for dear life as they played with her breasts. She was so consumed by what they were doing, it wasn't exactly a hand job, but he was much happier with her fingers wrapped around his dick than nothing.

Their server, a club submissive named Grace, appeared at their table, picking up the dishes Kincaid had pushed to the edge.

"Would you like any dessert?" she asked nonchalantly. The servers at Marquis were used to far more risqué behavior than something as simple as two men getting hand jobs while they played with the woman sitting between them.

Amy whimpered.

"Ice cream, please," Kincaid said, rubbing the scratchy lace against Amy's nipple as he smiled up at Grace. She nodded, smiling, and moved on, as if she hadn't seen anything out of the ordinary.

Damn, but he loved kink-safe spaces.

On the other side of Amy, Zach pulled down the lace of her bra, exposing the hard pink nipple completely.

"First clamp, my sweet slut."

Her eyes closed as he applied it, lips parting as she sucked in a deep breath, her chest lifting as she did so. A high-pitched whine came from the back of her throat, and her fingers tightened around Kincaid's cock like a death grip, causing him to moan in response. Zach did the same, so he had a feeling his boyfriend was receiving the same treatment.

As she panted, Kincaid pulled down the other side of her bra, hefting her breast in his hand and holding it up for Zach. Their gazes connected over Amy's gorgeous breasts, Zach looking into Kincaid's eyes as he put the second clamp on her nipple. She whined again, panting for breath through the pain, as Kincaid and Zach smiled over her.

Amy

Her Doms were jerks of the highest order.

What happened to all the orgasms she could handle? Right now, she'd be willing to kill for just *one* orgasm.

She was wetter than she'd ever been in her life, and they were alternating between eating ice cream and feeding her ice cream. For one shining, hopeful moment, she'd thought maybe they'd eat the ice cream off her pussy, but no. They just toyed with the clamps, occasionally tugging on them to tighten the clover clamps even more, sending another flash of pain through her body. Sometimes, they'd brush their fingers over the tips of her nipples, peeking out from the clamps.

Her chest throbbed, and her pussy clenched with need, but now that they'd gotten her fantasy out of her, both of them were apparently ignoring her pussy.

Jerks.

She kept squirming in her seat, pressing her thighs together, trying to get the pressure she needed to tip her growing arousal over the edge while they talked about some boring finance thing Zach was doing at work. Okay, it wouldn't be *that* boring if she could focus, but she'd be a lot more interested if she wasn't dying of sexual need between them while they talked finance! Not even jerking them off harder changed their determined conversation. They just fed her another bite of ice cream, which forced her to slow her movements.

Then the lights started to go down, and she perked up. The show was starting.

Thank the sex gods.

Music, heavy on the bass, slowly filled the air in a slow crescendo as dark figures made their way out onto the stage. It wasn't until the lights came up that Amy realized there were three of them.

She hadn't asked who was performing tonight, and she hadn't looked it up because she wanted to be surprised... so she hadn't known it was a threesome.

Masters Justin and Chris with their wife and submissive, Jessica. Talk about a fantasy come true. Just like Kincaid and Zach, they were tall, dark-haired, and very handsome. They'd been a little worn down after having their baby with Jessica, but it appeared they'd bounced back since then.

They circled around Jessica, who stood between them beside a spanking bench, hands at her side, with the most serene expression on her face. She wasn't quite as curvy as Amy, but close, and the way the two men looked at her made Amy ache... but not with envy anymore.

Kincaid and Zach looked at *her* almost exactly like that.

Of course, it couldn't be exactly like that. They weren't in love with her, after all. But it was close enough to make her ache, wishing that maybe...

Stop it. Don't go there.

She was rebounding. Of course, her feelings were all confused. Especially because Kincaid and Zach—just as housemates, friends, and sexual partners—acted as better boyfriends than Jeremy ever had. She needed to raise the bar of her expectations. She didn't ever want to go back to how Jeremy had treated her.

He'd *never* looked at her the way the three on stage looked at each other.

"Ow!" She jumped as pain throbbed through her nipple—unexpectedly coming from Kincaid's side rather than Zach's.

"I feel like you're not paying attention, princess," he murmured in her ear. "Maybe we need to give you something else to focus on."

Shoot, she really had missed some of the show, she'd been so lost in thought.

On stage, Justin had Jessica's arms behind her back, trapped between her and him while Chris was applying clamps to her nipples. Amy's breasts throbbed in sympathy, not that she had more than a moment to feel that sympathy before she was suddenly lifted up by both men and bent over the table.

"Ow!" Unlike in the Jail, she could use her hands to push herself up, so her clamped nipples weren't pressed flat against the hard wooden surface. She got her elbows underneath her, propping herself up so that her breasts hung down between them.

The tips of her nipples still brushed against the hard wood when she moved, stimulating the tortured buds without causing true pain. The position also meant that she could still see what was happening onstage, where Chris was now hefting a leather flogger in his hand. Justin still held Jessica in place, her arms behind her, his mouth moving up the side of her neck with kisses. Her head fell back against his shoulder, pushing her breasts out farther like an offering.

Behind Amy, she felt something hot and hard press against her slit, rubbing up and down the wet folds of her pussy.

Then he thrust forward, and she moaned, pushing back against whoever was starting to fuck her. It only took a glance over her shoulder to know that it was Zach sliding his cock into her. She could see Kincaid's head turned, watching from an incredibly advantageous perspective as Zach pulled back and thrust in again, his hands tightly gripping her hips.

She could feel him sliding in, stretching her muscles as they clenched around him, needily sucking him in deeper. The movements made her breasts sway, and she moaned as the tips brushed against the table beneath her, making her nipples throb as blood tried to push into them, only to be stopped by the clamps.

Onstage in front of her, Jessica was now moaning as she leaned back against Master Justin, the leather slapping against her breasts over and over again. She writhed against him as Master Chris turned her breasts from pale cream to a bright, blushing rose.

Amy was having trouble concentrating on watching them, though, because Zach was fucking her with long, slow strokes that made her senses go haywire.

"Oh, fuck…" Her fingers curled, nails digging into the wood as she panted for breath. She'd been so worked up, even before he'd bent her over the table, that her orgasm was ramping up again exponentially with every thrust of his cock. His balls slapped against her swollen clit, sending little sparks of ecstasy through her roiling pleasure. "Oh, fuck, oh, fuck…"

Suddenly, Kincaid was there beside her, one elbow on the table, his other hand fisting her hair and pulling her head completely upright. She was staring right at the stage but seeing nothing as he whispered in her ear.

"Come for us, good girl."

She cried out, shuddering and clenching around Zach as he kept fucking her, harder and faster, sending her on wave after wave of pleasure. Kincaid kept his tight grip on her hair, and she could feel his gaze on her, watching her as she came for them.

Zach

Amy felt like sweet heaven as he buried himself inside her, over and over again. He could feel her coming around him, her pussy grip-ping him even tighter than her fingers had while he'd been teasing her. Seeing Kincaid's head next to hers, his boyfriend's fingers buried in her hair, only turned him on more.

"Good girl," Kincaid said, loud enough for Zach to hear, though he doubted anyone outside the booth could hear. He let go of her hair so he could slide his hands under her body.

Zach knew the exact moment that Kincaid removed the first clamp from her nipple. He could *feel* it as her pussy rippled around him, even as her cry was lost in the noises from all around them.

He groaned with pleasure at the incredible sensation.

On stage, Justin and Chris now had Jessica leaning against Chris, her head on his chest, her bottom pushed outward, as Justin flogged her ass.

He could imagine him and Kincaid in this position but with more than a flogger. Maybe a whip or a cane. Amy would whimper and cling to Kincaid while Zach whipped her, and Kincaid would tell her what a good girl she was being for taking the pain for Zach.

Fuck.

Amy's pussy rippled again as the second clamp was removed, then Kincaid had his hands under her chest, probably massaging her breasts and sore nipples. Zach gripped her hips, fucking her faster and harder, rocking her against the table as she was held up by her elbows.

Then Kincaid released her breasts and straightened again, moving one hand back to her hair and pulling her head back up again so he could make sure she could see what was happening in front of them.

He felt her pussy spasm again when Justin dropped the flogger and unzipped his pants, stepping up behind Jessica. Chris held her in place as Justin moved into position and thrust his cock into her from behind, the same way Zach was doing to Amy.

His own need was bubbling up and over, breath coming in short, hot pants as her pussy clamped down around him again.

Kincaid turned his head away from the scene on stage, meeting

Zach's gaze, heat burning in his eyes. That was all Zach needed to send himself over the edge.

Caught in Kincaid's gaze, he buried himself in Amy, his cock pulsing against the wet, throbbing heat of her body. Still holding on to Amy's hair with one hand, Kincaid leaned over, wrapping his hand around the back of Zach's neck and kissing the fuck out of him while he emptied himself into Amy's pussy.

25

───────────

Holding on to both of his lovers as they came together was a heady experience. Kincaid didn't need to be inside either of them to feel his power over them, and he felt it right now. Felt them quiver together, felt them sag as they both reached their climax. Felt Amy sink down as her arms went weak, though her head was still up and watching the scene on stage, thanks to Kincaid's grip on her silky soft hair.

Ending the kiss with Zach, he grinned at his lover's slightly glazed eyes.

"My turn." He gave Zach another quick kiss before letting the other man's neck go, so Zach could disengage from Amy.

Both of them worked together to flip her over on the table, getting her into position with her knees toward the ceiling and in a spot where she could still watch the threesome onstage if she turned her head. The light in their booth was dim, but Kincaid could easily see that her abused nipples were now dark red from the clamps, her pink pussy glistening from her juices. White cum dripped along the dark pink folds, moving down toward her crack.

Sitting down, Kincaid draped her legs over his shoulders with

Zach's help, lifting her lower back off of the table to lift her pussy to his mouth. The scent of sex filled his nose as he cupped her buttocks, spreading them apart so he could start where Zach's cum had already dripped down.

Amy cried out, loud enough that he could hear it over the music and all the other people in the room, as his tongue pressed against her crinkled rosebud. He felt her legs flex, trying to escape, but he had a firm hold on her, and he wasn't going to let her get away from him just because she wasn't expecting a little analingus.

The salty taste of Zach's cum coated his tongue, along with the sweeter flavor of Amy's juices, and it was delicious. He moved his tongue over her little hole, teasing the sensitive nerve endings there, demonstrating his domination over her body as he didn't allow her squirming to deter him from what *he* wanted to do. Only after he'd felt her relax into it, no longer trying to wriggle away from his questing tongue, did he give her anus a last few licks before dragging his tongue upward, collecting more of Zach's cum along the way.

He felt her shudder when he reached her pussy, felt the way she moved to press herself more firmly against his mouth. The taste of cum and pussy was much stronger here, of course. Since Zach's cock had just stretched her open, it was easy to get his tongue inside her, questing for more cum in her sloppy pussy.

At some point, he was going to want to take turns with Zach, so he could feel his dick sliding into Zach's cum in her pussy. They could take her over and over again, one resting while the other fucked her, filling her with as much cum as they could until she couldn't take anymore.

Fuck.

His dick throbbed against the front of his pants.

Even though he was licking Zach's cum out of her, and it wasn't going to be quite the same, he still couldn't wait to take her again now, so soon after Zach had. Feeling her all soft and wet from her orgasm, knowing she was even more sensitive than normal, and having her wrapped around his dick.

He had no regrets about taking her mouth last time, but that wasn't what he wanted this time.

Sucking her clit between his lips, he enjoyed the way she tried to levitate against his mouth. He looked up along the length of her body to watch her soft stomach ripple as she panted for breath, squirming against his tongue. Zach had her arms above her head, reaching toward where he was seated on the other side of the booth, holding her wrists down with one hand while his other toyed with her breast. She was pinned in place between them.

Grinning, Kincaid gave her clit a last, hard suckle before releasing the swollen bud with a little pop. Getting to his feet, he kept her legs against his chest as he lined his cock up with her pussy and thrust in with no preamble. She didn't need it. Her pussy was sopping wet, already stretched from Zach fucking her, and his cock easily slid in to the hilt.

He groaned with pure pleasure as her wet heat wrapped around him, pussy muscles spasming as he slammed home. Amy cried out, her back arching upward, and Zach took full advantage to close his hand around her full breast, his fingers pinching her already sore nipple. Kincaid could feel the effect of the torment as her pussy clenched around him again.

Wrapping his hands around her thighs as he leaned forward, pressing them against his chest, he started fucking her harder and faster. He wasn't paying attention to what was happening on stage, and neither were Zach or Amy. Zach was watching Kincaid fuck her into the table, and Amy was looking up at him, her mouth open in a little 'o', eyes glazed, cheeks flushed as he pounded her toward another climax.

She felt so fucking good, her body quivering underneath his. Zach was still holding her hands down. He'd released her breast, sitting back to watch, which meant all her focus would be on the feel of Kincaid's cock sliding back and forth inside her. He shifted his own hand on her.

With the music, the long wait, he didn't want to have to hold back, but he did want her to cum on his cock. So, he splayed his hand out over her mound, his thumb dipping down to rub against her slippery clit with every thrust of his cock. Her head thrashed from side to side as he began to circle the little bud, his body slamming against his thumb to add pressure every time he thrust in.

Her scream of ecstasy was lost in the cacophony of sound that crescendoed around them.

AMY

She'd had the fantasy... she just hadn't realized it would feel like *this*.

Every part of her body felt like an erogenous zone; she was so sensitive after multiple orgasms. They'd gone from denial to overload, and she wasn't sure how much she would be able to take.

Each one felt like she couldn't possibly have another, then it happened again.

When Kincaid slid inside her, stretching her open, bending her in half, she'd been sure she was only capable of hazy floating on the cloud of pleasure that she'd already landed on. Then he'd put his hand on her lower body, this thumb on her clit, and she'd been launched into another stratosphere, sobbing from the agonizing ecstasy of another orgasm.

Zach held her down as she fought against him, her body completely vulnerable to them. She couldn't stop the sensual assault, couldn't stop the painful build of sensation, couldn't stop them from doing whatever they wanted to her.

Then Kincaid slid his hand away from her throbbing nub to grip her hips. Amy writhed beneath him, her hands now gripping Zach's forearms as he held her in place for his boyfriend. In the flickering darkness, Kincaid's features were foreboding, his concentration absolute, as he pounded into her.

"Please..." she begged, without knowing whether she was begging him to stop or to keep going. "Please..."

His fingers tightened, bruising her hips, and she cried out again as he slammed into her, his hard body rubbing against her oversensitive pussy and clit. It was heaven. It was hell. She sobbed as the pleasure and pain rose over her like a tidal wave and crashed, tumbling her senses like a tiny shell through the rolling waters.

Inside her, she could feel Kincaid throbbing against her clenching muscles, feel the heat as he came. She felt, more than heard, his low groan.

She was so wrapped up in him, in Zach, that she had almost forgotten there were people in the booths around them, that there was another throuple onstage. They had finished their show, and she didn't even notice until the lights went dark again.

"My turn for dessert," Zach whispered in her ear just as Kincaid disengaged in the darkness, his cock sliding from her aching channel.

Amy whimpered.

She must have been mad asking for this.

But she couldn't find her voice as they spun her around.

Couldn't bring herself to stop them.

Because even though she wasn't sure she could take it, she still wanted them to finish it.

Zach's mouth came down on her pussy, his tongue lapping up Kincaid's cum the same way Kincaid had done his. Hands closed over her breasts, cupping and massaging, squeezing the tender mounds. Kincaid was playing with her while Zach feasted on her.

She couldn't take anymore.

She really couldn't.

Then she felt Zach's finger rubbing through the combined juices coating her skin, felt him pushing against her anus. She cried out as his finger pushed inside the tight little hole, adding a whole new sensation to the litany she was already experiencing.

Crying out, Amy clenched, quivering. Slow tears slid down her cheeks in the darkness, as if the sensory overload was escaping through her eyes because it had no other way out.

She couldn't possibly cum again.

She couldn't.

Except she was going to.

She fought it, straining, trying to outlast the cleaning that Zach was giving her... but he was determined.

"One more," Kincaid murmured, leaning down next to her ear so she could hear him. "Be a good girl, and come for us one more time."

His hands massaged her breasts as Zach's tongue circled her clit. His finger worked back and forth in her ass, stimulating entirely new nerve endings.

Amy's head thrashed from side to side.

"I can't!"

"Yes, you can." Kincaid's hands became rougher on her breasts, his fingers pinching and tugging on her very sore nipples, sending a hot flash of pain straight through to her core. "Come for us, princess."

Zach sucked her clit, his tongue fluttering against the sensitive nub, and Amy cried out as a second finger pushed into her ass, stretching her. The sting, the burn, the hot bursts of pain mixed with pleasure...

It sent her over the edge again, and she sobbed as she fell, sure her body couldn't handle anything more, that the multiple 'little deaths' were the end of her.

Yet she didn't black out.

She felt Kincaid's hands gentle, felt the final caress. Felt Zach's final lick. She closed her eyes and floated, trusting them to take care of her, but she wasn't asleep, either.

She felt everything.

Heard everything.

The rasp of fabric over sensitive flesh.

The strong hands lifting her from the table.

The arms holding her securely against a broad chest.

They took the elevator down. It felt like she was falling again, but she could feel the presence of both men—one holding her, one beside her—keeping her safe.

Kincaid carried her to the car, then Zach held her in his lap in the back seat on the way home. She could tell who was who more by their smell than anything else since they were both quiet. They felt the same as they held her.

They both helped get her undressed, cleaned up, and into paja-mas, though she felt more like a ragdoll than a human being. Even though she was *aware*, she wasn't exactly functional. She leaned on them, sighing, humming, and occasionally whimpering when they touched a particularly sensitive spot.

Zach made her whimper far more than Kincaid did until Kincaid finally slapped his hand away from her sore nipple. Mentally, she thanked him, even if she couldn't find the words right now. She just sighed with relief.

They got her into her bed, between them, which was exactly where she wanted to be.

As darkness finally swallowed her up, she wistfully wished it could always be this way.

26

———————

AMY

Kincaid getting up from the bed woke her up. Zach was still breathing heavily on the other side of her, his warm breath wafting over her bare neck. She turned, wincing slightly, and looking up at Kincaid. He smiled down at her, his gaze soft.

"How are you feeling?" he asked as soon as he realized she was looking at him.

"Sore." She gave him a rueful smile. "But good."

"Good." His smile changed to just a little more smug, a little more like a smirk. It was all she could do not to roll her eyes.

Men.

He hesitated, and she got the strangest impression that he wanted to lean down and kiss her. Even though they weren't at the club or in the middle of a scene.

Or maybe her wishful thinking was getting out of control again.

"I'm going to go make breakfast," he said and hurried out the bedroom door, leaving her there with the still-sleeping Zach.

Well. That was... awkward.

Or maybe it was all in her head, like thinking he'd had the urge to kiss her.

With a groan, she flopped back down next to Zach, who didn't budge an inch. Her feelings were getting way more complicated than she'd expected. Was this what a rebound was like?

She didn't have much time to think about it because her phone started vibrating. Someone was calling her. Thankful for the distraction, she leaned over to check the screen, not even thinking for a moment that it might be Jeremy until her stomach did a weird swooping thing in memory of how he'd called her last weekend. Thankfully, it wasn't him.

It was her mom.

Amy scooted to the side of the bed, glancing over her shoulder. Zach was still fast asleep. Still. Better take it out to the hall.

Hurrying out the bedroom door, she stayed at the end of the hall rather than going down to the main room. Yeah, her parents knew she was staying with Zach and Kincaid, but since things had changed between them, she felt the need to... well, hide.

"Hey, Mom."

"Good morning, sweetheart. How are you?" Her mom's voice was filled with sympathy, making Amy's stomach flip, worried that something terrible had happened and she had missed it.

Then she realized—the terrible thing had happened to her. Her parents hadn't been able to do much more than email and occasionally text while on their trip. Her mom had no idea that Amy wasn't in mourning. That she didn't miss Jeremy *at all*. And that she was actually way happier than she'd been in years.

"I'm fine," she said automatically because saying 'I'm the best I've ever been' after she'd been a total wreck the last time her mom had seen her felt wrong. "How was your trip?"

"Oh, we had a great time, but I couldn't help but worry about you the whole time. I felt so guilty taking off like that." The guilt was evident in her mom's voice, making Amy feel bad.

Maybe she *should* tell her mom she was the best she'd ever been.

"Don't feel guilty. I would have felt way worse if you hadn't gone. I'm glad you guys had a great time. That's exactly what I wanted. And, really, I... this is going to sound terrible, but I don't think I was heartbroken as much as I was humiliated." She shrugged one shoulder, even though her mom couldn't see her. "The longer I've been away from Jeremy, the more I've realized what a terrible boyfriend and fiancé he was."

"About time," her dad muttered.

"Am I on speakerphone?"

"Yes, honey, we're both here," her mom said, and her dad grunted, as if her mom had just elbowed him or something. She probably had.

"Hi, honey," he said.

"Hi, Dad." She couldn't help but smile. Wanting a relationship like her parents might have been part of the reason she'd been so invested in getting married, but just being married didn't make the relationship. That's what she was waking up to now. If she had married Jeremy, it wasn't like things would have changed. She would have still been unhappy and unfulfilled; she just would have been even more trapped than before. "Well, seriously, don't worry about me. I did my crying, and I've moved on to the anger phase. My friends and I are getting together tonight to burn my dress."

"Oh, that sounds like fun!" her mom said brightly, just as her dad asked, "Why?" Amy didn't need to answer because her mother immediately did it for her. "Because it's cathartic."

"But we spent so much money on it," he complained.

Oh, shoot. They had.

"I don't have to burn it. I can..." Amy's voice trailed off.

"You can what? We don't need to resell it. We basically had to rip it off you. The repairs wouldn't be worth it, and no one is going to buy a dress that's that damaged, not at a price that would be worth selling it for. Burn it, sweetie." Her mom sounded very sure of herself. "Burn all that bad juju away."

Amy couldn't help but laugh, even as her dad huffed. He didn't argue, though. And her mom was right. She'd forgotten about the damage Kincaid had done getting the thing off her. She doubted she could even give it away. The repairs would cost enough that someone might as well buy a new dress rather than take her severely damaged one.

Catching up with her parents was really nice and being able to truthfully reassure them that she was doing just fine. She relaxed enough that, rather than standing in the hallway and talking, she wandered down to the main rooms. Kincaid looked up from where he was standing at the stove, flashing her a quick smile before turning back to his tasks.

And everything in the world was right again.

Zach

Being out without Amy felt weird. Even though he was having a great time, and so was Kincaid. His sister's new boyfriend was pretty great. His name was Thaddeus, but he went by Tad. Like Zach, he worked in finance, and like Zach he preferred to talk about anything else when away from the job.

Though if the two of them got alone, they'd probably have an interesting discussion about work.

He and Krista had met while LARPing—Live Action Role Play— one of Krista's passions. Zach had been dragged to quite a few Renaissance Fairs with her when they were younger.

Eventually, Zach wanted Krista to meet Amy, but obviously, tonight wasn't the right time. Tonight was about meeting Krista's new boyfriend, not introducing his sister to the girl he and Kincaid were scening with on the side. He wasn't even sure his sister would understand what was going on between them.

"And then she took off her helmet and said, 'I am no man' and stabbed me through the heart," Tad said, grinning. His eyes were for Krista and Krista only as he finished up the story of how they'd met on the battlefield at Pennsic. She beamed back at him. They were really cute together, Tad with his long, dark blond hair that he had tied back in a ponytail and his dark eyes, next to Krista with her black curls and bright blue eyes. They might have opposite colored hair and eyes, but they were clearly kindred spirits.

"So, you don't need the warning that she's a handful," he joked. "Sounds like you already found out for yourself."

Krista sniffed derisively. "I may be a handful, but so is this ass."

She leaned to the side so she could pat the ass in question, making Zach groan and cover his eyes while Kincaid cracked up. When Zach opened his eyes again, Tad was staring at Krista in a besotted manner, as if she was the most amazing thing he'd ever seen.

Yeah, he liked the guy.

"I think that's the best 'how did you meet' story I've ever heard," Kincaid said, lifting his beer. "Cheers to that."

"Cheers!" Everyone lifted their own drink and clinked them together, laughing. Once again, Zach wished Amy had been here. She would have died laughing at Krista's declaration about her ass. He'd have to tell her later.

As if his sister knew where his mind was, she asked about Amy as she was putting her drink back on the table.

"So, how is the friend that moved in with you?" She glanced over at Tad. "I think I told you about her. Her asshole of a fiancé eloped with one of her bridesmaids on her wedding day."

"Oh, yeah, that dickweed." Tad shook his head. "Who the fuck even does that?"

"Dickweeds," Zach and Krista chorused in unison, which made everyone laugh again.

"Hashtag: Siblings," she said with a smirk. "Seriously though, how is she?"

"She's burning her wedding dress tonight with her friends," Kincaid answered while Zach was still trying to come up with a response that didn't involve how complicated things had gotten with her. He was pretty sure his sister wasn't asking if they were fucking her. Why would she think that? But that was the first place his mind had gone. Thank goodness Kincaid was more on top of things.

"Oh, good for her." Krista lit up. "She sounds like my kind of girl. I need to meet her at some point."

"You two should come over for dinner sometime next week,"

Kincaid offered. "I'm sure she'd love to meet you. She's one of the friendliest people I've ever met."

Something about that idea made Zach want to bristle, but it wasn't like he could reverse the invitation now that it was out there. Especially when Krista's eyes lit up.

"I would love to. And I promise not to be too nosy."

"Ha," Zach answered, trying to cover up his unease. Why didn't he want Krista to meet Amy? What made him feel so anxious about that? He didn't know, but his stomach was starting to churn uncomfortably, the way it did when his mom bothered him about whether or not he'd met any nice girls recently. "You, not nosy? In what universe?"

Krista kicked him under the table.

"Ow!"

"Brutal," Tad said, shaking his head. "Just like my sister."

Thankfully, the conversation turned to how awful sisters were, though Tad somehow managed to walk the line of telling the horror stories of being a younger brother while maintaining that Krista had probably been an angel of a sister and that Zach had deserved everything he'd gotten. Which made Zach like him even more.

About an hour later, coming out of the bathroom, his own awful sister cornered him. She was waiting as soon as he stepped out of the door. He raised his eyebrows at her.

"Tad's great," he said, heading her off at the pass, though he wasn't sure why she felt the need to bother him about his opinion *right now*. She must really like the guy if she was this impatient to get his opinion.

Krista flipped her head, making her curls bounce.

"I know that. I just needed to tell you that Mom was bugging me about getting *you* hooked up to a nice girl again the other day after she met Tad."

Ice hit his heart.

"You didn't tell her..."

His sister glared at him.

"Of course, I didn't. It's not my thing to tell. But you need to tell her, and soon, because I'm not lying for you. I told her I thought you were seeing someone." She rolled her eyes at his groan. "You're going to have to tell them, eventually. Exactly how long did you think you could keep this all a secret?"

Definitely at least a little longer. Until he found the exact right way to tell them. Part of him almost wished Krista *had* told their mom. At least then, the Band-Aid would have been ripped off, and he would know what the reaction was.

He put his hand to his chest, which was starting to hurt, right where his heart was.

Krista's expression softened, and she stepped forward, putting her hand on his shoulder.

"They're not going to reject you."

"You don't know that for sure. Even if they don't, I don't want them feeling 'sorry' for me because my life is going to be harder or thinking I'm just going through a phase or changing how they see me..." He gulped in a breath of air hard. It felt like his chest was constricting.

"Of course, it's going to change how they see you, the same way it would if you quit your job and announced you were going to do something else entirely." She rubbed his upper back. "That doesn't mean it's a bad thing."

But it could be.

"Mom could decide it's great, and Dad could hate it. And then Mom would defend me. They'd end up fighting about it."

"Zach, it is not—and never has been—your fault when they fight, even if the topic they're fighting about is you," she said sternly.

The pain in his chest said it didn't believe her.

"You know, it's actually pretty egotistical to think that everything is about you. You always do this."

"What do you mean?" He turned his head to look at her incredulously. What did he always do?

She shook her head at him.

"When Mom and Dad separated, you were convinced it was about you."

"I was?" He didn't actually remember that. He barely remembered his parents' separation. He'd only been five when they'd separated, and they hadn't been separated for very long.

"Yes. Because the last fight they had before Mom kicked Dad out was about where you were going to go to kindergarten. You thought you'd done something wrong for weeks. Right up until Dad came back home. But it was never actually about where you were going to school."

"I... I don't remember." But his chest was hurting more than ever. Was this what a heart attack felt like?

Probably more like a panic attack.

Apparently the backrub was over because Krista took the opportunity to smack him on the back of the head instead.

"Ow!"

"Not. Everything. Is. About. You." She punctuated each word with a slap, even as he ducked away, putting his own hand on the back of his head for protection.

"Stop it!"

"Admit that not everything is about you!"

"Not everything is about me!" Saying the words should have been easy, but instead, he felt his stomach twist inside him with nausea. *I do know that, right?*

Right?

"You need to tell Mom and Dad about Kincaid."

"I need to tell Mom and Dad about Kincaid," he agreed, sagging slightly. At least he'd gotten turned around to face her so she couldn't keep slapping him upside his head. "I'm going to."

"When?"

"Soon."

Sooner than he'd meant to, thanks to Krista.

She crossed her arms and frowned, tapping her foot.

"I want a timeline. Because it's not fair to me that I keep having to lie to Mom and Dad, and it's definitely not fair to Kincaid."

He knew that.

"By the end of the month." Today was the second, so that gave him plenty of time.

Krista pressed her lips together, obviously displeased with that answer—probably too much time, in her opinion—but she nodded her agreement. The sick feeling in his stomach increased. He had till the end of the month to figure out exactly how to tell his parents that he wasn't straight. And that he'd been living with his boyfriend for the past year and lying to them about it.

Well, if I'd told them sooner, I wouldn't have been lying to them for a year.

Am I really afraid I'm going to break up my parents' marriage?

Maybe.

But he felt just as afraid that it was going to change everything.

"Deal," Krista said, uncrossing her arms and stepping forward so she could loop her arm through his. Obviously, she felt better now that the agreement was made rather than worse, like him. "Now, let's get back to our boyfriends."

She made it sound so much simpler than it felt.

27

———————

"Burn, baby, burn! Burn, baby, burn!" her friends chanted as she walked toward the fire, her arms full of fluffy whiteness.

Not just the initial friends she'd invited, either. Somehow—thank you, club gossip train—word had spread about what she was doing tonight, and the group of supporters had quadrupled. They were in Morgan and Asad's backyard because they had a fire pit, and the whole backyard was full of submissives from Stronghold and Marquis.

Amy couldn't help but laugh at everyone's enthusiasm.

And she had to admit, as she threw the dress onto the fire, her heart did feel lighter.

Everyone cheered as the flames flared up, hungrily consuming the fabric and turning it from white to crisp black in the blink of an eye. The smoke billowed up, and Amy stepped back, her shoulders sagging in relief.

There.

It was done.

Watching the smoke curling up into the evening sky, she imagined all her humiliation, all her pain, all her resentment, floating up with it and disappearing. Oddly, it worked. A sense of peace settled over her, the feeling of closing a door behind her on a chapter of her life she'd spent far too long in.

"So mote it be," Freddy said, coming up beside her and slinging his arm around her shoulders. Amy laughed, leaning her head against him. "Can I just say I'm a little disappointed that your douchebag ex hasn't called my office? I've been hoping I get to tear him apart a little."

"Sadist in the streets, masochist in the sheets," Sam teased from Amy's other side.

"Aren't we all?" Morgan asked.

"Oh, no, Amy is definitely not a sadist in the streets. A brat, maybe, but not a sadist."

"Hey." Amy turned her head to frown at Freddy, straightening up a little. "I can be mean."

"Your version of mean versus my version of mean are two very different things," he told her.

"He has a point," Sam admitted.

Amy sniffed. She could be mean if she wanted to. She just... didn't want to most of the time. Being mean didn't make her feel good and there was usually no point to it.

But she totally could be if she wanted to.

"Who wants s'mores?" Someone called out, and everyone cheered again, making Amy laugh. She looked around. It was quite the collection of people, not all of whom got along, but they were all here to support her.

Marissa and Carolyn were on one side of the yard, shooting looks over at the other side, where Leigh was hanging out with some of her friends. Amy didn't agree that Leigh had stolen Marissa's ex, but she also knew better than to think they would ever get along. The fact that they were both here and not causing drama was a big deal since, normally, they couldn't be in the same space together without Marissa doing something.

But she wasn't. Because tonight was about Amy.

As if Marissa had heard her thoughts, she looked over and caught

Amy's gaze. She turned to say something to Carolyn, then started walking over. Amy gave Freddy a little squeeze, then slipped out from under his arm so she could meet Marissa halfway.

"I've got to head out. I have an early flight," she said, which Amy already knew. She opened her arms for a hug, which Amy stepped into.

"Have a good trip." Amy hugged her hard. Marissa wasn't always an easy person to be friends with, not the least because half the time she wasn't in town, but Amy had been more grateful for her friendship than ever over the past few weeks. "When are you coming back again?"

"In a few weeks." Marissa stepped away, waving her hand. "Probably. I'm up for a part in California that's right afterward. If I get that, it'll be a few months."

"I don't know whether to wish you luck or not, then," Amy teased. "Since selfishly, I'm not sure I want you gone that long."

That made Marissa laugh.

"As if you could ever be selfish." She hugged Amy again, then walked away, leaving Amy feeling a little odd.

Was that how everyone saw her? She couldn't be mean, she couldn't be selfish... neither of those things seemed bad on the surface, but she couldn't help but wonder if that's how Jeremy had seen her, too. Not just unable to be mean or selfish, but as a doormat. Someone who wasn't ever going to stand up for herself. Someone who wasn't going to ask for anything for herself.

She didn't think she liked that idea too much.

"What's with the frowny face?" Morgan appeared in front of her, a s'more in each hand. She held one out, offering it to Amy. "You were happy a few minutes ago. What did Marissa say?"

"It's not something she said exactly, just... do you think I let people walk all over me?" she asked, taking the offered s'more. One of the best things about being friends with Morgan was that tact often escaped her. She was bluntly truthful, though she did her best not to be cruel or unkind.

"Sometimes," Morgan said blithely. She bit into the s'more in her hand and made an odd face. "Huh."

"What?"

Morgan looked down at the s'more in her hand, now slightly crumbled, and wrinkled her nose.

"I don't think I like it."

That... actually did not entirely surprise Amy. Morgan was the kind of person who ate salads because she liked them. She didn't like most sweets. And s'mores were very sweet.

As she frowned at it, Rae, Domi, and Iris were walking up, and the expression on Rae's face was even funnier than Morgan's.

"I'm sorry, did you just say you didn't like the s'more?" Rae asked, sounding scandalized.

Amy tensed a little, but thankfully, Morgan didn't take offense.

"Yeah, I don't think this is for me." Morgan held it out toward Rae. "Do you want it?"

Rae didn't even hesitate. "Yes, please," she said, plucking it from Morgan's fingers, then turning away from Domi, who had tried to reach for it too. "Mine."

"You can share! It wasn't even yours a second ago." Domi glared at her.

"Mine." Rae turned her head to take a massive bite out of it. "Go get your own."

They all turned to look toward the fire, which was barely visible because it was surrounded by people toasting their own marshmallows. Morgan must have been one of the first people to make one. And she'd managed to make two.

"How are you feeling?" Iris asked Amy. "Any better?"

"A lot better, honestly," she replied. "I know it's silly, but it felt really cathartic throwing that dress in the fire."

"I don't think that's silly. I've been thinking of burning some of the stuff from when Noelle and I were friends." Iris sighed. "I just can't decide if I would regret it or not."

"I don't. But that's also the only thing I'm burning for right now." She kinda wanted to go burn more stuff, but she'd wait to think about it. She didn't want to burn something that she'd regret not having later.

Granted, she couldn't think of anything to do with Jeremy that she'd regret not having, including pictures of the two of them together, but she wasn't going to make any hasty decisions.

"How is living with the guys?" Domi asked, chewing on the bite of s'more Rae had finally given her.

"And scening with them?" Rae grunted as Domi elbowed her in the side.

"Don't just dive in. You gotta work your way around to that," Domi admonished her, making Amy laugh.

"Great and great. They're really wonderful." Which was about all she could say without starting to gush, so she was just going to cut it off there. She didn't want anyone to realize that she was starting to get feelings for them that went beyond the scene or being housemates.

That would just make everything even more awkward.

Her phone buzzed in her back pocket, which, thankfully, gave her a reason to look away from everyone. Were they looking at her a little oddly, or was she just being paranoid? It wasn't like they could read her mind and know that she was getting too attached to Kincaid and Zach.

Pulling out her phone, she stared at the Caller ID, unable to believe her eyes.

"Holy shit..." Morgan breathed out the words. "That *bitch*."

"Who?" Rae stepped forward, looking down at Amy's screen, and even though it was upside down to her, she obviously had no trouble reading the name. "Cuntcake?! She's calling you?"

"The audacity!" Domi was equally furious.

Suddenly, the whole backyard was buzzing with energy, even more than her phone was, as the call continued to try to get through. Everyone knew Noelle was calling her.

Amy hit the button on the side of her phone, automatically declining the call.

"Wait, you aren't going to answer it?" Carolyn came up behind

Rae, looking almost aggrieved. "Don't you want to know what she was going to say?"

Yes. No. Amy didn't know.

"What could she possibly say that would make anything better?"

Everyone stared at her.

"It's not about her trying to make it better. She can't," Carolyn said after a long moment. "It's about you getting to say something to her."

"What would I say to her? Never mind, it's a moot point—" Just as she started to say that it was a moot point since she'd already declined the call, the phone started to buzz again.

"She's calling back?" Rae shrieked with outrage. "I'm gonna— Mmph!" Whatever she was gonna do was cut off as Domi wrapped her hand around Rae's mouth.

"Amy gets to decide what we're going to do— Ew! Stop licking my hand!" Domi squealed, pulling her hand away from Rae's mouth and wiping it on Rae's shirt.

"Ew, don't wipe it on me!"

"If you didn't want it wiped on you, you shouldn't have licked me!"

Amy didn't know if they meant to make her laugh or not, but they broke the tension in a big way. Noelle had turned out to be a terrible friend, but that wasn't Amy's fault. She'd given the other woman a chance, and she'd gotten burned, but it was Noelle's fault she'd squandered that chance.

Maybe some people would see being kind and unselfish as weak —maybe Jeremy and Noelle did, but she didn't regret giving both of them a chance. That didn't mean she was willing to give them another.

She sighed.

"I really don't want to talk to her."

"Can I answer it?" Rae asked, pushing past Domi. Her dark eyes were lit up with mischief as she reached up to pull a wayward braid out of her face.

"Um... you know what? Sure." Amy handed her the phone.

Clearly, Noelle was going to keep calling. The phone was still buzzing. If she got the message that she wasn't going to get to talk to Amy, maybe she would stop. There was nothing she could say that would change how Amy felt about her.

With an absolutely evil smile, Rae took the phone and swiped to answer. She didn't bother to say hello. Didn't bother to say anything at all. She just launched straight into "Hit the Road, Jack" at full volume. Not only that, but within three words of the first line, every single person in the backyard had joined her.

Pressing her hands to her stomach, Amy doubled over from laughing.

Under the singing, she could hear Noelle yelling furiously, and somehow, that just made it even funnier. Maybe it was mean... but she'd needed this almost as much as she'd needed to burn her wedding dress.

There were multiple ways to find catharsis.

Kincaid

Sitting in the front room, Kincaid looked up from the book he was reading as the lock in the door turned over. Amy came quietly shuffling inside, a sheepish expression on her face when she saw him sitting there.

"Hey... I hope you weren't up waiting for me. I should have texted to let you know I was running later than I thought I would be."

"I wasn't." He totally had been, but he wasn't going to admit it. He closed the book, keeping his finger on the page he'd been reading. "I just wanted to sit and read for a bit."

Because if he hadn't had something to do, he would have either been worrying about Amy being out so late on her own or stewing about why Zach had been so weird at the end of their dinner. He'd been incredibly quiet on the ride home and almost as soon as they'd got home, he'd said he was tired and needed to go to bed.

Since Kincaid hadn't been tired yet, he'd decided to do his own thing.

"Makes sense." She came over and sat down on the couch with a sigh. "Did you have a good dinner?"

"Very." He smiled at her. "Zach's sister's boyfriend was a lot of fun." Amy giggled as he'd intended her to. "How was the dress burning?"

"There were a lot more people than I'd realized." She grinned wide enough that he eyed her with suspicion. If she'd been drinking, she better not have driven home. "And then Noelle called."

Kincaid gasped. He couldn't help it. "Are you serious?"

"Oh, yes. Twice. I declined the first time, then she called back, so I let Rae answer it, and she sang 'Hit the Road, Jack' at her. Well, actually, everyone ended up singing it at her. The whole backyard, full of Stronghold subs."

He could picture that quite easily, actually. The subbies tended to stick together, and while Noelle had nominally been one of them, eloping with another sub's fiancé was definitely going to break that bond. Not to mention the fact that she'd taken pictures of Amy and Zach in the club. Even if she hadn't been kicked out, no one would have ever welcomed her back after that.

"Did anyone get a video of it?" Because he wouldn't put it past them.

"Angel did from one angle, and Lexie got it from another. They already emailed both videos out to all of us." Amy giggled again, leaning back against the couch and letting her head loll toward him so she could both rest and look at him. "I can show you if you want."

"Sure." He gave up on using his finger as a bookmark and put the actual one in so he could join Amy on the couch, sitting beside her and slinging his arm around the back of the couch so he could watch her phone's screen. Both videos. He grinned the whole time.

Now, that was what sisterhood was all about. He appreciated that karma had finally bitten Noelle in the ass.

"I almost wish we'd gotten to know why she called, but this is better," he said when the videos were over.

"Oh, I know why. She texted me, too." Amy swiped over the phone, bringing up the texts to show him.

> Noelle: Fine. You want to make me the bad guy; I'm the bad guy. I just wanted to reach out and try to extend an olive branch, even though you were so rude to Jeremy about paying the money THAT YOU OWED. Good luck with the rest of your life.

Kincaid laughed so hard that it hurt, which made Amy start giggling.

"Oh, no..." he said in a tiny voice when he managed to get himself semi-under control. He reached out in front of him with his free hand. "Don't go..."

He could only hold the seriousness for a minute, especially when Amy dissolved into a puddle of giggles beside him, which cracked him up all over again. It helped soothe some of the anxiety he was feeling over how the evening had ended with Zach.

"Okay. I should go to bed," she said with a sigh. "I am exhausted."

"I bet. Have a good night." He lowered his arm a little to give her shoulders a squeeze before releasing her. It took a bit of willpower not to give her ass a little slap as she got up, but he restrained himself.

Left alone in the room again, he took in a deep breath and let it out.

At some point, if things didn't change, they were all going to need to have a talk. Because there was a pink elephant in the room, and it wasn't disappearing. It was just getting bigger with every day that passed. First, though, he needed to figure out what the hell had happened between Zach and Krista this evening.

28

"Sorry I got weird last night." He felt awkward enough about it that he'd woken up when Kincaid did. Sleep hadn't exactly been restful. He hadn't managed to actually fall asleep until Kincaid came to bed, and even then, he hadn't been able to sleep very well. He'd woken up multiple times.

Not like him at all.

"What happened?" Kincaid asked. He should have expected that since he'd opened the topic. If he hadn't, Kincaid probably would have left him alone because he knew Zach needed time to think about things. Course, he hadn't been able to do much else last night except think. "Did your sister say something to you? Tell you that Tad's secretly a psycho stalker and ask us to save her?"

That made Zach laugh, which Kincaid clearly meant to do because Tad was so exactly the opposite of that.

"No, she just..." He shook his head. He didn't want to get into everything because he didn't want Kincaid to know that he was still struggling with the idea of telling their parents. "Somehow, we got on the topic of my parents' separation."

Kincaid looked up from getting dressed, alarm in his expression.

"Your parents are separating?"

"What? No, sorry. They did separate, for a very short time, back when I was like five years old. Krista said that I thought it was because of me because they'd gotten into an argument about me right before my mom kicked my dad out." Zach shook his head, and Kincaid came over to sit on the bed next to Zach's legs, facing him. "I don't remember much about it. I definitely don't really remember thinking that it was my fault they separated, but it feels right somehow."

Expression softening, Kincaid put his hand on Zach's leg or, at least, where Zach's leg was under the covers.

"That's got to be rough to live with."

Zach shrugged. "Is it? Like I said, I don't really remember, but she did. And she said something about me feeling like I'm still scared of them breaking up because of me."

"Are you?"

"I don't know. I want to say no because I know that's ridiculous, but..." He sighed and reached out to put his hand over Kincaid's. "It's kind of messing with my head, and I needed some time to think about that."

His boyfriend smiled at him, giving his leg a squeeze.

"I get that. Thank you for telling me this morning." He leaned forward and gave Zach a quick kiss. "I'm going to go get breakfast started."

"I'll get up and help you." Zach smiled wanly. "Since I'm up, anyway."

"That would be great." The smile on Kincaid's face turned more flirty than sympathetic, and he winked as he got to his feet, which made Zach's heart feel a little lighter.

He didn't want to be a downer, he really didn't...

Whether or not Kincaid realized the reason Krista had brought up her and Zach's parents' separation was because she was hassling Zach to tell their parents about Kincaid, he wasn't sure. His boyfriend was very good at reading between the lines. He might have. Maybe

Zach should outright tell him. Then he might feel better about knowing it wasn't him.

It was because Zach had this ridiculous fear that his parents would fight, split up, and it would be all his fault.

Again.

The hitch in his breath made him rub his chest.

He would tell them. By the end of the month. Just like he'd promised Krista. Maybe he'd see if Julie, one of the mistresses at the club and also a therapist, could work him in for a session. Give him some perspective. Maybe help him figure out how to talk to his parents about it. Couldn't hurt.

Yeah, he'd call her later today and see if he could get an appointment.

Yawning, he stretched and made himself get up. Might as well get moving.

By the time he made it into the kitchen, Amy was also up and sipping coffee as she watched Kincaid make breakfast. She twitched a little when Zach bumped Kincaid out of the way with his hip and took over. Though he didn't feel like cooking all the time, sometimes he wanted to make something a little special.

Today felt like a crepe day. Especially since Kincaid had most of the ingredients out. He'd been about to make pancakes, but Zach was in the mood for something fancier.

"Any plans for the day?" Kincaid asked Amy, obviously unbothered by being bumped out of the way.

She shook her head, though she wasn't looking at him; she was watching Zach. He'd started dicing the strawberries Kincaid had pulled out.

More importantly, he was dicing them correctly.

"Aren't you scared of cutting yourself?" she asked, watching in fascination.

"No." He glanced up at her, grinning as the knife continued to move, and she winced. "I've had a lot of practice at this. I worked in a restaurant through college and for a few years after. Kincaid loves cooking more than I do, but sometimes, I get in a mood. I can show you how to dice correctly, if you want."

Cocking her head, Amy watched him as he pulled another strawberry his way and got to work.

"Or you could just dice for me?"

Zach and Kincaid both laughed.

"I could do that, too, although you won't be able to do it this quickly at first."

"Can you dice some cucumber for me? I want to make tzatziki later."

"You sure you don't want to use your patented dicing technique?" he teased.

"Oh, no, that only works on zucchini, not cucumbers."

Zach froze as his brain blanked out because *they were basically the same damn thing,* and he didn't know how to respond to that. The knife hovered in the air as his thoughts bounced incoherently around his head, trying to come together in a way that made sense, except that it made *no* sense and...

And Kincaid and Amy were laughing at him.

He scowled.

"Your face!" Amy pressed her hand against her chest, gasping for air. "I'm sorry... I'm sorry... I couldn't help it... but oh my God, your *face!*"

"You are in so much trouble," he said, wagging the knife at her. That just made her laugh harder.

So much for being a threatening sadist. He couldn't help but smile, though he hid it, shaking his head and ducking his head back down to look at the strawberry he was dicing.

Kincaid high-fived her, which didn't help.

"I saw that," Zach said without looking up, making both of them laugh again.

Everything just felt so damn right...

He needed to call Julie later and talk to her about more than his feelings about his parents.

<u>*Amy*</u>

After breakfast, which was amazing, mad that Zach didn't cook more often and determined to change that, Amy decided to join Zach for some yard work. Kincaid was going to help, too, but he wanted to go for a run first.

"I didn't realize you were into gardening," Amy commented as Zach pulled on some gloves and grabbed some clippers from the garage. She was wearing an extra pair of his gloves, which were rough against her skin and brought back memories of being a kid, helping her parents in their garden, something she'd enjoyed.

Jeremy hadn't been 'into plants,' as he said. He'd had the barest lawn and only a few bushes that were as low maintenance as possible.

When Amy had seen Zach and Kincaid's lawn, she'd honestly assumed that they hired someone to take care of it, but apparently, Zach did most of the maintenance.

"I find it soothing." He grinned. "And I can take time to think, which is nice."

Kincaid came out through the door between the house and the garage, dressed in nothing but running shorts. Which, of course, made Amy think about the times she'd now seen him naked. And then, when he'd been inside her. Her cheeks heated with a blush.

Thankfully, neither man seemed to notice.

"I'll be back, then I'll help," Kincaid promised, giving Zach a quick kiss.

"Damn right you will," Zach replied in a threatening tone, though his expression made it clear he was joking around. Kincaid winked at Amy, then took off, jogging out to the sidewalk and down the street out of view. She had to push away the pouty feeling of not getting her own kiss from him.

Get a grip. You're not his girlfriend.

At some point, she really was going to need to get serious about getting out of this house. Her feelings were getting too confused, even for being on the rebound. She was getting attached. But who could blame her? Two gorgeous guys doting on her, feeding her, giving her multiple orgasms... No wonder she needed to get out of here, yet kept procrastinating on actually looking for another place to live.

"Okay, let me show you where to weed, and when you're done with that, you can start watering," Zach said, propping the clippers up against his shoulder. Suppressing a smile, Amy nodded and followed him out to the yard. She did like his bossy side, and she thought it was funny that he was turning out to be even bossier in the garden than in the club.

Though, as fond as her memories of gardening were, she quickly found she didn't love being left alone with her own thoughts and nothing else to do. Zach was clipping bushes far enough away from where she was weeding that she would have to yell at him to be heard, which she didn't want to do. Plus, he looked so peaceful whenever she glanced over at him, she didn't want to disturb that. She should have brought her phone out so she could turn on some music or a podcast or something.

But if she went inside, he might think she was slacking.

Sigh.

It probably wasn't a bad thing to have some time to herself to think. Except all she could think about were Kincaid and Zach and how perfect they were and how happy she was and how she wished things could go on like this forever. Well, like this, but with her actually a part of their relationship. Would that even be possible?

Would they even be interested?

Yeah, they were doting on her now because she needed their help, and they were good guys.

They were attracted to her. That much was clear.

But there was a very big difference between being attracted and wanting to be in a relationship.

One thing was very clear, though—she didn't want to stay here for months and months as their club plaything but a third wheel in the home. That's what she was really avoiding thinking about. The fact that she needed to figure her shit out and get out because, one way or another, this idyllic little bubble was going to end. It would be a lot better to end it on her own terms before she got her heart broken all over again.

Maybe once she had an out, she could ask them if they'd be interested in taking things outside of the club. She couldn't do that before she knew she had an escape route because if they weren't interested —or, worse, horrified at the idea—there was no way she could keep living with them. Not even for another night. Nope.

Pulling the last of the weeds out of the section of the garden she'd been working on, Amy glanced over to where Zach was still busily, happily trimming the bushes. He glistened with sweat, but he looked so happy. She wondered if Kincaid didn't like gardening and if he was taking an extra-long run, but she bet he would be back soon.

In the meantime... she needed to water the flowers.

It wasn't until she had the hose in hand that it occurred to her... poor Zach looked so hot trimming the bushes. He probably would appreciate a cool down.

Grinning, she let the water flow from the hose as she moved toward him, getting her thumb into position on the lip of the metal around the tube. As she came closer, Zach looked up, moving his forearms to wipe some of the sweat from his forehead as he did so.

"Hey, finished already?"

"Yeah, with the first part of the garden, I was going to water it when I realized you look a little hot."

His gaze sharpened with suspicion.

"No, I'm— Ah!" His words cut off as she lifted the hose and put her thumb over the nozzle, turning it from a steady flow to a spray that she could direct—straight at him. "Amy!"

He dropped the clippers and came at her while she shrieked and backed up, still sending the spray at him, soaking him completely. Now, he was holding his arms up in front of him to keep the water out of his eyes while Amy cackled. Suddenly, he went from taking one slow, solid step forward to surging at her. She shrieked, stumbling backward, and he caught her around her middle, lifting her up and over his shoulder.

"Got ya!"

Amy squealed as his hand came down hard on her upturned bottom, accidentally dropping the hose. Oops.

"I'm sorry!"

"No, you're not."

Well, she sort of was, now that she was getting wet, thanks to being over his shoulder and the fact that he was completely soaked. She was getting soaked by proximity.

"I was just trying to help!"

"No, you weren't— Oh, shit."

Oh, shit, what? Amy tried to push herself to the side so she could see whatever it was Zach was saying 'oh, shit' about, but she was moving through the air and back on her feet so fast, she almost fell over. Zach caught her by her arm, and she could feel the rigid tension in his fingers.

She turned to see what he was looking at—a man and a woman had just parked on the street and were getting out of the car. The woman was beaming at Zach. The man... well, he looked *just* like Zach but older with salt and pepper hair.

His parents?

"Zach! Hello!" The woman rushed toward them. Her hair was a coppery red with highlights shimmering throughout, her makeup perfectly done, and her classy outfit made Amy feel incredibly under-dressed. Glancing down, she hastily pulled the front of her shirt away from her breasts, where it was clinging. "Oh my goodness, this must be your girlfriend Krista told us about!"

Amy opened her mouth to correct the woman, but Zach suddenly pulled her against him, his arm going around her, fingers digging into her shoulder.

"Yes, this is my girlfriend, Amy."

What. The. Fuck.

29

____

Z*ACH*

Fuck, fuck, fuck.

He was panicking, and he knew it, but he didn't know what else to do. The words were out of his mouth before he could think about them. Before he could stop them. He didn't do well on his feet.

Krista had told his parents he had a girlfriend? Was that what she'd said? No, she wouldn't have told them that. Whatever she'd said to his mom, his mom had misinterpreted.

And now he'd just introduced Amy as his girlfriend.

Fuck.

She'd gone still beside him, but at least she hadn't immediately contradicted him and told his mom that he'd just lied to her.

"Oh, it's so nice to meet you!" His mom held her hand out to Amy, who took it, smiling weakly. "Oh, you're so pretty! Isn't she pretty, Stuart?"

"Last time I told you another woman was pretty, I had to hear about it for a year, so I'm just going to keep quiet this time," his dad said cheerfully, coming up behind his mom. He eyed Zach. "No offense, but I'll skip the hug this time, son."

Both of them were dressed for church, which they must have just come from.

"What are you doing here?" he asked, feeling a little desperate. He needed to know what they wanted so he could make them leave. Immediately. Preferably before Kincaid got back. Fuck. Forget sweating over the bushes; he was pretty sure the wetness on his skin was no longer due to the water Amy had just sprayed him with. He was leaking nerves out of every single one of his pores.

"Oh, you didn't get my text? I was going through the back closet when I found a box of your books this morning, and I remembered you telling me that you were looking for one of them a few months ago." His mom turned to frown at his dad. "Stuart, you didn't bring the books."

"Well, I wanted to come meet Zach's girlfriend first." His dad grinned at Amy, who smiled back weakly. "I'm Stuart, Zach's dad. Did Lauren introduce herself?"

"Um, yes," Amy lied. She cast a glance at Zach, which he ignored, keeping his arm slung around her shoulder. As soon as his parents left, he'd explain everything. Then he'd call Mistress Julie right away and see how soon she could talk to him because he needed to get this whole hot mess sorted asap.

Before it blew up in his face.

"Sort of," he told his dad. "Here, let me get the books, then Amy and I need to get inside and get cleaned up. We've been gardening this morning."

"Of course, we won't keep you." His mom peered over his shoulder. "Is that nice boy still living here, too?"

"Um, yes, Kincaid is still living here, too, but he's out right now." Zach stepped away from Amy, making a subtle movement with his arms to try to herd his parents toward their car. "We'll have you over some time. Soon."

"Oh, that would be lovely," his mom said, brightening. Since he'd just offered her something she wanted, she didn't put up a fight about moving away, though, of course, she did have one last thing to say to Amy first. "I can't wait to get to know you better, dear."

"Um, me, too." Amy waved, a strained smile on her face.

Fuck. He was going to need to apologize to her as well as explain to her.

"She's so pretty, and she seems nice, though I don't know if I approve of you hauling her around over your shoulder like that in public, dear," his mom said quietly as they approached her car. "That's more for indoor activities."

"In my defense, she had just sprayed me with the hose."

"Ah, is that how you got all wet?" His mom's lips twitched. "I like her."

"Me, too." At least that part wasn't a lie. "We'll have you over for dinner soon and talk about... everything. Okay?"

"Sounds good, sweetheart." His mom went up on her tiptoes to give him a kiss.

"Here," his dad said, lifting a small box out of the car and hiking it up on his hip before reaching up with his other hand to close the trunk. "Are you sure you want to carry this while you're that wet?"

"I'm sure the water won't work its way through the cardboard that quickly," Zach reassured him. Even if it did, he would rather have completely waterlogged books than have his parents stay here one second longer than they needed to. "Thanks for bringing them over."

"Of course." His dad winked at him. "Have fun with your girl."

Oh, fuck. That was probably why his parents were so willing to leave. They thought they'd just interrupted his and Amy's foreplay. That's why his mom had told him to keep things inside. He was so panicked, his brain wasn't working properly.

"Thank you." It was the only thing he could say. "I'll call you guys later."

"Of course. Bye!" His parents waved to him, then his mom waved to Amy as they pulled away. Zach turned around to see that she was turning off the water to the hose, though she did lift her hand to wave goodbye to his parents.

Pure relief slammed through him as he glanced up and down the street. Kincaid was nowhere in sight. He'd gotten through it. Somehow. He could have cried.

Except he didn't have time to enjoy his relief because Amy was storming toward him, and she was *pissed.*

"What the fuck was that?!" She shouted the words at him from halfway down the yard.

He stepped back, physically taken aback, because he didn't think he'd ever heard her cuss before. Not even on her wedding day at Jeremy or Noelle.

Having her curse at him wasn't on his bingo card.

"I... thank you for covering for me," he said, not entirely sure what had set her off like that.

"Thank you for letting you use me as a beard, you mean." She stopped about ten feet away from him, hands balled into fists, as though she couldn't get any closer or she might try to hit him. "Your parents think I'm your girlfriend? I knew you hadn't told them about Kincaid yet, but that's one thing. Telling them I'm your girlfriend? Are you *serious*?"

"I didn't tell my mom that, she assumed... I'm sorry, okay? I panicked. I didn't know what to do!" Now his voice was rising, too, some of the pent-up emotion coming out. Fuck. He was shaking so hard, he could barely hold on to the box, but he also couldn't let it go. He clutched at it with both hands, like a teddy bear, except it was far less snuggly and far less comforting.

"You tell them the truth! That I'm not your girlfriend!" She threw her hands up in the air. "How are you this dense? All you had to say was no, Amy is just a friend. She's not my girlfriend."

"I know... I know... I just..."

"And now, what am I supposed to say to Kincaid? How are we supposed to tell him that your parents think that I'm your girlfriend?" Amy's chest was heaving, and she looked on the verge of tears.

"We're not! You can't..." The panic was clawing its way back up his throat, making it harder and harder for him to think. Everything was falling apart. He didn't know what to do. He wanted to run, but there was nowhere to go. He wanted to hide, but eventually, he'd have to come out and face this. "Just... I need a minute to think."

If she heard him, Amy didn't give him any indication.

"What do you mean we're not? I'm not going to lie to Kincaid for you, Zach. You have to tell him! And you have to tell your parents that I'm not your girlfriend! You have to stop lying to everyone!"

The pounding in his head was so intense, he almost didn't hear the quiet words from the side.

"He won't."

Amy's face went pale, as white as Zach's felt, and they turned as one. They'd been shouting at each other so intently, so distressed, they'd blocked everything out.

Including Kincaid's approach.

He was pale. Stoic. Staring between Zach and Amy rather than looking at either of them.

"Kincaid..." Zach croaked his boyfriend's name, taking a step toward him.

"Don't." Kincaid held up his hand. "Just don't."

Fuck. Amy whirled around, dashing back to the house, leaving Zach and Kincaid staring at each other.

<u>KINCAID</u>

Hell of a way to end a run. When he'd seen Amy and Zach facing off across the sidewalk, Zach holding a box, he hadn't been able to figure out what the hell was going on. As soon as he'd gotten within earshot—which hadn't been hard to do considering they'd been shouting at each other—it had only taken him a moment to realize what had happened.

Zach's parents must have stopped by and seen Zach and Amy. Zach introduced Amy as his girlfriend. Amy hadn't outed him, and now she was pissed.

Maybe the two of them could form a club.

The 'We're Fucking Pissed at Zach Marshall' Club.

"My parents showed up and assumed, and I—"

"I said *don't!*" Kincaid shouted, holding up his hand in the universal gesture for 'stop.' He was too fucking pissed right now to

even attempt to try to understand or have sympathy for Zach's position. He took a deep breath, lowering his voice back down. "Like Amy
said, all you had to do was tell them she's not your girlfriend. It's not
like you had to admit that you have a boyfriend."

"Krista told them I was seeing someone! When they pulled up,
Amy was over my shoulder, and I'd just slapped her ass. They would
have thought I was cheating or something if I'd said she was just a
friend."

Heartsick sliced through Kincaid. "Well, weren't you? We sure as
hell never discussed you spanking her when I'm not around."

"It wasn't like that!"

"It never is with you, is it? You can't have it both ways, Zach. At
some point, you have to make a decision."

Zach was paler than ever, clutching the box in front of him like a
shield. Because that's who Zach was. He was someone who always
ducked behind a shield.

"I had, I was going to tell them, I promised Krista—"

"Oh, you promised Krista that you were going to tell them, so now
you were going to?" The heated rage that crawled up Kincaid's spine
took hold and wouldn't let go. "The fact that you promised me wasn't
enough?"

"It's not that! Krista told me that she was going to end up telling
them if I didn't!"

"Then *you could have just told them, Zach.* That was one of the
options." Kincaid threw his hands up in the air. "I don't know why I
would expect that of you, though. You never make a fucking decision.
You're so damn afraid of making the wrong decision, you'd rather not
make one at all."

"There's nothing wrong with needing time to figure things out! I
just want to tell them the right way."

"There might not be a right way! And while there's nothing wrong
with needing time to figure things out, eventually time is up." Kincaid
huffed. Fuck, this hurt. Because he did want Zach to decide. He
wanted Zach to choose. "I keep waiting and waiting along with you,
and every day you wait, I hurt. Every day you wait, I feel less impor-

tant to you. And you keep sitting there, waiting for something to happen so you can make the 'right' move or waiting for someone to do it for you. I wouldn't be surprised if you let the month run out just so Krista had to be the one to tell your parents, and you didn't have to."

"Your parents supported you. You don't understand."

"My parents supported me, and I was still scared to tell them at first. That's why I do understand." Fuck it. He was done coddling Zach. "I understand being scared of losing your family. But either you have to tell them, or we can't be together, no matter how long you put that off... that's what the end result is always going to be. I'm willing to wait for a while, but I'm not willing to spend the rest of my life as your housemate."

It was the same damn fight all over again. A little different. A little rawer, a little more vulnerable, a little more pointed. But the same damn fight.

"But I am telling them. Before the end of this month."

"Because Krista gave you an ultimatum."

"What do you want me to say, Kincaid? You wanted me to tell them? I'm going to tell them. I told my mom that we'd have dinner with her soon. I figured I'd tell her then. So, it'll be even before the end of this month. And then I might lose my family, if you even care."

"Of course, I care. And if you do, you'll have me." Even as he said the words, he knew it wouldn't be the same. Couldn't be the same. But they also couldn't move forward unless Zach told them.

"Will I?"

Kincaid stared at him. That was the last thing he'd expected Zach to say. If he'd said that having Kincaid didn't make up for the loss of his parents, that was something Kincaid could understand, but asking if Zach would have *him?*

"Why would you think you wouldn't?"

"You already left me once." The accusation hurled out like a knife. "You're asking me to trade in my parents, who have never let me down, for someone who already left once."

"I left because you weren't going to tell them!"

"And what happens if we break up again?" Zach heaved in a huge breath, tears glistening in his eyes. "What if I give up everything for you and *we break up?*"

Throwing his hands up in the air again, Kincaid shook his head. This hurt too much. He couldn't argue against a hypothetical. He couldn't reassure Zach that would never happen. Anything was possible. Did he think it would happen? No. But it wasn't like he could promise it was impossible.

He didn't know what to say, and it ended up being a moot point because Zach suddenly started in alarm, his gaze going beyond Kincaid. Spinning around, he turned to see Amy coming out the front door, still in the wet clothes that were clinging to her, carrying a suitcase.

"Amy—" They both said her name at the same time.

She held up her hand, in the same 'stop' gesture Kincaid had used, and kept moving toward her car.

"I can't be here right now."

"Amy—" He and Zach were like a fucking Greek chorus.

She came to a stop.

"No. Red." She pointed at Kincaid and then at Zach. "And red. I cannot be here right now."

They both stood there, helpless, as she got into her car and sped away. Kincaid stared after the car as it disappeared, feeling like they'd opened Pandora's Box, but instead of keeping hope locked safely inside, they'd just let it escape.

Fuck.

He didn't know what to say. Didn't know what to do.

Maybe there wasn't anything to say. Maybe the words didn't exist.

Feeling incredibly numb, he turned away from Zach and walked into the house alone.

30

Changed out of his wet clothes, his skin still felt clammy, and he didn't think it was because he was still damp. Kincaid was out in the main rooms. He'd been sitting on the couch, staring at the blank television, when Zach had come in. Not knowing what to say, Zach had just gone behind him.

Fuck.

He didn't know how he was going to face Kincaid. Didn't know what to say.

He also wasn't going to be able to think clearly. Not here. Not surrounded by his and Kincaid's things. Grabbing his phone, he saw the text from his parents and shook his head. If only he'd taken his phone out to the garden with him.

From now on, it was going to be freaking glued to his side.

He texted Brian. The same person he'd gone to when he and Kincaid had broken up.

Zach: Can I come over?

Now, he just had to hope that, unlike Zach, Brian hadn't left his phone somewhere away from him.

Thankfully, he didn't have long to wait.

> Brian: I'm at Marquis. Meet me here?

Not ideal, but better than spending one more minute in this house where Amy's absence gaped, and Kincaid's melancholy hovered in the air like a dark miasma.

Before answering Brian, though, he walked back out into the main room. Kincaid was still sitting on the couch, staring at the television. It was still off.

"I'm going to go meet up with Brian," he said, waiting to see what Kincaid's response would be. Kincaid didn't even twitch.

"Okay." His voice sounded hollow. He didn't ask where. He didn't ask if Zach would be back.

Fuck.

It was all falling apart.

Pressing his lips together to keep his emotions from spilling out, Zach went to the front door and grabbed his keys off the hook. He waited until he was outside to text Brian back and let him know that he was on the way.

Getting into his car, feeling like he was fully alone for the first time, Zach slammed his hands against the steering wheel.

"*Fuck.*"

Did he feel a little better? Not really. But at least he wasn't all pent-up anymore. He could drive. As long as he focused really hard on where he was going and didn't think about everything that had just happened. Which was a lot easier said than done when all his brain wanted to do was turn over every single word he'd said, every single place he'd gone wrong.

Right from the point of accidentally leaving his phone inside. That was the first mistake.

Stop thinking about it. Just get to Marquis. Just get to Brian. He'll know what to do.

Fuck. Was Kincaid right? Did he really expect other people to tell him what to do?

No. He just wanted to talk things out. And to get out of the house to think. He didn't actually mean that he would do whatever Brian told him to. It was just that Brian was a good sounding board. He knew the situation. He knew Zach. He knew Kincaid. He'd have good ideas.

The universe was finally on Zach's side when he arrived at Marquis, and he managed to get a spot right in front of the restaurant. He spotted Brian as soon as he walked in at a booth with Rae, Iris, Law, Nick, and Avery. Shit. Zach was interrupting a group date. He was so fucking selfish. Krista was right—he did make everything about himself. It hadn't even occurred to him to ask Brian why he was at Marquis.

It was too late to back out, though, because Brian had obviously been waiting for him. He saw Zach as soon as he walked through the door and was already getting up from his seat.

"I'm sorry," Zach said as soon as Brian reached him. "I didn't realize... I wasn't thinking..."

"It's okay. When you texted, I figured you needed me right away." Brian held out his hand for Zach to clap, and they came together in a bro hug. "I can see now that I was right."

"I..." Zach sagged as they broke back apart. "Yeah. Thank you for always being there for me. It means a lot."

"I know." Brian inspected Zach's face, his serious brown eyes taking in everything. "Come on, let's go over to the bar, and we'll talk about it."

"I don't want to interrupt."

"It's fine. I already told Rae that I'd be stepping away when you got here. We just paid, so everyone will be getting back to their day. Law and Iris are going to take her home."

Zach's eyes stung with threatening tears as Brian turned him toward the bar, hand on his shoulder.

"You're a really good friend."

"I know."

That made him laugh. At least he could still laugh.

They sat down at the bar where Shane, who seemed like a permanent fixture at Marquis' bar, was wiping bar glasses dry. A Dom, though he didn't scene at either club, he was as bald as Mr. Clean but sported a mostly grey goatee. With his position, he almost always knew what was going on between club members, though the gossip never passed through his lips; he was a vault of secrets. So, Zach didn't have to worry about or care about whatever he overheard. Thankfully, there was no one else at the actual bar, though there were a few people in the booths along the way.

"Have you eaten?" Brian asked, which made Zach's lips twitch in amusement.

"No, Daddy," he replied. Brian couldn't help himself; he was a Daddy Dom through and through, no matter who he was dealing with.

Brian sighed, shaking his head. "One day, I'll get over hearing that from my friends but never my girlfriend." He chuckled as soon as he said it though, his eyes light, and he glanced back to look at said girlfriend.

Despite being a Daddy Dom, he'd accepted that Rae was never going to call him 'Daddy.' Yet he was perfectly happy with their arrangement. If he could fully accept that from Rae, maybe he could help Zach figure out how to get Kincaid to fully accept him.

They sat down at the bar and ordered. Brian just got a mimosa, while Zach ordered a full meal and a coffee. Now that he was aware of it, he *was* starving. He also didn't want to start drinking because he had a feeling he wouldn't stop if he did, and it was way too early in the day for that. Plus, he wanted to be sober later if he was going to make up with Kincaid... or break up with him. His mind shied away from that possibility, even though it felt far too imminent.

"So. Tell me what happened," Brian said. He sat and listened without interrupting as Zach haltingly went through the events of the morning. Shane was listening, too, though he was pretending not to, as he'd gone back to polishing the barware.

He didn't spare himself. He knew that he'd fucked up. His

problem was that he didn't know how to make it right when Kincaid was unwilling to listen to him. To really hear him.

Brian sat in silence when he finished, breathing heavily, as if he'd just run a marathon. It kind of felt like he had. An emotional marathon.

"So... what do you think?" he asked when he couldn't take the silence anymore.

"That's... a lot." Brian scrubbed his hands over his face and gave Zach a look. "I think at the base of it, you have to really think about your motivations."

"What do you mean?"

"Like, what are you so scared of when it comes to telling your parents? That they'll get a divorce? You're not five anymore. You're old enough to know that they won't get a divorce over one argument. If you coming out as 'not entirely straight' to your parents and they get into a bad enough fight over it that they divorce, that's not on you. That's because they just learned something about the other person that they can't live with. If they both reject you, then... what? You've learned something about them."

"I don't like any of this." Zach propped his elbows on the bar and pressed the heels of his hands into his closed eyes, rubbing the sockets. It felt like there was something weighing down on his chest, even though he was sitting upright, making it hard for him to breathe. "I don't know what I'm supposed to do."

"That's because you're fundamentally insecure."

The bald statement made both him and Brian spin around in their seats. Zach stared at Olivia. The Dominatrix was wearing her signature red suit, which somehow *didn't* clash with her red hair, and her silvery gaze was uncompromising. She'd pinned him with it more than once during his introduction class, and it was all he could do not to shrivel down now, no matter how indignant he felt.

"I'm not insecure." He'd literally never been called that in his life. "I'm one of the most confident people I know."

"You're secure in yourself; you're insecure in how others view you," she replied, coming up beside him to sit down. She waved a finger at Shane, who immediately jumped to get her a glass of water. "You're so wrapped up in thinking about how other people think of you, you can't see straight. And when you think you're losing one of your support systems, you panic. The fact that you're possibly setting yourself up to lose two has sent that panic into overdrive."

Zach opened his mouth. Closed it. He didn't know what to say to that.

Taking a sip of her water, Olivia turned to him and raised an eyebrow.

"You've always been led by strong personalities, people with strong convictions because you think that they must have made the right decision. That's how you ended up being Roland's friend."

"That fucking asshole," Brian muttered from behind Zach as Olivia referenced Zach's ex-best friend.

Zach winced. That friendship was one of the greatest shames of his life. The one really good thing Roland had ever done for him had been to convince him to come take the Dom class at Stronghold—the class Roland got kicked out of after he couldn't take being taught by a woman. He was in jail now after stalking Olivia and attempting to shoot her.

"I didn't let Roland lead me anywhere but Stronghold," he argued. "I didn't support him."

"No, because you met other, better personalities that were also strong." She didn't break her gaze. "You're a good person, but you still had trouble standing up to him. It helped that Kincaid, Brian, and Mitch all did because you knew that they were doing the right thing."

"I don't sound like a good person when you put it that way," he muttered.

"You are. You wouldn't have kept supporting him. You know that. I know that. But you're bolstered by the people around you. It's not a bad thing. It's just that you're in conflict right now." Olivia smiled gently at him. "You're afraid of losing Kincaid. You're afraid of losing your parents. What Kincaid wants is directly opposed to what you think your parents want, and vice versa. And today, you pulled Amy into it. You keep waiting for the right moment, the right way to do it so that you don't lose anyone, but in trying not to lose anyone, you're risking losing everyone."

The heaviness that hit the pit of Zach's stomach made it impossible for him to argue. That was exactly what he was afraid of, and he didn't know what to do about it.

"Not me," Brian joked, clapping Zach's shoulder. "I'll still be here for you, brother."

Surprisingly, that was enough to lighten a lot of the tension that was weighing Zach down, and he barked a short laugh.

"Oh, yeah?" he asked, only half-joking as he turned in his seat. "And what do you think?"

"I think Olivia is right. You get tied up in knots trying to make a decision. You're always worried you're making the wrong one. You look at everything from every angle, so when you do finally make a decision, you've really weighed out every possibility. The problem is that when something is high stakes, you're so afraid of what will go wrong that you avoid making the decision at all." Brian shrugged. "That's why I'm going to refuse to tell you what to do. I'm here to listen, but you have to figure this out."

"Well, I'm not here to listen," Olivia said, hopping up from her seat. She smacked Zach on the back of his head, hard enough to sting and make him duck, though not so hard that it was truly painful.

"Ow!" He turned around to face her again.

"You're going to have to do more than talk to Kincaid. You're going to have to *show* him you're serious this time. Actions talk louder than words. Stop sitting on your ass and waiting for the universe to show you the way. You've had over a year to think about it; now, it's time to do something." And with that, Olivia sauntered away. Brian and Zach watched her go, Zach rubbing the back of his head as he turned her words over in his thoughts.

Then he frowned.

"Wait a second, how did she even know what we were talking about?" he asked.

Both he and Brian swung around to stare at Shane. The bartender studiously ignored their stares, focusing on the glass he was polishing in his hand.

"Traitor," Zach accused.

Shane just shrugged.

Fuck. Olivia was right. He needed to show Kincaid that he mattered. He needed to show Kincaid that he wasn't going to be a hidden part of Zach's life for the rest of their lives.

It wasn't enough to tell him that he would. He needed to do it. Now. Before he lost his courage.

He glanced at Brian.

"Not to sound like a complete pansy, but... I'm going to go talk to my parents. Can you come with me?"

"Shut that toxic masculinity bullshit down, and sure," Brian said with a snort. "You're not a pansy. You're about to go face down your fears. You're about to make yourself emotionally vulnerable. Anyone who thinks that's pansy is someone who's afraid to own up to their own shit."

That was true enough. Zach felt the tightness in his chest still, but some of it had eased. Brian was going to be there for him. He didn't know whether Kincaid would be there at the end of the day, but he was going to go tell his parents, anyway. He needed to show Kincaid that he meant every word he'd ever said, every promise he'd made, and that he wasn't just going to wait until the end of the month because of his sister's ultimatum.

It was time to do what he'd been too scared to do for the past year and tell his parents who he really was and who he really loved.

Then he needed to tell Kincaid, and probably grovel, as well as apologize to Amy.

"Do you think I should tell Kincaid I'm going beforehand? Or wait till after? No, shit, wait. Holy fuck, do I really expect everyone to make my decisions for me?" Fuck. Was that why he'd been drawn to Kincaid being a Dom? So Kincaid could make the decisions in a scene? He was always happy to follow Kincaid's lead when they were scening with a third. Fuck.

"You're just asking for feedback; I think that's normal." Brian shrugged. "I've asked for advice a time or two myself, you know. But if you're thinking about contacting him because you're worried, don't. After you texted me, I told Mitch to check in on him."

Well, that was a relief. Zach sighed.

"Good. Then let's go tell my parents, then I'll go grovel to Kincaid, and then, hopefully, we can figure out where Amy went, and I can grovel to her, too."

"You know... do you think you told your parents that Amy was your girlfriend because you wished she was? Your and Kincaid's girlfriend, I mean."

Zach groaned and pressed his hands back into his eyes. "Dude. Shut up. I cannot deal with that right now."

One thing at a time.

31

The knock on the door made him frown. Then he sighed in exasperation when it was immediately followed by Mitch's voice, muffled but recognizable.

"Little pig, little pig, let me in!"

"You've got to be kidding me," Kincaid muttered, but he pushed himself up from the couch. He'd finally turned on the television but then immediately turned it back off again when it offered the next Marvel movie. Just thinking about watching a movie without Zach and Amy made his stomach turn over.

He'd only been sitting here for... okay, half an hour.

Sighing, he answered the door. "Or what, you'll huff and puff and blow me?"

Mitch grinned broadly and winked at him.

"If that's what gets you off... no, wait, I know that's what gets you off." Mitch chuckled and shoved past Kincaid, not waiting to be invited inside. Pushy blond bastard.

"Who called you?" Kincaid asked dryly. He wondered where Zach had gone that it had gotten this kind of response. Actually, wait, that answered his question. "It was Brian, wasn't it?"

"You know Daddy gets worried when we're fighting." Mitch sauntered over to the armchair and flopped down. Looking at him, stupid grin on his face, totally relaxed with one leg hanging over the arm of the chair while he lolled against the back of it at an angle—the ultimate manspread—it would be hard to believe he was a sadist who enjoyed making his fiancé scream on a regular basis. He was like a sadistic golden retriever. Proof that appearances could be deceiving.

"Well, I'm glad Zach has someone with him." The words came out with more bitterness than he'd meant, and Mitch raised his eyebrow. To give himself time to collect himself, Kincaid moved over to the couch and sat back down. This time, he deliberately sat down on a cushion that was not the one he'd been sitting on.

"What happened?" Mitch asked once Kincaid was settled in.

Kincaid snorted. "What didn't happen?"

Closing his eyes, because it was somehow easier to talk about it that way, he leaned back against the couch and went through the events. Granted, he had to make some suppositions about how things had gone down with Zach's parents from things Amy and Zach had said, but everything from the moment he'd returned from his run was pretty much indelibly imprinted in his mind.

When he finished, he let out a huge sigh and opened his eyes to see how Mitch was taking it. His friend had a thoughtful frown on his usually smiling face. Then he hopped up from where he was sitting.

Kincaid blinked as Mitch went past him, heading into the kitchen.

"What are you doing?" he asked, surprised out of the melancholy that had settled back over him while he'd been talking. He sat up, turning to watch Mitch.

"Daddy texted and said Zach hadn't eaten lunch, so I'm assuming you haven't either."

"I... No. I'm not really hungry."

"Mm, well, I am. I haven't eaten either. I was... busy this morning." Mitch smiled the blissful smile of a happy Dom who'd had a happy morning.

Why can't that be me?

It almost had been. This was the part he hadn't told Mitch. While he was on his run, he'd been thinking about how to broach the idea of trying to be a real threesome to Zach and Amy. He wasn't sure if they'd be interested, too, but he was pretty sure. And after seeing Jessica, Justin, and Chris at Marquis... he'd realized he wanted that.

The three of them fit together. They worked well together. But he wasn't willing to pretend to be the housemate while Zach and Amy were the couple. He wasn't a damn third wheel.

"What's that face for?" Mitch asked, pausing as he looked at Kincaid over the refrigerator door.

"I..." He sighed. He might as well tell Mitch all of it. Why not, at this point? "I've been thinking about me and Zach... and Amy."

"Huh." Mitch's blue gaze unfocused for a moment, then he nodded his head, his lips forming a little half smile. "Yeah, I could see that."

"Sure, if I'm okay with Zach shoving me in the closet every time his parents come over so he can pretend Amy is his only partner." This time, Kincaid knew exactly how bitter he sounded. "He can't even handle telling his parents he's bisexual. Can you imagine him telling them that he's both bisexual *and* polyamorous?"

Mitch closed the refrigerator door, his hands full of sandwich meat and cheese. He'd been over often enough that he didn't need anyone to tell him where to go. He turned to the pantry to get out the bread.

"You know what your problem is? You're too sure of yourself."

"How is that a problem?" Kincaid asked, amused. Sometimes, Mitch's mind worked in interesting ways. "Especially for a Dom."

"Most of the time, it's not," Mitch admitted. "But sometimes, it is. Like right now. In a conceptual way, you understand what Zach's afraid of, but it's not something you really fear, so you can't really understand where he's coming from. You sort of get it, but it pisses you off at the same time."

"This sounds a lot like the talk we had the last time Zach and I broke up." Kincaid tapped his fingers on the back of the couch. "I'm not saying you're wrong, which is why we ended up getting back together in the first place. I needed to be more understanding of the fact that he's a very different person from me and isn't going to act the same way that I would. But exactly how long am I supposed to be willing to wait?"

"See, that's the thing. You're going to have your timetable. He's going to have his. They might not match up." Mitch opened up the bread bag and started pulling slices out. Then he paused and turned, leaning over to open the cabinet where the cutting board was before Kincaid could even say something to him. "Yeah, I know. Food on the cutting board, not the counter."

"Thank you," Kincaid said, though it made his heart hurt a little because that was Zach's rule, not his. "I don't want to wait forever."

"You shouldn't have to wait forever. I won't lie... Zach fucked up pretty big. He hit some trigger points for you, for sure. But... you're also not very understanding when someone doesn't do what you think is the 'right' thing."

That grated a little because what? He was supposed to be okay with people doing the wrong thing?

"I see that face," Mitch said in the kind of sing-song voice that he sometimes used with his soon-to-be six-year-old stepdaughter. "I didn't say the 'right' thing. I said what *you* think the right thing is. Sometimes, in some situations, there's more than one way to do the right thing, but you have a tendency to choose what you think is the one 'right way,' and woe betide anyone who doesn't choose the same way."

"Are you saying Zach did the right thing today?"

"No, but I *am* saying that he's not doing anything wrong by working on the timetable that *he's* comfortable with. Unfortunately, today that timetable bit him in the ass. You have every right to be pissed. But he also has every right to have waited this long. It's up to you whether or not you can deal with his timetable, but being mad that his is different from yours isn't going to help anyone." Mitch's tone was matter-of-fact.

Kincaid frowned.

Shit. He had been doing that, hadn't he?

"Also, I'm pretty sure you wouldn't be nearly as pissed at him if you hadn't been working up a whole throuple scenario in your head while you were on your run, only to come back and find that he'd tried to implement what you would feel was the worst-case-scenario of that arrangement. If you weren't afraid of exactly that happening, you probably would have been able to deal with everything better." Mitch grinned when Kincaid flinched at the direct hit.

"Ow," Kincaid complained, putting his hand on his chest. "Why don't you just punch me in the face next time? It would hurt less." He huffed. "I still don't think it's right that Zach hasn't told his parents about us."

"I agree," Mitch said calmly, plating the sandwiches. "I also don't think it's right that you keep pressuring him to. Mostly because it's not helping anyone; it's making Zach more insecure, and it's making you resentful. None of that is good for a relationship."

"Get a girl to agree to marry you, and all of the sudden, you're a relationship expert," Kincaid muttered.

"Hey, if anyone knows about what it takes for a relationship to fall apart, it's me. You want to end up like my parents?" Mitch wrinkled his nose. "I mean, they're blissfully happy now, but I don't think you want to spend ten years in a 'will they, won't they' situation while y'all get your shit together."

Having heard the entire story about Mitch's parents' divorce and reconciliation, Kincaid had to agree. Deep down, he'd already known that. Which was why he hadn't broken up with Zach immediately. He hadn't wanted to do anything rash while he was angry. He wasn't sure Zach could handle another breakup, especially after he'd accused Kincaid of leaving him once.

He wasn't ready to take that step.

"So what do I do?" he asked. Having to ask that wasn't normally his thing, but he truly didn't know what to do.

"I think you have to wait and see what Zach does." Finished putting the ingredients away, Mitch walked back into the living room and handed Kincaid a plate.

"I hate waiting," Kincaid muttered.

"Don't we all." Mitch snorted. "If you could wrap this up today while I'm here, so that I can tell Domi all the good, juicy gossip when I get back home, that would be much appreciated."

Taking a big bite of his sandwich, Kincaid flipped off his best friend with his free hand.

<u>Amy</u>

"I'm a homewrecker," Amy moaned into her hands while Morgan rubbed her back with one hand. She was sitting on Morgan and Asad's couch—where she'd probably be sleeping tonight—trying not to totally dissolve into tears.

As crazy as it was, this felt worse than being left at the altar.

"No, you're not," Morgan said soothingly, still rubbing her back.

"By the legal definition, you're definitely not," Asad said from behind them. "Kincaid and Zach both invited you into the relationship, you're living with them, and they both knew about you."

When Amy and Morgan both lifted their heads to glare at him, he put his hands up in front of him in a placating gesture and took a slow, careful step back.

"So, um, I'm going to step out and let you ladies have the house," he said. "Uh... I hope you're feeling better soon, Amy." He side-stepped to the front door and yanked it open, disappearing as fast as he could and causing both Amy and Morgan to dissolve into giggles. Amy's ended a lot faster than Morgan's did.

Technically, Asad was right. She wasn't a homewrecker. Not in the sense that Noelle had been. But she'd still messed up Kincaid and Zach's relationship, even inadvertently, which was the last thing she'd ever wanted to do. She felt like she'd wrecked things with her mere presence.

If she hadn't sprayed Zach with water, they wouldn't have been in the position his parents found them in. If she hadn't been there, if she hadn't taken over their guest room, they wouldn't have agreed to the club relationship, and it wouldn't have spilled over to real life. If she hadn't started yelling at Zach in the street, maybe he would have found the right time and way to tell Kincaid what had happened with his parents. Or, at least, a way that didn't involve her, so she wasn't partially responsible for that awful expression on Kincaid's face. No matter which way she looked at it, everything started with her.

"He is right, though," Morgan said delicately, returning to rubbing Amy's back. "I don't think we can call you a homewrecker. It was just a fight. A bad one. But you didn't do anything wrong."

"I... I shouldn't have yelled at Zach in the street." That was one she was pretty sure Morgan couldn't argue with.

"Sounds to me like he deserved it. And you were upset."

"Yeah, but I also wasn't thinking." Amy rubbed her face. "I should have thought about the fact that Kincaid was out on a run. That he might be back soon. That anyone could hear us."

"You weren't thinking because you were upset."

"That's no excuse," Amy said stubbornly, even though she knew she'd say the exact same thing to any of her friends.

Thankfully, she was saved by the bell.

"That must be the others," Morgan said with a sigh of relief as she got up to go answer the door. Amy had texted the group chat, and Morgan had immediately told her she could come over. She'd been the first to respond. Carolyn had been second—she was out of town with her husband. Marissa hadn't responded at all, but she was also on the other side of the country. Sam had texted back that she wanted to come help, but she was with Iris, Avery, Rae, and Domi... could she bring them?

After the humiliation at her wedding, such a small audience was hardly going to faze Amy. She'd said, 'sure.' Plus, she'd realized how nice it was to have so many people supporting her when she'd burned her wedding dress. She felt like she needed the support even more now, as crazy as that was, especially with both Carolyn and Marissa being unavailable.

When everyone came in, all of them immediately moving to her with sympathy and hugs and greetings, her heart felt so happy and warm, it was hard not to feel calmer. The support, even from newer friends she hadn't known for as long or as well, bolstered her in a way that she desperately needed right now.

"Okay, honey," Sam said, sitting Amy back down on the couch beside her, with her arm around her. Morgan was back on Amy's other side, and the others all arrayed themselves around the room with sympathetic expressions. "What on earth happened?"

Amy took a deep breath and started from the beginning—this morning when she'd started gardening with Zach and Kincaid had gone out for his run. Thankfully, everyone at the club knew Kincaid and Zach's history, so there was no need to explain any of that. They all listened quietly until Amy got to the part about Zach's parents showing up and being told that she was his girlfriend.

"No..." Iris gasped.

"What did you do?" Domi asked.

"What was I supposed to do? Out him to his parents?" Amy wrung her hands. "I don't know, maybe I should have."

"No, you definitely shouldn't have," Rae said, shaking her head.

"Might have deserved it for making Amy his beard," Sam muttered. Then she shook her head, too. "No, because he'd just slapped your ass, right? And you were over his shoulder. They saw that."

"Kind of hard to claim 'just friends' after that," Avery agreed. "Though he could have still tried if he really wanted to."

"Do you think he didn't want to because he does want you to be his girlfriend? I mean, not just his, but his and Kincaid's," Morgan hastily added on the second part when everyone turned to look at her. "Sorry, that's probably wrong. I'm not good at reading people."

"Oh, I think you might be better than you think," Sam said slowly. "I could totally believe that's part of it."

"Y'all, I do not need you to give me *more* problems," Amy said, shaking her head. "Besides, I don't think that's true. Even if it was, I'm not done. I started yelling at him as soon as his parents left when I should have just let us go inside to talk about it... but I was so mad—"

"Were you mad because you wanted it to be true?" Sam interjected.

Amy elbowed her in the side and ignored her, even though everyone else's expressions appeared to agree with her assessment.

"And while we were yelling, at some point, Kincaid showed up. And we didn't notice him." More gasps around the room. Iris actually lifted her hands to cover her mouth in shock. "I have no idea how much he heard, but enough to know that Zach told his parents I was his girlfriend."

"Oh, no..." Domi breathed out the words. Her husband was Kincaid's best friend, so she probably knew him pretty well. "What did he do?"

"Started yelling at Zach, which is when I realized what I'd done, and I ran into the house to get my stuff and get out of there before I could cause any more damage."

"And... what *did* you do exactly?" Avery asked, looking confused.

"Other than moving in and ruining their lives with my very presence, you mean?" she asked, throwing her hands up in the air.

Morgan looked pained. "See what I've been dealing with? I don't understand why she thinks it's her fault."

"Because she always blames herself for everything that goes wrong," Sam said. "Don't look at me like that. You do. You even blamed yourself for Jeremy being a huge jerk and leaving you at the altar."

"I should have realized he was a huge jerk before we ever got to the altar."

"Well, he was, but no one ever expected he would do *that*. We didn't suspect. I would have told you. Morgan definitely would have told you." Sam reached over and hugged her shoulders. "Carolyn would have told you. Marissa would have told you. Worst-case scenario, we thought he might not be as good of a husband as you deserved. And hopefully, if he was bad enough, eventually, you'd get divorced. But his behavior is not on you."

"Neither are Kincaid and Zach's," Rae said, picking up the thread. "They were messed up before you came along. There was some drama at Domi and Mitch's Jack-and-Jill weekend away, then they broke up, and then they got back together... all before you were doing anything with them other than an occasional scene with Zach."

"And none of those issues they were having had anything to do with you."

Amy opened her mouth. Closed it. That was true. She knew she had nothing to do with any of that. She'd been deep in wedding prep with Jeremy.

So, why did she still feel like it was her fault?

"I should have still been able to do something instead of running away," she said stubbornly. "If I hadn't been yelling at Zach, Kincaid wouldn't have heard what happened like that, and he might not have been upset."

"Pretty sure that he was going to be upset about Zach using you as a beard, regardless of how he found out," Iris pointed out. "And, again, Zach's behavior isn't your fault, and he deserved to be yelled at."

Rubbing her forehead, Amy frowned. "I just feel like I should have been able to do something."

"That's because you like to fix everything," Sam said. "But you can't always fix people or a situation, and sometimes, there's nothing you can do to help."

Ugh. She didn't like the sound of that at all. Especially because she realized it was true. As much as she was kicking herself over everything, the thing she was kicking herself over the most was running away instead of staying to try to help them. At that moment, she'd felt like she could help the most by getting out of there.

Now, she wasn't so sure, and she was feeling the urge to go back and try to put what she'd broken back together.

32

When it came time, it was almost easy. Maybe it was because he'd finally made the decision that it was time, maybe it was because Brian was by his side, maybe it was because he was too emotionally exhausted to be scared anymore. Whatever it was, when he showed up at his parents' house and told his mom that he needed to talk to both of them, he felt oddly calm.

They sat in the living room he'd grown up in, and though the couch wasn't the same as when he was a kid, all the décor was. He felt safe here. So, maybe that was why it was easier, too.

"So, what are you in such a hurry to tell us?" his mom asked, her gaze flicking to Brian, who was sitting beside Zach on the couch. They'd met before, just like she'd met Mitch and Kincaid, but Zach hadn't explained why Brian was with him. She was obviously confused, and he didn't blame her.

Zach cleared his throat.

"Earlier today when you met Amy and asked if she was my girl-friend, and I said yes, that was a lie. Amy is not my girlfriend. I don't have a girlfriend. I have a boyfriend."

"But..." His mom looked at Brian today. "Oh... well, we've always liked you, Brian, but I thought you had a girlfriend, too."

"Not me," Brian said, barely suppressing laughter as Zach jumped in at the same time.

"Not him, Mom. He does have a girlfriend. A real one." Zach took a deep breath. "Kincaid is my boyfriend."

"The... the man you've been living with?" his mom asked. On the other side of her, his dad was sitting with a fairly blank expression, thinking rather than asking questions, which was very much like his parents. It also made him worry because he wasn't sure what his dad was thinking.

"Yes."

"Did you become boyfriends after you started living together?"

Zach hesitated, but he was done with the lies. Even if his parents got mad at him. Having Brian's support at his side helped a lot.

"No. We moved in together after we started seeing each other romantically. I lied to you about that. I'm sorry."

"I... I'm confused. Why did you lie? Why not just tell us that you're gay?"

"I'm bisexual, not gay, and I wasn't ready to tell you yet because I wasn't sure how you'd react. I wasn't... I guess, honestly, at first, I wasn't sure if Kincaid and I would last, so I didn't want to tell you in case it didn't work out. Then, the longer it went on, the harder it was to tell you that I'd lied in the first place."

"You have a boyfriend, but you're not gay?"

Trust his mom to fixate on that point.

"No, I'm still attracted to both men and women, so I'm bisexual."

"But you have a boyfriend, so isn't that basically the same as being gay?"

Zach took a deep breath.

"Okay, so I should bring up this is another part of the reason I didn't want to tell you. Some of these questions you're asking are kind of invasive and... well, to be perfectly honest, they're a little ignorant. I didn't want you asking them while Kincaid was here. I didn't want you asking him any kind of questions like this. I was afraid he'd be scared off or insulted enough to walk away." Damn, he really was insecure. Not just about how his parents would react, but about how Kincaid might react. "Kincaid and I are both bisexual, so we are both still attracted to women and men, though we've chosen to be with each other."

"But you were flirting with Amy today. I saw you... you had her over your shoulder, and you touched her... her rear end. Were you cheating on Kincaid?" His mom looked indignant at the thought, which kind of amused Zach, considering she'd just found out that he was with Kincaid. "I didn't raise you to be a cheater, Zach."

"Mine and Kincaid and Amy's relationship is complicated. She is not my girlfriend, but we do have..." Fuck. Zach looked at Brian, wondering if he had a better way to explain it without having to get into all the kinky shit. He did not want to get into the kinky shit with his parents.

Especially his dad, who was still sitting there with that blank expression on his face, giving nothing away.

"They're both dating Amy, though they won't call it that yet because they're both afraid that the other one won't be interested, but really, all three of them are basically in love and just too stupid to look at what's right in front of their faces," Brian said casually, as if he'd just announced that Zach liked food rather than dropping an emotional bomb.

"Wait, so, if you're both dating Amy, is that because you're bisexual, because you need a man and a woman?"

Zach groaned.

This was going to be a long fucking conversation.

Amy

The afternoon descended into an impromptu chick flick movie afternoon, complete with junk food. Exactly what Amy needed. Was eating her feelings healthy? Probably not, but sometimes a girl needed to do what a girl needed to do. The most amusing part of the afternoon was everyone watching Morgan eat her salad, all of them with an expression on their faces that said they were wondering if they should have ordered something with vegetables on it.

"I should go back," Amy said finally, after the movie ended.

"Back... to Zach and Kincaid's house? You mean like to live or to talk to them?" Sam asked. "No judgment either way, just wondering."

"Mostly to talk to them. I have no idea how they ended things after I left, and it's bothering me."

"Me, too," Rae chimed in, shrugging when Domi smacked her with a pillow. "What? I'm nosy, and neither Brian nor Mitch have been sending updates."

"You didn't really expect them to, did you?" Domi asked.

"Brian, no, Mitch..." Rae left her voice hanging.

Amy sat up. "Wait, what?"

Domi and Rae exchanged a glance.

"We weren't sure if we should tell you, especially since you seem to be blaming yourself for everything," Domi said. "Zach texted Brian that he needed to see him, and Brian sent Mitch to Kincaid."

"Wait... so... Kincaid and Zach have been separate this whole afternoon?" Amy felt her emotions slipping back toward turmoil. "I left so they would have the privacy to talk to each other while I was gone!"

"Maybe they didn't want privacy. Or maybe there just wasn't much to say." Rae gave her a sympathetic look. "Or maybe they just need some time apart to think things over. Zach needs a lot of thinking time."

Zach did, but Kincaid didn't. Which meant that she'd left him alone. Sure, Mitch had gone over, but...

She shouldn't have left them totally alone. She should have stayed and tried to referee. What if Zach didn't come back tonight? What if they broke up again? And she wasn't there for them, either of them. She didn't like that thought at all.

"I need to go back."

"Mitch has it handled, I promise," Domi said, looking at her curiously. "He won't let Kincaid do anything stupid." She paused. "Well...

I mean, not anything too stupid. He won't let Kincaid wreck his life or anything."

"This better not be some kind of martyr thing," Sam said suspiciously. "You don't need to go over there because you think Kincaid needs to yell at someone or anything."

"No, I need to be there because... because..." Amy took a deep breath. "Because I love them. Both of them. And even if they don't feel the same way about me, I want to be there for them."

Terrible timing on her part, really. She waited for everyone to tell her that she was being stupid or that she was just rebounding, but that didn't happen.

"Finally!" Sam clapped her hands together. "I thought it was going to take way longer for you to realize that."

"It took longer than I thought it would," Morgan said, picking one of the olives out of her salad and handing it to Avery, who immediately popped it into her mouth, smiling approvingly at Amy.

"You three really do seem perfect together from what we've seen," Domi said, gesturing to herself and Rae. "We didn't want to intervene, though I bet Brian and Mitch finally say something to the boys about it."

"I'm pretty sure that's exactly what Brian planned to do because he assumed that's why Zach was texting him," Rae said.

Amy looked at Iris, who was the only one not jumping in with some kind of opinion. Iris shrugged, raising her hands palms up.

"Don't look at me. I don't know any of y'all well enough to think anything." She paused. "Though you would make a very cute throuple. And if you ever want to talk to another throuple, I know Jessica, Justin, and Chris would be happy to talk to you."

Well, that was good to know.

Amy looked around the room. Apparently, no one was going to stop her. Fine, then.

"I'm going back," she announced. Then she looked at Morgan. "But I can still come sleep on the couch if I need to, right?"

"Of course." Morgan smiled at her. "Any time."

That was the backup plan; Kincaid and Zach might not feel the same about her.

But maybe the reason she felt compelled to 'fix' them wasn't because she wanted to fix everyone... maybe she felt compelled to fix them because they belonged together, and they belonged to her.

***

Kincaid

The doorbell rang, causing him and Mitch to pause the videogame they'd started playing and look at each other.

"Were you expecting someone?" Mitch asked.

"No."

Putting down the controller, Kincaid got up to go see who it was, so they didn't start shouting through the door the way Mitch had. He peeked through the eye hole, but all he saw was the back of someone's head, as though they'd turned around after they'd rung the doorbell.

Opening it, he saw that he was correct—and she spun back around to face him as the door opened.

"Amy." Sheer relief poured through him at seeing her back at the door before a thought occurred to him, and he frowned. "Why are you knocking?"

She bit her lip, shrugging and looking incredibly uncomfortable.

"It felt a little weird just walking back in after... after this morning. I wasn't sure how you'd feel about me coming back."

Glad. That was how he felt. Glad and more settled, like she was supposed to be here, and now that she was back, at least one piece of the puzzle had been slotted back into its space. She belonged here, as much as he and Zach did, even if it had taken everything falling apart for him to realize that.

"Come on in," he said, opening the door wider and stepping back. "I'm glad you came back."

She walked in but came to a halt when she saw Mitch getting up from the couch. "Oh... I thought..."

"You thought..." Kincaid put his hand on her back to keep her from turning and running out the door, subtly pressuring her to keep moving inside.

"I thought Mitch was Zach for a moment." She sighed. "I'd hoped he'd come back, too."

"Not yet." Kincaid still had no idea where Zach was. Not much he could do about that, though. Would he be back? Would things change? He didn't know.

"I'm going to get out of here," Mitch said grinning, moving quickly enough that Amy couldn't protest.

Kincaid wasn't going to try to. As glad as he was that Mitch had been there to help him through the day, what he needed to talk to Amy about was better done alone.

"Take care of him, Amy. He needs it, even though he won't admit it."

Kincaid scowled at his friend's back as he practically ran out the door.

"Ignore him, I'm fine."

"Are you? Because I'm not. And I wouldn't be fine if I was in your shoes." Amy sagged a little, avoiding his gaze.

"Fine might be the wrong word, but I'll live. Your coming back helps. I'm sorry Zach and I basically chased you away." He sighed as he escorted her into the living room so she could take Mitch's seat on the couch, and he sat down beside her. They weren't cuddling exactly, just sitting very close together.

Amy's hands came together in her lap, her fingers fiddling with each other.

"You didn't chase me away. I left because I figured I'd already done enough damage, and I wanted to give you guys the privacy to talk to each other. I didn't realize Zach was going to leave, too, or I might have tried to stay."

"Hey." Kincaid reached over, putting his hand over her fidgeting ones. "Amy, look at me. You did not do any damage. Zach shouldn't have put you in the position of pretending to be his girlfriend to his parents."

"No, but I also didn't have to scream at him in the street afterward. You shouldn't have found out about it the way you did."

"I don't think there was a good way to find out about it," Kincaid said ruefully, giving her hands a squeeze. With another sigh, she leaned to the side, resting her head against his shoulder like she needed something to lean on. Being the thing she was leaning on helped him feel a little better. A little more like himself. "Even if he'd told me calmly, I would have been righteously pissed. But I know I'm being hard on him. He's caught in the middle, and while I have a right to my feelings, it's been a struggle to understand his, and that doesn't make things easier for any of us."

"I think he does want to tell his parents; he's just scared."

"I know." He didn't really understand why Zach was willing to go to the lengths that he was to avoid telling them for so long; it seemed like it just made everything harder. But, as Mitch had said, he and Zach were different people. They were going to act differently. Feel things differently. He either needed to accept that or get out of the situation.

And he wasn't ready to lose Zach.

As much as he needed to talk to Zach about that, he needed to talk to Amy, too. He needed her to know that it wasn't her fault. It didn't surprise him that she'd blamed herself. That was who *she* was.

"I think one of the hardest parts for me was realizing that I wanted to talk to you and Zach about us bringing our relationship out of the club and seeing if it would work at home, too, but then becoming scared that he would use that as a reason not to tell his parents about me." He couldn't tell what Amy's reaction was to all of this since she was still leaning against his shoulder, but he kept going. "That he would only tell them about you, and I would just always be... there. The housemate. An unacknowledged third wheel."

Amy sat up and looked at him, their hands still clasped on her lap. She looked utterly bewildered.

"You want me? With you and Zach?" Not just incredulous; there was hopefulness there, too. Some of the incredibility seemed as though it was coming from the idea that her hope was being realized.

He'd been pretty sure that both she and Zach would be interested in moving their relationship to the next level unless he'd been reading them both completely wrong, but it was still nice to get the confirmation that he was right.

"Yes." He'd meant to have this conversation with Zach here, too, but he might as well be honest. "You feel like you belong. Like you fit with us. I think I've been falling for you from the moment you moved in with us, even though I didn't know it at the time."

Amy stared at him for a long, long moment.

Then she suddenly leaned forward, reaching for him, and he reached for her, pulling her onto his lap as their lips came together in a heated kiss.

33

ZACH

When he finally left his parents, Zach still wasn't sure they completely understood. His dad had been really quiet for the whole conversation, though before they'd left, he'd given Zach a hug and told him he loved him, no matter what. His mom wanted to ask more questions, and Zach had made her promise to ask him or Krista and never Kincaid. Or Amy.

"You going to be okay?" Brian asked, giving him a pat on the shoulder as he walked Zach to his car.

"Yeah, I just feel wrung out. And now I need to go home and tell Kincaid that I've told my parents and see what he says. Then I need to talk to him about Amy. Then we can hopefully figure out where Amy went."

"Good luck." They'd reached the cars, and Brian stepped in to give him a bro hug—hands clasped between them, pulling each other in for mutual slaps on the back. "If you need me, call me."

"I will." Though he really hoped not to. He'd already pulled Brian away from enough of his day. Still, he appreciated knowing that Brian was there for him, no matter what. And if things went horribly wrong, Brian was exactly who he would call.

Getting into his car, Zach took a deep breath. That had been... hard. Though not as hard as he'd thought it would be. And his parents had taken it a hell of a lot better than he'd thought. Nothing that he'd been afraid of had come to pass. Now, he just had to talk to Kincaid to see if he felt the same way about Amy, then they could talk to Amy.

Those were all conversations he wanted to have in person.

On the way home, however, he had one more conversation to have, and that one he could do on the phone.

He started the call before starting to drive.

"Hello?" Krista's voice was amplified through the car dashboard.

"Hey." Zach pulled out of his parking spot and started heading home. "I just wanted to call and let you know that I just told Mom and Dad about me and Kincaid."

"Huzzah! Finally!" Even though he couldn't see her, it wasn't hard to imagine Krista throwing her hands in the air—or at least one hand if she was holding the phone with the other—as she cheered. "Took you long enough!"

"Yeah, yeah... a little too long, actually."

"What does that mean?"

Since he didn't know whether or not he still had a boyfriend, Zach wanted to prepare Krista for the possibility that Kincaid was going to dump him after this morning. It was no less agonizing going through it for a second time. Maybe a little more agonizing because his sister was a much less sympathetic listener than Brian.

"Oh my God, you are such a stupid little shit sometimes," she groaned when he got to the part about telling their parents that Amy was his girlfriend.

"Yes, just keep kicking me while I'm down, thanks."

"That *is* my job as your sister. If I don't tell you when you're being a dumbass, who else is going to?"

"I can tell myself plenty, thank you."

"Apparently not, since you're still doing dumbass shit."

"Anyway. I got them out of there as quickly as I could before

Kincaid got home, but then as soon as they were gone, Amy started yelling at me about using her as a beard."

Krista groaned. "Oh, no. Don't tell me. Kincaid came home *then* and heard her."

"At the worst possible time."

"Maybe not the *worst* possible time. The worst possible time would have been if he'd come up and heard you telling Mom and Dad that Amy was your girlfriend. Hearing about it secondhand is probably less painful than hearing you actually do it. Plus, this way, Mom wasn't there to make things even worse. And you know she could have."

"You know, that's a good point," Zach admitted. He could only imagine how that would have gone down, and to be perfectly honest, it was worse. His mom definitely would have tried to get involved, both trying to understand and attempting to play peacemaker without actually understanding.

He wasn't sure how his dad would have reacted.

Maybe by hiding in the car until it was all over.

Huh. Maybe he was more like his dad sometimes than he thought.

"I'm glad you told them, though. Maybe that'll help make things up to Kincaid a little."

"Fingers crossed." Zach sighed as he pulled into his driveway. "Things probably can't get worse, right?"

"Dude, never say that. Things can always get worse."

"You're such a ray of sunshine. Thanks," he said dryly.

"You sure Mom didn't beat you over there to reintroduce herself to Kincaid?" Krista joked, making Zach shudder.

"Don't say that, even as a joke." He wouldn't put it past his mom to do something like that with the best of intentions. Crap. The likelihood of her doing something wildly outrageous to 'welcome Kincaid to the family' was a lot higher after today's debacle. She was probably going to feel the need to try to make up for the misunderstanding, even though it wasn't her fault. "Have you ever thought about the fact that our mom is the definition of chaotic good?"

"Good intentions, questionable methods? Oh, yeah. That's her all over."

At least he wasn't the only one who saw it.

"I'm home. I'm going inside. Wish me luck."

"Don't fuck it up again!" Krista responded cheerfully, which was her very big sisterly way of saying 'good luck.' Strangely, it made him feel better.

"Thanks." He shoved his phone in his pocket and headed to the door, wiping suddenly clammy hands on his pants as he approached. His chest tightened, and he took a deep breath, giving himself a little shake to try to release the tension from his muscles.

Punching in the code to the lock, he opened the door and stepped inside... and nearly tripped over himself when movement on the couch caught his eye, and he turned to look.

Amy had returned.

Her car must have been out front, but somehow he hadn't noticed.

Amy had returned, and she was sitting on Kincaid's lap.

Amy had returned, and she was sitting on Kincaid's lap with his arms around her, and she'd just pulled away from him, and her cheeks were flushed and...

And they'd been kissing.

Without him.

AMY

What am I doing?

It wasn't that she didn't want to kiss Kincaid, but... it felt wrong. Zach wasn't here.

Kincaid must have had the same thought, or something, because they both pulled back from the kiss at the same time. His arms remained locked around her, though, holding her securely. Though their lips had pulled away from each other, they leaned against each other, foreheads touching.

"We can't do this before I talk to Zach," Kincaid said before Amy could catch her breath, proving that he had been thinking the exact same thing as her. "I don't even know what he wants yet."

"I know... I..." Something beeped, and Amy frowned. What was that?

It wasn't until the door opened that she realized she'd been hearing the keypad.

She jerked away from Kincaid, but when she turned her head, Zach was standing in the doorway, staring at her and Kincaid, white as a sheet.

"Zach!" She and Kincaid said his name at the same time, her trying to roll off his lap at the same time he stood up, which sent her tumbling to the floor. He stood beside her while she was on the ground.

"Shit." He reached out his hand to help her up, though his eyes were still on Zach. "I didn't know you were coming home."

Zach looked between Kincaid and her as she got to her feet, releasing Kincaid's hand as soon as she could.

"Clearly," he said in a hollow voice.

She felt Kincaid stiffen beside her, and she looked up to see him scowling.

"Nothing happened. Well, we kissed, but we both immediately realized that we shouldn't until we talked to you."

"Well, that's something at least." Zach didn't look at all reassured, and his words came out more sarcastic than sincere.

"It's better than telling someone that she's my girlfriend without talking to you about it first," Kincaid shot back.

"Hey, hey!" Amy was not having any of this. Zach had come back. That was good. She did not want anyone storming out again. "You are not to use me as a weapon between you or a way to get back at each other."

"I'm sorry," Kincaid said immediately, shamefaced. "That's not... If I did do that, it wasn't my intention. That's not why I kissed you, and it's not why I said that, but I can see how it could come off that way."

"I'm sorry, too." Zach sighed, the fight visibly leaking out of him.

He shut the front door, which helped Amy to relax. He'd gone from freeze to fight and, thankfully, had now shut down the avenue to flight. Hopefully, they could just talk now. The way they should have in the first place. "I really don't have room to talk today. I just..." He took a deep breath and looked at Kincaid. "It hurt feeling left out. I know I did it to you, and in a much worse way, and I was blindsided. But so were you, and I'm sorry. I'm the one who was out of line."

"No, like I said, Amy and I were both just saying that we couldn't do anything without talking to you. If our relationship is going to change, that can't happen if you aren't part of the conversation." Kincaid ran his fingers through his hair. "I do think we need to talk, though. Maybe just the two of us at first, then we can bring in Amy?"

Damn. Her heart sank a little, but it made sense. They were the original relationship. If they were going to bring her in, they needed to talk about it first. She wanted it. She knew Kincaid wanted it. She thought—hoped—Zach wanted it, too.

Her heart sank more when Zach shook his head.

"Amy might as well stay because I'm pretty sure you and I both want the same thing." He cleared his throat. "In the interest of full disclosure, I should tell both of you that I've been at my parents, telling them that Kincaid is my boyfriend and that I was not cheating on him with Amy the way my mom accused me of, then having to try to explain polyamory to her."

Her heart rose back up with every word he said, then the pained expression on his face when he talked about trying to explain polyamory to his mom made Amy laugh. Not just because it was funny, though it was, but because all the tension was bursting out of her and needed somewhere to go.

It was a laugh of relief, of joy, of hope.

Fingers closed around hers. Kincaid was holding her hand. He reached his free hand toward Zach, who took the steps to close the gap and take it. Amy breathed out a sigh of contentment.

Yes. This felt right. This is how they were supposed to be.

"So, everyone's in agreement that we want to be in a relationship with each other?" Kincaid asked with barely suppressed amusement.

"Yes. But only if we're in this together. I never want to be Zach's beard." Amy narrowed her eyes at him, joking but not really joking.

"You won't be. I promise I won't hide either of you. Which is going to make my company holiday party this year really interesting, but we'll have fun with it." He grinned at them. He looked so much more relaxed than he had in months, and Amy realized how much keeping the secret had been weighing on him. Now that the weight was off, he didn't seem eager to take it back up again.

"Well, I still have to tell my parents," Amy said, though considering her mom's reading habits and her suggestion at Amy's wedding, perhaps it wouldn't go too badly. "Um, which... I would like to wait a little before telling them, if that's okay. Just to make sure that we don't change our minds."

Zach smiled warmly at her, washing away her worry about him. Kincaid's expression was more serious, but he nodded.

"I'm not going to change my mind, but we can wait until you're more comfortable." He looked at Zach again. "I'm working on my patience."

"You were already really patient," Zach told him. "You had every right to be upset that it was taking so long to tell my parents."

"And you were working on your own timetable. You shouldn't have had to adhere to mine, and you would have every right to be upset that I was pressuring you." Kincaid sighed.

"So, both of you were in the wrong, and I'm the good girl," Amy quipped, looking to break up the pity fest a little bit. They'd just gotten things sorted out; she didn't want them arguing about who had done the other one more wrong.

Both of them laughed, just as she'd meant them to.

"You are the good girl," Kincaid said, his dark eyes lighting up. "And I think you deserve a reward."

"I feel like I'm getting off easy," Zach murmured.

Kincaid turned to look at him with a wolfish smile. "Trust me, you won't feel that way by the end of the night."

34

Everything felt right. As if it was supposed to be. Not that he and Kincaid had ever felt wrong together—they hadn't—but they hadn't felt *this* right. Zach knew it was partly because he was no longer holding back. His parents knew. His sister knew. Their friends knew. They didn't have anything to hide anymore.

It was also because Amy was with them now. If she'd been available, if he'd been available, he would have made a move on her a long time ago. He'd always figured she'd be an important part of his life once they'd started scening because he cared deeply about her.

Having her be a part of Kincaid's life, in the same way she was a part of his, felt like everything had fallen into place.

They held her between them, passing her back and forth while they stripped her down. Hands moving over her body, mouths stealing kisses from her lips, exploring her neck, making her moan when Kincaid had her lean back against him, lifting her breasts to Zach like an offering. One that he took full advantage of, ravaging her pert nipples with his mouth, using his fingers to twist and pull them.

"Lift your arms up around my neck, princess," Kincaid murmured in her ear, and Amy whimpered as she did as she was told. The position thrust her breasts out in front of her, the pink tips begging for more torment. "Zach, go get the clamps. I think our girl needs some jewelry."

"I agree." Zach grinned as he went to get the clamps he wanted. Nothing too harsh tonight. He wanted to focus on the pleasure rather than the pain for her. She didn't need harsh right now.

So, he picked out the tweezer clamps, the triad strand with one for her clit, all connected by a chain so that when her breasts bounced or moved, it would tug on her clit. He also knew it was Kincaid's favorite to use on a sub, confirmed by the way his boyfriend's eyes lit up when he saw what Zach was holding.

With one hand covering Amy's breast, the other down between her legs stroking her clit, Kincaid was already priming her. Zach went for the breast Kincaid wasn't toying with first, putting the rubber tips of the clamp around her pert nipple and pushing the slider up the tweezers to pinch. The closer the slider got to the rubber, the tighter the pinch, though it still would be a lot less than something like clover clamps.

It was enough to make Amy moan and lean her head back against Kincaid, who released her breast and moved his hand up to her throat. He held her in place, moving his lips along the top of her shoulder, while Zach lifted the breast Kincaid had been playing with and pinched the clamp around that nipple. Amy moaned again, shuddering as both of her nipples were trapped and tightly pinched.

Zach dropped to his knees in front of her, pushing her legs a little farther apart as Kincaid's hand retreated from there so Zach could clamp her clit. She leaned back on Kincaid, giving Zach more access to her sweet pussy.

"Look at our pretty little slut; she's soaking wet," Zach said, giving her pussy a stroke. The little nub of her clit was already peeking out at him, swollen and eager to be touched and rubbed and tormented.

"And she tastes delicious," Kincaid responded, licking her cream from his fingers while still holding her by the throat with his other hand. "Such a good, sweet girl."

"Thank you, Sirs," she said, a little sassily, then moaned long and loud when Zach leaned forward and sucked her clit between his lips.

He wanted it nice and hard and swollen when he clamped it. It only took him a moment or two, more of a tease than anything else, before he released the tiny bud and replaced his mouth with the clamp. Her hips jerked forward as she gasped, shuddering against Kincaid, her eyelashes fluttering.

"Ooooooh..."

Zach's cock jerked in reaction. Damn, he liked it when she made little noises like that. He reached out and tugged gently on the chain connecting her nipples to her clit, pulling on all three sensitive buds at once, and she cried out.

"Now that our pretty girl is decorated... on your knees, Zach," Kincaid said with a wicked grin. "You can let go of me now, Amy." He shifted her as her arms dropped, moving her to the side, though his fingers were still wrapped around her throat as he guided her to where he wanted her—right next to him.

Zach dropped to his knees in front of Kincaid, his mouth immediately watering as the bulge in the other man's jeans was right at face level. His own dick twitched in envy, but he was pretty sure this was part of his penance—being on his knees, taking Kincaid down his throat while he got nothing.

He'd eventually get what he wanted, but Kincaid was going to make him wait for it.

Freeing Kincaid's cock from his jeans, he didn't wait to be told what to do. He wanted to make today up to Kincaid. Gripping his boyfriend's cock by the root, he opened his mouth and sucked the length of it between his lips, taking him deep from the get-go.

Kincaid groaned, his fingers threading into Zach's hair to hold him in place. The groan was muffled after a moment, and Zach tilted his head back to look up. While he swallowed Kincaid's cock, Kincaid had turned his head and lowered it to take Amy's lips in a kiss. Her soft curves were pressed against his side, the chain hanging right next to Zach's face, as Kincaid plundered her mouth with his tongue.

At the same time, he gripped Zach's hair tightly, holding him in place as he began to fuck Zach's mouth with his cock, using Zach for his pleasure. Zach knew the rhythm—sometimes Kincaid liked to get off fast, so he could take his time with the next round without struggling to hold himself back from coming.

It meant he planned to use Zach's ass hard. He felt his cheeks clench in anticipation as he sucked Kincaid's dick harder, trying to give his boyfriend what he wanted.

———

<u>AMY</u>

Her nipples and clit throbbed as Kincaid kissed the ever-loving fuck out of her. She leaned against him, the gentle sway of the chain brushing cool metal against her skin but also tugging lightly on the clamps where it was attached to her. All the while, she was hyper-aware of Zach on his knees beside her, Kincaid's cock down his throat. The hot, wet sound of Kincaid fucking Zach's mouth was driving her a little wild, and as much as she wanted to keep kissing Kincaid, she also wanted to watch.

When Kincaid finally pulled away, groaning as his head fell back, she was finally able to look down. His fingers were still curved around the back of her neck, holding her beside him, making her feel like a little doll that he was moving around. She watched as he thrust deep into Zach's mouth. Zach's hands were on Kincaid's hips, his gaze trained upward.

He'd been watching Kincaid, but as Amy looked down at him, his gaze shifted and clashed with hers. The sight of Kincaid's cock between Zach's lips down to the root took her breath away. It was incredibly hot. She squeezed her thighs together, making her moan as the pressure on the clamp increased, and she winced in pained pleasure at the sensation.

Kincaid's grip on her neck tightened, then relaxed. She watched as Zach's eyes unfocused, his throat working, and knew Kincaid was cumming. Her own body was buzzing eagerly, her heartbeat a steady pulse in her clamped nipples and clit, and she whimpered, rubbing herself against Kincaid as he came. She felt so needy as his thumb stroked her neck while he let out a long sigh.

His hand in Zach's hair relaxed its grip, and he cradled the other man's head. Zach's eyes closed for a brief moment, then they opened again as Kincaid pulled back, his cock shiny from Zach's saliva and slowly shrinking back to its normal proportions.

"Good boy," Kincaid said, caressing Zach's head. His thumb moved against Amy's neck at the same time, and she leaned into it, wriggling a little.

She'd been a good girl, too, and she wanted a reward.

As if he'd heard her thoughts, Kincaid chuckled and turned his head to look at her.

"Your turn, princess. Get on the couch and lie back. Zach's going to fuck you, and you can cum as often as you can." He turned to look down at Zach, giving the other man's hair another quick, sharp grip. "You, boy, aren't allowed to cum until I tell you to. Got it?"

"Yes, Sir," Zach said, licking his lips as he looked up at Kincaid with a hot gaze. Then, that hot gaze shifted to Amy and turned into a blaze that heated her from the inside out.

He wanted to fuck her as badly as she wanted him to.

Kincaid gave her a little nudge.

"On the couch, Amy," he reminded her.

Oops. Right. She deserved the little slap he gave her ass when she started moving again, the sting adding to her arousal.

The couch was only a step away... but she hesitated, not sure exactly how he wanted her on it. As usual, Kincaid was on top of things.

"On your back, princess, so Zach and I can see your pretty face while you cum."

Her pretty face was immediately blushing, but she wasn't going to argue with him.

"Yes, Sir." She sat on the couch and leaned back against the cushions as Zach turned, not bothering to get off his knees. He didn't need to. The seat of the couch put her at the exact right position for his rigidly hard cock, and he was on her immediately.

While he might have gotten on his knees and said 'Yes, Sir' for Kincaid, that was not at all the Zach now looming over her, caging her in with his hands. His dark eyes pinned her beneath him as he looked down at her, his hard body between her spread legs.

"Hands above your head, little slut. I want you stretched out in front of me so I can pound your sweet little pussy." He grinned down at her.

Kincaid was off to the side, getting something, so Amy's entire focus was on the man who was about to fuck her. Breathlessly, she reached up again. The guys liked to have her immobilized, something she was quickly figuring out. Sure enough, as soon as her hands were above her head, Zach pinned them there with his own, holding on to her wrists to keep them in place.

The tip of his cock rubbed along the wet seam of her pussy, then he adjusted his hips, pulling back so he could line himself up with her body, and thrust in hard. Amy cried out as he filled her with one long thrust, her body arching upward. The chain on the clamps went taut and pulled on her nipples and clit, adding to the new sensations rippling through her. The blissful feeling of fullness left her shuddering, and she clenched around him, adding to that feeling.

At first, she thought he might take her fast and hard after that initial thrust, but instead, he slowly pulled back and thrust in again, taking his time—because he wasn't allowed to cum until Kincaid gave him permission. *She* was allowed to come... as much as she could, which wouldn't be much if she couldn't get Zach to move faster.

Though, every one of her movements made the clamps tug on her tender bits, which might move her along faster. And every time Zach slid home, his body rubbed against the ultra-sensitive, protruding tip of her clit. It throbbed painfully in the confines of the clamp, arousing her more and making her shudder at the contact.

"Oh... please..." She writhed, then jerked when Zach's body jerked against hers.

Opening her eyes, she saw Kincaid stand behind him, flogger in hand, bringing it down on Zach's shoulders. Zach shifted, moving her legs up, so they were pressed against his chest, protecting them from the flogger with his body as Kincaid swung again, the leather falling against Zach's buttocks.

It completely changed the rhythm of Zach's strokes in and out of her as he reacted to the flogger. She cried out as he hit her insides exactly right, sending her into her first orgasm. Everything throbbed, especially her nipples and clit, as the ecstasy exploded inside her and burst outward like a rocket going off.

35

ZACH

For someone who wasn't 'that much of a sadist,' Kincaid was a real fucking sadist sometimes.

Zach gritted his teeth as Amy's pussy clenched and rippled around him, her lips parted, body arching to thrust her breasts into the air as she came. Fuck, she was beautiful when she came. The flogger didn't hurt so much as it was making his whole body feel extra sensitive, hyperaware, especially his shoulders and buttocks.

Watching Amy come and having to hold himself back?

That was the real pain.

Fingers gripped his hair, pulling his head back. Zach shuddered, panting for breath as he fought off his orgasm.

"She's so pretty when she comes, isn't she?" Kincaid asked, watching Amy writhe for them. His cock was right at Zach's face height again, slowly thickening. "Does she feel good coming on your cock?"

"Yes," Zach gritted out from between his teeth.

Such a fucking sadist, even if he didn't get off on causing physical pain. Kincaid released Zach's hair and ran his fingers over the sensitive skin on Zach's back.

"Keep fucking her, but remember... no coming, or I'll fuck her ass instead of yours."

Fuck. Zach groaned as Amy's pussy clamped down around him again, her expression lighting up as she tuned back into the conversation. It looked like she liked that idea. But fuck that. This was Zach's chance to earn his fantasy—Kincaid's cock in his ass while his was buried in Amy's pussy—and he was not going to lose out on it.

He just had to think about anything else to keep him from coming.

Football.

No, baseball, because that's what was in season.

Not that he followed either.

The new recipe he wanted to try out.

The way Amy diced zucchini.

That did it.

He took a deep breath in as Kincaid started flogging him again, and he started fucking Amy again, thrusting in and out of her as slowly as he could, keeping her hands pinned. At least he could keep her hands off him, so she couldn't try to speed things along that way.

It was hard enough to keep himself under control with her wiggling and arching against him, her pussy squeezing and rippling around his cock. Every lash of the flogger made him jerk as his skin grew more and more sensitive under the leather. When Kincaid stepped forward to run his hand across Zach's shoulders, then down to cup his buttocks, he leaned forward with a groan, his groin pressing against Amy's clit, chest brushing against her nipples, and she cried out as she came again.

Fuck.

He panted, holding back his own orgasm with sheer willpower, even the mental image of her ridiculous dicing technique not entirely combating his need to come. Her legs pressed against his chest, almost as though trying to push him away—she might be as the second orgasm was going to make her exquisitely sensitive, which made holding his position all the more enjoyable... and all the more difficult to hold back his orgasm.

"My turn," Kincaid said from right behind Zach, his voice a low murmur.

Amy cried out as Kincaid pulled the chain, tugging the clamps, then shrieked when he jerked hard, removing them all at once. Her pussy gripped Zach like a vise, not that either of them were given more than a second to recover as Kincaid pressed his hand down on Zach's back, pressing him against Amy. Which was likely why he'd removed the clamps the way he had. It would leave her ultra-sensitive and throbbing after the initial sting of pain, and if he'd left them on, they would likely be painful in an un-fun way as Zach's groin was completely flush with hers now.

Zach groaned as he felt the slick tip of Kincaid's cock press against his anus. His own cock jerked and throbbed inside of Amy.

His boyfriend had taken his fantasy and was turning it into pure erotic torture.

Gripping Zach's head, Kincaid pulled it back toward him, nipping at Zach's earlobe as he began to slowly bury himself in Zach's ass.

"Don't forget, boy, you can't come until I tell you to."

"Yes, Sir." Zach panted as he was stretched open, struggling with the overwhelming sensation of being sandwiched by pure pleasure. Yes, it hurt a bit to have Kincaid sinking into him, the slight burn of being invaded, but it felt so damn good, too. With his own cock buried in Amy, it was the most intense pleasure he'd ever experienced.

How the fuck he was supposed to keep from coming, he didn't know, but he didn't want to disappoint Kincaid. Not after everything they'd been through today. All he wanted was to give Kincaid exactly what he desired.

So, when Kincaid started to pull out, then thrust back in, pulling Zach with him, then pushing him in deep to Amy, using Zach like an extension of his own cock to fuck her, Zach held onto his orgasm by sheer willpower.

His brain fuzzed out as he was caught between his two lovers, Amy wrapped around him, Kincaid going deep inside him, both of them pouring more heat and pleasure through his body. Closing his eyes, he gasped and groaned as they moved against him, inside him, around him, all of his focus on not coming until Kincaid told him he could.

<u>*AMY*</u>

This was too much... it was all too much... yet she didn't want it to ever stop.

Her position on the couch meant that even though both men were on top of her, she wasn't bearing all of their weight, but they took her breath away, regardless. She could see Kincaid moving behind Zach, feel Zach's cock moving inside her, and it was happening at the same time, which meant her brain was processing it as both of them moving inside her. Both of them fucking her. Both of them making love to her.

Zach's new position also meant he was grinding against her poor clit, which was now smashed against his hard body. The wiry hair on his chest abraded her swollen nipples. All the little buds were throbbing from the clamps that Kincaid had yanked off her, and she was just glad it was the tweezer clamps because, while there had been a sharp burst of pain, at least those came off.

And because of how her body reacted to things, the pain had almost immediately transmuted into sheer pleasure, especially as Zach's weight had pressed against her. She rubbed herself against him, everything that was so sensitive lighting her up like a Christmas display gone wild.

Kincaid's gaze met hers over Zach's shoulder as he groaned between them, his own eyes closed, his expression screwed into a grimace as though he was focusing inward. Probably trying not to orgasm while Kincaid fucked him into her.

She whimpered at the thought.

"How many orgasms have you had, princess?" Kincaid asked, still moving, still fucking Zach with long, slow strokes that had the other man rocking in and out of her pussy to the same rhythm.

"Two," she replied, shuddering as her pussy clamped down around Zach's cock.

She was already on her way to a third, and she didn't know if she could handle much more than that. It seemed like they both wanted to push her limits on pleasure. Too many orgasms'r'us.

Kincaid smiled, a slow, almost sadistic smile. She was starting to think that Zach wasn't the only sadist; Kincaid just hid his type of sadism a little better.

"Let's see if we can do at least two more."

Zach groaned again. "Fuck."

He was panting. Two more orgasms were going to take some effort... and time. Time Kincaid definitely had because he had already orgasmed once. She was starting to understand why he'd wanted that quick and dirty blow job from Zach; it made it a lot easier for Kincaid to take his time now. And Amy could have as many orgasms as she could handle, maybe even more than she wanted. But poor Zach was having to hold himself back in edging hell. Kincaid had not been kidding about making Zach pay for it, and he clearly hadn't been talking about anything harsh like a cane or a whip.

Hell, Amy would have preferred the physical impact punishment over what Zach was going through.

Note to self: don't piss off Kincaid.

While he and Zach might do the Nice Dom, Mean Dom thing to play off each other, Kincaid was more like a Sneaky Dom coming in with the mean streak after your guard was down.

And he was *mean.*

The rhythm he used was hard enough to slowly rock Amy to her third orgasm, making her cry out and writhe underneath Zach, her pussy squeezing him over and over again as the pleasure rippled through her. He was panting and gasping and moaning, struggling to hold back his climax while she reached hers for the third time... and she wasn't sure she wanted another.

She felt limp. Satisfied. Satiated. And incredibly oversensitive. The sensations were becoming too intense, ready to tip over the edge from pleasurable to painful. She squirmed underneath Zach, trying to get away from the overstimulation of her poor clit, which needed a break more than it needed another orgasm.

Too many orgasms for her, not enough for Zach, and Kincaid was grinning with pleasure as he continued to work himself in and out of Zach's ass, fucking his way to his second climax.

"Last one, princess," he said to her over Zach's shoulder. Amy shook her head.

"I don't think I can."

"You can. And you will." The utter confidence in his voice was enough to make her pussy spasm. "One more time for us, princess."

He didn't give her a chance to answer; he just started fucking Zach harder, making Zach cry out as his cock retreated, then plunged into Amy, his body moving to Kincaid's whim. Starbursts shot through Amy's body as Zach's thrusts slammed him against her clit over and over again, and she cried out, arching beneath him, held in place by his hands and cock.

He was rigidly hard inside her, and she knew he wasn't going to be able to last much longer.

<u>KINCAID</u>

Wearing out two subbies at once wasn't easy but it sure as hell was fun.

Zach's ass gripped Kincaid's cock as he buried himself inside his boyfriend again, their girlfriend moaning in half-protest, half-pleasure as she started the journey toward her fourth orgasm in a row. Amy was getting tired, overstimulated; Kincaid could see it. He wanted that last orgasm, though.

One more to go with his and Zach's.

So, he switched things into high gear, pounding into Zach's ass with abandon, forcing him to go along with the new pace. Amy's reaction was gratifying. She might be fighting the final climax, but she was going to lose.

"Oh, fuck…" Zach started chanting, his ass spasming around Kincaid's cock. "Oh fuck, oh fuck, oh fuck, oh fuck…"

Kincaid didn't give him permission to come yet, though. They needed Amy closer to her climax. She was writhing, straining beneath Zach, panting for breath right along with him, though for an entirely different reason.

"That's it, princess. We're both fucking you right now." Kincaid crooned. "And when we put you between us, you'll have us both inside you, one in your pussy and one in your ass while we split you open. We'll make you come over and over again until *we've* had enough."

The volume of Zach's chant increased.

"Oh fuck, oh fuck, oh fuck…"

"Sometimes, we'll pass you back and forth, our dirty little slut, filling you with so much cum that it's dripping down your legs, then we'll lick it off you before filling you up again."

"Oh, fuck."

Zach didn't just call Amy their little slut because she liked it; he called her that because he did, too. And Kincaid could tell that hearing him say it was almost too much for Zach. He bucked backward, impaling himself on Kincaid's cock before jerking forward to bury himself in Amy's pussy. Kincaid thrust in hard to pin him there while Amy let out a sharp cry as her eyes glazed over, pleasure slamming into her along with Zach's cock.

His own pleasure surged, balls tightening as his need pushed at him. He had full control of both of them, sending his arousal to a fever pitch.

"Come for me." It wasn't a demand; it was an order. "Come for me, both of you."

The cry that ripped from Zach's throat was almost inhuman as he was freed to move in the way that he needed—the rhythm was wild, inconsistent, pushing himself back on Kincaid's cock, thrusting himself into Amy. He only managed a few thrusts before he buried himself in her entirely. His ass clamped down around Kincaid's cock, increasing Kincaid's pleasure as Zach shuddered with ecstasy. Amy was crying out, too, slow tears leaking from her eyes at the assault on her senses, her lips open as she panted with overwhelming ecstasy.

Kincaid thrust hard into Zach, rocking him against her, prolonging both of their orgasms, using Zach's hole as hard as he wanted to reach his own peak. He tumbled over it, freefalling through the orgasmic bliss that started from his core and swallowed him up.

The three of them moved together, rocking in unison, as the last dregs of pleasure were wrung from each of them.

For the first time, Kincaid felt completely whole.

36

"So, you're rebounding with both of them?" Amy's mom asked her, her voice and expression thankfully free of judgment, though Amy's dad seemed to be taking things a little harder. He'd kept his mouth shut and his hand over his eyes while he listened to her explanation of what was going on with her housemates and why she'd moved into their bedroom instead of moving out.

"If it's a rebound, I hope I don't ever get back up again," she responded truthfully. The past few weeks had been a dream. A really good one. It was just like before except she was sleeping with Kincaid and Zach in the main bedroom every night, all of her things had been moved in there, and the sex was no longer confined to the club.

When she'd complained that her vagina was getting sore after the first few days together, Zach had taken her mouth while Kincaid slowly fucked her ass instead. It had been hot as hell.

It wasn't just all the amazing sex and orgasms, though, because that really would have been just rebound material. It was everything else. The way they listened to her. The way they remembered things about her. When she'd had her period, instead of having to suffer through it without complaining—while listening to her boyfriend whine about how 'moody' she was despite her silence—they'd gone into caretaker overdrive.

Midol and hot pads when she was cramping, Kincaid had made sure every bathroom in the house had every menstrual product known to woman. They'd stocked the freezer with three different kinds of ice cream, and Zach had brought home a different candy bar every day. Not one word of judgment about any of her cravings or her pain.

With that kind of treatment, she'd had the least 'moody' period of her life. It was amazing what a difference a little support made.

Zach also helped her figure out how to block Noelle's number because she'd started calling *again*. Amy didn't know why, and she didn't care. At least Jeremy had gotten the hint—or maybe he was just afraid of Kincaid. Or maybe he'd looked Freddy up as a lawyer. Regardless, she was glad not to have to deal with him, and she'd like the same from Noelle.

She'd gotten past the anger. Getting dumped had been the best thing to ever happen to her because it had led her to where she was now. She didn't wish any ill upon Noelle, but that didn't mean she had to forgive her, and that didn't mean she wanted Noelle in her life ever again. She hoped Noelle lived a very nice life somewhere else, far away from her.

The fact that she'd been kicked out of the club was a relief because that was the only place they were likely to run into each other. Otherwise, Amy didn't expect to see Noelle anywhere.

"Are you sure you can't choose just one of them?" Her dad asked, finally lifting his hand from his eyes. "Or choose a guy who doesn't come with a boyfriend?"

"No," she said firmly. "But don't worry, I'll be the one to tell Grandma."

His sheepish expression gave away that that was exactly what his biggest hangup was.

"No, you won't," her mom said, making Amy's dad groan. "He can handle telling his mom, and I'll handle telling mine." She glanced at her husband. "Maybe we'll wait a bit, though... put it on the family Christmas card rather than making a phone call."

"Oh, I like that idea," Amy's dad said, brightening.

"However you want to handle it," Amy said, amused.

Her mom tapped her finger against her lips. "I think I'll suggest one of the Bliss books for the next book club. That might help, too."

"Have you read the Trinity Masters?" Amy asked. Her mom gave her a scornful look that halted anything else she might say.

"Of course I have. I'm no newbie. Have you read Bianca Sommerland's Dartmouth Cobras?"

"No, but I'll put that on my list." She grinned. Bonding over smutty books was not something she'd expected to happen with her mom.

Wait a minute... her aunts and grandma were all part of the book club her mom was referring to. Shit. Nope. She didn't want to know what they were all reading. She could handle her mom going all fifty shades of kinky books; she wasn't sure she could handle her grandma.

"Just don't get ideas," her mom said, glancing at Amy's dad again. "I don't think he can handle more than two boyfriends."

"Definitely not. And I'm starting to think that I should be paying closer attention to what you're reading," he said with a scowl.

"Oh, as if you don't benefit," her mom scoffed. "Last time I checked, you love it when I read these books because it gets my motor running and then—"

"Hey, hey, hey!" Amy put her hands to her ears. "I don't need to be hearing this!"

"Don't be a prude, dear. You should be glad your parents are... active. Life doesn't end at fifty, you know." Her mom winked at her dad.

"I'm glad you guys are... doing whatever it is you're doing, but that doesn't mean I want to hear graphic details about it. I promise I won't be sharing any graphic details about my sex life." Talk about awkward. Especially when her mom looked a little disappointed.

"Well, we're very happy for whatever makes you happy. And, I have to say, I liked those two boys much better than I did Jeremy," her mom said, reaching over to pat Amy's knee. "Can we have them over for dinner sometime to get to know them a little better?"

That put the grumpy expression back on Amy's dad's face, but he didn't protest.

"I'm sure they'd be happy to," Amy said. They'd actually wanted to come over for dinner with her today when she'd told them she was going to tell her parents, but she'd said no. She'd had the feeling her parents would take it better if they weren't confronted with two boyfriends face-to-face immediately.

Giving them time to settle into the idea before she brought her boys over had seemed like the prudent decision, and she wasn't regretting it. It would give her parents time to let it all sink in before she made the formal introduction.

She also had the feeling that Jeremy's shitastic treatment of her on their wedding day and the way Zach and Kincaid had stepped up at that moment also helped with her parents' acceptance. The contrast was pretty stark.

<hr>

KINCAID

Dinnertime without Amy was odd. They'd gotten used to having her around. It didn't help that they were waiting to hear from her on how telling her parents had gone.

"Is it weird that it feels lonely here with just the two of us?" Zach asked suddenly, breaking the momentary silence. There'd been a few lulls in the conversation already. "It was just the two of us for a long time, and it didn't feel lonely then."

"It does, and it's not weird," Kincaid reassured him. "We've gotten used to having her around.

"I think I'm also freaking out a little that she's going to come back and say her parents couldn't accept her dating two guys and that she's moving out and leaving us," Zach admitted. He'd gotten a lot better about sharing his feelings and fears over the past weeks, something

Kincaid really appreciated. He might not be able to do anything about them, but he was glad Zach wasn't keeping it all bottled inside anymore.

"I doubt she's going to do that, but even if she did, I'm not going anywhere. We'll just be lonely together for a little while." He reached out his hand to take Zach's, making the other man pause in eating. Not that he'd been eating much, to begin with. "But I really don't think that's going to happen."

Zach took a deep breath.

"I don't either, but I can't stop thinking 'what-if?' And I know, Mistress Julie said to do exactly what you just said and actually answer the question, not just leave it hanging. You're right. We'll be okay. Just... sad." Zach sighed. "If she does, I don't want to go looking for another third."

"No, I don't either. I think if we're going to be a trio, Amy is it for us. It only works with her," Kincaid agreed. He and Zach would make it on their own if they needed to, but he hoped they wouldn't have to. Being with Amy made them feel even more complete.

His phone buzzed, and he released Zach's hand so he could pull it out and check the text. He frowned as he read it.

"What's wrong?" Zach asked, concern and some confusion laced through his voice. He probably assumed it had to do with Amy, but it didn't.

"Don, Cassidy's ex, seems to have disappeared," he said grimly. "He hasn't been at his job for a few days or any of his usual places. Patrick wants me to see what I can find out."

He'd also text the information to Lincoln and David. If Cassidy was in danger...

Maybe they'd gotten lucky, and the asshole had gotten arrested or something and was out of their hair for good. Kincaid didn't believe in that kind of luck, though. He looked up at Zach.

"Sorry, I don't want to interrupt dinner, but do you mind if I make a few calls?"

Zach's expression was as grim as he felt.

"Do it. I'm not that hungry, and neither of us is going to feel like eating while you've got asshole Don hanging over Cassidy's head. I can make some calls, too, and see if anyone knows anything." The gossip train at the club wasn't just for the fun stuff; members had been keeping tabs on asshole Don, which was probably why Patrick knew the jerk hadn't been to work.

Nodding, Kincaid got up from his seat while Zach pulled out his phone and started texting people.

Half an hour later, they knew that no one had seen him since Wednesday, the lease on his apartment had ended, and he was in the wind. Not the news that he wanted to call Cassidy about, but she needed to know. It was even worse when she answered the phone with a chipper tone that indicated she was having a good night.

"Hey, Kincaid! How are you? I was going to call you tonight!"

"You were?" He blinked in surprise.

"Yeah, I wanted you to know that I finally got a job! I applied for a job being someone's personal assistant, and I got it... and you'll never guess who it is... David's grandmother. He didn't want her to hire me, but she did, and now I have a job!" Cassidy's glee traveled easily over the phone and made Kincaid feel even worse because he was going to have to burst her happy bubble.

"Is David giving you a hard time about it?" he asked, because if he was... But Cassidy just giggled. Fuck, he was really going to hate raining on her parade.

"No, she won't let him. She's amazing. And, to be fair, he had good reason for not wanting to hire me. I kind of accidentally showed up to the interview high."

"You what?" That *definitely* wasn't like Cassidy. "How do you accidentally get high?"

Zach turned to look at Kincaid, a baffled, questioning expression on his face, and Kincaid waved his hand at him. Obviously, he couldn't stop to explain right now.

"Oh, it's kind of a long story... What did you need?"

Damn. Guess he couldn't put it off any longer, but she did need to know. He was absolutely getting the story about how she accidentally got high later, though.

"Cassidy, I have some... well, we're not sure it's bad news yet, but it's not good news," he said gently.

"Oh... oh. Damn." Her energy immediately dropped in reaction, and her next question had a small, fearful quiver to her words. "What did he do now?"

"We're not sure. He seems to have disappeared. He hasn't shown up for his job, although he didn't quit. The lease on his apartment ended, and he's no longer there." Kincaid sighed. "We're not sure where he is. We're going to do our best to find him quickly and make sure he's nowhere near you, okay?"

Cassidy took a deep breath and let it out slowly before she answered. "Okay. Do you think he's coming here?"

"There's no way of knowing. Maybe he pissed someone off and is on the run. Maybe he got a new job somewhere else and needed to move and didn't care that he was leaving someone in the lurch."

"Or maybe he figured out where I am and is coming after me here," she said quietly.

"Maybe."

"Do you think I should quit my job? I don't want to put Brenda in danger."

"No. Because there are a lot of other things it could be," he said firmly. "But I do want you to keep an eye out, just in case. I'm also going to let Lincoln and David know that Don has fallen off our radar so they can keep an eye on you."

"I'll tell Jensen tonight, too." She sighed again. "This sucks."

"It really does. I'll keep you updated as I get new information."

"Thanks, Kincaid, I appreciate it."

He could tell she was sincere, but he still felt like a jerk for having to ruin her day, especially when it sounded like she'd been having a good one. Other than getting accidentally high. But he didn't feel like he could ask her about that right now. She clearly wanted to get off the phone, probably to take some time to think or process or maybe cry.

Fuck. He hated this. Cassidy didn't deserve this shit. He gave her the reassurance that he could, but there was only so much he could do. The best thing they could do was find Don as quickly as possible and hopefully discover that he was far, far away from Pittsburgh.

After calling Cassidy, he called Lincoln, then David. He didn't ask David about Cassidy's new job. No point in making things harder for her. The other man didn't offer up any information about it, either. He really was going to need to get the full story from Cassidy as soon as he could.

Getting off the phone, he looked over at Zach, who appeared frustrated.

"Nothing?" he asked, already knowing the answer.

"Nothing. I'm sure now that everyone's on the lookout we'll find something soon. And some of those subs should be hired by the FBI because... damn. I'm pretty sure Domi and Rae were on a computer before I even finished my first sentence." He shook his head. "If someone doesn't figure out where he went in the next twenty-four hours, I'll be surprised."

Kincaid hoped so.

The sound of the keypad on the front door made both of them look up. Despite the shitty turn of the night, just knowing that Amy was home made him feel better.

"Hey, guys," she said, walking in with a smile and pushing the door shut behind her. Almost immediately, her expression changed. "What's wrong?"

"Cassidy's ex is in the wind," Kincaid said. "We're talking to some people to try to figure out where he might have gone."

"Oh... that's awful. Do you think..." Her voice trailed off.

"We don't know," Kincaid said firmly. Part of him feared that Don was doing exactly what they were afraid of, but there were other possibilities as well. He wasn't going to have anyone panicking until they knew they had reason to. It was always possible the guy had just disappeared off the face of the planet, which would not be the worst thing, as long as he never resurfaced.

Callous? Yes. Kincaid didn't care. Cassidy deserved peace, and Don didn't deserve shit.

"How did dinner with your parents go?" Zach asked. It almost felt wrong to change the subject, but there really was nothing more they could do for Cassidy right now. As soon as he had a lead, Kincaid would pursue it. They just didn't have one at the moment, and... the most pressing issue within his personal life was the result of Amy's dinner with her parents.

Sometimes, it felt wrong not to be able to do more, but he'd long ago had to accept that life continued. A really fast way to burn out was not to let himself live his life because someone else's life was fucked up. Cassidy wasn't in immediate danger, and even if she was, she needed the team up in Pennsylvania. He wouldn't be able to do more than drive up there and miss everything, anyway.

"Dinner was good," Amy said, perking up a little. "They want to meet you. Again. More formally, as my boyfriends, I mean. My dad is a little weirded out by it. I think Mom is taking it a lot better, but she's still not seeing it as 'real' in some ways. Having dinner with you will make it more real."

"Interesting." Kincaid chuckled. "Sounds a little like my parents." Though his parents were more of the 'we're determined to be open-minded no matter what you throw at us' type. They'd been a little taken aback by his announcement that he was now poly as well bisexual and that he had both a boyfriend and a girlfriend, but they'd quickly rallied and voiced their full support.

"Mine are getting used to us," Zach pointed out. "Although Mom still asks some weird questions when you guys aren't around."

"Just make sure you never let it slip to her that we're also part of a BDSM club," Amy teased. "Can you imagine what kind of questions she'd come up with after that?"

Zach groaned. "I don't even want to think about it. Not a hint of talk about kink near her. *Ever*."

"Speaking of, are we still going to go to Stronghold tomorrow?" Amy asked, looking over at Kincaid. "Or will you need to work on finding the douchebag? No problem if you are. Cassidy's safety comes first, but I'm just wondering."

"It'll probably depend on how things go," he admitted. "I might not know until the last minute."

"That's okay. As long as I know that's the plan," she said with a smile. That was something else he'd noticed about her. Even though Amy preferred plans, she could be very flexible as long as she knew that's what was needed.

"And if you do need to go, and I can't, Zach can always take you."

She and Zach exchanged a glance. "I don't need it. If we go without you, it'll be just to hang out."

Damn, he was so fucking lucky.

"You can have sex without me, you know," he teased.

"We know," Zach said, coming up beside him, grinning. He reached out to slide his hand up Kincaid's back. "It's just more fun with you."

"Oh, is that so?" he asked, very aware that he was being manipulated by the other two, much to his consenting amusement.

"A lot more fun," Amy said, coming up on his other side. "I think we should show him."

Well, who was he to argue with that?

Not that he let either of them be fully in charge, but he enjoyed them crawling all over him before he finally took back the reins and put Zach on his knees with his face in Amy's pussy while Kincaid fucked his ass.

It was a damn good night.

37

Saturday night and Amy was headed to Stronghold with her boyfriends.

Corsets weren't as uncomfortable as movies sometimes made them out to be, but they weren't exactly comfortable while sitting in a car, either. Cars were not made to accommodate women in corsets. The butt plug they'd inserted in her ass before leaving for the club also did not lend itself to comfort, which was why it was such a relief to arrive at Stronghold and be able to get out of the car.

Her boobs looked great, though, and she was finally going to get fully sandwiched between them, which made it all worth it.

"You look fantastic," Zach said with a grin, opening her door. It was his turn to drive, so Kincaid had been in the back with her, teasing her with gentle touches, though they hadn't gone for a full-on makeout session like she and Zach had the last time it had been Kincaid's turn to drive. She was kinda hoping to get to be the chauffeur during backseat blowjob when it was her turn to drive and the guys were both in the backseat.

"Thank you. You're looking pretty good yourself," she replied, running her hand over his abs, which were showing through the opening in the leather vest he was wearing.

It was warm enough out that they hadn't bothered to put anything on over their club wear. Since they were at Stronghold instead of Marquis, they didn't have any restaurant patrons or even anyone on the street walking by and seeing them. The parking lot was pretty much members-only since it wasn't in an area with other shops or restaurants, unlike Marquis.

"Hey, now, save that for the club," Kincaid teased as he got out on the other side of the car, shaking his head. "Or I'll have to punish you both."

"Oh, no," Amy sassed, sliding her fingers through Zach's as they moved around the car to meet Kincaid on his side of it so they could head into the club together. "A punishment. Whatever will I do."

"Try to earn one, apparently," Kincaid responded, amused. He took her other hand, and she grinned up at him. She loved being able to walk around with the two of them like this.

As they walked toward the front entrance, a door to another car opened, and Noelle stepped out. Amy jerked to a halt, which pulled the guys to a stop as well. She was so used to familiar-looking cars in the parking lot that she hadn't even registered that one as Noelle's.

Her ex-friend looked exactly the same. Blonde. Pretty. And her eyes filled with tears the second they met Amy's.

"I'm so sorry!" She practically yelled the words. "I messed up, Amy. I'm sorry."

Beside Amy, Kincaid and Zach bristled, but this wasn't their fight. She tightened her fingers around both of theirs.

"Yes... you did mess up," she said slowly. She really had not expected to see Noelle here. Yes, she'd had to block the other woman's number because she'd been calling, but she'd figured that would be the end of it. She sure as hell hadn't expected Noelle to show up here, at Stronghold, where she'd already had her membership revoked. "Thank you for the apology."

Zach snorted, but she ignored him. She wasn't going to let Noelle back into her life, but she was *owed* that apology, dammit.

Sniffling, Noelle stepped forward, raising her arms and coming toward Amy as if she thought she was going to get a hug. Amy stepped back, shaking her head—not that she needed to go far to retreat because Kincaid and Zach practically jumped in front of her to keep Noelle from being able to reach her.

"Amy!" Noelle moved back and forth, trying to see Amy through the small space between Kincaid and Zach's beefy arms. "I said I was sorry."

"I heard you. I accept your apology," Amy said stiltedly. This was... seriously? Beyond the broad shoulders in front of her, she could see the main door of Stronghold opening, and people started pouring out.

That's right. There were cameras in the parking lot.

Great. Now, they had an audience.

"So, you'll accept an apology but not a hug?"

"Um... no offense, but I really don't want to hug you." They were the first words that came to mind, and they popped out of Amy's mouth before she could stop them, even though they were kind of mean. They were also true. "Accepting your apology does not mean we're friends again."

"Why not?" Noelle sounded sincerely shocked.

Amy shoved through her boyfriends, staring at Noelle. She wanted to be able to see Noelle's full expression, wanted Noelle to be able to see hers. She didn't need her boyfriends standing between them. She could handle Noelle on her own. Even if she wasn't entirely on her own, with her boyfriends at her back and her friends standing in a semi-circle around the parking lot next to Stronghold, listening to the conversation. If she needed them, they were there. Every sub in Stronghold, it looked like.

"Are you high?" Had she somehow forgotten what she'd done to Amy? "You eloped with my groom. On my wedding day."

"I did you a favor, showing you what an asshole he is!"

"*Now* he's an asshole? You *married* him!" Not that Amy wanted him, and she did agree that he was an asshole, but Noelle was attempting to rewrite history with pure fiction.

"And now we split up." Noelle sniffled again, lifting her hand to wipe away a sudden tear. A very convenient tear, considering a second ago she hadn't had any. Or maybe Amy was being too cynical, but she still felt unmoved, even if Noelle really was crying. "Why do you think I've been trying to call you? He fooled me. He fooled me, and he used me, and I'm so sorry I betrayed you that way… but he fooled and used us both."

Two months. They'd lasted all of two months. Suddenly, Amy felt like laughing. God, Noelle really had done her a favor, showing her not just Jeremy's true colors but her own. They had deserved each other for the short time that they'd made each other miserable.

"I think you're forgetting that you also fooled and used me." Amy shook her head. "You are not my friend. I'm not sure you ever were. I'm sorry if you got hurt, but that doesn't change how you hurt me, and it doesn't mean we can be friends again."

"God, what is with this place?" Noelle stomped her foot. She actually stomped her foot as she flung her arm at Stronghold—the building, though the gesture encompassed all the people now coming out of it. None of whom were looking at her with anything in the way of welcome or friendship, though she didn't seem to care. "You come here, get dickmatized by a pervert, and then bam, you think you're too good to be friends with me, just like Iris."

"Everyone here is too good to be friends with you," Rae yelled out.

Noelle jerked in surprise, as if she really hadn't realized that the whole club had come out to listen to her. Maybe she hadn't. They were all behind her.

Noelle spun and turned in a slow circle, taking in all the people glaring at her.

"Screw all of you," she yelled. "You think you're so much better than everyone else just because you do weird shit during sex."

"Don't be bitter about losing your membership or anything," Lexie, the club owner's wife, retorted with a snort. "You freaking begged us not to kick you out, or did you forget that, too?"

"You're all a bunch of awful bullies!" Noelle shrieked. She spun around to face Amy. "Fine, you don't want to be my friend? Fuck you then. You can go whore around with two men all you want. They'll leave you in the end, too."

"Shut up, Noelle," called out Jessica, who Amy hadn't ever really interacted with. She was standing there with her husbands, Justin and Chris. "You're just mad Amy's got two hotties, and you couldn't even hold on to her leftovers."

Everyone's jaw dropped at that one. Jessica winked at Amy.

Noelle sputtered. Actually sputtered, her lips coming together and vibrating, little droplets of spit popping off of them. It was the most amazing thing Amy had ever seen.

"Fuck all of you!" Noelle finally came up with, yanking her car door open. "You can all go to hell."

She pulled out of the parking lot with the window down so she could hold her middle finger high in the air, flicking them all off—but it also meant she'd be able to hear all the cheering as she went.

Amy pressed her hand to her stomach, which felt a little queasy after the confrontation. That had been... bad. Bad enough that she almost felt sorry for Noelle. It couldn't be easy seeing an entire club of people cheering your departure.

"Stop it," Kincaid said in her ear.

"Stop what?" She turned her head to look up at him.

"Stop feeling bad. She doesn't deserve your pity. Literally, everything that's happened to her, she's brought on herself."

"Damn right," Zach agreed. Despite the cheering around them, he'd obviously heard what Kincaid had said.

Amy huffed, but she couldn't argue. She still felt a little bad. Noelle was going to go through life in perpetual victimhood and probably never find happiness, whereas she, Amy, was blissfully happy. In some ways, her happiness was because of Noelle and the shitty way she had treated Amy. She wished Noelle was able to also find happiness, but Kincaid was right. She kept bringing things on herself and blaming everyone else, and as long as she couldn't see what she was doing to others and herself, she was never going to be happy.

None of which was Amy's problem. *Not my circus, not my angry monkey.*

It seemed like everyone wanted to come by and tell Amy that they all supported her and thought Noelle was awful. Everyone was happy for her that she'd gotten together with Zach and Kincaid.

The last to come say hi were Jessica, Justin, and Chris.

"Thank you, seriously, for getting Noelle to back off," Amy said to Jessica. The way the other woman had come to her defense, even though they didn't really know each other, had helped her feel a lot better. They weren't the only poly group at Stronghold, but as far as she knew, they were the only two groups of three that were all in a relationship together rather than having separate relationships.

"Hell, yeah," Jessica said, her hazel eyes twinkling as she grinned at Amy. "We've gotta stick together. I don't often get hassled about having two boyfriends anymore, but you get pretty quick on your feet with the comebacks after a while."

Amy wasn't sure she'd ever be *that* quick, but who knew? "If you want to share any of your comebacks, I'll be happy to steal them from you."

Jessica laughed. "We can definitely do that." She reached out and hugged Amy, and Amy hugged her back hard.

It didn't matter that they'd never really interacted with each other; there was a sisterhood among the subbies at Stronghold. Something Noelle had really never understood. And, again, Amy ended up feeling sad for her, because she probably never would. Only Noelle could change her future, though, and she didn't seem to want to.

Justin and Chris were talking to Zach and Kincaid, but they wrapped things up so they could give Amy hugs and a few words of support, too. Then they went back into the club, leaving Amy in the parking lot with her boyfriends again, so they could have a private moment.

"How are you feeling?" Kincaid asked sympathetically. "Do you still want to scene tonight?"

"Oh, yes." Amy narrowed her eyes at him. "You guys aren't getting out of finally sandwiching me."

"Trust me, we don't want out of it," Zach said, slipping his hand down her back to her butt to give it a little pat. "But we can wait if we need to. That was not exactly how we expected tonight to go."

"Life is full of the unexpected. And some of the unexpected things unexpectedly turned into the best things. Like being left at the altar for my bridesmaid." She wrapped her arms around her men as they stepped into her, tilting her head back to look up at them. "Noelle really did do me a favor, saving me from marrying Jeremy. If it wasn't for her, I would have married him that day and would probably be completely miserable right now. Instead, I'm about to be the middle of a hottie sandwich, and I've never been happier."

It was about time.

38

———

The showdown with Noelle before coming into the club had been unpleasant, but he thought it was needed. It didn't affect Amy nearly as badly as he'd worried. She was still smiling sincerely, and though she seemed sad about Noelle, it wasn't the kind of sadness that ate away at her insides. She seemed to have finally accepted that Noelle was beyond her help.

Noelle was beyond anyone's help as far as he was concerned.

Now that they were in the club, it was easier to put her out of their minds. Focus on what was important—Amy and Kincaid.

Amy looked damn good in her corset, her breasts pushed up high, the short, pleated leather skirt she was wearing swishing as she walked. The hem ended just past her ass, so if she bent forward even a little, her cheeks peeked out—if she bent over far enough, they'd be able to see the string of her thong straining against the base of the plug in her ass. Her hair was pulled back in a ponytail that would be perfect for gripping.

She was sex on two legs, and she knew it.

She wasn't the only one. When they'd gotten into the club, Kincaid had stripped off his shirt and handed it over at the front desk, leaving him in nothing but his leathers. Zach hadn't bothered with a shirt because he liked his vest, but he loved seeing Kincaid bare from the waist up and clad in nothing but leather pants. It was fucking hot.

They'd thought about going to Marquis tonight for the privacy, but they'd wanted to be able to hang out with their friends after their scene if they wanted to. They'd still gotten a private room, though—the fantasy royalty room, complete with a throne and a huge bed for them to share. It was decorated in lush red velvets and wall hangings, making it feel like a sexy movie set.

Kincaid had chosen it for the bed, but it did come with another handy attribute—from the center of the room, there was a long chain hanging down with a set of cuffs at the end. Perfect for putting Amy's wrists above her head and cuffing her into place.

"Can we lower this a little?" she asked, tugging on her wrists. She was stretched out completely, with no slack. Her breasts were high in the corset, practically popping out.

"Nope," Zach said, grinning. "I like seeing you like this."

"Me, too," Kincaid chimed in.

Amy made a face.

"Kind of hard for you to get between my legs when I have to keep them closed if my hands are going to be up this high." She pouted at them.

"Oh, don't worry, little slut," Zach said, walking around behind her and giving her ass a smack that sent the hem of her skirt fluttering. "We'll get to your pussy... eventually."

"Let's get this corset off you first, though, princess." Kincaid stepped up to unhook the front of the corset. The one she was wearing today was nice and easy to pop open. The clasps were actual hooks that curved down through a little ring on the other side of the corset, so all Kincaid had to do was run his finger up the center, pulling the hooks out of the rings, and boom... boobs. "I like this corset a lot. Very easy access."

He grinned over Amy's shoulder at Zach as she gasped and arched her back, indicating he was doing something to her breasts. Zach grinned back and stepped up behind her to unzip her skirt.

"This can come off now, too. I want to whip this pretty ass before Kincaid fucks it."

Amy moaned, panting for breath at both his words and whatever Kincaid was doing to her. They were working in tandem, Kincaid providing the pleasure while he provided the pain—point and counterpoint to give her everything she needed.

While Kincaid played with her pretty breasts, squeezing and pinching and heightening her arousal, Zach started spanking her. He wasn't going to whip her very much, but he wanted to mark up her ass before Kincaid used it. A few nice weals across that pretty surface... but he needed to warm it up first with a good, hard spanking.

Because of the way she was stretched out, there wasn't much room for her to move around, so she couldn't do more than twitch in place as he spanked her. Even when she lifted her feet, trying to dance away, there wasn't anywhere for her to go—especially with Kincaid in front of her. The other man was now bending his head, sucking her breasts as Zach spanked her harder and harder. Her bottom was turning a nice, hot pink, all the blood coming to the surface under the punishment he was giving her.

"Ready for the whip, slut?" he asked, his hand moving down to the undercurve of her ass, right on the sensitive spot where her cheeks met her thighs. Amy squealed, jerking in place.

"Yes, Sir. Please." There was real pleading in her voice. For someone like Amy, this kind of spanking was more of a tease than real satisfaction. She wanted the leather... and he wanted to hear her scream. "Oh!"

That last little 'oh' was for Kincaid, not for him. No need to be jealous, though. She was about to be a lot noisier for him.

He went to get the whip, a nice long, braided single tail that would sting like a bitch but was also thick and thuddy enough to leave a lasting impression. As he got into position behind her, Kincaid lifted his head, standing straight up and moving in close to Amy so she couldn't go very far.

"Hold her still for me?" Zach asked. Amy would hold perfectly still if he asked her to, but he had a feeling she'd like the way Kincaid wanted to do it.

"Of course." Kincaid's dark eyes glinted with mischief as his gaze met Zach's, and Amy bounced upward, letting out a little squeak. Zach knew that Kincaid had just slid his fingers between her legs, taking up space she didn't have and holding her in place by her pussy just as his other hand went around her throat. "Go ahead, partner. She's ready."

Amy whimpered before the whip even touched her, and that whimper turned into a shriek that made Zach sigh with satisfaction when the whip cut across her ass. A nice dark red weal rose up where the leather had bit her, and he stepped forward to rub his hand over it.

"Now that's very pretty," he said. "Too bad you can't see it, Kincaid."

"Oh, I'm perfectly happy with my view," Kincaid responded, glancing down at Amy's front side. She shuddered and whimpered against him. "That's our good girl."

"Three more," Zach said. "For our pretty little slut."

Three more perfectly placed lines across her pinked ass, which had his cock standing up straight to attention and throbbing. He'd love to fuck her ass now and feel her hot flesh against his groin, but Kincaid had requested the back door for tonight, and Zach had agreed. He'd get her ass when they double-teamed her another time.

They had their entire future together for him to be with her in every way possible.

Kincaid

His boyfriend had done a gorgeous job on Amy's ass. Bright pink cheeks crossed with dark red welts that were almost perfectly evenly spaced. If he hadn't seen the whip, he might have thought a cane was used instead. Watching her straddle Zach, who was lying on his back on the bed, was a hell of a view. Such a pretty pink ass with stripes, waiting for him to fuck it.

They'd taken out the plug before she'd gotten on the bed, and her little hole winked at him from between her cheeks, just above where Zach's cock was now impaling her. Kincaid gripped his own cock, spreading the slick lube all over its length and grinning as Zach moaned and reached up to Amy's breasts. She gasped, her downward momentum halting for just a moment before she suddenly sat down all the way, taking him inside her.

"Ride him, princess. I want to see you bouncing on his cock," Kincaid ordered, climbing onto the bed behind her.

"Yes, Sir. Ow!" Amy squealed again, arching her back. Zach's hands were busy on her breasts, which Kincaid had already made extra sensitive with all his pinching and pulling, and he knew Zach was a hell of a lot meaner than he was. They weren't using the clamps tonight because they wanted her focused on how their cocks felt, but her breasts were too pretty for either of them to ignore entirely.

"Now, slut," Zach demanded, even though he'd barely given her time to get started. Not that it mattered. Kincaid knew Zach had just wanted the excuse to pinch her nipples hard. As soon as he gave the order, she started moving, whimpering the entire time. From the way Zach's hands moved with her, it was clear he hadn't relinquished his grip on her nipples even as she started riding him.

The mattress sank down under Kincaid's weight as he got into position between Zach's spread legs, coming up behind Amy. Looking over her shoulder at Zach as she moved, he was suddenly struck by overwhelming emotion at the realization that he had everything he wanted. Right here, right now.

"I love you." The words came out without meaning to. Words he'd said to Zach before and meant, but somehow, they felt like they meant even more now. Because they'd been through hell and back together. They'd shown each other. And now those words included Amy, too.

Amy paused in her movements, turning to look over her shoulder at him with a frown.

"Shouldn't Zach be the one making random declarations of love?" she asked. "You aren't even inside me yet."

Kincaid barked out a laugh. She was such a damn brat. She squealed as Zach slapped her breast, though she thrust them out as if asking for more. Leaning forward, Kincaid kissed her shoulder, sliding his hand around her throat, the way he knew drove her wild.

"Not if I want you to know I mean it. I love you. Both of you. This is... everything. I'm not saying it because we're about to have insanely hot sex, although we are. I'm saying it because I couldn't hold it back." That was the full and honest truth.

"Oh..." she said softly, as if she really hadn't realized that he meant it. And maybe she hadn't.

"I love you both," Zach said. "You *are* my everything. Both of you. There were some seriously rough moments getting here, but I wouldn't change any of it because it led to this." He winked at Amy. "And I'm not just saying that because I'm balls deep inside you."

Amy threw up her hands. "Well, how am I supposed to follow that?" She shook her head. "I do love you. Both of you. And I wouldn't change anything, either. Not even being dumped on my wedding day. You two are the best thing that has ever happened to me, and I hope we have the longest rebound ever. Now, are you going to fuck me or what?"

Giving her throat a little squeeze, Kincaid lined his cock up with her ass and growled in her ear.

"Sassy brat... You might be my princess, but brace yourself... I'm about to fuck you like a dirty little slut." He thrust forward, pushing his cock into her ass, and she cried out as she bent toward Zach, panting with breath as the two cocks slid alongside each other. She was exquisitely tight, the ring of her sphincter gripping every inch of him as it slid past, her muscles spasming against the invasion.

Then he was in, his cock nestled alongside Zach's inside her, only a thin membrane separating them, while she sobbed and panted between them. The heat from her skin seared his groin, her channel massaging every inch of his cock. He could feel her swallow against his fingers.

His gaze met Zach's over her shoulder, and he gave a little nod... and began to move.

———

Amy

Two cocks at once was too many, but she didn't want it to stop. She was so incredibly, insanely full. Too full. It was so much more than just having a cock and a toy. So much more than having anal sex. Part of her had really thought it wouldn't be that different, but it was.

Two of them. Thick. Hard. Hot. Throbbing inside her.

And *moving.*

She could feel them sliding against each other as one retreated and the other thrust in, playing havoc with her senses. All the while, Kincaid's hand around her throat kept her in place, making her body pulse with his dominance over her.

The men moved.

Beneath her.

Atop her.

All around her.

They thrust in and out of her, as though they were passing her back and forth between them, yet they were simultaneously pleasuring her.

It was too much, a sensory overload that made it feel like she couldn't possibly orgasm. Her climax was too far away... or she'd gone too far beyond it... she didn't know which was which or what was up and what was down. She was spiraling through the sensations, caught in the maelstrom and struggling to right herself.

"Oh, please..." she begged. "Oh, please... oh, please..."

That was all she could say, over and over again, not entirely sure what she was begging for as they used her. Their rhythm was steady, pounding, sending her soaring. She heard their groans, their guttural pants, as their own need began to rise, and the rhythm started to falter.

Felt them surging inside her. No longer completely in tandem. Sometimes alternating, sometimes thrusting in together.

She screamed their names as the ecstasy hit her, the tension breaking across her body as fireworks burst in her core. Everything felt bigger, fuller, more intense. Pure bliss wrapped her up, curling her toes, sending her reeling as she gasped for air. Hot liquid poured into her, cocks pulsing inside her, and she felt herself go limp between her two men as the world turned upside down.

My two men.

No one was the third wheel. They were a triangle, and they were meant to be shaped this way.

Best rebound ever.

EPILOGUE

1 year **later**

Amy.

It was the second time in her life she'd had a ring sparkling on the third finger of her left hand, but the first time Amy was completely sure she was marrying the right people. People, not person. She beamed from between the two of them, her beringed hand holding a plastic champagne flute as Kincaid made his speech.

"Thank you, everyone, for coming to celebrate our engagement. We cannot express how much we appreciate all of you—our families and our friends—for all of your support. For loving and accepting us for who we are. For being there for us even if our lives and our love look a little different from what you're used to."

Amy saw Zach's parents give each other proud looks. The engagement had brought up a few more questions from Zach's mom, but mostly logistical ones about who was going to actually marry who and how that would all work. They'd decided that Kincaid and Amy would get married because that would get her on Kincaid's health insurance plan, which was way better than hers. Zach's was fantastic, so he didn't need Kincaid's. All of them would have power of attorney for each other, and they'd have all the legal documents drawn up for them to share everything equally.

The state might not recognize Zach as part of the marriage, but that was just a piece of paper. Everything they needed for each other, they had.

"Thank you for being our people." Kincaid raised his glass, then turned his head to look at Amy and Zach. "We were lucky, not just to have found each other, but to have all of you in our lives. Not everyone like us gets to have this kind of turnout at their engagement party, and we are so grateful to be here today, with all the people we love, celebrating *our* love with you. Cheers."

"Cheers!" Everyone chimed in, lifting their own glasses. Amy's mom wiped a tear away from her eye, and her dad slung his arm around her mom, both of them grinning ear to ear. Her dad had definitely been a little wary at first, but eventually, he'd decided that two men pampering and taking care of his daughter were way better than one shithead making her take care of him all the time.

And that was a direct quote.

Kincaid's parents had flown in for the engagement party, and they were both beaming proudly at their son. Amy adored them, though she hadn't gotten as much time with them as she had Zach's parents. They were here for the whole week, though, and she was looking forward to spending that time with them. Both Zach's and Kincaid's moms had been thrilled to be invited to go dress shopping with her.

"Now, who's ready for cake?" Zach's mom asked excitedly. She'd insisted on making their engagement cake, which Amy had accepted because she was an amazing baker. It was clear where Zach got his skill in the kitchen from.

Multiple 'mes!' were shouted out from around the room, causing laughter, and everyone started breaking up into their little conversational groups again. Amy laughed as she saw Rae and Domi making a beeline for the cake. Morgan, unsurprisingly, was hanging back with Sam and Iris. She looked around for her last bridesmaid and, after a moment, spotted Avery beside Nick, talking to his brother and sister-in-law, as well as Cassidy and her boyfriend, who had come down from Pittsburgh to be here. She wanted to talk to Cassidy, too; she'd only gotten bits and pieces from Kincaid on how Cassidy and David had gotten together, and the little bit she'd heard had been wild.

Mitch and Brian were right behind Rae and Domi for the cake. They were Kincaid's and Zach's best men, of course, and all the partners of her bridesmaids were their groomsmen. Two groups of friends had truly come together and become one. It was a newer group, but she'd wanted Rae, Domi, Iris, and Avery to be her bridesmaids because she truly believed it was a group of friends meant to last.

More bridesmaids than she'd had last time... but better ones in a lot of ways. She'd asked Marissa, but she had recently landed a movie deal and wasn't sure she'd be able to be at the wedding, much less commit to the events. Filming started tomorrow, which was why she'd missed today.

Carolyn had fully embraced her stereotype, running away with her pool boy, and was currently going through a contentious divorce. Mistress Camille, Freddy's girlfriend and Domme, was representing her, much to Freddy's relief that Carolyn hadn't asked him instead. She and Monet were currently enjoying life in the Bahamas, and she, too, had sent her regrets, though she hadn't seemed all that regretful. She had promised to attend the wedding, though, even if she wasn't going to be a part of it.

"Penny for your thoughts. You're frowning... if you need to run, I'll block any chasers." The big man who sidled up next to her threw his arm around her shoulders. Connor, formerly Master Connor, was built like a linebacker and probably could have blocked the whole party if he wanted to.

"Are you supposed to make offers like that after agreeing to officiate the wedding?" she teased.

He winked down at her.

"That's *exactly* why I'm supposed to make offers like that." It was clear he hadn't been serious, though. He knew she didn't need it. Not this time.

"If only you'd been my officiant last time."

"Well, you made a better choice this time." He looked across the room where Zach and Kincaid were getting some cake. "In more ways than one."

Truth.

Amy smiled as Iris, Sam, and Morgan approached, coming to join her and Connor. They'd all refilled their champagne flutes after the toast.

"Hey, Amy, do you need anything?" Iris asked. "I feel like I'm failing as a bridesmaid; you never ask for anything."

"Yeah, I was hoping for a little bridezilla action to film this time," Sam teased.

"Oh, I'm sorry I'm such a chill bride." Amy rolled her eyes. "I didn't mean to make things so easy for you. Someone, go get me some cake or something, but not the cake that's here; it needs to be a Smith Island cake, and I want it in thirty minutes."

Which was a clear impossibility, and it made everyone laugh.

"We were just talking about how I've made better choices for this wedding," Amy said, tipping her head toward Connor. "Officiant, grooms, bridesmaids."

"Much better choice in bridesmaids," Sam said enthusiastically. "Anyone know what hole Noelle slithered into?"

"Nope and don't care." Amy actually hadn't thought about the woman in months.

"It's weird. I almost feel like I should thank her," Iris admitted. "Yeah, she was an awful friend, but if it wasn't for her, I wouldn't be where I am now... and I'm really happy with where I am."

Amy laughed in surprise.

"I've thought the same thing," she agreed, though Sam was wrinkling her nose like she didn't like the idea. Amy smiled at Sam. "I'm not saying I want her here so I can thank her, just that I am really happy with where I am and grateful to be here."

"Then let's thank her in absentia." Sam raised her glass, and the others did as well. Connor looked bemused, but he didn't protest. Amy had never gotten the impression he liked Noelle very much, either, even though he'd had very little to do with her. "To the double stuffed cuntcake... thanks for bringing us all together."

No one could take the drink because they were all too busy laughing at Sam's play on the insulting nickname Noelle had originally been dubbed with.

Of course, Zach had to turn up and ruin it.

"Double stuffed cuntcake? Mmm, that sounds delicious," he said, sliding in next to Amy's side and looking down at her speculatively. Connor was already moving away, so Kincaid could take his place on that side. Zach had two plates of cake, and he handed one to her.

"Oh. My. God. Way to ruin a perfectly good insult," Sam complained.

"Insult? It sounds like a sex position. One that we could try out." Zach raised his eyebrow.

"Double stuffed, then eat some... cake?" Kincaid grinned. "Sounds good to me."

"Um, do I get a say in this?" Amy asked because she was pretty sure they weren't talking about one in her pussy and one in her butt. "I'm not sure you'll both fit in there."

"If Asad can fit his fist in my vagina, I'm sure you can accommodate two dicks," Morgan offered by way of reassurance. It was not actually reassuring, but it did take the attention off of Amy and her men as everyone turned to stare at Morgan.

"Yeah, okay, I'm going to need details about that," Rae said from behind Morgan. "I've always wanted to write a fisting scene."

The laughter that engulfed them had some of the parents wandering over, which meant the conversation immediately shifted. Wedged between her two men, Amy happily ate the piece of cake Zach had brought her.

She couldn't wait to see what the future held for all of them.

THANK YOU SO MUCH FOR READING MY MASTERS OF MARQUIS SERIES. I have loved this series from beginning to end, and though I'm going to miss *it, I'm also really excited about the Black Fox Security Doms series and seeing Cassidy finally get her HEA in <u>Danger and Dominance</u>.*

If you aren't ready to leave Marquis just yet, thank my Patreon subscribers because they agreed so I wrote a little extra something and you can sign up for my newsletter for a bonus scene where Kincaid and Zach end up paying a little visit to Jeremy.

Take care and stay sassy,
Golden Angel

The End

ABOUT THE AUTHOR

Golden Angel is a USA Today best-selling author of heart and bottom warming romance.

She is happily married, old enough to know better but still too young to care, and a big fan of happily-ever-afters, strong heroes and heroines, and sizzling chemistry.

When she's not writing, she can often be found on the couch reading, in front of her sewing machine making a new cosplay, hanging out with her friends, or wandering the Maryland Renaissance Fair.

www.goldenangelromance.com

BB bookbub.com/authors/golden-angel

g goodreads.com/goldeniangel

f facebook.com/GoldenAngelAuthor

o instagram.com/goldeniangel

ACKNOWLEDGMENTS

I have a lot of people to thank for helping me with this book.

My amazing beta readers, who are invaluable in helping me catch mistakes, doing the initial grammar and word checks, identifying continuity issues, and working through problems with me. Marie, Candida, Karen, Marta, Rara, Piper, and Katherine – you all make these books so much better!

My Patreon subscribers, whose comments and assistance keep me motivated and bring me so much joy.

Another extra special thank you to Katherine, who got me started down this career path and has been by my metaphorical side ever since.

Thank you to my husband for his continued loved and support. I could not do this without you.

And, as always, a big thank you to all of you for buying and reading my work... if you love it, please leave a review!

OTHER BOOKS BY GOLDEN ANGEL

Contemporary BDSM Romance

Venus Rising Series (MFM Romance)

The Venus School

Venus Aspiring

Venus Desiring

Venus Transcendent

Venus Wedding

Venus Rising Box Set

Stronghold Doms Series

The Sassy Submissive

Taming the Tease

Mastering Lexie

Pieces of Stronghold

Breaking the Chain

Bound to the Past

Stripping the Sub

Tempting the Domme

Hardcore Vanilla

Steamy Stocking Stuffers

A Sassy Christmas

Entering Stronghold Box Set

Nights at Stronghold Box Set

Stronghold: Closing Time Box Set

Masters of Marquis Series

Bondage Buddies

Master Chef

Law & Disorder

Switch Play

Legally Bound

Shallow Submission

Hidden Away

Secret Submission

Third Wheel

Black Fox Security Doms

Outfoxed by Love

Outfoxed by Passion

Dungeons & Doms Series

Dungeon Master

Dungeon Daddy

Dungeon Showdown

Dungeons & Doms Boxset

Daddies Everywhere

Chef Daddy

Foosball Daddies

Taco Daddy

Cheese Daddy

Garden Daddy

Little Villain

Historical Spanking Romance

Domestic Discipline Quartet

Birching His Bride

Dealing With Discipline

Punishing His Ward

Claiming His Wife

The Domestic Discipline Quartet Box Set

Bridal Discipline Series

Philip's Rules

Gabrielle's Discipline

Lydia's Penance

Benedict's Commands

Arabella's Taming

Pride and Punishment Box Set

Commands and Consequences Box Set

Deception and Discipline

A Season for Treason

A Season for Scandal

A Season for Smugglers

A Season for Spies

Desire and Discipline

A Season for Bliss

A Season for Desire

A Season for Christmas.

Indecent Dukes

The Duke's Indecent Scandal

Bridgewater Brides

Their Harlot Bride

Standalone

Marriage Training

The Duke's Pursuit

Rogue Booty

Sci-fi Romance

Tsenturion Masters Series with Lee Savino

Alien Captive

Alien Tribute

Alien Abduction

Standalone

Mated on Hades

Shifter Romance

Big Bad Bunnies Series

Chasing His Bunny

Chasing His Squirrel

Chasing His Puma

Chasing His Polar Bear

Chasing His Honey Badger

Chasing Her Lion

Night of the Wild Stags

Chasing Tail Box Set

Chasing Tail... Again Box Set